Let Me Come to You Tonight . . .

Slowly Chantal nodded her head. Then her eyes followed the movement of his body as Simon rose from the couch and came around to where she sat. Standing above her, he reached down and, one by one, removed the tortoise-shell pins from her hair. His touch was expert, swift and sure. His fingers sent an exquisitely sensual current tingling down her backbone. Something blocked within her chest and she began to breathe rapidly, unevenly.

He murmured, "Extraordinary," as her heavy red hair fell to her shoulders. As he had done one time before, he smoothed back the hoyden wisps that strayed across her forehead. All the while, Chantal sat very still, wondering what she would do if she really forgot how to breathe.

"May I?"

She could barely hear his voice. . . .

Dear Reader:

We trust you will enjoy this Richard Gallen romance. We plan to bring you more of the best in both contemporary and historical romantic fiction with four exciting new titles each month.

We'd like your help.

We value your suggestions and opinions. They will help us to publish the kind of romances you want to read. Please send us your comments, or just let us know which Richard Gallen romances you have especially enjoyed. Write to the address below. We're looking forward to hearing from you!

Happy reading!

Judy Sullivan
Richard Gallen Books
8-10 West 36th St.
New York, N.Y. 10018

The Sudden Summer

MURIEL BRADLEY

PUBLISHED BY RICHARD GALLEN BOOKS
Distributed by POCKET BOOKS

Books by Muriel Bradley

Tanya
The Sudden Summer

Also published by RICHARD GALLEN BOOKS

The Silver Kiss
  by Lynn Erickson

Fortune's Choice
  by Eleanor Howard
The Perfect Couple
  by Paula Moore

A RICHARD GALLEN BOOKS *Original* publication

Distributed by
POCKET BOOKS, a Simon & Schuster division of
GULF & WESTERN CORPORATION
1230 Avenue of the Americas, New York, N.Y. 10020

ISBN: 0-671-43346-6

First Pocket Books printing July, 1981

10 9 8 7 6 5 4 3 2 1

RICHARD GALLEN and colophon are trademarks
of Simon & Schuster and Richard Gallen & Co., Inc.

Printed in the U.S.A.

For
Betty and Ed Grant
with love

The Sudden Summer

Chapter One

It was six o'clock on an early June evening. While the disagreement between the two women continued, Chantal was clearing out her desk for the final time. She refused to lose her temper. Doro Kentz, story department head at Twentieth Century-Fox's Tri-Symbol Productions, was leaning against the door of Chantal's office.

Doro stubbornly repeated all the arguments she'd lined up against Chantal's leaving. "I still say you're making a mistake to walk out on the company and freelance on your own. It's a big, wide, rotten world out there. I'm not sure the door will be open for you here if you want to come back. Don't forget, there're a lot of eager kids fresh out of film school panting for what you're throwing away."

Chantal raised her head from the packing cartons and looked at Doro, her face impassive. Then her lower lip jutted and she blew upward vigorously, causing the heavy, reddish-colored bangs that had fallen across her forehead to rise.

Doro Kentz paused in disgust. "Why am I spieling such crap! You're the best researcher and story analyst Tri-Symb's ever had. Anytime, Chantal—come on back."

Chantal lifted the thick hair from the nape of her neck and twisted it up into a tousled ponytail that sprayed out wildly. Bending down, she continued to stuff personal files into the two large boxes. "I appreciate what you've just said. If Lee and the new reader you hired weren't so good, I'd have given you more notice. Certain things came up—"

Chantal stopped abruptly. She didn't want to say too much. It would be a mistake to soften up and start explaining matters to Doro. Chantal knew the code: keep the personal out of the business at hand. If one didn't, it had a way of sweeping back when least expected, like a riptide in sunny waters that could reach and yank one beyond professional depths. It wasn't always easy to rescind confidences given. Chantal was glad when the phone rang.

Doro took it. "Kentz speaking." She put on her regretful face. "Charlie, I've been after my people to read your script, but they've been awfully busy and we're short-handed." Doro glanced meaningfully at Chantal. "The report did come in late this afternoon. Unfortunately, it's not affirmative. They feel it's a project we shouldn't attempt to go forward with right now." Doro listened keenly. "No. Don't pick it up here. I'll see it's sent out to your house first thing in the morning. Call me sometime soon. We'll have lunch." Doro cradled the instrument, scribbled on a memo pad, hung up, then walked across the hall and stuck the note into her secretary's typewriter.

Chantal knew what the instruction would say. "No

calls from Charlie L. for awhile. Thanks, Pat. Doro."

Chantal picked up the last of her belongings—the bud vase and the desk plate with her name on it. *Chantal Jerrold.* She scrubbed her forearm across the metal, blew on it. The genuine brass was wearing off.

Kentz came back into Chantal's office. The story editor was tall and intelligent-looking, with an engaging grin that spread all over her narrow face yet somehow never managed to reach the cool blue eyes that now surveyed Chantal. "You *will* do this last project for me tonight, won't you?"

"I said I would." Chantal stood up. She was small and tenderly voluptuous, her appearance made more so by the clothes she was wearing. She tucked her pink shirt into well-tailored khaki cotton pants and tightened the narrow leather belt with its free-form silver buckle. She glanced at her wristwatch. "You said six-thirty, Projection Room A. What's the running time?"

"Forty-five minutes. They're only screening the first reels. I want you to tell me exactly what your impression is of this foreign actor. He's being considered for *The Assaulters.* You read it."

"All seven hundred pages."

"The full report's in the file, isn't it?"

"No. I only did the résumé. You thought that was enough."

Doro frowned. "At the time I did. I wonder . . ." She looked speculatively at Chantal.

"Too late now," Chantal reminded her, and put the cover on the one-thousand-dollar studio typewriter. "By the way, if someone named Mark Duffy gets lost and calls me here, you'll tell him where I am?"

"Didn't you leave his name at the front gate with a drive-on pass?" Chantal nodded. "Then he won't get lost. Isn't he the brainy one who has nothing to do with films?"

"That's the one."

"You better hang onto him." This time Doro's smile almost reached her eyes.

Seated in the darkened screening room among all the other rapt viewers, Chantal didn't hear Mark softly hissing her name. He was late. He walked down one aisle, then the next. Several people hissed back at Duffy to shut him up. Chantal, three seats from the end row and saving a place for Mark, continued to concentrate her attention on the screen.

Surrounded by the absorbed faces of her one-time co-workers, Chantal was as mesmerized as they were by what she saw. She told herself she was here for business reasons, not to be bewitched by an image on film. Still, she felt the same erotic pulse that the rest of the group did. Her visceral self shivered each time the star actor turned those deadly blue Germanic eyes toward the camera . . . and thus out of the screen and into the insides of his audience. Into Chantal.

Each time the star hitched himself forward and twitched a shoulder neurotically in that oddly mannered style of his, the sophisticates in Projection Room A quivered uneasily, though most of them had seen and done everything there was to do in life twice over.

Mark found Chantal and sat down. "You're breathing hard," he noted. ". . . Me?"

Chantal didn't look at him. She kept staring at the action being unleashed on the screen. Her hypnotized attention held, she finally whispered back, "Doro asked me to do a report for her on this man from Munich."

Mark's own eyes on the screen, he grunted, "Tell me, Chan, what *do* you see up there?"

"I see a demon—unreal. It's fascistic. Know what I mean? Autocratic, savage. Maybe its time has come."

"Why *it?* Why so impersonal? Doesn't he have a gender?"

Chantal peered toward Mark in the darkness. "Observe. See the reaction to this German? These people in here are totally fascinated by him. They're not an easy bunch to impress. Yet look at them! Hardened as they are, right now you're watching them form a cult for this man."

Mark whispered, "Is that the sort of thing you'll write in your report?"

"What I'll say is that he could be the hottest property the studio ever signed . . . if an American director doesn't ruin him!"

The film action plunged on. Mark slid his long frame farther down in the seat. "I don't know. He affects me like a combination Mick Jagger and Greta Garbo. You ever see any of her pictures, or were you too young for the late-night shows on the tube?"

"Shut up, *please!*" Chantal glanced sideways. "Remember, Duffy, I said it nicely."

Afterward they spoke several goodbyes to people to whom it was necessary to be very, very polite. As they strode along a walkway outside the projection room building, he lit a cigarette. Chantal, barely glancing at him, reached up, removed it from between his lips and tossed it away.

Mark grinned, sidestepped, ground out the butt under his heel and spoke pragmatically. "The guy you just saw on the screen is Polish, not German. I read that in one of your scholarly film journals."

"I know, but I'd rather believe he's Teutonic. It's got a more decadent feel to it. It suits his style, suits *him*."

Mark looked up at the darkening sky. "How does a nice woman like you come off with ideas like these?" He sounded mournful.

"I'm paid to think weird. I'm in the industry, y'know." Maybe now was the time to say it. At least she could begin. Either way he was going to be hurt. "Marko, you and I really shouldn't hang around together. You're too normal. That's a word my father would use. A word that's not exactly my choice. You've met my father. He doesn't smoke. He goes in for health and the environment."

"I guessed that, among other things."

Chantal looked sharply at Mark. "I don't have a father fix, if that's what you're thinking." Her father, Jason Jerrold, was more the immature man-child than a father figure. Mark Duffy hardly knew the truth about Chantal and her family.

Mark continued. "Why do you say I'm normal?" They were walking toward the parking lot. He started to take the pack of cigarettes out of his pocket, then slid it back.

"For one thing, you have a useful occupation. You're a seismologist." Chantal's gray eyes sparkled. "I like to say that word. Think of it! A geophysicist who specializes in earth movement. You're from Boston. I'm from L.A." She quickened her steps to match his longer ones. "I think you're just staying in town waiting for the big one they say is coming."

"Funny, nobody who really lives here ever calls Los Angeles a city."

"What's so funny about that? It isn't."

They reached Chantal's Datsun. Mark held the door shut against her entrance. "When are you going to invite me to your apartment . . . like the last time? We could have a sincere conversation for once. I can demonstrate my craft." His strong hands wedged fingers together and undulated them. "I can explain it all—the phenomena of earthquakes. You, as a native daughter, should learn about things like tremors. We can manage a little natural vibration between us, just to see how it is. We can—"

"We have already." Chantal looked away from him. "It can't be tonight. I have to work." She knew she was putting off what had to be said forthrightly between them. She reached around Mark, trying for the door handle. Duffy held it tightly closed with his fist. Chantal looked up at him, her roan-colored eyebrows intent and straight, the sweep of her black eyelashes veiling the expression in her eyes. She went on, talking fast. "Tonight I've two novels to skim . . . and a screenplay I have to do an in-depth on, as well as this last-minute report for Doro."

This is hard, she thought. He really doesn't understand. Why should he? Every female in his life before I came along was an impeccable lady from the eastern seaboard whose reflexes he could depend on. When Mark went to bed with one of them, it was probably love, and they did it because he was the right man. Mark is a very right man!

He was talking. She'd have to listen. Mark explained it patiently. "You said if I met you over here tonight, we'd have dinner together. You had something important to tell me. That was the idea." He sounded plaintive. Even though one was supposed to, she didn't care for vulnerability in a man.

Chantal leaned against the car door. Where had her head been that night she'd let it all go a little too far with Mark? They'd gotten involved too fast. It should never have happened. Mark was too perfect. Trim, tall, dark-haired, brown-eyed. What a marvelous smile he had. Just . . . not for her.

Mark did his smile. "Let's go to your place and argue. We can't stand here."

Chantal looked around her. "You're right. It's haunted."

The Twentieth Century lot, which was the umbrella for various production companies like Chantal's own recent home, Tri-Symbol, appeared big and drafty, a lonely stage in the summer dusk. Of course, not as big as it had once been. From a distance the lights of the Century City high-rise apartments and office buildings winked brazenly through the lingering twilight. The tall buildings grouped and soared where mansions of the deep South, New York streets and Marseilles wharves had once stood as permanent sets. Where Shirley Temple had played, where Betty Grable had danced and sung. It had all happened before Chantal was born: the transfer of the prime land of the studio's huge back lot in exchange for those millions of ventured capital. Today it would be billions. She mustn't think about mistakes like that. It was too uncomfortably close to the problems her family faced at home.

As an extension of her musings concerning plantation mansions bulldozed under for the sake of real estate dollars, she spoke aloud. "Magnolias and mammon—they don't mix."

"What the hell does that mean?" Mark sounded less sensitive than he had a few moments earlier.

Chantal shrugged. Mark Duffy could never look

close enough inside her to see the mischief, or even the fear. She doubted that any man could. She tried to play it lightly. "That means material profit can have a debasing influence on the beauty of the earth, and on the character of the people one meets."

"Chan, are you trying to con me? I know exactly where you come from. I've seen your parents' house." He waved an arm. "Hancock Park! The enclave of the privileged, the old-monied. The quiet money set that lies low, hoping to keep itself out of the way of those awful people moving in just south of Wilshire Boulevard. Grab the racquets. Man those tennis courts that run north and south—the debasers shall not pass!"

Chantal laughed out loud. She pushed back the dark red hair from the places where it clung damply about her forehead. She held it up and out to let the June breeze cool her skin. A mocking, very pretty face looked up into Mark's. Curiously, each of Chantal's features possessed its own special individuality. In Chantal's case there was a blend of disparate elements that worked. Her smoke-gray eyes tilted slightly upward at the corners. Her nose was wide, yet short and straight. Her lips were sensuously full, yet sweetly, delicately, curved. Her skin was ivory-colored, yet it glowed. There was a touch of magic about her. Chantal was not beautiful, she was lovely.

Duffy took in all this grace and pleasure beaming up at him and wondered why he felt desolate inside, where it didn't show. Somehow, for some reason, he knew he was losing her.

Chantal's eyes still gleamed with amusement at Mark's pat summing up of her background. "You're right, Mark. That's where I come from, right off those ivy-covered walls. And don't think I don't carry the load around with me. Here"—she indicated her heart—"and here." She tapped her temple.

Chantal put a fond hand on his arm. She did like him a lot. He was a good person. One more evening together, providing they kept their distance, wouldn't hurt. Then she'd have to tell him it was over. "I'll fix something to eat at my apartment. It'll be quicker than going out."

The feeling she had for Mark was one of respect and interest. That kind of feeling, by itself, wasn't important enough. On the other hand, what Mark felt for her was too important. She'd have to stop running the situation around in her mind . . . and act.

Mark opened her car door for her. "I'll follow in my wagon," he said.

From behind the steering wheel, Chantal declared, "Tonight you leave. At ten o'clock."

The apartment building was old. That was the way Chantal liked it. It was situated on the west side of town above Sunset, where the winding boulevard curved toward the sea next to the Santa Monica mountains. The tawny-colored Villa Apartments had been built during the forties. The architecture was Spanish, the craftsmanship excellent. The walls were thick, cool in summer. The roof was red-tiled. On winter nights the rain ran off it with a beautiful sound, rhythmic and primitive. Inside, the apartments were spacious, with high ceilings, hardwood floors and deep fireplaces that took eucalyptus logs and turned them into smoky fragrance. Outside there were graceful, drooping-branched pepper trees, flame-orange hibiscus bushes and scented honeysuckle vines.

Moonlighting at several different jobs made the west side location possible for Chantal. The rent was one she could afford, providing the economics of her family situation didn't worsen. Hancock Park! If Duffy only knew the truth.

Standing in the kitchen making bay shrimp crêpes with fresh asparagus on the side, Chantal thought about how much she loved this place where she had lived for three years. She liked being alone in the apartment. Mark would say this made her an eccentric. Mark, being healthily, breezily free of any intellectual neurosis, would say the usual: One needs people. . . .

She glanced at Duffy, whose splendidly featured face was intent as he opened the wine bottle. He caught her look, spilled a little of the wine into the waiting, chilled glass, took a sip and pantomimed, "Superb!"

Chantal smiled brightly before she turned back to fold the crêpe on the griddle. Something argued in her brain: was she making a mistake in dismissing Mark's devotion? How often in this town does one meet a man who walks the Southern California hills looking for its earth faults; who carries instruments with him to register shocks that are barely perceptible on a Richter scale; a man who can call most of the professors at Pasadena's California Institute of Technology by their first name? Looked at in a different light, Mark Duffy could be considered an exotic, rather than what he actually was: a well-integrated, conforming individual whose touch didn't accelerate her pulse, nor cause her heart to leap or her mind to spin with restless, creative fancies.

Chantal had to say it aloud. "Marko, you're an impressive guy. Why is it that you didn't keep on with that psychiatrist from UCLA you were with the night we met? She was prettier than I am, and smarter too."

Mark put down the wine bottle, took a swift step toward Chantal and pulled her close. As always, her head fit neatly under his chin while he murmured, "She didn't have divine breasts, or hair that reminds me of autumn leaves in the Berkshires, or a lower lip which is a devastating eight point seven!"

Chantal moved away suddenly. She wanted to laugh, or cry. "What a rotten thing to say! Why can't you be romantic about my lower lip? Or, at the very least, sentimental?"

"I thought I was sentimental. I thought that was one of the things you didn't like about me."

Chantal shot Mark a surprised look. Had she been that transparent? She decided to let the remark pass. "You said eight point seven," she reminded him. "You once told me a magnitude of eight point five could wreck everything."

"You're learning." Mark clicked off the stove's gas burner. Before she could protest, he reached down, picked her up as easily as one would a weightless tumbleweed in a field of sage and carried her into the living room.

Chantal loosened herself from Mark's grasp and slid down to stand beside him. "Why did you do that? What about our crêpes? Aren't you hungry?"

"I have an appetite, all right . . ."

"Mark!"

He spoke hastily. "I'll give you another answer. I like to heft someone who weighs a hundred ten pounds, has bronze hair and classy brains and—" Suddenly he stopped. Nothing seemed fun anymore between them. He was too anxious. "I love you, Chantal." He said it humbly.

Oh, dear God, she thought, why couldn't he be mean, dumb, psychotic even? Anything but probably the nicest man I'll ever meet in this town.

Now had to be the time. She swallowed hard. "Marko, I like you so much. More than that, I respect you—your mind, your character, the way life seems to work for you."

His eyes weren't really puzzled, and even though he asked the question, he knew the answer. "What are you talking about?"

"Don't say you love me, Mark, because I can't say it back to you."

Duffy touched her lower lip with a gentle finger. Standing there in front of him, she appeared very small, very worried and, at the moment, inarticulate. "It's all right, Chantal," he reassured. "It's not *exactly* all right, you understand, but that's the intent."

Suddenly and fiercely, Chantal was angry with herself. "What's all right? That I let you make love to me when it wasn't real for me?"

"It was real for me."

When he swept her into his arms a second time, she didn't protest. She was still fighting the sense of what she called her own lack of chivalry. Mark carried her down the short hallway in the direction of the one bedroom. He was hopeful.

Feeling the savage blood-rush in his own body, the hot need to enter Chantal, to find her bold and playful and ardent, as she had been those first weeks, he could not believe that she couldn't be caught up once again in their driving need for each other. He would accept her on any terms. If she didn't love him, she could *learn* to love him. He would prove this to her. Any other resolution of their relationship was unthinkable. He could never say goodbye. His body trembled and sought hers.

Light from the street lamps outside filtered through the lacy pepper trees, across the second-floor balcony and into the room, to touch antique furniture, a dark rose carpet, a pearl-skinned Chantal lying beneath Mark's body on the bed.

He had stripped her swiftly, making her aware of her utter nakedness, both in emotion and in desire. It was happening, and she would let it happen—the slow, deep kisses that warmed her lips and parted them, that joined both their mouths in sweet excitement. His arms folded under her shoulders, bringing her up to his hard chest. Her nipples tingled. She could feel the deep, steady pound of his heart. She could not stop the quickening of her own breath, which rose in rhythm with his while his fingers touched her breasts, exploring as lightly as wind strokes her tightening nipples.

His head bent down beneath hers as he ran the tip of his tongue around the aureole of each nipple, teasing, attacking, suckling. His heartbeat, his breath were explosive in the sexual surge which he was controlling, as he had often done before, in order to carry her along with him.

It was too late to begin a dialogue of why this shouldn't be happening to them. She couldn't do that to Mark at this moment. She couldn't refuse his arousal of her body, even though her damnable honesty said this was wrong because she didn't care enough. She tried to relax. She couldn't. Worse, she was rigid as though with distaste.

His hand moving down her belly abruptly checked, too sensitively aware of the signal it was receiving from her body. Through the half-dark he looked up and stared into her face with an intensity that almost seared. "You really did mean what you said to me back there. You don't care at all."

"I . . . I . . ." She made a strange, strangled sound.

He swung himself away from her. "I've never raped anyone. I'm not about to begin now." He attempted to subdue his heightened sexual tensions before moving aside. After a moment he heaved himself upright to stand near the bed. She could hear the breath expel harshly from his lungs, could almost hear the pounding blood-surge in his body. She turned her eyes away from the outline of his tumescence.

"I am sorry," she whispered. "I was willing, this last time."

"Willing? My God, willing!" When Mark could move without a spasm of pain, he began to stumble about the partially darkened room, finding his clothes, pulling on the knit shirt, the navy jeans. "What kind of man do you think I am, to take a woman who's merely *willing?*"

Chantal put her hand over her mouth, raised the sheet across her body. She was shaking. She clamped her thighs tight together.

His voice low, toneless, Mark spaced each word. "I am in love with you, Chantal. We've known each other seven weeks and three days. I want to marry you. And all this time you were only *willing* to let me touch you?" He paused. "Was it that way in the beginning too?"

She couldn't reply to that. And he didn't really want to hear what she had to say. Now, fully clothed, he snapped on the bathroom light. It flooded into the bedroom, in Chantal's direction.

She turned over onto her stomach, her face smothered in the pillow. The light was like the dragon light of doom.

Mark bent over her. His eyes glittered with anger; then, unaccountably, they softened. He stroked the bright hair that flowed across her naked shoulders. He wanted to touch her skin itself. He refused the impulse. "You couldn't help it, Chantal—that I wasn't the one."

He knelt beside the bed to bring his face on a level with hers. "Promise me you'll never be kind to anyone again in the special way you were kind to me . . . unless it *is* real for you."

Chantal kept her face hidden. She couldn't compound the wrong by telling Mark she admired him, that he was different from most men she'd known, that she had wanted to care seriously for him, that she had hoped the response would happen. But it hadn't. She couldn't tell him all that. She could only wait for him to go away so that she could be alone with her contrition.

Finally she heard him leave the room, walk down the hallway. For a long minute he paused in the foyer of her apartment. Silence. She knew Mark would be standing just inside her living room door. Was he waiting for her to call him back?

Chantal raised her head from the pillow and listened tensely. He mustn't return to her side with fallible arguments, with post-mortems that wouldn't help. He'd made his commitment to her; she'd been unable to accept it, or him. At that moment she heard the front door open, close. Mark Duffy was irretrievably gone.

Chantal eased out of bed. She ached with her body's throbbing arousal that had not been fulfilled.

She shivered, thinking of Mark's own physical distress and unhappiness. She looked out over her narrow balcony to the street below. At the curb a car went into gear, moved off into the night. There was no calling back a future with Mark Duffy. A future that practically any other woman she knew would have accepted with joy.

Chantal walked slowly to the bathroom. Mark's desire just didn't blaze for her, it didn't consume. It comforted and warmed, and that was all. Not enough to settle for!

She stepped into the shower, turned on the faucets and let a mixture of hot and cold roar down upon her head. Streaming with rivulets of water, her hair swirled across her face like a dark veil hiding her tomorrows. So she remained, eyes closed, leaning forward, the weight of her body supported by both arms outstretched, palms and fingers pressed against the green tile squares of the shower wall.

Where her back ached, just above the buttocks, she let the hot water plunge its comfort. An unintended, unexpected orgasm shuddered through her womb. It was the final demeaning gift that Mark Duffy had left her this terrible evening of her life.

After a time she opened her eyes, reached for the loufa mitt and vigorously scrubbed the length of her legs. She should be feeling sad. She wanted to feel sad—sad and romantic and yearning because she had lost a love. That at least would be ennobling. What she felt was dynamic relief.

Chantal turned off the faucets and reached for the big towel that hung over the side of the shower rod. Wrapped in terry cloth and blow-drying her hair, she was unprepared for the long, steady rings of the extension phone in the next room.

Doro Kentz's voice on the other end of the line was husky and apprehensive. "Thank God, you're home! Were you in the sack? Or alone?"

"Alone. Completely. What's up?" Chantal sounded businesslike.

Doro responded in kind. "If you haven't started that report on our Munich star, forget it. Something urgent has come up. You remember *The Assaulters?*"

"Seven hundred pages. A course in speed reading. How could I forget?"

"We were considering optioning it. Merely *considering,* mind you. I just found out we already *have* an option on the property. Some bright lawyer in our New York office did the legal bit. No one thought to tell us out here."

"What happened to your lines of communication?"

"Can't you guess? Everyone's too damned efficient. Let's not discuss it now. Are you prepared to work tonight?"

"Sure. I've got on my bath towel. I was going to type until midnight."

"If you do this favor for me, I'll never forget it. Tri-Symbol will never forget. And there's a big bonus."

"What . . . is . . . it?"

"Don't tense up, Chantal. Please get dressed, take what notes you have on *The Assaulters* and drive out to the Valley, to a bungalow office on the Universal Studios lot. There'll be a pass at the gate for you. It's Simon Bryce's office you want, Bungalow A, B . . . something like that. The guard at the drive-in gate will direct you. They're interested in the book out there. Here, they've decided they don't want it! That German actor you saw tonight in the screening, remember? His agent just told us he doesn't speak English well enough for an American film. Fluent in six languages but not in English, can you imagine? So now everyone's scrambling to trade off the option."

"What's the hook? What am I supposed to do?"

"No one over at Universal has really read *The Assaulters*. They just know it's hot. Chantal, there's a priority rush on this. Our vice president in charge of creative affairs, who shall be nameless, wants to get rid of the option New York dropped on us and which he was supposed to know about."

"Keep it simple, Doro. You're getting repetitive."

"It's up to you to do a verbal synopsis of the plot so Simon Bryce's outfit will buy! He's a thirty-seven-year-old independent producer over there who does quality work. You've got to be absolutely marvelous. Bryce's development exec and a couple of his assistants will be watching and listening. As well as the great Simon himself."

"It will cost you."

"We're prepared. We'll pay anything, Chantal . . . anything within reason, that is. We'll be forever in your debt. Think what that means. You're going to freelance. We'll throw a lot of business your way."

"No, you won't, Doro. Just make tonight's check big enough. And I'll do it."

"Five hundred?"

"Five percent of the option price. What was it?"

Doro whispered a figure. Chantal told her it was a deal. Before hanging up the phone, Doro came back with a cautionary "You know you're gambling. The company will pay that big only if you bring it off."

Chantal smiled, a slow, secret tightening of her lips. She'd do it. She needed the money. Her family needed the money. As her Latina friend, Blanca, would say, "The *problema principal* with you, Chantal, is that you are too tied to the life stream of your family; you are captive."

Chantal could put it more factually. The *problema* in her life right now—aside from Mark, and that was solved—was the really awesome financial bind the Jerrold clan was in. She had to help rescue them from their hard luck. Plus, she had to enhance her own career. She spoke into an empty phone line. "It's done!"

Chantal replaced the receiver, then dressed quickly in a delicately feminine gray silk suit, its gray eyelet blouse matching her silvery eyes. She stopped in the kitchen, drank a glass of milk, put the cold crêpes aside and ate a hard roll.

She was thinking ahead. She'd done this sort of thing before: a verbal exposition of material under consideration for a film, or for a TV project. But never had she done it without adequate preparation. Never, unexpectedly, in the middle of the night. Or practically middle-of-night for a place where everyone went to bed early in order to rise early to fight the freeway system. She glanced at the clock. Nine-thirty. Depending on the traffic, it would certainly be after ten before she reached Universal.

Double-locking the apartment door behind her, she sent up a swift petition to whoever was looking after Chantal Jerrold: let me do well, be self-confident. Let this be a beginning. . . .

Chapter Two

Chantal drove her car up the San Diego Freeway, through the Sepulveda Pass, made the turnoff to the right onto the Ventura. Deliberately she kept her mind away from the strenuous session ahead of her. Instead, now that she was no longer awash in guilt, she could think about Mark, coolly and even with some humor.

Her family had met Duffy once. She knew what they had thought—her mother, her father, her sister, Ardis, an aunt or two, a cousin, a family friend, whoever had been there that day in Hancock Park: Mark Duffy seemed an intelligent, agreeable man, more traditional in appearance, occupation and background than the others Chantal had brought around.

To her family, it seemed that Chantal specialized in collecting strays. There'd been black-belt Tony, who'd bench-pressed three hundred pounds in the

Jerrold driveway; grim-faced Steven, who'd lectured them all on the evils of nuclear power; there'd been that attractive young man who composed classical music and who was on lithium to control his mood swings—which was fine with the Jerrolds except that he'd insisted on going into clinical details concerning his condition, which only he seemed to find fascinating.

Chantal exited at Cahuenga Boulevard, driving south toward Universal Studios' tall office building, known as the Black Tower because of its dark glass conformation. She had finally allowed her attention to veer away from family and toward *The Assaulters*. Before leaving her apartment, she'd reviewed her file of notes and the résumé on the galleys. She timed herself. It would be twenty minutes before she drove onto the studio lot, found a parking space near the Simon Bryce bungalow, walked inside to introduce herself to the strangers waiting for her. Twenty minutes was long enough to plan the campaign, but not long enough to allow stage fright to tie its stranglehold on her—which could happen if she let it.

The security guard at the gate wrote her name in the log-in sheet, spoke on the interstudio phone and motioned Chantal past him with the instruction "First turn to your right. Next to your left. Straight ahead to the brown building—Bungalow C. Plenty of parking this time of night, right in front. G'night, miss. See you on the way out."

She was unprepared for the tall cypress trees, the marble steps leading down into a secluded garden, the fountain splashing in the night. She followed a winding path that led to a massive oak door bearing a bronze knocker.

Before Chantal had time to pull the knocker, the

door pushed open, seemingly by itself. Startled, she moved cautiously inside, to a foyer whose walls were paneled in pale birch. Overhead there was indirect, golden-toned lighting. An antique hat rack, standing to the right of Chantal, bore an unusual assortment of headgear: a Foreign Legionnaire's kepi, a fur busby resembling the bearskin hat worn by a British guardsman, a gentleman's black silk opera hat, a pith helmet, a scarlet fez with a gold tassel, various leghorn straws and a plumed toque.

Chantal reacted in stuttering astonishment as a darkly handsome youth leaped unexpectedly from behind the opened door. He was wearing a one-piece garment zipped halfway up his bronze-skinned torso and expensively tailored to exploit the masculine thrust of his body. Like a spiteful imp, he grinned at Chantal. Grasping the fur busby, he set it atop his head. Then rakishly and with panache, he saluted her.

Helped along by the towering bearskin hat, and by a projection of some private alchemy of his own, the small figure appeared to grow a foot in height. He truly seemed to become Her Majesty's guardsman. His bearing military, his manner stern, he wheeled ahead of Chantal. With an impeccably British accent, he commanded, "Follow me . . . to the inner chamber."

Chantal remained motionless. Distracted by the young man's playacting, she was fast losing the poise she'd hoarded for herself on the drive to the Valley. Abruptly the fellow turned back to her, removed his headgear and tossed it toward the rack. He waited, fingers at the ready, to catch it if he erred. But the busby whirled on its peg, settled and scored. The man regained his sly grin, sank to his former stature. His eyes were beautiful and brown. His delicately chiseled, strikingly handsome face was oddly familiar.

Chantal whispered, "Peter Tark!"

"You've seen my films?" Universal Studios' biggest box office attraction seemed raptly pleased with Chantal's involuntary reaction. "You *know* me."

He was secretly laughing at her, making fun of her astonishment. Coolly, Chantal answered, "I'm here on an assignment for Mr. Bryce. Which way shall I go?" She would refuse to bow and flutter at his celebrity status. Perhaps it was humorless of her, but she had real business at hand.

"How do I know, dear, which way you should go? Some pretty girls go this way." Peter Tark nodded to the left. "Others go directly to the office." He looked Chantal up and down, his velvet-brown eyes insolent. "Dream, if you were coming to see *me,* I'd say left, march! You're probably too intelligent, though, so right it is!"

"Peter!"

A lithe woman, beautifully dressed and discreetly ash blond, hurried into the foyer. On seeing Chantal, she halted. "You must be Miss Jerrold." She put out her hand. "I'm Larette Howell, in charge of creative development. Mr. Bryce and a couple of his assistants are waiting for you. *Peter!* Aren't you coming back inside to listen to this?"

"Why should I?"

Larette moved her hands helplessly. "Because he expects you to."

"He's not going to cast me in the lead and you know it. The Black Tower told him to give a nod in my direction, and that's as far as it takes us. Number one, I wouldn't do a picture with him. I hate his goddamn good taste—no exquisite money in it. Number two, give me incest, or a costar who's a nubile twelve-year-old, and then I'll listen. Good night, Larette.''

Peter Tark grabbed his left arm with his right hand, upped his forearm with fist clenched in salute and departed.

"Oh, Jeez, that little squirm!" Larette collapsed against the paneled wall. "If I don't net that tiger butterfly, if I don't come back with him . . ."

"What will happen?" The expression in Chantal's eyes deepened into curiosity.

Larette didn't answer directly. Instead, she said, "Arrogant, abrasive bastard! But you should see that face on the screen. Of course you have—and the body too! When the camera locks on him, that Peter is magic. Despite all the women he's had, his only continuing love affair is with an Arriflex. Oh, well, who needs him."

"Don't you think we'd better go?"

Larette straightened and returned her attention to Chantal. She became crisp in her manner, discreetly casual, her smile polished, her blue eyes clear. No hint remained of the frustration she'd shown following the departure of Tark. The pale and perfect face glowed earnestly. *"So* glad you're here. Wonderful of you to come out this way, and so late too. Any difficulty finding us? Would you like to go to the john before you meet with the others? Sometimes one becomes nervous. You know?"

"I'm okay."

They walked to the right, into a wide corridor containing a fireplace whose cream-colored mantel held a Tang ceramic horse. Larette nodded in response to Chantal's query. "It's the real thing. As well as the bronze over there . . ." She nodded. "And that marble piece at the end of the hall."

"Should I tiptoe?"

"Just don't wave your arms around too much."
Larette paused. "By the way, do you do this sort of
thing often? It must be extraordinarily difficult to
spell out an entire book verbally. I mean, give space
to the plot, color to the protagonists . . .?"

Though Chantal's gaze was as untroubled as
crystal, she was beginning to feel the inner tautness
of anxiety. First Peter Tark and his patronizing
ironies. Now this sleekly dressed woman's tension-
producing questions.

Chantal squared her shoulders, which brought
Howell's speculative stare to the gentle outthrust of
Chantal's breasts. Chantal quickly caved in her
shoulders, removing the bosomy outline. "I don't
expect to have any difficulty," she replied stiffly.

"You're right. Don't let those people in there
intimidate you." With this final jab, the executive
moved ahead of Chantal. The set of Larette's
smooth blond head was perfection, the swing of her
white linen blazer a sonnet. Uneasily, Chantal raised
a hand to push back her own hair that suddenly felt
oppressively heavy and unruly. Her forehead was
damp. She was perspiring. Her throat clicked dryly.
She watched Larette's graceful back. What a diaboli-
cally clever putdown of a suggestion: *Don't let those
people in there intimidate you.*

She was becoming paranoid. What purpose could
possibly suit Larette Howell to see Chantal Jerrold
fall flat on her face, professionally speaking? It
would be to the creative development exec's interest
to have it all work well, wouldn't it?

As Chantal entered the large office a pace behind
Larette, she was certain the air conditioning unit had
been turned off, or, at the very least, lowered
several uncomfortable degrees—perhaps in respect

to the studio's energy quota for the day. Quietly she removed her tailored jacket and placed it over the arm of a leather chair. If she wore it a minute longer, she knew she would break out in an undistinguished sweat.

Her face serious and intent, Chantal was unaware that she was being watched, unaware that to someone else her small form might have a grace and sensuousness that she herself had never recognized. She was not a floating blond goddess or a sable-haired beauty who moved like a panther. She had never regarded herself as having any particular physical distinction. Someone else thought otherwise.

The individual sitting in the shadows watching Chantal as she slipped out of her jacket was reminded of the limpid fluidity of a figurine in a porcelain group he had once observed in the Victoria and Albert Museum in London. At that time he had been beguiled by the graceful, eighteenth-century nymph, her perfect breasts spilling out of sculptured draperies. He had never forgotten the statuette. But porcelain was not flesh and blood. This striking creature was *here*, in this room with him, wearing a sheer, pale gray blouse, bending to adjust the jacket and handbag. He wondered what color her eyes were—a fact that didn't really matter. She had merely addressed his senses for the moment, had stirred a long-ago imagery. He folded his arms and sat back.

As if responding to some silent signal, Moira, one of the assistants present, asked Chantal to begin. Chantal was aware that there was a listening figure behind the shining table top that served as a desk. She knew there were the two assistants, a man and the woman, as well as Larette Howell, all shadowly present in the background. She knew she must do superbly well to earn the fee Doro had promised.

Because Chantal's former employers wanted to rid themselves of the property, she must make Bryce and his people buy the whole deal on *The Assaulters*. The illumination in the room was soft and deliberately indirect. Chantal let her gaze flow from point to point, from person to person, yet still she could not actually see anything or anyone. It was as though she were behind footlights. The listeners out there were a blur, but an attentive, dangerous blur. One she must conquer.

She began to talk, recounting the story from all those pages she had read, which none of these people would ever have the time or the inclination to do, though their company would eventually pay six figures for the privilege of buying first the option and then the book to put on film. All of this would happen *if* she were successful tonight in what she was doing.

Carefully Chantal colored with words and expressive phrases, tracing in descriptive framework and dialogue, varying the emphasis by the use of her voice tones, pausing at the explosive scenes to give full value, playing up the book's valor, violence and eroticism. She held her audience. It was hers, and she discovered in the telling of the tale that the story, too, belonged to her. When she neared its conclusion, she sensed a stir followed by a quiet that seemed to hang intently on each word.

Always there was the man behind the table top, watching, listening. The office was vast and dim. The face of the listening man was obscured; only the eyes gleamed. Sexuality was tied in with the type of success Simon Bryce had attained. It was a bridge, a strumming, a kind of drumming communication of the senses. Standing before him, Chantal began to feel the pull of emotional intimacy between them. She continued her rush of words, the descriptions, the action, yet all the time she was aware that someone, some *impulse,* was reaching out to her. It was a carnal quivering she must ignore. It was too sharp a divergence from the matter at hand.

She talked on, weaving words into compelling mental pictures for her listeners to visualize. She did well because it was her business to do well. She also sweated. All of her was damp—her armpits, the hollow between her breasts, the small of her back, the secret places of her body. She felt consumed, not by her task but by the sensual magnetism projected by the listening presence she could not see.

She had done well. She knew it when the last gun died, when the book's hero and heroine were doomed, yet gazed at each other knowing that together they had achieved. Still, there was always the frantic hope that they would survive, but the fiery blast at the end destroyed that hope . . . and there was no more.

The room was heavy with silence. Chantal's voice had lasted for the full hour without a hint of hoarseness. At the conclusion of the story, its tones were still vibrant. After several long moments of silence there was a spatter of congratulatory applause. Larette and the two assistants purred, though not too loudly, because Bryce had not yet given his verdict. He had neither spoken nor moved.

Chantal picked up her jacket and handbag, feeling a surge of dislike for this silent listener. It was cruel and unnatural of Simon Bryce not to rise, not to come forward, not to make himself known to her. Or rather, to make his satisfactions known.

It was possible he was *not* pleased. It might not be "a deal" at all. She could not resist shooting one swift glance into the dark behind the desk. Nothing. No response. She could not reach him, nor could she tear apart the noncommunicative shadows surrounding him.

Larette Howell and Dean, the male assistant, followed Chantal down the office corridor. When Larette murmured good night and again thanked the younger woman, this time she appeared genuinely friendly. Chantal was certain she knew why. Simon Bryce's independent production company was going to take over Tri-Symbol's option on *The Assaulters,* though no one had committed himself to it.

Chantal had won.

Larette turned and walked swiftly back toward her own office in the bungalow. Dean asked for Chantal's phone number. His request had an official ring to it. "I'd like to let you know our decision on this."

A week earlier Chantal had received her newly printed business cards. She reached into her bag. Dean took the proffered card and read it carefully. "I'll personally see to it that you have plenty of assignments," he assured her. "Perhaps more than you can handle." He was young, and he looked eager.

Chantal smiled to oblige him. Though she was weary, she spoke confidently and with a lurking mischief. "I'm very fast, and very good."

"I'm sure you are." His tone lingered. "May I use this number to call you socially sometime?" He sounded well mannered in a dated fashion. She assumed—correctly, as it turned out—that he lived in San Marino, the "establishment" area of Pasadena.

To her own surprise, Chantal responded, "I . . . I think not. You do understand?" He didn't. Actually, neither did she. He was nice. It would have been pleasant to go to dinner, or to see a film, with him.

But something unprecedented had happened to her tonight. Whether it had been back in her own apartment with Mark, or whether it had been here in Bryce's small world, Chantal wasn't quite sure.

She couldn't resist asking, "Is your boss always so . . . stoic?"

Neither heard the footsteps behind them until Bryce spoke. "I'd like Miss . . ."

Hiding his surprise, Dean quickly supplied the name. "Jerrold."

". . . Miss Jerrold to come back to my office—if it isn't too late for her."

Simon Bryce looked directly at Chantal. In the goldly glowing foyer, she, in her turn, saw his face for the first time.

His eyes were extraordinary, a melding of blue-black like the sea at its farthest, deepest depths. The nose was proud, the cheeks faintly grooved with fatigue. Simon Bryce's lips were long; in their lack of expression they were as teasingly inviting as the carved lips of a statue. His hair was thick and dark.

He had a magnificent physique. Broad shoulders tapered to a lean waist; the line of thigh was straight and strong and hard. Of course, Chantal mused, it's his tailor who is impressive. No one who sits hours at the conference table could keep a muscular torso so splendidly under control. It has to be done with expensive fittings. Actually, she admired his conservative dark suit.

"Why are you smiling?" Bryce asked. Without waiting for her answer, he turned toward Dean and nodded him away, then looked back at Chantal.

"Are you tired after your . . . shall we say, exhibition tonight? You know, you were very good."

"I know," Chantal said mock-humbly.

They both laughed, were suddenly silent.

"You can come to my office, can't you?" he coaxed. "I have something to say to you."

This time Bryce's office was brilliantly lighted. Quickly Chantal looked around. One thing she knew immediately. The furniture was not leased. Taste and the patina of age were evident in the antique cabinets, the mahogany breakfront bookcase filled with leather-bound volumes, the wing-backed chairs, the brass chandelier, the Chinese vase, the original Modigliani.

Simon indicated a chair near his desk. Chantal seated herself. "A drink?" he asked. "You must be thirsty after crossing that Sahara of talk. Or would you like tea, Perrier?"

Chantal shook her head. Knees together, fingers gripping the strap of her handbag, she glanced fleetingly across Simon's desk, where papers now lay scattered. Reading production reports upside down was a bad habit of hers. She could discern the total minutes of shooting on a particular day, the number of setups, the amount of film used and the amount of film printed to date. Sometimes this was an invaluable bad habit when assessing the progress of a rival company.

He noticed the involuntary flicker of her eyes along his desk. He leaned forward. "The first call of the day was for eight-thirty, the set dismissal at seven-fifteen."

Chantal colored. "A long day's work, wasn't it?" Her chin lifted challengingly. "You didn't allow me time to see the starting film inventory."

"Just as well." His tone was dry. "You'd accuse

my production unit of waste. Let's stop being technical, even if I definitely appreciate your abilities in matters like these. I don't find you devious, though, Miss . . ." He paused thoughtfully, his mind scrambling for the girl's full name that Larette Howell had given him during a briefing. Having solved the problem, he went on. "Chantal, I find you interesting. It hasn't taken me long to make up my mind about you. But be candid with me, if you can, and give me a truthful answer. Do you yourself believe in *The Assaulters,* or is what you did tonight a ploy to remove its option from Tri-Symbol's schedule and add it to mine?"

Though she might never see him again, she knew that Simon Bryce's face, person, the sound of his voice, would be recalled to her in private fantasy a hundred times over. For this reason, she then told him exactly what she believed, and what she knew to be true.

"The book is excellent material. However, the one man who could do the lead role full tilt is not available. He's a Polish actor who does his best work in German films. I saw him earlier this evening in a film with English subtitles. His English isn't fluent enough yet for an American audience, but they would be stunned by his talent and charisma."

"I know the work of the actor to whom you're referring. He did that Peruvian river thing." Chantal nodded. Simon Bryce continued to probe. "You see no one else in the role?"

"Second and third choices, perhaps." She named names.

"What about Peter Tark?"

Chantal's reply was an explosive "No!"

Bryce smiled widely and leaned back in his chair. "I'm certain there would be a three-way agreement on that among you, me and Tark. No question of it. Later, I would like you to assemble reasons for me why he shouldn't be cast in *The Assaulters*, should I decide to take it over. In that way, I can transmit that solid 'No!' of yours to the executives in the Black Tower. They have the unreasonable expectation that Peter Tark should be next seen in what they think of as an 'artistic success.'"

He stood up and began to pace. "I never guarantee what's going to happen to what I put on the screen—my private vision. My *product* is known as quality. Quality can fail amazingly at the box office . . . and often does."

"Mr. Bryce, I don't understand your connecting any further services of mine with your projected plans."

"You're coming to work for me as an associate." He looked at Chantal almost in surprise, as if she hadn't known this fact, or hadn't understood the implication of their conversation.

"I . . . no . . ."

"What is this 'I,' 'no'?" Seemingly he was amused. "You may not have had time to consider what an association with me would mean to you at this point in your career." He paused. There was no answer. "Have I acted too quickly? Let me see another of those business cards of yours. The same one you gave to Dean."

Wordlessly Chantal again reached into her purse.

Simón Bryce scanned the small, stiff card, then handed it back. "Do you intend to spend the next year of your life reading, by the hundreds, other people's scripts, their book galleys, their agents' presentations—all on a freelance basis? You can do the same thing for me on a far more selective scale. I make only one film a year—sometimes one film in two or three years. The financing is no problem. There's never a rush in the production or in the evaluation of material. Aren't you, like other women, working toward taking an important part in the creative preparation of film properties?" Bryce stared down at Chantal, his gaze quizzical. "Here, with me, you would find an ideal base for your very authentic talents. I decide quickly. When I make a business proposal like this to a relatively inexperienced young woman, it is because my instinct tells me my faith in her will not be misplaced."

"You do make a rapid contract." Chantal watched with alarmed interest as the man resumed his pacing. His profile resembled that of a hawk assessing its territory.

Simon halted, looked sharply at her. "What is it, Chantal? Most people in your position would give an immediate 'Yes' to an opportunity to work closely with me in my organization."

"Most people would. I agree." Chantal added warmly, "I do appreciate the offer you've made to me, but . . ."

"But what? Is it because we haven't talked money? The income in a deal like this would be substantial. Shall we get down to that?"

"No, please!" Chantal jumped to her feet. "There is a very specific reason why I can't tie myself to long hours, to a rigid schedule. I know what film work entails. I've had production experience, not as an associate to a producer such as yourself, but I've done it all—call sheets, production reports, cast calls, coordination of the actor's wardrobe, hair, script; writers' changes, revisions, mimeo, even coordination of post-production scheduling: dubbing, looping and musical-scoring arrangements."

"Look! I want your brain, not your coordinating

ability. What else did you do—AFTRA contracts and payments? Time cards? Shooting schedules?"

Again they were both laughing as Chantal took up the chant: "I've done observation of booth timing, video blocking, staging and tape direction."

"You see? You're an all-around genius type, and you don't know it."

Chantal grinned. "*I* know it, Mr. Bryce." She sank back into the leather chair.

"Simon."

She absolutely couldn't call him Simon. This big, magnificent man must be a little mad. She knew, in a triumph of vision, that this late-night conference of theirs would remain with her as the wonder of her life. Slowly she looked up at the lean, expressive face glaring down at her. A man like this deserved the truth.

Almost shyly, she began to explain. "I told you there was a reason why I couldn't accept any type of assignment that didn't allow me to come and go freely. It has to do with a situation in my family. My parents need my help now."

Simon bent over Chantal, his hands resting on either arm of her chair. "Where does your family live?"

"In Hancock Park."

"Then you don't mean that they need your financial help. What is it—an emotional problem? I didn't know your generation looked upon family as a responsibility."

"It's . . . many things." The short statement was inadequate, but it was the best she could do.

"You prefer not to talk to me about it?"

Chantal nodded, intensely aware of the close proximity of his arms to her body, of his face on a level with her own. She looked at his lips. She could breathe in the masculine scent of him. She edged farther back in the chair in an attempt to appear more at ease than she actually was. And then, shocking her with its suddenness, she felt his touch.

With the palms of his hands he smoothed back her unruly hair, sleeking away the heavy bang that had fallen across her forehead. "I want to see your face." Deeply startled, Chantal stared up at him, her eyes very wide. "They're gray," he murmured, as though in response to an earlier question that had been cornered somewhere in his mind.

He stood up and moved slightly away from her. "Well, little Chantal, I would like to have you with us. You possess qualities I value—a distinctiveness, an originality of thought. I observed them while listening to your synopsis of that vast book—which, incidentally, I *have* read. I'm well aware of what you did with it, cutting its length, emphasizing the drama. Are *you* aware of the certain capabilities you have?" He moved still farther away, his back to her. "Also, you are loyal. I like that. I understood it when you mentioned your duty to your family. Even before dedication and discipline, that loyalty of yours is to be prized. I would like to see it expended in my behalf." He shrugged, turned back. "But do what you have to do. We'll keep in touch."

It was the casual tone of that final phrase that awakened Chantal from the hypnotized attentiveness she had given Simon. He might be like so many of Los Angeles' independent film makers, a spellbinder. One needed that quality to secure financing, to seek distribution, to woo creative writers, directors and stars.

But where Simon was concerned, she really didn't think that was true. Simon Bryce was unique. He has to be, she told herself, because it seemed to her that she was, in part, forever lost in the sea depths of those somber eyes.

Earlier, before starting out to the Valley, she had surmised that tonight would be a beginning. It had turned out to be that. But only in career terms, she reflected hastily. Not in reference to anything personal. Yet she acknowledged that in saying goodbye to Bryce, in walking out of this office, away from Bungalow C, she would be taking with her an image of a man who had unsettled her without—she was sure—any intent on his part. A man who—

Her reverie was interrupted as he gave her hand a businesslike shake. At that moment there was a genteel tap at the door, and a smoothly functioning Larette Howell glided inside Simon's office.

Larette smiled evenly. "It's midnight. Dean and I are getting ready to send out the cables to Paris and Vienna so we can catch our people there before they go to lunch. Could I have your okay, Simon?"

"Good night, Chantal." Simon Bryce spoke in absent dismissal, not looking at her. "Oh . . . and thank you."

Chapter Three

The house was a classic English Tudor. It sprawled over three-quarters of an acre in the prestigious Hancock Park area of Los Angeles. It had been passed down through three generations, to end finally with Jason Jerrold.

Early in the morning Chantal parked her Datsun in the driveway and stared at the house. She had grown up with its inlaid hardwood floors, its beveled, stained-glass windows, its nineteen-foot ceilings. There were eight bedrooms, marble baths in each suite, a spiral staircase and a gourmet kitchen with oak cabinets and floors. French doors led to aged-brick pathways and patios in the rear and to the side. At one time, when Jason was flush, he'd added a pool and a spa, and in the kitchen a microwave oven, a trash compactor and other modern conveniences.

The championship north-south tennis court had been in place since the turn of the century. Helen

Wills Moody and Bill Tilden had played there in Chantal's grandfather's time.

Chantal knew the area's real estate brokers would describe the house and environs in terms of "gracious, comfortable living; tasteful elegance on a quiet, tree-shaded street." The truth was something else.

Millicent Jerrold met her daughter at the front door. She was nearing fifty and was still beautiful in a rather bizarre fashion. Twenty years earlier her reddish hair had shown signs of gray. This mischance of nature had been taken care of by the frosting skills of a Beverly Hills salon that had transformed her into a striking pale blonde. She wore her long hair coiled high on top of her head. Her eyes tilted upward at the corners, as did Chantal's, but their color was an indefinable hazel shading to smoky topaz. She was a small woman, barefoot at the moment, wearing a flowing caftan and carrying herself and her voluptuous bosom with the exotic grace of a lovely pagan.

Chantal was amused. Her mother always made her think of silver waterfalls and foreign shores. She was a woman whose body scent seemed redolent of island spices. Chantal looked down at Millicent's bare toes, which should have been tinkling with the rings of tiny bells. Chantal could not imagine where her father had found her mother. Actually, it had been on the campus of the University of Southern California, and Chantal had long known this prosaic fact.

Millicent drew Chantal inside the house and kissed her warmly, something she had never done with any of her children while they still lived at home.

"Look at this!" Millicent thrust a sheet of paper

into Chantal's hands. The large block letters printed on the lined tablet paper read: FIRST ONE HOME SKIMS THE POOL.

Chantal's eyebrows raised. She recognized her father's outsized script.

"Jason left this note on the kitchen table, then went off jogging with Cy Barlow. Jason refuses to assume responsibility for that pool." Millicent moved toward the bay window in the outer hallway. "We had to let the gardener go. George Sunada had been working for us for twenty years. Look out there! Lush landscaping? It's a jungle. The neighbors must think we have something to hide. As a matter of fact, I suppose we do."

"You say Jason's off with *Cy Barlow?* Wasn't it Cy's bank that refused to extend Jason's loan when the broker called that stock he'd bought on margin?"

"Darling, don't blame Cy. He knows your father too well. They were Sigma Chi fraternity brothers. They played on the football team and all that. Cy's very, very fond of your father socially. He just won't do business with him."

"Doesn't that attitude sort of impede their friendly running schedule?"

"Of course not. Jason still belongs to the Los Angeles Country Club. That's a very big plus as far as Cy's concerned." Millicent inspected a brass bowl filled with pale pink peonies. Reflectively, she sniffed the faint fragrance of the round blossoms. "Jason should have lived in the eighteenth century— or was it the nineteenth?—when it was fashionable for gentlemen of substance not to pay their bills."

"You're thinking of Beau Brummell and his tailor. What's this about the pool?" Chantal crackled the paper she still held.

"Jason let Dick Sparkleclean's pool cleaning

service go. Or rather, the bill wasn't paid for six months, so Sparkleclean terminated us. Your father said he'd take care of the chlorinator and the algae and all the rest of it. Of course he hasn't."

"Do you love Jason?"

"Certainly. Don't you?"

"He's my father."

"He's my husband."

Smoky amber eyes met those of gray. The two women smiled at each other in conspiratorial pleasure. They linked arms, sauntered past the drawing room and along the downstairs corridor. Chantal glanced into the formal dining room.

"That sterling silver tea set on the buffet should be worth several thousand dollars. It's massive. And what about those pastoral landscapes? You never liked them. Someone might bid for them if you sent them off to Sotheby Parke Bernet's auction rooms."

"I simply couldn't do that. At least Junior mails us a check for a thousand dollars every month, which barely covers the grocery bills, Jason's club and the utilities. Jay Junior's a generous boy—and only twenty-one years old. Chantal, where do you suppose he makes his money?"

"I'd be afraid to ask, if I were you. Maybe he's become a whiz at cornering the glassies market." In reply to her mother's questioning look, Chantal said tersely, "Marbles! Remember, he was the champion on the block when he was six. I guess Jay must be adept at other games by now."

"Not very funny, Chantal." Millicent frowned, then raised a hand to smooth her brow. "Do you realize I don't have my son's telephone number— only his answering service?"

"Mother, I've tried to explain why."

"You mean because of his affair with Kiki Dalton? I don't think he lives at her house. What do you suppose a forty-year-old woman sees in a twenty-one-year-old man?"

"It's understandable. Jay is gorgeous. As Uncle Edward used to say, Fairy Godmother hit him with the beauty stick. He got *all* the looks in this family, and that's considerable if you think about his being a combination of you and Jason. Ardis and I were left out."

"You look very nice, dear. I mean, you're healthy, and you do have an attractive figure. And Ardis has definite chic."

"But Jay is beautiful."

"I hope he doesn't know it."

"I think he does."

Mother and daughter grinned at each other. Millicent reflected that Chantal had always been her favorite child. One wasn't supposed to have favorites, but Jay seldom appeared at home, and Ardis was petulant, really quite mean-tempered at times. Understandable, perhaps, due to the unfortunate involvement with Boy Farrell. Chantal was whimsical, kind and dependable. Definitely the one Millicent could talk to candidly.

Aloud, Millicent recounted the disastrous ventures of the past week. "The travel agency job fell through. My math isn't up to figuring airline schedules. And I failed the state's real estate exam for the second time. I can't afford to take that course again. Your father doesn't know."

"Then you haven't told him you've been trying to find some type of work? He wouldn't like it. I hate to say this, but though he's purse-poor, he's even more family-proud. The Jerrold name and all that."

"My dear, *I* wasn't born a Jerrold, I merely married one. I'm not too proud to want to pay the bills in this financially distressed household of ours." Millicent glanced out a French door. "Here they come. Your father may not have a head for finances, but he's certainly a fine-looking man. Look at that stride of his. Diet, exercise, vitamins and meditation do it all for him."

Chantal joined her mother at the glass door. "He's wearing a different running outfit."

"You mean a *new* running outfit." Impassively Millicent ticked off the items. "Digital stopwatch, nylon shorts, Adidas TRX Competitions."

In wonderment, Chantal shook her head. "Wrist, torso, feet—everything for the well-heeled runner."

"An extravagant charmer, your father. Let's make him some hot tea with honey and lemon. He'll want his papaya too."

They walked into the kitchen. As she watched her mother fill the copper kettle, Chantal was curious. "Don't you miss the garden club, the bridge tournament stuff, the volunteer work you used to do? What does Father think of your dropping out of all that? He must notice. He doesn't know the reason for it, does he?"

"I told him I was writing a novel."

"You did *what?*"

Millicent curled her legs around the rungs of the kitchen stool and looked fixedly at her bare toes. "Why not? I'm thinking of enrolling in Oliver Larch's writing group at the university next September."

"How did you and Oliver Larch make contact?"

"I saw him last week at the benefit garden party the Blakeneys gave. We talked. Then a day later we had lunch at Perino's. I brought along some short stories I did years ago. He says they show promise."

"Perino's? Who paid?" Certainly not Oliver Larch, whom Chantal knew slightly. She was sure he could barely afford the dollar—or was it now two dollars?—for valet parking at the luxurious, pricey restaurant on Wilshire Boulevard.

Millicent sighed. "It was our good fortune that Boy Farrell happened in with Ardis. Your father always says timing is everything. Boy and Ardis joined us, and he insisted it was *his* treat—such a generous man. It's unfortunate that he's been married twice before. He seems to be happy the way he is now. Free. But Ardis is twenty-five and it's time they married. They've been engaged for five years."

Chantal spooned honey into her teacup. "Engaged?"

"Don't upset me, Chantal. I know Ardis isn't a virgin. I don't want to think about it. Here's your father."

Jason Jerrold charged in through the screen door at the rear of the garden porch. He ran in place for a few seconds in order to cool down. Reaching out, he tapped Millicent affectionately on the shoulder. Keeping up his pace, he kissed Chantal. Next, he paused in his gait long enough to pick up the porcelain teacup and drink down his tea. He held up the cup to the morning sunlight, admiring its translucent quality.

"Chantal, I have an old Pennsylvania Dutch expression for you. It goes, 'I Like fine things Even when They are not mine, And cannot become mine; I still enjoy them.' Yes, that's how it goes." Jason appeared very pleased with himself. "However, it happens this fine cup is mine—ours, rather. It's part of a set that serves thirty people and has belonged in this family since my grandfather's time." Jason put down the cup. "Chantal, how *are* you? You look ravishing. Whom have you ravished lately?"

Her father made her feel beautiful, womanly, spirited and wise. She was grateful to him for this. But now her cheeks became as pink as the peonies in the outer hallway.

"Look at the child light up. Milla, our younger daughter must be in love. Oh, where's the honey . . . the honey, and my papaya."

Millicent served the fruit. Jason gave his wife a kiss full on the lips. He winked at his daughter. "Let this demonstration be a lesson to you. You see here, in your mother and me, two products of a happy marriage that has lasted twenty-six years, an eternity in this town."

There was a small mirror in a baroque frame to the side of the kitchen door. Jason stopped by it and inspected his handsome, graying head. "On Melrose Avenue they want fifty dollars for a hair trim."

"I wouldn't pay it, Jason. Let me shape it for you." Millicent ran a finger over the back of his neck.

"This penurious woman is after me with her manicure scissors. Chantal, I want you to look at this thigh of mine." He gave its muscularity a hard chop with the side of his hand. "Have you seen anything like that in a man fifty-two years old?"

"You want me to say you can't possibly be fifty-two?"

"Certainly. What do you suppose I was leading up to?" He gave Chantal a rib-cracking bear hug. "You're not smoking, are you? I mean grass and such. You going light on the wines?" He turned to

Millicent. "Keep Chantal here for lunch. I'm going upstairs for a shower. We'll talk when I come down."

Jason vanished.

"He won't be down for an hour," Millicent said. "He'll do his meditation now."

Chantal was pensive. "Can you believe Jason? We all love him, but he's such a child. Was he always this way, Ma? I don't seem to remember."

Millicent stared thoughtfully across the room. "I don't think he was when I married him. He was a few years out of college then, and working in an investment firm. He always had marvelous social contacts, so the stocks and bonds sold well. That is, they sold the first time around. Then he retired to go into property management—his own property! In the last few years he's retreated from the realities that the rest of us face. He feels that he's failed us, failed his blessed Jerrold name. Everything he inherited is dwindling fast—the property leases, the stocks, the investments. Everything that came from your great-grandfather originally. *He* was a monument of a man."

"What about Jason's father?"

"A lot like Jason. Right after World War Two, your grandfather Jerrold sold the acreage west of the Sunset Strip. It was a field of poinsettias in those days. It didn't occur to him that a meadow filled with flowers could be valuable for anything but aesthetic reasons. You know what's there now?"

"A couple of high-rise buildings."

"Exactly." Millicent tied the strings of an apron around her small waist, causing the crinkly material of her caftan to billow out in shades of muted lilac and blue. "It's not that Jason cares all that much about money for its own sake. He knows he's mishandled the estate left to him and that we, who are his responsibility, are all suffering for it."

Chantal looked around the handsome kitchen. "A lovely place in which to suffer." She didn't want to dispute her mother, but the reality was that none of them was Jason's responsibility any longer.

Millicent continued. "This lovely place, as you call it, may not be ours for long. Jason's thinking about a mortgage on the house. He has always picked the wrong lawyers and the wrong accountants to advise him. I'd never admit this to anyone but you, Chantal."

Chantal knew that her mother's tone was rueful rather than bitter. "I'll come home to live if you want me to. I know you had to let Beulah go."

"Let's say Beulah retired. It was time. She'd been housekeeper here for thirty years, long before I married Jason. I still have weekly cleaning help. Don't come home, Chantal. It's enough that Ardis will be here."

"I didn't know about Ardis!" Chantal was totally astonished. Ardis had been content living at the Marina on Boyd Farrell's boat.

"She plans to spend the summer with us at EdgeMont. Boy will come out there for awhile. I invited him right after he paid for our lunch at Perino's. The bill was a hundred and thirty-eight dollars for the four of us. Of course, it included wine. And tips to the maitre d' and the waiter."

"That's terrible. You're putting yourself in bondage to that man. Boyd Farrell has always wanted to buy EdgeMont. Ardis and he must be working on you and Jason to sell the country place."

"Jason will never sell EdgeMont. Don't suspect Boy's motives. I'm hoping he and Ardis will marry."

"So is Ardis."

"Can you blame her?"

"No, I can't. He's rich, eligible, still cute enough to be called by that silly nickname. *Boy!* It sounds like a first-grade primer: Ardis wants Boy. What does Boy want? Boy wants our country place—the whole two hundred and eighty-five prime acres. His construction company will bulldoze the citrus, the vineyards, the sage fields and the canyon. He'll build houses, roads, a sewage system, and put in gas lines, electricity and a shopping center. He'll make himself another fortune. I think I had better go to Edge-Mont for the summer along with the rest of you."

"I can keep an eye on things, Chantal. I won't let anything wrong happen out there." Millicent opened the refrigerator door and peered inside.

"Can I trust you, Mother?" Millicent didn't answer. Chantal was impatient. "What are you doing?"

"Jason likes an early lunch. I'm preparing Mediterranean salad. Artichoke hearts, black olives and alfalfa sprouts with a wedge of goat's milk cheese."

Chantal chained herself to a painful silence.

Cheerfully her mother continued. "Did I tell you my friend Athalie, who runs a modeling agency downtown, has asked me to come in part time and help with her trainees? It doesn't pay much. Still, it may be my grand entrance into the business world."

Millicent spoke the last phrase with an exaggerated lilt. She pouted her lips, raised her eyebrows, made a funny little clown face which was meant to reassure.

Chantal felt a protest rising. Mothers shouldn't have to try to cover up their fears with brave evasions. Mothers should be strong. Forever.

Her father had said it: timing is everything. It was

at that moment that the coder in the breast pocket of Chantal's denim blouse beeped loudly.

Millicent started in alarm. "It's a remote-control device," Chantal explained. Her voice was steady. For a moment back there, she'd almost made a ridiculous mistake. Millicent's spirit was great; there was really nothing pathetic about her mother. Relieved, Chantal went on. "It means someone's called me at my apartment and has left a message on the answering service. I'll use your phone here to pick up the recorded message that's on the system there."

"When was all of this installed?"

Chantal had not yet told Millicent she had left Tri-Symbol Productions to allow herself freedom to come home when needed. Over her shoulder, Chantal replied, "Don't worry. It wasn't expensive, and it's deductible. I'll tell you about it later."

She sat down at the hall phone, dialed her apartment number at the Villa, then listened intently to the message being played back to her. When she hung up, her heart beat a wild tattoo.

He had only had to say her name: "Chantal?" She had known who it was, known an immediate sensation of bitter-lingering sweetness. He had dismissed her coolly the night before, but what matter? She dialed the number he had left for her on her machine. When he answered, she said, "Yes, certainly I'll be there." Carefully she wrote down the address. She also wrote down Simon Bryce's phone number, knowing it would be unlisted.

In Encino, at the top of the high hill ridge, Chantal drove west on Mulholland, her eyes on the sharply winding road ahead. She did not look, but she knew there were spectacular views on either side of the canyon's crest. To the north, the busy mélange of the San Fernando Valley, combining its home communities and its industry; to the south, the city itself; and far beyond, the Pacific Ocean sequined in the early-afternoon sunlight. The day was a clear one, no smog, but with a strong movement of the Santa Ana wind in the air.

Chantal's thoughts preoccupied her. Why had Simon Bryce summoned her so urgently? Who were the others whom he had mentioned as being present for the meeting at his house?

There was no need to glance down at the piece of paper that lay on the front seat beside her bearing the instructions on how to reach his home. Her mind, trained to memorize, functioned sharply. As she would never forget Simon Bryce's face, she seemed to know inevitably her way to his presence.

The wind was blowing strongly, a real norther. She turned the car to the right. The descent was steep. The few houses to be seen in the folds of the canyon were of a 1940s vintage with pale walls and Spanish tile roofs, their second-floor balconies encircled by strangling vines of copa de oro, whose huge gold flowers opened in daylight to drink in the sun's rays.

Farther below in the canyon, where her destination lay, there was deep shadow as the sun disappeared beyond the arm of the mesquite-covered ridge. Chantal drove through an open iron-grille gate to a horseshoe-shaped driveway in front of a large house that appeared silent and remote. A handsome place of indeterminate style, its lower windows were barred by ornamental iron scrollwork. The curving arch of the front entrance was decorated in an arabesque, with flower, animal and figural designs in the intricate and mysterious patterns of the East. Tall eucalyptus trees formed a windbreak behind the house. Even here, in the canyon's depths, the wind blew, though more gently, as it stirred the tops of the shiny-leaved eucalyptus trees and swirled the profusion of untamed shrubbery—oleander bushes grown tall and lush, giant hibiscus and trailing lantana that snaked through thrusting green vines.

Several cars were parked in front of Chantal's. She moved among them—a Porsche, a Mercedes, a Toyota, a pickup truck, a vintage Continental—and glanced down at herself. She was wearing the same clothes she'd worn to her parent's house this morning; a denim-style shirt created out of thin, imported French fabric, pleated blue cotton pants caught to her waistline by a drawstring, thong sandals on her bare feet. She'd left the phone beeper in her woven handbag on the car seat. No other call could be more important than the one she had received a half-hour earlier.

Chantal took a deep breath to still a wild heartbeat. At her age, an auricular fibrillation? Chantal laughed at herself. At sixteen years, yes, but Chantal was twenty-three.

She rang the front doorbell. Moira, Bryce's assistant, opened the door. Dean was behind her shoulder.

At the sight of them, Chantal knew she needn't have been concerned as to the appropriateness of her own attire. Moira was barely into a tank dress, and with her wet brown hair looking as sleek as a seal's pelt, she must have just climbed out of a pool a few minutes ago. Dean stood tall in cowboy boots, a green and brown plaid shirt and rusty-brown denims.

They greeted Chantal with rival warmth and led her toward a sparsely furnished conference room. Three men seated at a long table rose at Chantal's entrance. Chantal surmised two were Europeans and the other man near her father's age.

Wearing tinted glasses and a three-piece business suit, Simon sat at the head of the table. He reached out an arm toward Chantal, took her hand and drew her close to him. It was merely a gracious gesture and slightly protective, of that Chantal was certain. She bit her lip to hide its tremor and smiled blithely. Introductions were made. She, who was trained always to remember names and put them together with faces, recalled nothing except that Simon's warm, strong fingers held hers and that a heady scent of June roses was drifting in from somewhere outside.

An instant later she had composed herself and was seated, as Simon had indicated, at his right side. A young man brought her a glass of freshly squeezed orange juice. Chantal breathed normally and listened precisely.

"We're buying *The Assaulters.*" Simon's smile was a brief gleam. "I've told my associates that you're unable to work for us on a—what was it you said . . . rigid schedule, long hours?" Chantal managed to nod, then was dismayed that her auburn hair fell like a loose sheaf across her intent face. Simon continued. "We're willing to have you do what you can for us on a part-time basis. We'll need a plot breakdown and a projection of major scenes, which must come from someone like yourself who is technically proficient and familiar with the book. A procedure like this isn't usual, but it's the way I like to work. You can do it, can't you?" Simon asked. "And have it ready for the writer we'll assign to the film?"

Chantal answered firmly, though her voice didn't sound familiar. It was pitched too high, it glided too rapidly. "Yes. No more than a one-hundred-page breakdown is required, wouldn't you say?"

"I would say." Again that splintered gleam of a brief smile. He didn't really look at her. He had achieved what he wanted, as he had expected to. He had hired Chantal. For confirmation, he glanced at the three men seated at the table. "We can work from that? It will give us an idea of what we'll need before the budget is finally okayed."

One of them asked, "In three weeks? How does that suit Miss . . . Chantal?"

Riveted by tension, Chantal thought, I can't! It's impossible! There's not enough time. Aloud, she confirmed calmly, "I'll deliver the script breakdown by July fifteenth."

Bryce's face was without expression. "Satisfactory, gentlemen?" The three nodded in unison. Bryce continued. "We can get on with our work on the preliminary budget, then." Three heads nodded. "Chantal, Larette is in the library. She and Dean can draw up the financial arrangement with you. You're certain that this type of assignment falls in with your . . . plans for the future?"

Chantal detected a sharp edge of amusement, even sarcasm, but his lips continued their amiable smile. She was unable to read the expression in the eyes hidden behind those tinted glasses. She wanted to. She couldn't.

The man who had served the orange juice made

his second appearance, this time to guide Chantal to the library. Larette Howell sat behind a huge desk, looking as immaculate and stiffly efficient as she had the night before—except for that incredible instant in the bungalow's foyer when she had appeared driven to a fury by Peter Tark's insolence. She regarded Chantal gravely.

"It seems you made an impression." From the tonelessness of her voice, it was impossible to tell whether the comment was meant as a compliment or whether it was said acidly. Chantal wondered what system of signals existed between employer and employee to enable Larette so swiftly to comprehend the meaning of Chantal Jerrold's presence in the library.

It was Dean, seated on the lower rungs of a ladder leading up to the high reaches of the bookshelves, who urged impatiently, "Don't be cryptic, Howell. After last night's masterly interpretation, we could all assume Chantal would be joining us."

"On a temporary basis, right, Chantal?" Larette's smile was honeyed.

"That's what I've agreed to. Exactly that, Larette, and no more. Shall we discuss terms?"

Outside, the wind gave a small, shrieking wail, while Dean snorted and turned away his head. Obviously, he was delighted with Chantal's answer to the executive in charge of Creative Development.

The unscreened, open library windows began to rattle with a monotonous metallic clang. Gusts of wind appeared to be rising in force. Annoyed, Larette crossed the room to crank open the casement hinges. The windows swung solidly outward once more. A sultry breeze riffled inside the room, stirring papers on the desk.

At that moment Moira's single scream from the patio stilled all movement within. Dean was the first to reach the windows and stare up at the hillside. With one lunge, he was over the casement ledge and racing across the grass. Oak and buckthorn on the steep canyon side behind the house were ablaze with the suddenness of a match touched to dry tinder.

The rising wind swept down the gully. Smoke and brush-crackle filled sight and sound. A tongue of flame broke from its comrades and raced crazily through the low grass at the rear of the house. Chantal and Larette ran to join Dean outside.

Almost immediately the automatic roof sprinklers on top of the house came on in full force drenching slate roof, stucco walls and the three women standing below in the outer patio area. With the deluge of water, Moira and Larette fled in panic around the side of the house.

At the first sight of that lighted cigarette carelessly tossed out of someone's car to ignite the dry grass, a canyon resident farther up the hill had telephoned the alarm. The floating warble of fire sirens could be heard as the crews pounded their engines up the steep road from Ventura Boulevard below.

The acrid bite of smoke was riding the Santa Ana wind, which had been blowing since dawn. A melon of color swept up into the sky. Action engendered by experience sent Bryce and the other men to moving out the cars in the driveway, yet not far enough to impede the progress of the fire trucks circling the curves of the canyon road.

Chantal watched the servant and Dean as they spun lengths of hose equipped with heavy-duty nozzles. They quickly sprayed streams of water across the back of the house, wetting down walls and shrubbery. Chantal grabbed up the only available, smaller garden hose, turned the faucet in the patio to its limit and noted that the water pressure had not yet dropped. Ash and burning leaves swirled about her. She stood up close to play the gush of water toward the space where ground brush stopped within one hundred feet of the house, as prescribed by the fire department.

Her hair and clothes laced with powdery residue and mud, Chantal dodged only when a pair of deer bounded out of the undergrowth, skittered across the brick patio, avoided the pool and disappeared into the foliage of the front gardens. The animals weren't frightened at the sight of humans. What they had seen, heard and scented behind them was a far greater enemy.

Staring above her, Chantal was shocked at the rapid destruction. She could see black char, the twist of smothering smoke, the vomit of heat. Yet suddenly there seemed to be a shift in the ominous atmosphere surrounding her. The burn no longer seared in the tops of the eucalyptus or reached out toward the house. The pace of flame grew uneven. The fire was indulging itself in a giant pole vault from treetop to treetop, spanning yards of oak and mesquite at a single bound. Crazily it had changed its course. Fortunate for those in Simon Bryce's house. Unlucky for the others in the next canyon.

It was still hot. Deadness lay across the horizon. But it was also dry, dry as the skin which crackled over Chantal's flesh. The quiet air sighed and split with the dehydration taking place. Chantal looked at the sky. It was a sinister wash of gray; nothing stirred. Her throat tightened. A tremulous weak-

ness stole through her body, she felt as though
the air were dying in her lungs. Her hands
lost their strength. The hose dropped from her
fingers to the ground, twisting like a snake from
the force of the water still shooting through its
length.

As she stumbled backward, someone caught her
trembling body. She was held close, then half
carried, half dragged along as she and the man made
their way around to the front of the house. There
they both stood gasping for fresh breath.

On the opposite ridge, there was an explosion of smoke and flame. Chantal swung away
from the awesome sight, her hands covering her
face. She leaned close into the scorched cloth
of someone's shirt, her face buried against a
male chest. Powerful hands held her to still the
quivering terror that pealed through her body
in reaction to the devastation she had witnessed.

"It's all right, Chantal. Everything here is safe.
They've got it under control. The field truck came
by to say they've started the chemical drops
from the big copters. You can hear them—see
them!"

It was true. Along the next ridge, the giant sky
birds were swooping low to discharge the full tanks
of retardants that would help deaden the conflagra-
tion below.

Small, disheveled, her shirt and pants stained and
torn, Chantal slowly looked up into black eyes
searching hers. No, not black, she sighed tiredly, but
eyes like the dark, far reaches of the sea. She
remembered nothing more. Chantal Jerrold had
never fainted in her life. She did not faint now. She

simply slid gratefully into semiconsciousness, still aware that she was being picked up by strong arms and carried easily into the house, up the stairs, to be laid peacefully on a wide bed. She sighed again and turned over, her lips crushed softly against hands that held her close.

Chapter Four

Chantal awakened suddenly, her heart pounding as though in an escape from the gross arms of a scarlet nightmare—flame, lashing wind, splintering heat.

Still dazed, she shot into a rigid sitting position, arms extended out behind her, alone in the vast bed. She looked about at a room darkened by the mysterious green-vine shadows of late afternoon. Who had brought her here?

She was not sure what had occurred after she had stumbled with weariness in the patio below. She remained in Bryce's home, of that one fact she was certain. She looked down at the clothing she was wearing. Ragged rips in the fabric of her once-elegant shirt revealed an ash-smudged bra.

She slid out of the bed. The pleated blue cotton pants she had worn were a disgrace, and with the drawstring somehow loosened, they fell to the floor in an untidy heap that she was glad to step out of.

Wearing only her bikini underpants with a narrow

lace crotch and a curvet of fine embroidery surrounding her upper thighs, Chantal padded across the room to the adjoining bathroom. She washed her hands and face at the basin, then combed through her tangled hair with a silver comb and brush that were on the small dressing table.

She splashed water on her upper body and refastened the straps on the lace bra that the voluptuous heaviness of her breasts demanded she wear. She had often wished for her sister's skinniness; Ardis could go braless with the freedom of an eleven-year-old girl. At the age of eleven, the much-smaller-statured Chantal had already been crossing her arms about her bobbing chest in gym class.

Chantal found her thong sandals, one by the doorway to the outer hall, the other upside down under the bed. She shook her head wonderingly, then explored the wardrobe for something she could wear—a man's shirt, an extra pair of lightweight slacks. She knew that nothing she would find could possibly fit her. And exactly nothing hung in the closet.

She'd have to put on her own ash-blackened clothing. As Chantal considered this, she walked to the window to scan the scorched hillside. But Chantal did not realize the bedroom was on the opposite side of the house. Her view was of the driveway. Only one car remained, her Datsun. Where had everyone gone?

Chantal was angered with herself for having passed out. It wasn't like her. She'd always stood up to stress in a definitive manner. She liked to believe she'd inherited the emotional steel of her great-grandparents.

She leaned farther over the window ledge and this

time looked down into a secluded walled patio at the side of the house. The miniature garden quarters were landscaped in a manner that provided a sybaritic and luxurious privacy. From a grotto of pure-veined stone a gentle waterfall splashed into the depths of a sunken outdoor bath, a pool large enough for several people to bathe in. Chantal was fascinated. Her gaze traveled to some ferns and draping willow branches, where a redwood-staved hot tub had been installed. Even from this distance, it was apparent to Chantal that the tub's soothing sorcery was at work. It frothed and foamed and bubbled, its waters pale green and opaque, as though recently put to use.

Suddenly a figure emerged from the overhanging greenery in the tub's vicinity. Though she knew she could not be seen, Chantal drew back. Then once more she peered curiously over the window ledge. A man, totally nude, his body starkly masculine in the width of shoulder and the brown length of leg, stepped directly into her line of vision. He strode across the grass to slide with one powerful thrust into the cooler waters of the marble pool. He floated face upward, his muscular body blurred beneath the shimmering movement of the water.

Chantal was unable to avert her gaze. Astounded at her own reaction to what should be a natural sight, she felt a hot rush of desire. It was as though the flames of the canyon fire again lashed out at her while a seething excitement tingled and licked within her. She was embarrassed by her voyeurism, and was even more surprised at her disturbingly physical response.

She had admired Simon Bryce. She had been both intellectually and emotionally attracted to him during their somewhat constrained encounters. She had not believed it possible to feel such a compelling need to be close to him.

Chantal stepped back from the window ledge and her vision of the naked and overpowering male. She must get out of his house as quickly and silently as possible. There must be no trace of Chantal left behind, no scent of unexpectedly urgent desires. Since she had accepted this present assignment with Bryce, there must be no sexuality to betray her own interests or his.

She threw on her garments, remembered that her handbag and ignition keys were in the car below. As she cinched the drawstring of her blue pants, she wondered why she was being assailed this way, both by physical desire and by the necessity for flight. It was unfair. She was Chantal, in thrall to no one. Yet she'd known from the very beginning that Simon's face, his person, his voice, would be recalled to her in private fantasy a hundred times over. She repeated this thought now, exactly as it had claimed her once before.

She looked around her. This house itself was not a private fantasy. She must get out!

Soundlessly, she raced down long stairs to the entrance hall. A shadow preceded hers and fell across the inside of the massive front door. He was here, clad in a white cloth robe, his black hair curling and wet, his face smiling and kind. Looking at Simon Bryce, Chantal knew she had lost her freedom forever.

"Where are you off to so fast? I thought you were still asleep. Now I find you running away like those deer escaping the fire."

That's exactly what I'm doing, was Chantal's inner response. She could only stare at him, her eyes huge and remorseful. He had not known she had spied upon his privacy, that she had deliberately assessed the deliciousness of his maleness. He did not know that he was looking at a woman raked by a longing to touch him, to fondle his beauty.

His expression changed. "What is it, Chantal? What's happened?"

The world has slid open and I have slid into it, to a far deep inside, burning like a hell, and the blaze is within me and cannot be quenched, and I shall die of it. . . . So ran Chantal's bemused, mad reflections as, voiceless, she stood before Simon Bryce.

It was as though he understood her frantic thoughts. Perhaps he would always understand her, and that was her curse. No matter what happened, no matter what events drove them apart, there would always be his comprehension of her. They *would* be driven apart. There was no doubt about that. Chantal had never been lucky with men. The men who were considered right for her had always adored her. But she had not wanted them. Chantal did not expect luck to be on her side in matters like these. She did not challenge Fate to be kind.

Simon touched Chantal's face, soothed the place where her hair fell wildly about her forehead. Swiftly, with a strong hand on her shoulder, he stopped what would have been her violent departure. His fingers gripped deeply, and Chantal thought she would cry out and turn and sink her teeth into that hand that held her life captive.

"The others have all gone. I wanted to talk to you, to learn more about you. We saved this house together, remember. I had thought we could go to dinner somewhere." It was spoken so casually.

She attempted a small joke, holding out the sides of the smudged, pleated pants as though she were a little Dutch boy. "Wearing these?"

"We could have gone to your place. You could have changed your clothes."

Could have . . . ? Wasn't it going to happen now? Perhaps he had already sensed her irrationality where he was concerned, and her attempted flight displeased him. There was nothing she could do. Chantal stared at Simon, shame for her sentimental imagination and desire for his person quivering in her gaze. Her eyes were as pure as a child's, yet they told Bryce nearly everything about her. They did not beg for protection for herself, they asked for a part of his life.

Bryce's own eyes grew bleak. He almost did comprehend everything. He glanced up the stairway to the second floor. He was sure then of what she had seen from the window.

It was not meant to be simple between them. Not meant to be merely a quick physical joining and then goodbye. From their first meeting in his office, Simon had been aware of depths in Chantal. He knew she was drawn to him and that he could become an obsession with her. He too was to blame. There might have been some deliberateness on his part, though he had never intended that anything between them should go further than a business association that would be rewarding to both. He had wooed her interest in him for that reason alone, but now . . . ? What was to be done?

He would give in. Very simple. It wasn't hard for Simon to convince himself, not with that beautiful womanly face and body asking for love, his. It would be this one time, though, and never again. Could this bright and honest young woman understand Simon Bryce's determination never to involve himself totally in anything except his own career?

"Come with me," he said. She hung back. "Come," he insisted. And he led her outside.

Darkness had filled the private garden, but the surrounding patio walls still gleamed with the last rays of daylight. The marble of the sunken bath shone ghostly pale. The high walls of the house reflected mirrored spaces of white that dappled down on them. It was here that they paused and looked at each other. As though giving permission to Bryce to do what he wished with her, Chantal nodded.

She did not know that her eyes filled with tears as he discarded his robe and stood un-self-consciously before her. Gently he removed her shirt, the blue pants and the lace bra that held breasts so full and enticing for so small a girl. She watched him catch his breath as he looked at her. He was seeing his nymph in the flesh, that porcelain figurine whose form was now coming so alluringly alive for him.

She was unaware of her scream as his hand moved swiftly around her breasts, committing her body to a circle of pleasure. She felt his hand slide down her belly and into the private parts of her waiting desire. She knew that he was making no effort to tantalize either her or himself, no effort to control the turgid surge of his manhood. It was there to be used.

He drew her to the ground, where she sank back into the enticement of surrender. He took her quickly, making his entrance into her body in a manner that was both impelling and yet strangely abstinent.

With half-closed eyes, he watched her face as he partially withdrew and stroked again until it was time. His mouth came down on hers as he held her shaking limbs. In pure delight and rising excitement, Chantal felt the riveting, powerful inner spiral of her rapturous response. It was good, good—wonderful, beautiful—she adored him!

Afterward, quiescent, she lay beneath him on the secluded grass enclave. She whispered wild and foolish words, saying that she loved him, that they had come together in rare beauty. She poured out passionate phrases, holding nothing back. He was the possessor of her love, of her body, of the essence of herself. Inflamed by her own ardor, she talked and talked. It was as though she were articulating the substance of her soul.

Then the night descended fully, and it was quiet. Though she lay in his arms still, she grew aware that he was watchful only. Was he merely being patient and . . . consoling?

Suddenly Chantal was ravaged with embarrassment. He was being very kind. He was being the man behind the desk, listening gravely to a girl who spoke of her raging love for him. Chantal realized then that she had made all the mistakes of being strongly attracted to a man whom she barely knew. Yet for her there was no one else! Unswervingly, unthinkingly, she had cast herself into the fierce fires of passion.

Later, alone, driving home in her car, she recognized the terrible truth of what had happened to her. But not to him, she told herself, trembling. Not to Simon, just to Chantal. *She* loved. *He* was kind. And yet why? she puzzled. He had led her by the hand to the garden. Why had he answered the folly in her eyes, the desire in her body? He did not have to. But he had. Would she ever know the answer?

Jason Jerrold, Jr. had been trying to reach Chantal for the past twenty-four hours. All he got was her damn answering machine, playing background music. There would be a beeping sound, time enough for a spoken message would pass, then there would be another beep—and then nothing.

The thing was expensive and probably was broken, he told Kiki Dalton, who merely threw a naked leg across his haunch and said, "Do it to me again, Jay—with a double ratchet this time."

After she said this, Kiki fell over on her back, laughing. "You know where I first heard that? I was waiting for my attorney in the Polo Lounge, and an ancient guy I knew, a friend of my mother's from World War Two, came over and sat down and started buying drinks and talking. A bore, but kind of likable. You know the type—you can't just snuff 'em, it's cruel. He told me he used to go to the Mocambo nightclub on Sunset Strip and sit at the bar and listen to Lena Horne sing 'Begin the Beguine.' When he was drunk at parties, he'd say it over and over, 'Do it to me with a double ratchet!' D'you suppose that meant something dirty in those days? I never knew."

"Mocambo? What's that? Sounds like a rum drink. I never touch the stuff."

Kiki thought it was funny the way Jay always managed to bring the conversation around to himself and his likes or dislikes.

"Mocambo was a nightclub when they had nightclubs here," she explained. "It must've been torn down years before you were born, Jay. My mother used to go to those places when she was dating. It was a big thing then. Mocambo was the place where Louis B. Mayer discovered Judy Garland singing. Or maybe it was the other place, the Trocadero."

"Kiki, I hope you aren't old enough to remember all the stuff you're talking about. I'm not really interested."

"Well, I am. I've been asked to put some money into a small saloon on the Strip. I'm thinking about whether its past could be revived, as they say, or whether it's too late for that sort of thing."

"What's the matter with that crappy answering service? I want my sister, and I want her now."

"How do you mean, you *want* your sister?"

Jay closed Kiki's wide mouth with a kiss, the kind that started with licking her lips, then sought her teeth, rubbed them tight and moved in with his tongue strangling hers. If he went farther down, she'd yell. He made her yell. "God, I love you, Jay."

Jason Jerrold, Jr., twenty-one years old, sat up in the tumbled bed and looked at Kiki Dalton. "I love *you*, Kiki."

The way he said it made her want to cry. She was rich and successful and smart and terrific. And this twenty-one-year-old wimp could make her cry!

She sat up also, blowing her nose with Kleenex tissue and remembering to hold her shoulders back so that the heavy-nippled, slightly drooping breasts would stand out straight. Consciously she held in her stomach, though she hardly needed to, after all that punching and pummeling at Trim and Touch. Trim and Touch, that was good. It reminded Kiki she'd have to tell the instructor-manager there that he'd better stop touching the customers, or she'd pull out her investment. Some of her friends had even complained to her. Oh, that goddamn business.

"Jay," Kiki asked, "why do you want to find your sister? And which one is it? The thin one who's trying to marry Boy Farrell and his boat and his millions? Or is it the other one, who's bright but not bright enough?"

"You're talking about Chantal, and she's the one I'm trying to reach. She and I are working together on a family problem of ours. I have to tell her I put Dad into a joint account with me at the bank and within two weeks he was overdrawn. So I'm going back to the old routine. Chantal has to know."

"Sending home a check for a thou a month?"

"Right."

"Do they know where your money comes from?"

"Not a chance."

"They know about me, and about you and me. They know I'm rich. Maybe they think it's me who's feeding the old folks."

"God, no, Kiki. Or they wouldn't take a cent. They don't like you."

"Why do you say things like that to a beautiful, loving woman like me?"

"Love me, beautiful woman, and I won't ever say bad things to you again."

"Like this?" Kiki ran her feather-long eyelashes across his bare nipple.

"Oh, Jeez, Kiki."

She moved farther down his body, her rear a hunch under the silk sheet as she nibbled. Jay looked happy. He was happy. Kiki had been nineteen years old when Jay was born. Sometimes he wished he'd known her at nineteen. Or he wished she were nineteen now to his twenty-one. No, it wouldn't be the same. He liked her the way she was. He liked the shadows under those big dark eyes of hers, the little lines spraying out from the corners of her eyes when she smiled, when she laughed. The droop to her lips, the droop to her breasts when she thought he hadn't noticed. He noticed everything about her. He knew everything about her. He loved everything about her.

She was rich and smart. Though not as smart, he was on his way to being rich, and he could have any young kid, male or female, he wanted to lay a finger on. It was Kiki he wanted, and that made her priceless.

"Ow! No teeth now, Kiki. It's a delicate place down there. Careful."

Kiki crawled up from under the covers. She was wearing nothing except her great-grandmother's pearl necklace, real pearls from the southern seas, enough of them to wrap twice around her neck. "These are the kind the natives dove for a hundred years ago," she'd explained to Jay. "They're not cultured."

"Can anyone tell the difference?" Jay had an interest in deceptive appearances.

"Not very many people can."

"How do I know you're not lying to me about your pearls?"

"Would I lie to you, baby?"

"You sure as hell would."

That had been then. Now they grappled, kissed, got serious for five minutes, and then Jay jumped up and off the bed. "Gotta pick up the new cinematographer at LAX. He's flying in from London. His plane better be late, because I am."

"In your business, Jay, I wouldn't call him a cinematographer."

"Okay. Cameraman. He can do beds, beds and more beds, from every angle you ever thought of. That's his specialty."

"You are . . . a . . . star, my love, and so handsome. Too bad your family can't see you in one of your best films."

"My best shows are on Santa Monica Boulevard. The Jerrolds don't even know where that is."

"They like the checks you send them."

"They do that. Damn, I wish Chantal would

answer her phone, or record a message, or do something with the beep coder she's got. I told her how to use it."

"Maybe she doesn't want to be found."

"What makes you think she's lost?"

"Because *Variety* already has it she's tied in somehow with Simon Bryce Productions. Have you ever seen him?"

"No. Why should I? Anyway, she wouldn't tie in with any one company because her plan is to chaperone the family this summer at EdgeMont. She doesn't want the old place sold, not even a spare twenty acres of sagebrush. You know how it's all going to end up? A big fight among Chantal, Ardis, the old man, Mother and Boy Farrell. Somebody else is in it too. Chantal's ex-boyfriend Ric Milland is the local land developer out there at Rancho Cucamonga. He's got his eyes on EdgeMont as well as on Chantal."

"You sound like what's-his-name in the *Hollywood Reporter*. Small-town gossip."

Jay was looking for his trousers. "These need a press."

"Sally!" Kiki shouted. "Come in here."

The maid came in, looked the other way and took Jay Jerrold's trousers.

"She's shy," Jay commented.

"I pay her not to be." Kiki stood up. She was six feet tall and absolutely magnificent with her blond hair and black eyes and nearly perfect figure.

She walked to the huge glass window that overlooked Century City and stared straight ahead toward the tower where her offices were. She picked up a pair of binoculars. "I can see my office from here, and that new secretary isn't where she should be."

"Where's that?" The maid had returned Jay's trousers. He put them on over his bare skin.

"She should be making it with the attorney from next door on our floor. He's got some interesting land leases in Arizona I want to know about."

Jay looked shocked. "You hired her for *that?*"

"I pay her for that," Kiki snapped, and put on a long Oriental robe. "See you sixish?"

"I'm shooting tonight." Jay's grin was that of a slightly depraved urchin.

"Maybe I'll come watch."

"I wouldn't if I were you."

"Oh . . . a little thigh-grappling with the camera looking on?"

"Don't be vulgar, Kiki. Leave that to men. Be a woman and go out and make a million dollars today."

"I love you, Jay."

"I love you, Kiki. Wait a minute." He came close, kissed her gently. "I really do love you, woman."

Kiki Dalton watched Jay Jerrold depart. Or "Jay Jonas," as he was known in his trade. Her face softened. She walked back to the glass window and again looked out toward her office in the building opposite. She wondered what she'd ever done to deserve Jay, except to take care of herself and say three Hail Marys every night of her life. Kiki was an exceptionally lucky person. She firmly believed in prayer.

She walked to the TV set and snapped it on. A news announcer was talking about a canyon fire on the Encino side of the hills. It had been doused by some new type of chemical flown in from Canada and recently purchased by the Los Angeles Fire Department. Kiki reached for the memo pad on the table beside her bed and made a note to herself to look up Standard and Poor's index on that Canadian company.

The boat was a forty-three-foot sportfisherman that had been out of the Marina only twice this year for runs down to Cabo San Lucas to indulge in a couple of catches of marlin.

Boyd Farrell was revolving this sullen fact in his mind while he sat below in the lounge watching Ardis Jerrold stuff her gear into a duffelbag. She zipped up the canvas and sat back on her heels to regard him defiantly. Ardis loved Boy, stubbornly. She also loved his money and his power. She'd been patient for five long years. Another five years and she'd be frightened and alone. A small voice asked: more alone than you are now, trying so hard to make it permanent with Boy? When he isn't trying at all?

Ardis indicated the duffelbag. "There! The last of me! You satisfied, you bastard?"

Farrell spoke quietly. "We'll have the whole summer for the two of us. That was agreed. You know the deal we made."

"And after that—if the deal doesn't work?"

Farrell shrugged. "We split. It's time. You should be on your own, Ardis. And I should attend to my own life."

"Commerce." She spit out the word. "You're a pig financier."

"I've never made a secret out of what counted with me. *Número uno*. I've always told you that."

Abruptly the woman's hostility faded. "But you have attended to business. Always business. No one ever stopped you. My living here on the boat with you hasn't kept you from going to your office in town. Whenever you've wanted to, you've had your associates here for conferences. I've served them

superb meals out of the galley. Look at this place—
the perfect hospitality suite!"

They both glanced in the direction of the wet bar
and sink, at the galley beyond, complete with its ice
cube maker, its refrigerator and freezer, its range
with oven and rotisserie.

Ardis's body rocked forward onto her knees. On
her knees she moved fast across the small space that
separated the two of them. "We can't give us up,"
she pleaded. Farrell remained silent. Ardis's eyes
slanted. "You mean you *can* give us up? What are
you planning to do?"

This character trait of Ardis's, the way she could
veer from an attack on him to a kind of plaintiveness
concerning them both, always unsettled him. She'd
fall back to a position where she'd be defending
herself; then, verbally, she'd shoot hard at him
again, looking for whatever vulnerability she might
detect in him.

Farrell reassured himself that he wasn't particularly assailable. He couldn't be damaged. He
couldn't be wounded. To encounter defeats like that,
one had to care a great deal about something or
someone. The *thing* he cared about, business, Ardis
couldn't touch. No woman could.

"What are you planning to do?" Ardis repeated.

"After this summer?" He was giving himself time
to parry.

She nodded.

"In the fall I might run over to Kona on the big
island of Hawaii, do some sport fishing. That's what
this boat's intended for, not just for living aboard,
not just for bed stuff." He didn't mean to hurt her.
Or did he? "Christ, Ardis, I've got to have time to
myself . . . for awhile."

She gibed at him then. "To do what, Boy? To

read, to think, to meditate with that big social consciousness of yours?"

Again he shrugged, but he watched her closely. She was circling. Like a piranha.

"Over in Kona, are you going to pontificate, Boy? Are you going to deliver oracular utterances to the natives?" She knew she made him uneasy when she hung out her Scripps College shingle. "You could install a newsprinter here in the salon. Have a Reuters commercial wire clicking night and day. Some fun! And as for relaxing . . ."

Ardis continued to stare at Boy for a long moment. Then, without taking her eyes from his, she reached down to her hip level and began to roll up the navy-and-white-striped top she was wearing. Boy's eyes didn't leave hers, but Ardis saw them flicker warily as the material of her T-shirt rubbed over and above her dime-size nipples. She felt the heat between her legs and knew her nipples were becoming taut. Though he kept himself from looking directly at her chest, his pupils expanded like a cat's as his peripheral vision caught those pointing breasts of Ardis's, so small and firm that she hadn't worn any underwear in years except an occasional party-type camisole.

Still on her knees, still holding his gaze, Ardis unzipped the front of her shorts. She stood up swiftly, stepped out of their encumbrance and remained motionless in front of him. Ardis knew she was a delectable nude, though with her extreme slimness she probably looked better in clothes than out of them.

When Farrell didn't quiver, didn't move an inch, she leaned forward and closed her hand over the bulge in his pants. She grinned. "You going to give me up for those damn fish in an on-deck holding tank at Kona?"

Farrell threw back his head and roared, "Who says I have to have you in my bunk?"

Ardis smiled cunningly. She was aware of Farrell's tastes. She had to be. "Have me any way at all. On the cover boards next to the toe rails. How about us locked up together in the head? And that time over at Catalina . . . underwater . . . remember what happened?"

He was out of his clothes, kneeling over her. "Keep talking," he said. "Just keep it up!" He pushed her down on the carpeted floor of the lounge.

"I let you have me at Ma Maison. I let you make me come with your finger in me under the table-cloth, and I sat up straight and nobody knew. I was wearing the diamond earrings and I kept sitting there talking . . . and dying. You make me die, Boy!"

His hand was working her, and though sometimes it was difficult for her to be moist and ready for him, this time she was panting and it was definitely all right. She was grateful for that, because she had to be good for him. Doing it unexpectedly on the floor this way was sexually exciting to him. All the odd places they found to do it enabled him to reach full arousal. That was why, with Boy, she had to keep her imagination working overtime.

For Ardis, this type of erotic inventiveness didn't come easily. Boyd Farrell had been the first—and he was the only—man in her life. A virgin at age twenty when she had first slept with him, she had wanted to keep him ignorant of her status at the time. Otherwise he would have left her alone and moved on to someone else. That was his code. She'd told him that the red seepage of her virginity was her period coming early.

Right now, with Boy Farrell inside her, Ardis forgot the scheming and hoping. How do you snare a man who doesn't want to be caught? Any way you can. Ardis's arms wrapped around Farrell's chunky shoulders. Her thin, darkly tanned legs entwined around his body, higher, higher, clutching him to her. Locked together, they rocked in a funny kind of rhythm with the gentle dip and swell of the waters beneath the slip where the boat was moored.

"Say it. Say it," he demanded.

"Rock your baby," she crooned. "Do it to your baby. Hit your baby good. A-eee!" She was at the apex, just ready for the big slide down, when he came first and crumpled. It was okay. It was really okay, she told herself hurriedly. She held him tight and close, and in her frustration whimpered just a little.

Much later, after he had heaved himself off her, Boy sat silent while Ardis knelt beside him, petting him, running her thin fingers back and forth across the sandy-colored hair that grew low on the nape of his neck. At times like these, she wondered what he was thinking, or even *if* he thought, because he never said.

Making it a firm statement so he'd agree with her, she whispered, "Five years and it's still the best." Actually, what did she know! She'd never had anyone else, so she had no means of comparison.

Boy's brow crinkled. "You turn me on like no one else, Ardie. But I've got to level with you. What I can accomplish in the real world turns me on even more. I've never pretended otherwise, have I?" He stood up.

Dangling, she thought, I hate the way it looks

when it's limp. She turned her eyes away and began
to listen to him. My God, what was he saying now?

". . . you. Or my other life. Why can't Farrell
have both? If I hadn't been married twice before, I'd
say, 'Sure, Farrell can have both, so let's make it
permanent.' But I know better. It—you and me—
gets in the way of what I want to do."

Ardis reached up for Boy's waterproof jacket that
lay on the nearby couch. What was he talking about
anyway? She never, never interfered in his business
world. She didn't want to. She'd learned to read *The
Wall Street Journal* and remember what she read only
for his sake. It was all some big excuse he was
making up so he wouldn't have to marry her. She
huddled the jacket over her body, pulled up her legs,
wrapped her arms around her knees. She sat there
looking like an unhappy gnome, her short reddish
hair cut in a caplike fringe around her forehead and
ears. Her pale brown eyes were unwinking.

"How old are you, Ardis?"

"Twenty-five. You gave me the diamond earrings
for my birthday."

"I should turn you loose to find another guy."

"I don't want another guy." As she had many
times before, she studied Boy. Built like a middle-
weight boxer, he was a man of medium height. The
freckled face had smallish features. The sun-
streaked hair was shaggy. Though he was nearing
forty, his nickname suited him. He did look like an
ingenuous kid, which might have accounted in minor
part for some of his success. Seeing only the youthful
appearance, business adversaries often didn't take
Boy Farrell seriously enough. This impact of his
usually worked to Boy's advantage.

"I know you want to get married," Boy soothed.
"Hell, every woman does! But if you wait too long,

the guys who feel the same way you do about playing
house, with a ring and a license to make it legal . . .
all those fellows are going to be snatched up."

"Oh, my mother told me that," Ardis murmured,
but so low he didn't hear her.

"I love you in my way, Ardis—as much as I can,
that is. Still, I don't want to be any kind of barrier to
what *you* want out of life. It just doesn't happen to
coincide with what I want. Which is total freedom. Is
that wrong?"

Ardis tacked expertly in another direction. "You
said we'd have the summer together. A firm promise?"

Farrell put out a hand to pull Ardis up close to
him. His jacket fell off her shoulders. He ran his
sun-browned hand down her arm, searching out her
hand. "Shake on it." Standing there in the boat's
lounge, naked, they shook hands.

To keep from laughing, to keep from thinking
about how they must look, and glad that none of the
crew was around, Ardis made herself contemplate
her family. Because it was the Jerrolds who were
involved in this solemn promise. Ardis questioned
whether she was being disloyal if she tried to do for
Boy what he wanted her to do. The Jerrolds needed
the money. Her father would receive a lot of money
if he sold EdgeMont to a financier-developer like
Farrell. Not to mention the even larger profit that
would eventually be Farrell's.

As though to reassure herself, Ardis spoke out
loud. "What has sentiment got to do with any of
it—just because Jason's granddaddy owned the place
before Jason did? Think of all those other people
who need the homes you'll be able to build for them,
Boy. You'll make it possible for young families to

have shelter, schools, shopping centers." She paused—dubiously? "Of course, they'll have to have triple-A credit ratings."

"That's my girl." Boy's open palm smacked sharply against Ardis's bare rear. He added in conclusion, "You know that high ground up near the canyon? We'll nudge the zoning commissioners into granting two- and three-acre lots there. The buyers can have corrals, their own riding horses." His smile was guileless. "We can put those properties on the market for around six hundred thousand dollars."

"Too bad land values aren't as high in San Bernardino County as they are in Orange County," Ardis amended.

Boyd Farrell brushed this aside. "If it all happens, Ardis, you'll be Mrs. Boyd Farrell. It's what you want. All you have to do is help me get what I want."

Ardis's lips thinned. Farrell could make this proposition because he was convinced there wasn't much chance of getting the Jerrold land. She'd show him. And after she'd shown him, she'd be a good wife to Boy . . . and all that lovely money of his. Since she'd never known another man in the carnal sense except Boy, he had to be the man she loved and intended to marry. Wasn't that the truth of it?

Ardis looked around her. She had to admit other truths were beckoning her. Such as the power from a pair of GM Diesels running quietly in a fully insulated engine room. The spacious, expensive, air-conditioned luxury. The music out of an AM/FM eight-track stereo system. A teak deck above. All of this priced according to power.

"Come on, get dressed, little crybaby."

The way he said it, with the faintest hint of

contempt, made her squeeze her eyes shut tight. Power, she thought. The price was high. But she would marry Boy Farrell; that was all she knew.

When Ardis was alone, she pulled on the navy-and-white-striped top and zipped up her shorts. No doubt she looked a mess. She could do something about herself physically—a fast shower and a change of clothes and she'd be okay. But emotionally? She wasn't so sure. She'd tried once to get help—to explain to herself, at least, why having Boy for keeps was the most important goal in her life.

She'd gone to the psychiatrist on Roxbury Drive in Beverly Hills three times a week for nearly five months. She'd gotten the money from Jay, making up a story about why she needed such big bucks. Her brother hadn't believed her, but he had come through, the way he always did. Perhaps she should have told Jay the truth about why she had wanted the money, perhaps not. With Jay, one never knew. His Kiki Dalton was so sane and smart, he expected everyone else to be like her. He was only twenty-one, after all.

Ardis's final session with the doctor had been last December. That was the time she had used the entire box of Kleenex that sat on the corner of his desk. She could still hear herself sobbing, "He demeans me, so why do I love him?"

The doctor had asked evenly, "Do you love him?" Always his question in reply to her question.

With tears spurting wildly, Ardis had cried, "But that's what this is all about! That's why I'm seeing you three times a week—to find out why!"

The doctor had said nothing to that, and the silence in the room had become so empty she had had to fill it with her own voice saying terrible things: "I'm willing to help him con my parents. But,

Doctor, they need the money, so selling the home place isn't so bad, is it?" Ardis had added more desperate sounds to that silent room: "My parents love my sister best, but if I marry so much money *I'll* be a success in their eyes. At least I'll have accomplished something. I won't have wasted five years, even though I'm not warm like Chantal, or handsome and independent like my brother. Don't you see?"

The doctor had remained expressionless. She'd jumped to her feet. "You think I don't love Boyd Farrell." She'd pounded on the desk. "That's your answer, isn't it? That's the terrible secret, isn't it? He makes me suffer. Someday I'll make him suffer."

"I did not say that, Miss Jerrold." With that remark, the fifty minutes had elapsed.

"I'll show you!" she had stormed. "*I'll show you!*"

She hadn't known what she was going to show the doctor, but she had never gone back to Roxbury Drive again. She had resolved to love Boy harder than ever, and not to try to find out why it was so important to her that she love him. Sometimes it was better, safer, not to look for answers.

Chapter Five

Tilda Gorman quickly answered Chantal's call for help. Tilda was Chantal's best friend outside the industry. Tilda had been in graduate school at UCLA when Chantal was a second-year student. She had sponsored Chantal in the club to which they both belonged. It took Tilda less than twenty minutes to drive into West L.A. from Santa Monica.

The two sat across from each other drinking Herb Lady's Celebration Tea. Tilda looked disbelievingly at the box's label. In an attempt to mute Chantal's flow of revelation, which was by this time getting unhealthily close to the self-recrimination stage, Tilda read the label aloud. "Chamomile, fennel, mint, sassafras. Is this what I'm drinking? Channie, you don't happen to have any old-fashioned vodka and tonic around, do you? Or maybe . . . hemlock?"

Tilda hadn't gotten through to Chantal. Chantal

still sat, elbows on the table, fingers laced through the untidy coppery lengths of her hair, both hands supporting a head that was aching unbearably.

For Chantal, yesterday's events at Simon Bryce's house continued to unreel tormentingly. Played through her mind, the episodes would rewind and start again, grouping into scenes that exploded, fragmented, then swam crazily together to interlock like the sections of a jigsaw puzzle.

By talking to Tilda, Chantal could escape the proscenium in which guilty thoughts scurried, confused. The night before, two Dalmane capsules of thirty milligrams each hadn't hypnotized her into sleep. They'd merely agitated and exhausted her brain and her emotions.

Tilda listened with sympathetic understanding. Chantal seemed to have arrived at a brilliant noon of passion. Tilda had a tendency to think dramatically. After all, she was an English Lit teacher at Santa Monica High.

Chantal stood up to pace nervously. "It's good to be able to talk to you, Tilda. Especially good because you're not involved at the studio. There, it's one gossip binge after another. Do you know what I mean? Personal confidences laid out, every detail." Tilda nodded comprehendingly. Chantal went on. "The trouble is, we not only hear each other's cries for help, we spread them around. It's, 'What did he mean by what he said?' 'What did she mean by that comment?' Or, 'Is a certain fellow gay . . . ?'"

"And that must be the reason he didn't call back for a second date, right?" Tilda sighed. "That type of reasoning sometimes keeps a gal from feeling too rejected when the phone doesn't ring and she wants it to."

"Who waits for the phone these days?" Chantal challenged.

"Oh, sure, there's always the bar at the Ginger Man. Isn't that where the chic singles go?"

"What do you think?" Chantal asked abruptly.

Tilda didn't have to ask about what. She neatly followed the segue. "I think you don't really want to know what I think. You didn't ask me here to supervise your life. But I can offer an observation if you really want it."

"I really want it." Chantal poured tea out of the brown earthenware pot.

"No more for me, thank you. God, how can you drink that stuff? Here's what I think. Remember, I'm not one to believe in overidentifying, so I'll be as impersonal as possible. This guy had a sexual relationship with you—bang—excuse me—like that. And you wanted it."

Miserably, Chantal nodded. "I must have."

"Was it good? For you, I mean."

Chantal's answer came out in a fast blur of words. "What have I been saying for the last hour? It was good. It was wonderful. It was afterward that I was awful. I wasn't cool. I kept telling him I loved him. And all the reasons why I loved him. How did I know any reasons? We'd just met. I mean, I really let go verbally."

"As only you can." Tilda rose and stalked the refrigerator. "Ah . . ." She'd found the chilled bottle of wine left over from two nights before. She poked her head around the door. "Okay if I have some?"

Chantal waved her hand. "The shelf above your head there."

Tilda retrieved a long-stemmed, Mexican goblet.

Measuring with a practiced eye, she estimated that the wineglass held a good five ounces at a clip, without even being filled to the rim.

She returned to Chantal. *"Salud,"* she said. "Do you want me to go on?" Chantal nodded. "I think what's bothering you, Channie, as much as your exotic love confession to this man, is that you don't understand your hero's motive in taking you the way he did. But look at it this way. The two of you had been through a kind of fireball experience together, and there you were alone in this house. You did your peeping Tom act. Maybe he arranged it so you'd see him nude?"

"No! That's disgusting. He wouldn't."

"Sssh . . . all right. I'll back off on that one. Anyway, there you stand in front of him—a bright, questing young woman with passion in her gut. The same shining out of telltale eyes. You're at the ready, the sacrificial lamb. So your bronzy man-god with a red lantern held to his heart accepts the sacrifice. Why not? He's straight, I hope. After it's all over, you tell him the truth about your purple feelings for him. From way up there on that altar where he sits, where you've placed him, he looks down at you and he listens. Tell me, why is he going to think any less of you because you confirm what is probably his own opinion of himself—that he's a great guy, a great stud . . . ?"

"No, no, no!"

"Okay, okay! I'll keep it on a higher plane. I repeat—his own opinion of himself that he's a clever fellow, a philosophical intellect, a man of purpose and achievement. With an icing of sexual attractiveness thrown in. Is that better? Have I said it right this time? Anyway, Chantal, if you acknowledge his superior splendors, why should he be disgusted with you because you see him in that light? A really terrific guy! No man would object to that."

"I made a big, big mistake, Tilda. Thank you for trying to make me feel better about it, but it's lying there flat in front of me. Absolutely inexcusable."

"From what you've told me, I was under the impression that he could have a spectacular meaning in your life. Am I wrong?"

"No, you're right."

"You were merely being premature, then, in pouring out your honest feelings about him."

Chantal sat, shaking her head, fumbling with the teacup and a Kleenex tissue.

Tilda said, "Gee, I wish I hadn't stopped smoking." She picked up a handful of raisins from the dish between them. "Ugh!" She put down her wineglass and glanced toward the phone, saw the wires and the flat machine with its insides whirring, whining and unwinding. "Is someone trying to reach you on that thing, do you suppose?"

"You're changing the subject."

"So I am. So sorry, Chantal."

Chantal looked toward the recorder. "I disconnected it when I came home. I don't know why. I even took my speech part off, where I say, 'This is so-and-so, and I'll get back to you and so forth.'"

"Think of all the interesting calls crawling around on that thing that you may be missing. Why don't you connect it up again?"

"Not till I decide what I'm going to do."

"What's to decide? Simon Bryce offered you an assignment. You agreed to take it. You don't know what you're going to be paid, because the brush fire cut off that part of the negotiation. Anyway, you agreed. The way you tell it, you've got one hundred pages of story breakdown to do by the fifteenth of July. You're committed. Tell me this. What was his attitude—*after?*"

"I've told you."

"Oh, yeah, that's right—like a professor who's just concluded a successful seminar."

"That's a rather crude way of putting it, but still, *you* might look at it that way."

"And the class applauded?"

"Tilda, are you really my friend, or are you trying out for a stand-up comic role?"

"Excuse it. I'll start over. *Afterward* there was nothing personal from the professor, like 'It's been nice meeting you. We must do this again some-time'?"

Chantal remained silent. Angered.

Tilda stood up. "You have a lot of work ahead of you. It probably won't be necessary for you to check in and see him for nearly a month. By then it won't seem such a big deal to you."

"I don't see how he and I can work together. I'll have to write a letter refusing the assignment—"

"Don't do that, Chantal," Tilda interrupted. "It's your career too, you know. Why break the cup just because you're not drinking from it? You didn't attack the man. A kind of natural lust got out of control between the two of you. It happens. He'll forget. Don't look wistful, now, and say you don't want him to forget."

"You're not exactly offering what I'd call friendly compassion. At least you didn't tell me I made a mistake professionally by getting involved, which is the truth of it. I did make a professional mistake."

Tilda sighed. "All right, I agree. But just remember I didn't say it, you did." She put her arms around her friend. "It can't be undone, Channie, obviously. So try to stop letting it squirrel around inside your head. God knows what was in Simon's mind. Maybe he was destructive, maybe he was exploiting you. For your sake, I hope not."

"I was an equal partner, and anyway, he's not that kind of a man."

"Good. That's what I wanted to hear. Think the best of him and you'll think the best of yourself. And that last is important. It may sound like first-grade primer talk, I know, but write in to Aunt Tilda anytime at all."

Together they hooked up the phone recorder, and then Tilda left. Almost immediately, Chantal received a call from her brother's secretary.

"Jay has been trying to reach you," the woman told her. "He had to go to the airport. He'll call you first thing tomorrow. He says it's important."

"Do you know what it's about, Ellen?"

The woman sounded apologetic. "A Jerrold family matter, I think. I'm not sure."

Chantal hung up hastily. The message gave her something to worry about besides herself and Simon. She thought about Jay and Kiki. Chantal knew that Kathleen Dalton Enterprises was heavily invested in video cassette players, and with more than a million of these machines in homes all over the country, owners were buying tapes by the dozens. All that Jay had ever said about Kiki was that they had met during the time when he had been doing videotapes, and Kiki's company was engaged in the distribution and sale of the machines themselves. The explanation had sounded legitimate and made Chantal feel better about Jay and where his money might be coming from. The headlines in the business section of the newspaper indicated this new industry's sales were setting records.

She looked across the room at her four-hundred-and-fifty-dollar leather attaché case. Jay's present to her last Christmas, purchased from a shop in Beverly Hills' Rodeo Drive. She walked across the room and tentatively touched the case. It contained galleys, a manuscript, a reader's report and a résumé, all the material she would need pertaining to *The Assaulters.* That is, if she were going to sit down and start work on the breakdown. If . . .

Simon's day was full. The reoptioning of *The Assaulters* had been taken care of to Tri-Symbol's satisfaction. The rights to the original manuscript had been sold by its author to Simon Bryce Productions. Certain that all would go as anticipated, Simon had put Larette on the trail of the screenwriter he wanted, someone with whom negotiations had been initiated sometime earlier. If a need for revisions when the final draft was completed should arise, or if a rewrite might be necessary, a list of writers' credits, with agents' phone numbers appended, was secure in a top drawer. Simon didn't expect to have to go to this list. He relied on persuasion, and he had faith in the writer selected. Yet even after many story conferences, one never knew for certain how the final scripting of a property would turn out.

There was no problem concerning financing. It was set, with worldwide distribution assured. He'd had to give points. Arrangements were not quite as flexible these days because of interest penalties, but the gross would be high, especially in Europe. Simon had in mind a clever director who owed him a film, and who would shoot two versions of *The Assaulters* simultaneously—one for United States distribution, one for Europe.

Simon was aware of the foreign star Chantal had mentioned. A contract for the actor's services had been submitted to his agent and was expected to be back in Simon's hands within twenty-four hours. At the moment, language was no problem. The charismatic actor would appear as the lead in the foreign version only. By the time his second film was readied for production, his English would be perfected.

Simon did not eat lunch. He went to a meeting with a trio of writers working on a script in the development stage, held a four-way conference call with New York, Chicago and Beverly Hills, spoke to Hong Kong in order to establish feelers for some necessary prefinancing on a future project, interviewed a colleague's niece whose college thesis had interested him and then hired the young woman as a part-time reader.

At the end of the day he closed his associates out of his office, told his secretary to hold all calls, opened the door to his private exercise room, shucked off his clothes and began his daily workout. He did fifty push-ups and fifty sit-ups. He could easily have done more, but there was no time. He accomplished some extraordinary feats on the parallel bars for a man his size, six feet two and a hundred ninety pounds. He worked out naked, as the Greeks had done in the early Olympiads. At Chantal's first sight of Simon in his office, she had been mistaken about him. It was not his tailor, but nature and his own Spartan regimen that gave him his impressive physique. Now, sweating and lithe and bare-torsoed, he stood upright working at weight pulleys while he reviewed the mental disciplines he'd set himself.

He knew that the precepts he lived by had a certain simplicity, but long ago he'd acknowledged himself to be a simple man. Let others think him subtle and complex, as many surely did. Simon knew better. He understood what impelled him toward the goals he'd set for himself. Abruptly he dropped this line of thought as being antiproductive. He pulled back hard on the tension weight. It slammed upward, then down again. His muscles rippled sinuously along chest and shoulder.

It was far more productive to turn his attention to his advantages—health, appearance, tenacity and faith. Here he was on safe ground. Did he truly have talent? He would not pursue that will-o'-the-wisp either, when so much talent sprang from mere craftsmanship and bravado and the willingness to take a chance—furthered by the magnetism in a handshake, the tone of voice, the carriage of one's body.

Simon turned away from the weights, picked up a towel and rubbed his face, the back of his neck, his black hair curled tight with perspiration. Intelligence, a mastery of detail and a willingness to assume responsibility had enabled him to become a successful leader. These qualities might have placed Simon Bryce behind an executive desk to head a giant industrial complex and gain him a column in *Fortune* magazine. Instead, he was here, in his own exercise room in his leased office-bungalow space on a major studio lot. He had no chairman of the board, no group of hard-eyed directors, watching him. Here in his tent of make-believe, he alone held the office of sultanate. He liked the analogy. It amused him. If he had any talent at all, it was for the depiction of images—the placing of visual experience on film—in a manner to awe or sustain the audience he sought. Actually, he was a magician with a tumbler full of splendid blocks, colorful toys to spill out, to rebuild with, to catch a child's fancy. . . .

Disadvantages? Those were his too.

Wiping the sweat from his naked body, Simon was at this moment making a herculean effort to dilute the memory of another afternoon, another nakedness. He had been so sure he could exorcise the picture of the foolish, ardent, ridiculously lovely girl he had taken on impulse. He had made a mistake. He appreciated a close cerebral, even emotional, attachment in joint creative efforts, but nothing more than that. And now, by his act of passion, he might have jeopardized what could be a very good working association with a bright young woman who had much to offer.

He reflected harshly that there were negatives in his personality. He was manipulative, selfish, often unconcerned with the gentle aspects of another's feelings and personality. Simon stepped into the shower, savagely turning its nozzle to full force. He took the battering of the water in his face and against his body. He mistrusted these leapings of memory that he was indulging in. Why should he think again of Chantal Jerrold? If she refused to work for his organization—a week had passed and no word from her—better to know it now! That had always been his creed, to rid himself quickly of the weak ones.

He stepped out of the shower, toweled off and began to dress in the fresh clothes he kept in his wardrobe at the studio. The words of love she'd heaped on him were purely the result of their physical act. She was the type to consider herself as whoring if she did it without love. So, of course, she had to believe she loved. She had even needed to say it embarrassingly aloud. Very simple. That was the way it was.

The way it was also, Simon discovered to his chagrin, was that his body was beginning to charge with a rigid excitement. He recalled Chantal's lovely limbs on the grass beneath him, her full breasts and tender thighs exposed to his eyes and to his hard embrace. It was as though his manhood possessed a memory of its own in its desire to once more claim Chantal's body.

Almost in anger, Simon shoved his arms into the long sleeves of a heavily textured fisherman's shirt, settling it over his head, pulling at it until his dark, still-wet head appeared through the collar opening. He looked down at himself. His grim face registered disgust. This arousal wasn't supposed to happen. She was just another woman. They were all made alike, weren't they? He knew he was being deliberately vulgar. Same tits, same ass—what the hell was different?

He knew what was different. She was bright and sensitive and she cared, goddammit!

In the outer office, Simon took the messages his secretary, Marilou, handed him and told her to go home. It was after seven o'clock. He'd return any calls himself, the ones that couldn't wait until morning.

He glanced down the list. An invitation to a screen preview at the Directors Guild, Coppola's latest— that could wait. A call from the special effects office. He looked at his wristwatch—too late to dial their extension. A couple of suits he'd ordered were ready for a fitting. That could wait. Long distance, London. Who was Patrice Holliday? He remembered. Someone who wanted an interview for a British film journal. Did the American film maker believe that black and white was more artistic in terms of depicting the terrors of city life than color film—*that* could wait! The next to the last on the list—Chantal Jerrold. The name only, followed by a telephone number. Chantal! He closed his eyes, opened them as if expecting to see that wild sweep of roughened red hair, the full, frightened lips, the pure smoke-gray eyes. His face expressionless, Simon Bryce reached for the desk phone.

She had done it! The breakdown was three-quarters completed. She'd eaten out of cartons; lived on Chicken Delight, cold potato salad from the deli; drunk juice, strong black coffee. No time for her usual health-food kick. In order to exercise, she'd raced quickly around the block after dark, hiding among the honeysuckle vines when a car or an infrequent pedestrian approached. Chantal refused to take any chances on being raped or robbed. There weren't enough hours in the day or night for her to go to the West Los Angeles police station to fill out a complaint. *The Assaulters* assignment came first.

Since she could listen to incoming phone calls before answering them, she had remained incommunicado to most of her friends. Only when Tilda checked in did Chantal whisper, "I can't talk. I'm working."

Tilda understood. "You're doing the breakdown? Everything's all right, then?"

Chantal hesitated. "Everything's fine, Tilda."

"Call me when you're free," Tilda answered.

Chantal hung up the phone, thinking beleagueredly, When I'm *free . . . ?*

She could work night and day, but she had to sleep, even for five hours. In sleep she was not free. She was besieged by restlessness and nearly always by the same dream. She would be wandering in a countryside that looked like France. Then, in a forest of pine trees, Chantal would come upon a clearing where an old chateau stood. She would enter the massive front door. On the first floor there would be many empty rooms. On the second floor all the rooms were empty. A small staircase led upward to a third floor—an attic, also empty. A place to put all the impedimenta of living.

Then came the part that always awakened her and caused her to recoil in terror. In the far corner of the otherwise empty attic there was a handsome room set aside. It was furnished with the trappings of a powerful, well-connected law firm. Behind an enormous desk a man sat in darkness wearing a judge's black robes. He would rise slowly and she would stand before him. She would look over his shoulder, and there she would see the Modigliani—the one that belonged in Simon Bryce's office!

The tall man would raise his arms, the flowing black material of his robe resembling great black wings. To see his face close, closer, she would be drawn to him. He would say, "I am the Black Angel, the Assaulter, and I have come for you."

She would scream herself awake then, because it was Simon's face and Simon's arms, and she wanted those arms to enfold her. She knew what would happen in the dream when they did. Under that black robe he was nude, and the garment would surround them both while he swiftly undressed her. They would stand close together, and he would reach down and part her legs, and he would thrust into her with that powerful member. . . .

Awake, she was furious and strong. Asleep, the dream pursued her and she was feeble, imploring Simon to take her. Chantal didn't let herself sleep very much, sitting instead for long hours at her Olivetti typewriter, working on the plot breakdown of *The Assaulters*. As page after page piled up on the desk beside her, she knew she would finish much sooner than the July fifteenth deadline.

No matter what she had told Tilda about that afternoon at Simon's house, Chantal still had expected in her heart that he'd telephone her and make an effort to see her. He had promised nothing of the kind, of course. But she had been so sure he would come and seek her out. When he didn't, she grew angrier—angry at him, at men in general and at herself for being so weak, so desirous of a man who obviously had no real interest in her. They had lain together. As far as he was concerned, she was a conquest, and nothing else.

Chantal had called Simon's office and told his secretary only to let Mr. Bryce know that the finished assignment would be sent by special messenger to the studio during the week. When Marilou had asked for Chantal's phone number, she had given it but had specifically repeated that she *did not want* Mr. Bryce to call her. It wasn't necessary. He was merely to be told that Chantal Jerrold was sending in the breakdown sooner than expected. It might make a difference in his scheduling of the screenwriter's starting date on the script.

But Marilou had been in a hurry. The phone had rung with the last call of the day. The wife of the chief executive in the Black Tower had been calling to invite Mr. Simon Bryce to her daughter's bat mitzvah. Hurriedly, Marilou had written down only Chantal's name and number. She had forgotten the remainder of Chantal's message, for Simon had come in at that moment from his exercise room with a face as dark as thunder. Marilou had hastily handed him the list of early-evening calls he'd received, and when Simon had suggested it, she'd rushed out to catch her ride home.

At seven twenty-eight that same evening, when the phone rang in Chantal's apartment, she was rereading her copy. Before checking to see who the caller was, she unthinkingly reached out her hand and picked up the instrument. After she said, "Hello?" it was too late.

She heard the sigh, then the male voice she instantly recognized. "Chantal?" Shaken, Chantal could not respond. Simon's voice continued. "Have you decided what you're going to do about *The Assaulters?* I've had no word from you; neither has Larette. We're wondering whether you're dropping the assignment. Is that why you called?" He waited.

So that was what they thought of her! She was a professional, but Simon and his Creative Development executive believed she might be undisciplined enough, *unprofessional* enough, not to complete an agreed-upon project. Chantal was so wrathful she still could not speak.

"You're not answering me?" The silence length-ened, palpable this time. "You're angry?"

While she sought her exact reply—cool, efficient, biting—Simon spoke again. "I believe a confronta-tion between us is indicated."

Over the phone, Chantal could sense his mocking smile.

Chapter Six

They met for lunch at La Serre on Ventura Boulevard. Neutral ground. A restaurant frequented by the executives from Universal, Studio Center and Marble Arch Productions. On each table there was a small metal plate with the name of whom the reservation was being held for. Only regulars would be seated between twelve o'clock and one-thirty.

Chantal was early. She didn't mind. It gave her an opportunity to look around. She'd never been to La Serre before, but she had always heard the atmosphere was attractive and the food excellent. The restaurant's interior walls were painted a light green latticed over in diamond patterns of white wood, giving it the charm and the cool feeling of a New Orleans summerhouse.

There were several small, intimate dining rooms. Moss-filled baskets trailing grape ivy and ferns hung from the ceiling. Behind the miniature bar's mirrored wall surface, sparkling glass shelves held clear vases, each containing an individual bouquet of fresh-cut flowers—purple irises, fragrant carnations, tall spears of salmon-colored gladiolas. It resembled a verdant garden. On the desk in the foyer was a massive arrangement of American Beauty roses, deep crimson, the scent rich and fragrant. All this hothouse perfection created the perfect background for deal making and ego stroking.

A couple strolled by Chantal, the man in designer jeans with the name label elaborately stitched on his tidy rump, a leather tote slung over his narrow shoulder; the woman in a conservatively tailored suit, her brown hair in a neat bun. Chantal recognized the man as a rising recording artist; the woman was probably his producer. Standing near the waiting couple, Chantal was unable to avoid overhearing the pair's conversation. They were newly divorced but planning to live together again. They were about to order their favorite roasted veal with Calvados brandy and fresh apples. Remember the good times?

While she waited, Chantal stood quietly doing her usual, which was refusing to think ahead to the impending meeting with Simon. She'd done enough meditating on the situation while showering, shampooing, manicuring and dressing. It was unlike her to convert so much precious time to the choice of a dress, to the fresh appearance of her skin, to the styling of her hair. But she'd had to undo the ravages of one week of solid work and—insufficient sleep.

She felt a touch on her arm, turned, looked up. It was he. Though she'd prepared herself for this moment, her eyes were dazzled at the sight of him. Her heart pumped frantically. It was a hot day in the Valley. She was wearing a thin, lilac-colored dress of pure silk, floaty, romantic and expensive. She hated herself for this gesture, but she'd run out last night after he'd called and bought it at an exclusive boutique on Sunset whose owner had promised to keep the shop open until she arrived.

Her bright hair was held back by small combs, and last season's spindle-heeled sandals brought her up almost to his shoulder—to the height of his heart. God, she was being stupidly sentimental—again! She had to pull herself out of this sticky rapture.

Simon said, "Sorry to be late. Traffic—"

"I was early," Chantal interrupted. Absolutely scintillating, wasn't she? Then, unaccountably, a burnished scoop of her hair loosened, falling down over one eye. She captured it, tucked it back, took a deep breath and, in chagrin, heard her stomach rumble loudly, nervously. She hoped Simon hadn't heard. Hastily she went on. "I've never been to La Serre. I wanted to look around first anyway."

"Quite a place, isn't it?"

Chantal nodded. "Do we need a green thumb to eat here?" Not very sharp repartee, but they smiled at each other. It felt good.

The hostess knew Simon and led them to the rear of the main room. Yet they were very much alone, very much à deux at a small table behind redwood boxes banked with azaleas that separated them from the rest of the lunch crowd.

"*Bon appétit,*" the hostess said, and left them.

A handsome waiter appeared to recite the day's specialties—Les Hors d'oeuvres, Les Entrées, Les Salades, Les Desserts. Listening to that impressive accent, it was Chantal's guess that the young man had been imported from Central Casting.

They discovered that neither drank vodka and both liked tequila, so they ordered Bloody Marias.

"The cream of celery soup is excellent here," Simon advised. "Let's order later, unless you're very hungry."

This was fine with Chantal. She wasn't hungry. Since Simon had once deciphered telltale signals in her eyes, this time Chantal tried to keep her gaze subdued. She appeared to be examining with interest the yellow tablecloth, then the hand-painted service plates. She was trying to retain some kind of composure while seated across from this stranger whose body she had known intimately for a brief hour in a garden.

Simon reached across the table and took her hand. She let it remain in his with the feeling that at any moment she was going to expire.

"Chantal, I have to know something. Are you with us or not? If it's yes, Larette will be in touch with you about salary terms so that you can start on the project we planned."

This time she could look at him. In a quite natural manner, Chantal released her hand from his. She spoke in a businesslike voice and hoped the expression in her direct gaze would remain unreadable. Not even a tiny touch of triumph must be allowed to show. Now she must behave like a professional.

"I've broken down the story line into master scenes. It's nearly completed." She was speaking with admirable poise. Fortunately for her, Simon was unable to see her hands, clenched tightly together beneath the napkin on her lap to hide their tremor.

"What did you say?" Simon stared unbelievingly at her. The Bloody Marias arrived to relax the moment. He raised his glass in grave salute. "You amaze me. You're as disciplined as I'd expected you to be. More so."

What, exactly, did he mean by his use of the word "disciplined"? Did he mean she'd already recovered from the emotion-charged affair at his house? Chantal hoped that wasn't what he meant. She didn't want him to remember, nor would she let herself remember what had happened between them. Or *why* it had happened.

Simon continued to look at her admiringly. His long, thoughtful face glowed with pleasure. "You *are* a mover. I'm even more impressed with you than I was when you did the exposition on the book. Tell me something, did you have it in mind that my company would be right for *The Assaulters?* Or were you merely trying to get Tri-Symbol out of its option?"

Chantal recalled that Simon had quizzed her once before in a similar fashion. She answered reflectively. "My first consideration was Tri-Symbol, of course. But as soon as I knew about the project, I realized it was overly ambitious for them. Their film arm isn't geared to this type of material. They haven't the resources. Oh, money—yes. Twentieth Century will help out there. But they've recently lost a couple of good people at the top." She hesitated. "Personally, I feel very close to the book. I've followed it through the galleys. It was assigned to me, as research analyst, rather than to one of the readers whom Tri-Symb employs. There was deep interest in it there, I'm sure."

"And you? How did you feel about it?"

"I've said. I love the story. I think I can see how it should be filmed. From the reputation of your production company, I believe you can do it with the understanding, with all the raw excitement, that it deserves."

She hoped Simon wouldn't think she was trying to

court his favor. Her words might have sounded that
way.

Simon smiled. "Does all that enthusiasm indicate
your commitment to this film? If it does, I'm glad."
He raised his glass. "Drink to it?"

He's taking a lot for granted, her instincts clam-
ored. The man certainly isn't modest. He's prideful,
forthright, egotistical—he has to be. She sipped her
drink, but not in commitment.

Simon's strange, sea-dark eyes regarded her. "I
believe we can make an exciting film. When we're
ready, it'll be like stepping into another dimension,
we'll create a world. . . ."

Was he putting her on? Aloud, Chantal had to
remind him, "It seems to me the author of the book
has provided a map to that world." It was an
imprudent remark, perhaps, but in honesty she had
to say it.

Belatedly Simon agreed. "But a flat map only,
Chantal. Oh, yes, a map with words, ideas, a certain
philosophy. But we build on that. We soar. I said we
must create. And *that* is visual."

There was a silence. Did he believe what he'd just
said? He appeared very serious. Leaning forward,
he continued. "What is *The Assaulters* about? It
deals with the forces that surround two human
beings—our principals. They are besieged by the
elements because of the hemisphere in which they
live. They are threatened by a political and military
power they cannot control. They must contend with
the eccentricity and the ill will of the milieu in which
they find themselves struggling. Who among the
citizens in the story will believe these two people
when they attempt to show their fellows the truth of
what is happening to them? Particularly when that
truth is unpalatable—the diminishing of the land

mass which they inhabit; the failure of crops; the pollution of food and water; the choking, stagnant air; and a population brought to a standstill by an insidious chemical inability to reproduce."

"Is it commercial?" Chantal ventured.

"Of course it is! Our story is set two decades ahead. *That* will draw the audience into the theater. Remember, rending the veil of the future is a great seducer. Look at the belief in fortune tellers, palmists, seers, numerology, astrology, a crystal ball. We'll do the magician act, Chantal, and in the process we'll show them truth. Oh, I know—*we* won't. Your original author, for whom you have so much respect, will show them in his plot, I grant you that. Then it will be *his* time—we'll use his words, his mind, his forecast. But we'll be the ones to create the actual force, the ambience. Say ten thousand people read his book. Twenty million to see the picture? We can project an audience of many millions more—worldwide distribution and the eventual sale to television will take care of that."

"I don't believe you!" Chantal was sitting back in her chair laughing at him.

Simon waved aside the waiter hovering with the menu. "You'd better believe me. Because, Miss Chantal Jerrold, this is the way it's done! Now, shall we eat and talk about the sensible world?"

Chantal didn't recall what they ate. Whatever it was, it was marvelous. He was marvelous. And this euphoric feeling wasn't because she'd touched her tequila again. She hadn't. Nor did she taste the wine he ordered. They both forgot the carafe. They talked of many things. Politics. Art and Europe and Picasso. They both agreed they loved Mexico. But in the summer on the coast, out of season, the climate could be appalling. Too humid, with the wet threat of hurricanes offshore. February was the ideal month, but February brought too many tourists to explore that exotic land. Yes, out of season was best. One could suffer through the climate, then, because one could live closer to the bone of the country.

After lunch they walked outside, to see the Rolls-Royces lined up along the curb. A proud clientele. Simon's car was also at the front curb, sitting under the watchful eye of the valet parking service. It was a classic, late-thirties Bentley convertible, gleaming steel-gray in the sunshine. Chantal's Datsun, along with the less fashionable Cadillacs, Mercedes, Volvos and Honda Accords, was parked in the lot behind the restaurant.

When her car was brought around, Simon tipped the attendant for her. He helped her inside, gave her a pleasant smile, said he'd see her at the studio. The veil of the future he'd mentioned earlier seemed heavy and murky now, with all camaraderie vanished. Chantal wondered. And yet, she thought gratefully as she drove away, Simon had put her so much at ease that no one would ever suspect that on a twilight afternoon they'd once lain naked, making love on the summer grass of a secluded patio.

Several days later, sitting behind his table-desk, Simon Bryce thought back to that lunch at La Serre and reflected that he'd managed the interlude well. He'd kept their meeting on an impersonal level, and he'd amused Chantal. It had already occurred to him that he was going to a great deal of trouble to win the trust and cooperation of a young woman whom he merely wanted to work with him. In a way, and probably for the first time, he was sorry he'd allowed sex to intrude between them.

Special messenger had delivered the results of Chantal's work. She'd accomplished the breakdown very expertly and with a certain touch of well-placed drama that he hadn't expected. Simon wondered whether she'd been spurred by anger at him or by a desire to please, by personal ambition or by resentment of his actions. He couldn't be sure. Those disturbing eyes of hers had told him nothing during their lunch. Still, she'd done a fine job of blocking in the book's main scenes. An unusual procedure, perhaps, but this was the way he liked to prepare his films.

Looking down at Chantal's neatly bound page copy, he wasn't surprised at its excellence. He had suspected that Chantal would do well; that is, if she decided to do it at all. And that he hadn't known until they'd met the other day and she had dropped her little depth charge with the casual announcement that her assignment was nearly completed.

He touched the intercom switch. Larette's voice responded. "Simon? Yes?"

"Do we have large enough quarters here in the bungalow for Cesar Williams, or will we have to lease space for him in the Writers Building?"

"His agent says Williams prefers to work at home."

There was a silence. "See that he has an office here on the lot. Something decent, with a private bathroom if possible. I don't want him holding his conferences down the hall." "Down the hall," always the secretary's euphemism for the men's room.

"I'll put Moira on it right away."

"Good. Thanks." He switched the intercom off.

These days, when young people seldom remained a year in their current posts before making a move up the ladder of studio rank, it was unusual that people of the caliber of Larette and Moira and Dean stayed with Simon's organization, presumably loyal to him. No doubt the reason was because he gave them an extraordinary amount of freedom by seeing to it that they had an important part in the supervision of his films, and always with single screen credit as associate producer. In their case the title carried authority because it meant that they had earned it. The associate producership was not something handed out to the brother of the star, or to the secretary-girlfriend-flunky of the line producer. Further, Simon expected his assistants to concentrate on bringing in fresh talent. They were paid well, and in no sense could their positions be considered lower-level.

Simon stood up and began to pace restlessly. He'd made a well-considered decision that the Jerrold woman might be the best of the upwardly mobile young people with whom he surrounded himself. He hadn't anticipated she might have other ideas, such as that ridiculous freelancing plan of hers. Nor had he anticipated he would feel more than a professional interest in her. Simon told himself that it was merely a temporary involvement, a functional eroticism that he'd have to control.

There was a knock on the door. He knew it was Larette, since she was the only one allowed to approach his inner office without first being announced by Marilou.

"Are you going to put the writer on payroll earlier than planned?" Larette asked. "Moira's arranging an office for him in Writers Building A."

"Read this." He tossed Chantal's bound copy over to Larette and sat down behind his desk. She took it, glanced at Simon. As usual, Larette was perfectly turned out, her hair gilded close to her head, her countenance impassive.

"It's good?" she inquired.

"Excellent. I don't want to hear an argument from Cesar Williams about his having to work from a breakdown like this. It's the way *I* like to work. Jerrold has done everything I asked of her. She has a touch for this sort of thing."

"Then why don't you have her write the treatment instead of Williams?"

"My dear Larette, it *is* an adaptation treatment, as you should recognize by now. This will allow Williams to go right into the first draft."

"You're a signatory to Writers Guild contracts. Do you think you can get away with this?"

"I don't have to get away with anything. Draw a check for Jerrold according to Guild scale, and sweeten it."

"By a thousand?"

Startled, Simon glanced at Larette. His eyes narrowed. Larette's tone of voice was even, her face expressionless. Was the rather generous monetary suggestion a contrived bit of sarcasm on her part? If so, was there some sort of implication in what she'd just said—one that he didn't want to think about? Jealousy? Or was Larette promoting a sister's interests? Not for a minute did he believe the latter.

Simon spoke coldly. "Halve that, Larette. Five hundred additional will do nicely, on top of the payment for an adaptation. Remember too, the work Jerrold has done for us will help her get into the Writers Guild, if that's what she wants." Almost to himself, he murmured, "I really don't know what she wants."

Larette turned and left Simon's office. Outside his door she halted, reflecting. I know what she wants, if he doesn't. The first goddamn mistake I've made with him in five years, not since the very beginning. I shouldn't have made that crack about the extra thousand. Where are my smarts?

She hurried past Marilou, her stride uneven, her shoulders bunched tight. Glancing up from her IBM Selectric, Marilou wondered what had happened to mess up Larette's composure and tax her usual model's glide.

Chantal studied the check sent to her by the Simon Bryce Productions accountant. It was very generous, a far greater amount of money than she had anticipated. Worriedly she wondered if what she considered to be an overpayment for the work she had done meant that she was being put under an obligation to Simon's company—one that she didn't want to assume. But then, nothing else had been asked of her, so presumably this was a cutoff, like and extra severance pay.

She placed the check on her antique desk, alongside the scripts that had arrived from MGM the day before. Having completed the assignment for Simon ahead of schedule, she planned a week's work in her apartment; then she'd go out of town.

Millicent had called that morning to say the family was closing up the Hancock Park house for the summer and they were all leaving for EdgeMont, where their expenses would be less for the next few months.

"Ardis has moved home from that boat in the Marina." Millicent's voice had floated along on a barely concealed sigh. Chantal's ears sharpened. Mrs. Jerrold went on. "She'll spend the summer with us."

"Boyd Farrell too, I suppose."

Her mother's sigh had turned into a definite, gusty reproach. "With the example of Jason and me in front of him, I expect Boy to do the right thing and ask Ardis to marry him. Jason and I have mutual duties as parents. I've invited Boy to come and stay with us. He said he would as often as his business commitments permit."

"He says! Ma, he'll be practically living there. He'll be in on the ground floor with you and Dad. Ardis is a serpent's tooth. You know she wants you to sell the place."

"Ardis is in no way ungrateful, as you imply." Millicent had giggled. "She's just looking out for her own interests."

"How about snake's belly, then? Devious? I'll settle for that."

"I wish you and your sister got along better."

"I don't trust her. She's skinny and mean."

"Chantal! Enough."

"You love me best," Chantal had teased.

"Darling, you mustn't be so candid. You'll make things difficult for yourself, honest as you are. I thought you had to develop tact, dealing with all those weird film people. Come out to EdgeMont on weekends, Chantal. Help your father with his organic gardening. You'll always be welcome then."

"Weekends! I'm planning to stay longer than that. Someone has to watch Farrell. Somehow I can't trust you. I think you'll agree to anything to keep the peace."

"Why do daughters think the worst of their mothers? Don't answer, Chantal, I have to hang up. I've only this to say. These days one can't count on a man for support, either emotionally or financially.

You do have a career to consider and you'd better stay with it. It's difficult enough for me, trying to marry off Ardis." Then, as usual, the balance of the scales had tipped the other way as her mother relented. "Chantal, come and stay with us for the entire summer, if that's what you want."

Dean Davison was a walking compendium of film deals, TV deals, current ratings and the status of entertainment stocks—their volume, advances and declines. He knew who was creating and developing and financing the new shows, which pacts were being ratified and what films, if any, were racking up an outstanding gross. Even more important, which ones were having a terrible box office. And the reasons why.

Anticipated film sales, predicted revenues and nets, who would be fired and who was replacing whom—in board rooms, in the industry's executive offices and in its Porthault-sheeted, king-sized beds—all this was part of Dean's field of knowledge. A *précis* that made him invaluable to Simon Bryce.

Dean was a "fan" with brains, with a memory that never failed him. Living with rich parents in a guest house on their estate in San Marino, he didn't have to hustle. He was dedicated to Bryce. Probably Dean's most important asset, aside from his inventory of categoried information, was that he was more ambitious for Simon, and for the company's product, than he was for himself.

He was smooth-mannered and very handsome, but he was an escort, not a lover. His social advantages had deprived him of that gut hunger which can either be purposely hidden or be monstrously used to magnetize fortune and followers. Thus he had no real propelling force to urge him to strive for material success and its concomitant power.

Earlier that day, and without comment, Larette had passed Chantal's plot breakdown to Dean. Whether Chantal had intended it or not, Dean quickly recognized her work to be a well-thought-out story treatment, one that could be used as the basis for a first draft of *The Assaulters*. Chantal's knowledge of production and camera technique, which she had acquired early in her career as a gofer and a production assistant, had enabled her to structure the principal scenes, emphasize action and characterization, omit plot irrelevancies and tone down much of the original author's too-specialized viewpoint.

Later, Larette stuck her ash-blond head into Dean's office and asked, "What did you think of it?"

In the usual manner of close associates, Dean knew immediately what she was talking about. He smiled innocently. "Cesar Williams isn't going to be happy."

"Deanie," Larette whispered softly, "it'll be up to you to be your most humbly persuasive with our writer. Simon is aware that what his new little protégée has done is an initial adaptation treatment."

"You think she did it on purpose?"

Larette shrugged. "If she didn't, she's stupid. I don't think she's stupid."

"She might be naive."

"Oh, come *on*." Larette was impatient. "When Cesar reads this he'll be furious, hurt, mortified, chagrined . . . whatever other literary adjectives he can think of. You'll have to go over to the Writers Building and sift numbers at him, sprinkle him with poppy juice. You'll have to convince him that what somebody's little girl here has written is what the big Paymaster in the Sky is going to want to see in Cesar's first draft."

"You think I can do all that?"

"Of course you can. You can give him the bit about how he'll have to refine this girlish thesis, but with his insight and genius for dialogue, that should be easy for him to do, et cetera, et cetera, et cetera. You're very good with et ceteras, Dean."

"You're not bad yourself, Larette. But you know something? This isn't a girlish thesis."

"I know it isn't, goddammit! It's very good."

"Not so incidentally, why don't *you* do the number on Williams instead of having me adjust his crown of thorns?"

"Because you're part of the fraternal bond, fella. Man-to-man stuff. Williams is over fifty and considers himself macho."

"What's happened to your sense of equality?"

"I never had it. You don't suppose I believe all that feminist stuff, do you? Not for one blinking instant."

"Well, now, that's interesting, Howell. Sit down and tell me about yourself."

"Oh, stuff it, Dean." Larette started to close his office door. "Go back to your quotients. And after you figure out the sum of the whole in that computer brain of yours, go and see Williams, like I said. If you can't handle him and spread butter on his manhood, I will." She gave Dean a derisive grin. "It's not equality, bub. It never was."

"Superior bitch."

"You've got it right!" Larette laughed and slammed the door.

Dean chuckled. He liked Larette most of the time. He couldn't picture sleeping with her, but he liked her. He sat and thought about Chantal Jerrold's hundred-page treatment. That was definitely what the plot breakdown, so called, had turned out to be. He knew the screenwriter assigned to *The Assaulters* would protest having to follow this anonymous and fairly complete óutline. But before Williams got on the phone to scream to his agent, Dean would try to soothe Cesar's ego. In the meantime, there was another problem about which his spies had informed him. He buzzed Marilou on the intercom.

"Can I talk to your boss?"

"It's *may* you talk to my boss. What about?"

Because Marilou always asked, and he never told, and she knew it, Dean muttered in what he believed to be his best Bogie voice: "A raise for you, sweetheart. Know what I mean?"

"I'm not wearing a skirt today, even if you could do what you imply," Marilou snapped. "And you may see him in fifteen minutes."

Simon was ready for Dean. He knew all about the problem. He'd attended the bat mitzvah for the Black Tower's chief executive's daughter, and while the string quartet had played and the caterers had catered, it had been explained to Simon Bryce that the studio would consider it sensational casting against type if he used Peter Tark as the lead in his next film, *The Assaulters*.

"The male lead?" Simon had asked in order to give himself time for a properly evasive reply.

The chief executive's black eyes had turned beady and suspicious. "I don't catch a smart-ass insinuation in what you just said, do I?"

Simon's eyes, even blacker than the executive's, had glittered in turn. "Howard, I don't know what your imputation is. But you've read the reader's report on the book, haven't you? There's the older man whom the young girl is in love with. It's his knowledge, his nobility of character, his worldly experience, that get her—not his manly beauty. So you can't be thinking of Tark for that character. The other male role isn't impressive enough, unless the part is built up in the rewriting. If we do that, we add two months to the script budget and—"

The executive had interrupted hastily. "We'll talk about it tomorrow, Bryce. I merely mentioned it because the idea originated in the penthouse."

"You can't go much higher than that," Simon had agreed seriously.

"Good comprehension." Howard had turned away. Tomorrow he'd get the story department in and find out what the hell that reader's synopsis had actually said about the lead characters in the five-page, single-spaced outline on *The Assaulters*. The trouble was, Simon Bryce was on the Universal Studios lot but had his own financing. There wasn't much pressure that could be put on him to influence his casting procedures. Except maybe, and Howard had grinned sardonically at the thought, take away Bungalow C's parking privileges. He'd raised his glass of Scotch, drunk it down, crunched ice between his teeth and gone over to speak to Peter Tark—who had seen him coming and disappeared.

Chapter Seven

Chantal's desk was finally cleared. The completed script analyses for MGM had been sent on their way. It was time to pull the suitcases out from under the bed. Starting to pack, Chantal came upon an old sweater that Jay had loaned her. She remembered the day they'd spent together at the beach, one of the few times she and Jay had really talked.

Her brother's life was a busy one, but lived at a mystifying level. He and Chantal spoke on the phone at odd hours. Jay rarely called her from home, instead from a public phone booth on Sunset Boulevard, from ship to shore on a yacht traveling to Acapulco, by wireless satellite from a condo on Maui. Chantal suspected his companion was the glamorous Kiki Dalton, whom she'd seen a few times with Jay. Yet Jay always explained he was "on the job"—at some unspecified task.

Chantal didn't question Jay's occupations. Whatever they were, they were his own affair. Anyway, their joint concern was really their father, Jason; always Jason.

Jay had told her, "You back up those two parents of ours with moral persuasion. You're good at that. I'll send money." And he had.

She should have asked how a twenty-one-year-old made so much money. But Jay, to his credit, was just tough enough so that Chantal didn't dare probe.

No matter. Chantal shrugged, put Jay's sweater aside and continued packing. The two suitcases were slowly filling up with her ranch clothes. She packed Levi's, cool shirts and a few cotton skirts, boots and sandals. She was reaching for her swimsuits when the phone rang.

"Chantal!" Moira's finishing-school voice was softly accented. "How *are* you?" Told that Chantal was fine, Moira's whispery tone hastened on. "Could you come to the studio today and see Simon? At once."

"I'm going out of town, Moira. Is it really urgent? Couldn't we discuss it over the phone? I had a very nice letter from Simon yesterday. He said the assignment I completed for the company was more than satisfactory, so whatever it is can't have anything to do with *The Assaulters.*"

In her office, Moira listened to Chantal's reply, and in her turn thought, That man! That duplicitous, deceitful, opportunistic man! Still, she was crazy about Simon—as a boss. She queried Chantal, "Simon said only that it was *satisfactory?*"

Sensing that Moira sounded somewhat critical of Simon, Chantal laughed. "The letter said *more* than satisfactory."

There was silence from Moira's end. She was thinking that Chantal Jerrold had saved Simon's company six weeks' time with her scholarly, well-written interpretation of that enigmatic novel they'd bought. It was Chantal who had actually put them ahead of schedule. Moira wondered whether the younger woman was aware of this. Probably not.

She clutched the phone tighter. Rather desperately, because she was always expected to accomplish whatever was asked of her, Moira ran the palm of her hand over her forehead and through her seal-sleek, short brown hair. She quickly smoothed her hair down again and purred, "It's important, Chantal, that you come over here to the lot." She'd been saving the *coup de grâce*, but now, since the moment seemed appropriate, she delivered it. "It's something to do with Peter Tark."

Chantal's attention was caught, as Moira had intended it should be. "Tark? What is it with him? They haven't chosen him for the lead, have they?"

"If you intended that remark for a jokey joke, you might be half right."

"What . . . ?" Chantal was astonished.

The unseen Moira smiled complacently. She'd baited the hook, now she'd draw in the line. "It seems the first night you were here you gave Simon a strong list of reasons why Peter would be impossible as the hero in the film."

"Yes, I recall that."

"Simon wants to go over them with you. An improbable situation has developed here. The studio is pressuring us to cast Peter. We don't want him, and he doesn't want us. It's a freaky situation."

"Very. Anyway, I remember the discussion."

Doggedly Moira continued. "Simon would like you to enumerate once more the negatives you lined up against Tark's playing the part of Auguste." Normally she would never have said this much over the phone, but Chantal was proving stubborn in her reluctance to drive over to Universal.

"Is the studio ignoring the basic fact that the lead is a much older man than Peter Tark, more mature in every way?" Chantal asked.

"They want us to rewrite to that." Moira paused. "None of us has been able to come up with anything like the cogent reasons Simon says you gave him. He doesn't expect you to convince the Black Tower in person, Chantal. He merely wants you to develop a written argument that he can use as if it's his own. As if it came right off the top of his head," Moira added, somewhat to her own private satisfaction.

"But I'm leaving town."

"Can't you delay it?"

Since Moira seemed implacable in her insistence, Chantal repeated, "Is it really necessary that I come in? Look, I'll try to get my thoughts together here. I'll put something down on paper and send it over. How's that?"

Moira's voice rushed on ingratiatingly. "That's very cooperative of you. But Simon needs to talk it over with you first. When Larette asked me to call you, she was pretty explicit about that, Chantal."

Chantal had fought the memory of Simon. In a brief span of time, she'd managed to refocus her life. It hadn't been easy. She was afraid of the nights and of the vivid dream . . . for the dream still remained. . . .

Chantal gasped into the phone, "I'd like to help, but I really can't." It would be madness for her to return to the bungalow and see Simon again.

But Moira would not be put off. She continued to plead in her soft voice. "Don't let us down. Please. It's so, so important. For all of us."

While she listened to Moira, on another level Chantal was thinking of that day at La Serre. Simon had been funny and dramatic and clever and entertaining. He had laughed at himself and coaxed her into laughter too. He had shown her his awareness of the absurdities he was propounding when he'd plunged into the richly articulate account of what could be done with the script. That day couldn't have been all pretense, could it? Or had he only shown her the Simon Bryce he had intended her to see? Why was she so afraid now, when that other day had been so pleasant?

Moira sighed patiently into the phone. "Are you still there, Chantal? You're not saying anything."

An hour later Chantal sat across from Simon Bryce in his office. If Moira had not convinced her, Chantal had finally convinced herself that she could handle this meeting. She would do what was needed. At the same time, she'd stand aside and judge Simon coolly, because she knew him for what he was—a glorious charlatan who could work his magic on her as he chose, as well as on the wide-eyed theater audiences. But now she was stronger; now she was armed with knowledge of him. Though she could be disarmed, she thought to herself contemptuously, because she was still fascinated by the man. That was one reality. The other was that she couldn't let her life be consumed this way. She'd have to stop running.

Simon was talking to her, explaining the situation with the studio and with Peter Tark. She must concentrate on what he was saying. She sat up straight, looking alert.

Simon stood and began to pace the room. She

knew she should be listening to his words, but she was more conscious of his tall, lithe figure than of what he was saying. The muscular strength of his broad shoulders and sun-bronzed chest was revealed beneath the open mesh of his white pullover. The stride of his long legs encased in their close-fitting, white denim trousers mesmerized her gaze.

". . . so, because of the stand certain executives on the lot are taking with regard to Tark's contract, and also because of the involvement of Tark's own production company with the studio, I'm in the middle. They're trying to use me to settle their flap with Tark. I won't let them, of course, but it's going to require diplomacy and some damn good, strong, persuasive arguments." He halted and looked at Chantal. She nodded numbly. He went on as though he were talking to a perfectly reasonable person. "You can give me some of the ammunition I need if you'll do a recap of everything you told me about Tark. We've got to be guarded, conciliatory. We can't be unflattering or stress Tark's inadequacies. You understand all that, of course—studio politics are involved."

Again Chantal nodded her head. What had she previously said in regard to Peter Tark's unsuitability for the role? Could she remember *anything?*

Simon's brow furrowed. "Are you paying attention, Chantal? I haven't had any input from you in this conversation." He grinned suddenly. "Or has it been one-sided because I haven't given you a chance to say word two?"

"Oh, no, no. Please go on."

Simon sat down again across from Chantal and looked at her intently. "That's what I don't want to do—repeat what I've just said. It's your turn now."

He waited, then laughed abruptly. "We should have taped our conversation when we spoke before. Too bad we didn't."

"I . . . I'll have to think."

"Do you want to go into Larette's office, use her typewriter, outline an approach? Larette's in a production meeting." There was a pause. Simon stared at Chantal. "Is something wrong?"

Yes. Something was very wrong. She looked directly at Simon, not answering. She was unaware that at this moment her eyes were speaking for her, giving her away. She couldn't prevent the enthrallment that shone in her gaze as it sped toward Simon on the other side of the table. Memory quivered along her veins. She felt its lash in the moisting, sweet deeps of her body. They had made love in that savage green twilight at his house. How could one *forget?* There in that garden, lying beneath his body, she had told Simon her truth—that he would live in her heart, in her fantasies; that she would never forget him.

Almost in panic she started to her feet. She should never have returned to the studio. Instinctively she knew she had been right in refusing Moira's request; wrong in finally agreeing to come here. The silence between her and Simon was lasting too long. She could hear the clock ticking. Hear the soft hum of the air conditioning. Or was it the sound of her own uneven breathing that she heard?

Simon stood up. He made a sudden strange and compelling gesture. In anyone else it would have been theatric. Perhaps he meant it to be; perhaps he intended to lighten the moment that hung between them, tense and waiting.

Startled, she watched as he bowed his head very

low in her direction. He curved the fingers of his right hand to his brow, then touched his fingers to his lips, then to his heart, as though in ceremonial obeisance to her.

"I have learned from my research group that this greeting indicates Peace. Is there ever going to be peace between us, Chantal?" He straightened his body and looked at her searchingly, dark eyes glowing.

He couldn't possibly be serious. Yet, trembling, Chantal returned his look, unable to control the racing beat of her heart. Why did his face, his voice, affect her so?

Simon moved around his desk toward her. His expression questioning, he came very close. Chantal rose to meet him like a moth drawn to light. And then, as his hand reached out tenderly, tentatively, to touch her breast—her heart—she glimpsed over his shoulder, as though in her dream, the ritual elegance of the Modigliani. . . .

Next she was in his arms and weeping wildly, held gently by Simon while his kisses covered her face. Slowly, deliciously, his lips comforted her lips, moved to her eyelids, to her throat. His hands caressed her body as though to soothe. He whispered, "I understand, Chantal. The beginning for us, for you and for me, was all a mistake. It was my fault." His voice husky, he murmured, "Let me come to you tonight."

Overcome with a tidal sweep of emotion, Chantal was unable to speak. Her face averted, she nodded her head, an agreement without words.

Simon took her hand and indicated a private exit from his office. Chantal went swiftly outside, hurrying through the side area where the fountain splashed. She got into the Datsun, her hands shaking so that she could barely insert the key into the ignition.

As she started to back the car out of the parking space, a recklessly driven Jaguar almost ran her down. The Jag nosed into the empty slot beside Chantal, and a very tall woman with white-blond hair hanging to her shoulders jumped out, paused, stared curiously at Chantal's tear-stained face and then strode off in the direction of Bungalow C.

Recognition was like a plunge into icy water. The woman, angular, beautiful and six feet tall, was Kiki Dalton. Through tear-drenched eyes Chantal read the Jag's license plate: KD WIN-R.

Kiki Dalton's vanity license plate was appropriate. Kiki was a winner. With an excellent education and a hundred thousand dollars inherited from her grandmother at age twenty, Kiki, two decades later, had turned her windfall into multiple enterprises and several million dollars.

Following her unexpected glimpse of Jay's sister, Kiki opened the door to Bungalow C and walked into the birch-paneled reception area. An extremely alert and curious woman, she wondered why Chantal had left Simon Bryce's bungalow in such ragged haste that she'd almost bashed Kiki's beloved Jag. Plus, it was apparent Chantal had tears in her eyes. Now, who or what on the Universal Studios lot would make Jay's sister cry?

Kiki greeted Simon's secretary graciously. It never hurt to be polite to underlings. She knew Marilou was admiring her Calvin Klein pull-on pants and sleeveless, silk crêpe de Chine blouse with its one-button jacket slung carelessly over her broad shoulders. Kiki adored being as tall as she was, and as statuesque. With her snow-queen hair worn unfashionably down to her shoulders, no one could ever miss Kiki in a crowd.

"I'm sorry I'm late for my three o'clock, Marilou." Kiki glanced at her wristwatch. She wasn't late at all. She never was.

"Why, you're not late, Miss Dalton. Chantal Jerrold is still inside."

Oh . . . ? Kiki thought. So that's it! She knew about the private exit.

When Simon buzzed a moment later, Marilou said, "Miss Dalton's waiting." Marilou looked surprised. "I'll send her right in." Marilou nodded at Kiki, and Kiki walked inside.

Kiki was determined to find out more. Jay hadn't told her there was any hanky-panky going on between his sister and Simon Bryce.

She and Simon greeted each other. They were old friends. Kiki noted that Simon appeared absent-minded as she opened her attaché case and took out the portfolio dealing with the small publishing house they were both interested in. Last week they'd discussed the controlling shares that were available in this West Coast shoestring operation. When Kiki had told Simon it was possible to get into the venture without too much of an investment, he'd seemed enthusiastic. Now his voice was curt and his handsome face subdued.

For awhile she tried to discuss the prospectus. Finally she sat back in her chair and asked him straight out what the matter was.

Simon shrugged. "I'm tapped out today, I guess. Been working too hard."

"Doing what?" Kiki asked idly. "I did see in the trades that you'd bought the rights to *The Assaulters*." She had also read that Chantal Jerrold was tied in there somewhere, and she'd forgotten about it until this very moment, though she'd told Jay at the time. She must be slipping!

"There's some beef about it with the studio and Peter Tark, but nothing that can't be fixed. How's Jay?"

Oh, boy, Simon led right into that one, Kiki thought, amused. "Jay's fine. I read that his sister is working for you."

Simon was a little vague. "Jay's *sister?* My God— Chantal *Jerrold!* Even with the same last name, I didn't connect her with Jay. She did a little freelance reading for us, that's all."

"She won't be continuing here?" Kiki asked, disappointed. Then she brightened. That *was* it! The girl had gotten the heave-ho. Kiki had settled that one. Nothing big to report to Jay after all. Merely a job termination. Not a terminated amour, as she'd suspected.

Kiki ran her tongue over her lips. Her saucer-round dark eyes sparkled. "If you've had it for today, why don't we talk about this publishing deal another time? It'll keep. You should take a vacation, Simon—run down to Mexico. That's your thing, isn't it? It'll be easier to get away now than when you actually go into production, right?"

Simon was grateful for Kiki's perception, though he wasn't sure where it came from. He stood up. So did Kiki. She lacked two inches of Simon's height but made up for it with her two-inch heels.

"Good girl." Simon gave Kiki a light kiss on the cheek. "Thanks for being so understanding. I *am* bushed this afternoon." He tapped the portfolio she'd left open so he could read its contents. "I'm still interested in this thing, you know. Doing business with these people, I might get my hands on some original material from writers hidden away up in Grass Valley or Modesto. Don't go into it without me."

"I won't," Kiki promised. "If you don't slip off to Mexico or to Palm Springs, we can talk about it next week. The principals will be hungrier by then. We can probably make an even better deal. I have the inside track. They don't dare make a move without first talking to my lawyer. I own the building they're in." She glanced at her Cartier watch. "Gotta run. I have a four o'clock in the Black Tower."

Simon raised his eyebrows.

"I'm selling a Universal exec that little two-bedroom *casa* in Beverly Hills, the one that was left over from my third divorce. I gave it to Jerry as part of the settlement. He couldn't keep up with the taxes, so he gave it back to me."

"How much, Kik?"

"A mil' seven hundred thou. Remember, it's in Beverly Hills on Carmelina. And look at the rare history that was made there! Errol Flynn built the place originally."

"But one point seven million for two bedrooms?"

"That's the ticket. See you, Simon."

Kiki gathered up her portfolio and her attaché case, blew Simon a kiss and departed, satisfied. But not for long. Getting into her Jag and sliding along the leather seat behind the steering wheel, Kiki sat still, tapping her inch-long, bronze-lacquered fingernails on the wheel's imported wood. She recalled Chantal's tear-spattered face, and that made the earlier explanation she had reached seem too easy. Jay's sister would never weep up a storm over a little thing like the loss of a job. Something far more catastrophic had caused the tempest in those gray eyes and the exquisite trembling in those full lips.

Kiki's curiosity was alert to signs of passionate involvement.

Slowly she backed up the Jag, and while she drove over to the Black Tower's VIP parking lot, her thoughts scrambled as furiously as any NFL quarterback's.

She did business with Simon Bryce, as she did with many people. The association between the two was close and friendly. In the Hollywood vernacular, they were "pals." But only to a certain point. The bottom line was not loyalty, but profitability. If Kiki could get something on Simon she could use, she would. *If* it would benefit her. Simon was often touted in *W* and other smart publications as being an exemplar of all that was commendable in the new Hollywood. He was considered the best possible exemplification of honor, taste and integrity. No one ever spoke a word against him, neither associates, employees, former employees nor rivals. In a town where gossip endured and salivated, Bryce was held up as a man to respect.

Kiki's eyelids curved sleepily over her black eyes as she braked her Jag to a stop. She sat meditating for a couple of minutes. The publishing house that was up for grabs had a secondary line that made it of truly high value to Kiki. She had intended to divulge the existence of this sideline when she and Simon finally got down to serious negotiating. Initially she hadn't wanted to scare Simon off. Some people called him Simon Pure. Now, suddenly, she decided against sharing this knowledge of hers with anyone, particularly Simon.

Secrets were better kept to oneself. Kiki pursed her luscious lips and glanced skyward in a whisper of gratitude. She was lucky she'd caught that glimpse of small, voluptuous, tear-sodden Chantal Jerrold. It might change many things—it just might. Kiki grinned wickedly. Great fun, to bring down someone's respectable reputation. And maybe trash it—just a little?

As happens on summer evenings, the weather can change in hours. The July heat lifted and the fog blew in from the Pacific. It swirled over the palisades, through the pines and eucalyptus and bougainvillea, crept up the Santa Monica Canyon and along winding Sunset Boulevard, past what had once been the polo fields where long-gone Will Rogers and Darryl Zanuck the Senior had galloped their imported ponies. It misted along the Santa Monica mountains, and its chill caused windows to close and fires to be lit in fireplaces.

The Villa Apartments was no exception. The red tile roof began to drip moisture. The ornamental iron of the balcony railings grew damp to the touch. Chantal wadded up newspaper and pushed it under the oak logs and pine kindling left in the fireplace from the previous cold spell in early May. How different it had been then. She and Doro Kentz from Tri-Symbol, and a couple of other friends, had gathered for a potluck dinner in front of Chantal's cozy hearth.

They'd had a four-way discussion, both serious and light: the feminist movement, many pros, a few cons; the men they knew, or would like to know; inflation, and the amount of taxes deducted from their paychecks; their individual careers and where they were headed. And what was this about mentors to help guide one's career and give one a boost? None of them had ever had a mentor.

The month before—April—Chantal had first met Mark Duffy. They had already become intimate, and she'd been expecting him later at the apartment after the others had left. She'd also been feeling ardent and secretive that May night, eager to share her feelings and tell her friends about Duffy, but of course she hadn't. Their romance had been new and special at the time—a kind of "knock on wood" hope—and she'd had the usual faith that the relationship with Mark would be the important one. It had turned out not to be. One of companionship, yes, warm and kind, but . . . nothing more.

And now—everything! Simon Bryce.

Whether theirs was to be friendship, or a deeply emotional affair—complicated, murderously unhappy—or a time of serenity, a riotous high, none of that seemed to matter. Whatever would happen, let it! To Chantal, Simon represented her headland of rock, the immovable one, her verity.

Let me come to you tonight.

Chantal shivered in anticipation of what this might mean for both of them. She bathed, changed into a long robe and lay down with moistened tea bags propped on her closed eyelids to rid them of the puffiness caused by earlier tears. It had been absurd of her to lose control that way and fall into a storm of weeping in Simon's presence! She was ashamed of her conduct, humiliated by it. Yet she couldn't undo it. It was the measure of the passion she felt for him.

Let me come to you tonight.

She fell asleep, dreamless this time. Within the hour she awakened quickly. With foreboding, she sprang up and ran into the living room. The crackling logs behind the fire screen had burned down to glowing embers. No damage was done. The room was warm and fragrant with pine scent. Chantal looked at the desk clock. It was well past seven.

Back in her bedroom, she threw off her robe and dressed hastily in a form-fitting, gray velvet top, its neckline deeply curved, leaving her arms bare and lovely. She pulled the long-torsoed line down over the waistband of her floor-length gray skirt made of the softest challis. After putting on velvet slippers with the new, lower heels and then being concerned that she still appeared diminutive, she coiled her dark red hair high on her head and secured its heaviness with tortoise-shell hairpins. Tonight, if she were going to face Simon with her dignity restored—and she had to do that for her own self-respect—she would need height and presence.

She was happy, excited, not at all fearful. Her gray eyes sparkled. He was coming here. Beautiful Simon.

An hour later she brewed a pot of tea for herself, poked at the dying logs and looked nervously at the tiny finger sandwiches she had made and arranged on a plate, their crusts neatly trimmed as Millicent had taught her. Chantal could see that the thin bread was drying up. She placed a dampened napkin over the plate. Feeling disgust, she thought she might as well have played pat-a-cake and baked a pan of cookies.

Two hours later she heated a can of soup for herself, which she left on the stove and forgot about. She checked the telephone for the third time that evening. Pacific Telephone was working perfectly, as it had been the other two times she'd tried the line. She called downstairs to the building manager's apartment to check whether the security system was in order. The manager, young herself, went outside to test the buzzer. It rang in Chantal's apartment.

"Thank you, Susan," Chantal apologized stiffly. Obviously, he wasn't coming. She went into her bedroom and started to uncoil her hair.

The sound of the buzzer once again ripped through the apartment. If Susan was going to invite Chantal to come downstairs to have her Tarot cards read, she would go. She was not going to stay in her apartment alone and be miserable, forming conjectures.

Chantal walked slowly to the living room door and leaned against the wall intercom. "Yes, Susan?" she sighed into the box.

"Chantal?" A man's voice. Chantal's heart exploded.

Simon, disdaining the elevator, ran up the stairs to the second floor. At Chantal's door he appeared his usual self, formidably tall and stunningly olive-skinned, only this time his black hair was curled tight by the moisture in the foggy air outside. He was wearing a pale suede jacket, its collar turned up high around his throat. He had not changed his clothes. Since he was so fastidious, this was unusual for Simon. He was still in the pullover sweater and the white pants he'd had on in the afternoon.

His attitude was as natural as the vigorous wind that seemed to blow in with his entrance. "God, I'm sorry, Chantal. I was at a meeting in the Tower until half an hour ago. I couldn't break away to get to a phone and call you. Then, when I could, I tried information, but your number's unlisted. I had to go back down to the bungalow and look you up on the Rolodex. The studio switchboard was closed by then. My outside line wasn't working either, so I said to hell with it and drove over here on the off-chance I'd find you home."

Chantal burst out laughing in nervous relief. "It sounds like it's all my fault, Simon."

She was truly relieved. She'd been fighting that scoundrel feeling of rejection. Now that Simon was here, she was released from self-doubt and despondency. Set free, Chantal felt as though she'd been turned into a spinning top of excitement. She tried to keep the Fourth of July sparklers out of her eyes and hoped he wouldn't notice. Where was the dignity she'd been striving for in order to erase the horrible impression she must have made on Simon this afternoon? At one time he had appeared to regard her as a colleague who could do excellent work. Now she wasn't sure what he thought of her. She wanted to get back on that sane, sensible footing again.

"You must be hungry," Chantal said, then realized she sounded anxious, like all the mothers in the world. But Simon didn't seem to notice her lapse into total womanhood.

"I am starved," he announced, "and at the moment I'm floating in Perrier water." He looked around. She grinned and gestured down the hall. Momentarily he disappeared. Thank God she'd put out her best soap and hand towels.

When Simon returned, Chantal said casually, "I have some tired old sandwiches around."

"Well, trot 'em out, ma'am." For almost the first time since he'd entered her apartment, Simon Bryce looked closely at Chantal. "You look gorgeous," he said spontaneously.

If she did look gorgeous, it was all for him. Her gray eyes shone, her smile beamed, her complexion was like pale silk against the auburn mass of her hair.

She was standing on a tiptoe of delight. He was here. In her apartment. She wanted to show him every-thing—her antique desk, her favorite painting, her books. She wanted him to say, "It's a lovely setting you've made for yourself, Chantal." She wanted him to know her and her life. She wanted him to stay forever.

She brought in the sandwiches, played hostess, wished she had champagne on ice. It was that kind of feeling. That kind of night.

She tried, but in her euphoria, she couldn't swallow even one of her sandwiches. There were Jarlsberg cheese and Black Forest ham, egg slices and carrot curls, watercress and avocado. So she sat happily by, watching Simon while he ate everything.

Simon seemed at home. He sat on her couch, leaning over the tray on her small coffee table. His suede jacket was tossed over the back of her rosewood chair. He'd told her not to bother to hang it up. She wanted to stroke that masculine jacket; it looked as if it were imported from Spain and would feel as soft as a kitten.

As Simon drank the straight tea, not sassafras or mint, she'd prepared for him, Chantal studied his face. He looked tired. A groove of fatigue had deepened on either side of his long, thin lips. The thick black hair hinted a frost of gray above each temple. It occurred to her that Simon, at thirty-seven, was considerably older than she.

They began to talk. It turned out to be a time that was easy and relaxed. Never mentioning Chantal's earlier behavior, Simon treated her as an interested and interesting equal partner and business associate.

He told her about the meeting in the Black Tower at which Peter Tark's lawyer, Tark's agent and Tark's business representative had been present, in addition to the studio representatives from the contract, legal and business affairs departments.

"There they were, negotiating new contracts between Peter and Peter's own production company and the studio. A new share of profits—net share, though, not gross. Profits from the gross would mean a bigger piece of the pie without all the expenses the studio tacks on. I don't think Peter's lawyers caught that one. Some of it got tough, but most of it was everybody stroking everybody else's ego. I sat there holding the best property that's been on the lot since Zanuck and Brown were there with *Jaws*. So they tried to use me to bring Peter into line. It won't happen again, any of it." In answer to Chantal's question, Simon continued with, "It's been in the back of my mind to move off the lot sometime in the future."

"That won't be easy, will it? There's not much vacant space to lease around town, and you do have a good relationship with the people at Universal, except perhaps for what just happened."

"That's right, it won't be an easy move. Not one I want to comtemplate either. Particularly since my slate of pictures is lined up for the next three years, and I'll be shooting in Brazil next year if conditions permit."

"Will you go there too . . . on location?"

"Part of the time. I might even be line producer on that one."

Chantal was silent. Brazil! A continent, an ocean away.

Simon stretched both arms massively. "I'm feeling better. How about you?" Without waiting to hear the answer to his question, he added, "I'm really sorry I didn't get here sooner." He appeared slightly curious. "You did expect me, though?"

"Well, I . . ." Chantal perceived that the evening's mood was changing.

Simon leaned across the coffee table to the opposite side where she sat on a hassock. He took her chin in his hand. "You knew I'd come tonight, didn't you?" he asked softly.

Slowly Chantal nodded her head. Then her eyes followed the movement of his body as Simon rose from the couch and came around to where she sat. Standing above her, he reached down and, one by one, removed the tortoiseshell pins from her hair. His touch was expert, swift and sure. His fingers sent an exquisitely sensual current tingling down her backbone. Something blocked within her chest and she began to breathe rapidly, unevenly.

He murmured, "Extraordinary," as her heavy red hair fell to her shoulders. As he had done one time before, he smoothed back the hoyden wisps that strayed across her forehead. All the while, Chantal sat very still, wondering what she would do if she really forgot how to breathe.

"May I?"

She could barely hear his voice.

Again not waiting for her answer, he placed his hands around the curve of each bare shoulder and eased the velvet top downward. It caught above the rising swell of her breasts. He knelt beside her and gently pushed the velvety material down over her bosom and arms. His fingers unzipped the back of the top. At the same time they released the hook of her lace brassiere. Every article of clothing fell away at once, leaving the lush, round, erect mounds of Chantal's white breasts exposed to Simon's gaze. He stared for long moments, then bowed his head beneath her trembling throat.

Chantal looked down at his dark head and shivered as she felt her nipples extend like wet buds under his searching tongue. She could not move from the hassock. She felt a blaze of heat rise within her body, felt its warmth spread through her limbs and into her loins, then swell upward in a fiery tide past her belly.

The lassitude of her own desire held her motionless, as though she were a small and flawless statue sitting bound to the hassock, her upper torso bare and lovely and belonging to Simon's caress. Yet she was flesh, alive and ardent under his mouth and hands. Those hands of his which at first had moved as lightly as silk but which now, in his strong arousal at the sight and the feel and the scent of her, grew heavy and possessive.

With one arm's tensile strength, Simon raised Chantal to her feet and held her against his chest while his fingers loosened the band of the skirt she was wearing. The sensuous fabric fell unnoticed to the floor as, with a moaning whimper, Chantal's arms went around Simon's neck, straining him to her.

His mouth closed down over hers. Warm and seeking, his tongue parted her lips. Their bodies moved together, searching, eager. Chantal became conscious of his hard strength thrusting against the thin lace of her underpants.

Simon swung her up into his arms, and carrying her easily, started down the hall toward her bedroom. As instinctively as he knew his way about Chantal's body, he seemed to know his way about her small apartment. He kneed open the half-closed door, crossed the room in one stride and laid her gently on the bed.

The light from the street below glided across the bedroom ceiling. Its illumination revealed Simon's strong physique as he stood erect, pulling the sweater over his head, unzipping the white pants. He was lean and powerful. He moved with the ease and grace of a sleek, long-muscled cat.

There was nothing between them now. Simon lowered his body and Chantal cried out as his chest ground down almost hurtfully on her breasts. His kisses covered the places that were bruised; his fingers lingered within and soothed the places he desired.

As though to remember her body, the palms of Simon's hands curved like a sculptor's around her small, perfectly defined waist, then moved back to measure and confine the rounded, womanly buttocks. As his hands spread beneath her hips to lift her torso to his, Chantal knew the fire of the enchanter's touch. Please, now! she cried silently, but he did not enter her as she expected him to. Instead, once more his hands surrounded her soft flanks, moved within the insides of her thighs, touched her intimately, until again her still voice cried out that it was time. Her body begged for the pulsation of his strength inside her. Yes, yes, now, she pleaded inwardly.

Not now.

Again his hands explored, and as they moved across her belly, raising her breasts, nuzzling them, his lips followed the movement of his hands along her body. In frustration this time, Chantal gripped his fingers in her own, surprised at her strength. Almost angrily, and still holding his hands tightly to keep them from exerting such an unbearable excitation upon her, she fastened her lips onto his. As though to punish, she bit softly at first, then sharply, tasting blood. "Now!" she cried aloud.

This time his whispered answer could be faintly heard. *"Not now."*

Chantal's body continued its demand. She arched her back, pressed her hips against his in a kind of beseechment, a lusting plea. She could feel herself spinning in a maelstrom of sweet, savage, young desire. Yet gradually, as he held her back, led her tantalizingly, she began to comprehend what his body was trying to show hers. The blaze of their physical needs must not be assuaged with the immediacy of quick passion. Both of them must learn the intoxicating path they could take to an utmost shared sensation.

Float free, Chantal . . . abandon yourself.

His words? His thought? Whichever it was, she didn't know. She only did as she was told; relaxed under his touch and waited and was fed by him. Then, as his hands rocked her hips gently, as his mouth moved upward along her body to linger on the firm, full points of her breasts, she knew the final explosion within her center—knew its spiral of sensation that whirled and spread and shuddered— and the *now* was here! The dream was here as he came into her for that final thrusting joy. The great soaring dream would no longer frighten her. She would never fear the blue night again, nor sleep.

"Simon . . . I love . . ." Exhausted, languid, Chantal closed her eyes.

"Chantal, you mustn't . . ." he warned softly, but she didn't hear him. She was asleep. Simon turned to look at her. As he watched her, his face became grave and absorbed, almost without expression. Then he folded his arms behind his head and stared into the darkness. Simon did not close his eyes until it was almost dawn. He heard the start of the summer rain, heard it gradually fade away over the desert to the east.

Chapter Eight

They awakened together in bright morning. Chantal
raised her head from the pillow beside Simon's. He
had surprised her by staying the night. Now he
moved upward and close beside her. With his dark
head propped against the padded headboard, he still
looked sleepy, but younger, relaxed. He rubbed his
hand over his forehead and down along the side of
his face to where his beard had begun to show. In
self-conscious amusement, Chantal thought he
looked more the bandit-hero than ever. Resignedly
she wondered why she was unable to restrain her
imagination.

Simon glanced down at her, yawned hugely, then
apologized. "It's not the company, I assure you."

He reached for her. Chantal laughed tantalizingly
and sprang out of bed, the sheet swathed loosely
around her naked-body. Her supple movement
stripped off his own covering.

"You've left me no modesty," Simon complained.

But he did nothing about it. He remained stretched out, his long legs and dark-thatched chest and middle exposed to her gaze.

Chantal wanted to say, "You're a beautiful man, Simon—you don't need modesty," but she kept still. Smiling a caress, she tossed him her terry robe. It looked very small on his big frame.

He sat up. "Why are you out of bed so fast? It's only Thursday. I want to talk to you."

"You mean you want our conversation to last until . . . the weekend?" Her gray eyes silvered into mischief.

"Wouldn't it be a good idea?" His gaze lingered on the pearl-like sheen of her shoulder. The rest of her was hidden, but deliciously profiled, by the sheet. He closed his eyes and breathed in as though to absorb her essence. Chantal could not keep from glancing down along the outline of his body. He opened his eyes suddenly and caught the path of her gaze. "Come back to bed," he ordered.

Tentatively Chantal placed one knee on the side of the bed and leaned toward him. She was trembling. Golden languor seemed to flow through her veins. "What about your office? It must be after ten o'clock. Won't they wonder where you are?"

"They can get along without me. They have before."

"Oh?"

He grinned wickedly. "Oh, yes. But not for any reason such as this. Tell me, Chantal, are you more interested in whether I'm missing a meeting at the studio—or in satisfying other preoccupations of mine? Of ours?" His exploring hand traveled inward to her thigh, surrounded it and brought her closer to him. "I think we should confer between ourselves." Shamelessly he indicated the now-powerfully impatient reason for that conference. She knew she shouldn't laugh, but she couldn't help it as, with abandon, she threw herself into his arms. The white sheet no longer covered her, but floated away like a great cloud to drift onto the floor near the bed.

Soon it was noon, and the yellow arc of sunlight flowed directly into the room to warm their bodies and awaken them . . . again. This time Simon watched Chantal as she sped into the bathroom, clanging the shower door shut behind her.

"I'll give you five minutes. If you're not out here by then, I'll join you," he called after her.

But Chantal was quick. She emerged breathless, made a piquant face at Simon and dressed swiftly in jeans and a plaid shirt. She slung moccasins on her bare feet, aware that his dark eyes followed each of her moves with interest.

"You next," she said, indicating the bathroom. "I'll make coffee."

Showered and dressed, his beard showing even darker, Simon joined her in the kitchen. The refrigerator had been cleared out in preparation for Chantal's trip to the country. Still, she'd come up with very good coffee, sliced oranges and pumpernickel toast spread with guava jelly.

"Share a hard-boiled egg?" She held it up.

Simon shook his head and sat down at the small table. They ate together in companionable silence. Chantal kept glancing at him. She couldn't help it. He was here, and she was in love. Afterward Simon stood up and leaned against the tile counter to drink his second cup of coffee. He winked at her. "It's not entirely the coffee that tastes . . . delicious."

All at once Chantal's oval-shaped face glowed;

her eyes shimmered, moist and brimming luminously with love for Simon. Impulsively she started to speak.

Simon looked at her with sudden intentness. "Wait!" It was as though his hand had chopped the air, cutting off whatever was to come next.

In dismay Chantal checked herself.

"You like me, don't you?"

"Like you?" Chantal stared at him, astonished. "Like" was such a feeble word. Simon had made bliss shudder through her body last night, this morning. He had brought her to the peak of physical and emotional sensation. Far more importantly, she adored Simon for himself—for his understanding, his intellect. He would lead and she would follow. She would learn from him. Her reaction was far removed from anything she had ever felt before. It was almost one of abjection. She did feel a certain amount of self-ridicule at what this mad storm of love had done to her. Disgraceful, but it was true. She wanted to sit at his feet, in worship of her beloved prophet, who would teach her all the wonders of the world—its sensual delights, its exotic wisdoms, its age-old truths.

So now she repeated aloud, "Like you! Simon, you know that I—"

She had been about to describe her encompassing love for him, but the sentence died on her lips. Instead, she stared at Simon a long moment. Strong currents of unease began to caution her. It was as though she had received a rattled warning. She shivered, beginning to understand.

Carefully she tried out her next sentence. "I like you." She said it simply, without emphasis. And watched him from beneath her sweep of shining hair.

His face unreadable, he answered, "That's better."

Better? What did that mean? It meant that she had said only what he wanted to hear, no more. A terrible comprehension began to grip Chantal. *She was not to love Simon.*

He sighed. "We have to come to an understanding, you and I," he said softly.

Not quite sure how she managed it, Chantal replied lightly, "That sounds ominous." She stood up and moved to the sink with dishes in her hands. She sensed that what was to come next might bring devastation to her heart.

"First I want to apologize for my actions toward you at my house after the fire. I think you know what I'm referring to. You've been a totally gallant lady, Chantal, and you haven't said anything about my behavior. It was pretty rough of me to take you the way I did. It's something I'm not proud of."

Chantal watched him gravely. What revelation would come next?

But what he said was merely, "What are those half-packed suitcases doing in your bedroom?" His tone was remote.

"I'm leaving town for awhile," she replied raggedly. Would he ask her not to go? Simon said nothing. She concluded, "I'll be at my parents' place in San Bernardino County."

"You're closing your apartment?"

He's making polite conversation, was Chantal's frantic thought. She answered dutifully, "For the rest of the summer anyway. I've mentioned it before." .

He remained silent. At the sink, Chantal clattered coffee cups nervously. Simon walked over and looked out the kitchen window toward the street below. "You have a nice view," he remarked. "I suppose you could sublease if you wanted to."

Was she hearing right? Was she going crazy?

"It rained last night." *That* she was surprised to hear. She must have slept through it. He continued. "I didn't sleep, Chantal, until almost morning. I was thinking about us. Perhaps I was thinking more about myself. You see, I am trying to be honest with you." He glanced over his shoulder at the silent woman. "You feel like calling me a bastard?"

Wordlessly Chantal nodded.

A smile flickered across his face. "Then why don't you?" When she didn't speak, he went on. "This does need to be said. I don't make commitments. Ever. Do you understand what I'm saying to you?"

Chantal turned to dash water into the emptied pot. She threw coffee grounds into a paper bag. At this moment, to Chantal, pride was not a thing of the spirit. It was a physical summoning. Pride resembled an interlocking upright support to lean against. Pride was crowned with painful stakes which could impale if one did not move warily. Or perhaps, and more aptly in Chantal's case, pride was a cloak that must be gathered brightly about one's self.

Her reply to Simon had an unreal quality to it because the situation itself was turning out to be unreal. "I understand you exactly, Simon. I'm not a stupid person." She paused, reflecting that love had really turned her into an idiot, but no use letting the loved object know how much of an idiot.

She attempted to put it gracefully, but knew her words came out sounding like bad dialogue in a bad script: "We played a tune last night, a very good one. I promise there will be no echoes to trouble

either one of us. Don't concern yourself about that."
She was, of course, promising only for him—not for
herself.

If what he intended was a smile, it turned out to be
merely a thin shift of his lips. "You're an original,
Chantal. What else could I have expected?" He
hesitated. "I had to explain how I felt about all this
because I don't want you to be hurt in your
association with me. You're too important an individual. You're desirable in every way. Yet I don't
want you to expect more that I can give. I don't want
you to give more than I can accept."

How thin the membrane between passion and
disaster. Chantal hung up a dish towel, swiped at the
sink with a sponge. She didn't look at Simon. Her
voice at a controlled level, she said, "I'm glad the
Tark thing turned out well. You didn't need my
arguments against his playing the role of Auguste,
did you? You had your own. They must have proved
strong enough to satisfy everyone, from what you've
told me about last night's meeting."

Simon's dark brows raised speculatively at the
turn their conversation was taking. He watched
Chantal. "I was able to put something together and
take the heat off, yes. But, as I told you, they were
actually using me as a ploy to get Tark and his own
production company to re-sign on the studio's
terms."

Coolly, Chantal returned Simon's look. But when
he started to approach her, she backed away, almost
imperceptibly. And what was the bastard—as he had
so aptly portrayed himself—saying now? Wearily
Chantal listened.

"After you think about what I've said, you'll see
we can still go on together. I've been truthful. I said

what had to be said." He paused. "There's no need for an ending between us."

"For now I think it is an ending, Simon. I have responsibilities I've already told you about. I'm leaving town. I won't be back until the fall."

It was a decision made on the instant. Earlier, it had not been Chantal's plan to spend the entire summer at EdgeMont. Nor would she have left town at all had matters turned out differently between her and Simon. She knew that. At least I'm honest with myself, she thought in consolation.

"Chantal, last night and this morning were very special for me. I hope they were that way for you too. As long as we understand each other, there's no reason why we can't continue."

"Because I have to go away," Chantal repeated. In its simplicity, hers was a sentence carefully constructed, thoughtfully spoken. It did not actually say, "I love you too much to settle for the little you have to offer me."

Chantal had been taught, both by experience and by the sophisticated advice of others, never to close a door entirely, particularly a professional door. There was always the possibility she and Simon might work at the same studio at some point in the future. The "industry" was its own small world. Tempers flared, insults were hurled, promises were broken, financial mishaps occurred. But no matter how cruel the circumstance, when the call came to do a major piece of work, to sign a fulfilling contract, to leave on a lucrative, far-distant location, you did it . . . together! The film business was one of reconciliation, expediency—hard and cynical fact.

Chantal assured herself that, in the physical sense, she would never return to Simon. But it was possible they might work together again one day. Thus, whatever his assumption, she would not storm, protest, cry out the truth—that she loved him, hated him; that he was unfeeling and cruel and selfish!

Simon started out of the kitchen toward the living room—away from Chantal. This time her heart really did despair. She thought, It can't be happening this way. *I love him.* Why can't I accept the little he has to give and be satisfied with that? Could she change his mind, change the man? Of course she couldn't.

Simon stopped at the door leading into the outside corridor. "You'll let me hear from you?"

Chantal said nothing. Finally she nodded. It was a lie. He would not hear from her. Simon walked back across the room to kiss her lightly on the cheek in farewell. To show him that there were no hard feelings, that she was a sophisticated woman, Chantal's smile was a bright flash, a reminder of pride's bright cloak.

Chantal drove along the San Bernardino Freeway, her summer possessions stuffed in the back of the Datsun. She drove carefully, impatient with the moisture that blurred her eyesight. She blinked angrily. Forget Simon Bryce! There were more important considerations in life.

Like what, for instance? she asked herself with irony. What, really, was more important to her than Simon? Was it her career? She knew she had a lot to learn and a long way to go. Eventually she wanted to write her own scripts, and then, if she were very lucky and a lot tougher than she was now, she'd put together a package—financing, a director, a star—go to a studio head and sell her idea. But that was in the future. Now was now. She accelerated and passed a truck. It loomed behind her and she went faster, keeping pace with her thoughts.

What else was important? There was her family, even though everyone didn't always get along well. It was difficult for Millicent and Jason to remember that the children were no longer children. No, Chantal was no longer a child. That was for sure. Which brought her full circle once more to Simon Bryce. With Simon, she'd grown up a lot, and in a hurry. One thing she knew for a certainty. She had no rival—no female rival, that is. Simon was a footloose man and he intended to stay that way. His most intense satisfaction seemed to be with his work. He'd been willing to give Chantal one small corner of his life. She recalled Simon's words: "I don't want you to expect more than I can give. I don't want you to give more than I can accept."

More important matters in life than Simon Bryce? There have to be, she told herself, and became aware that the truck behind her was blinking its lights. She let it pass her as she began looking ahead for the Archibald Avenue turnoff.

Soon Chantal was off the freeway and driving due north, up the avenue that led through the few remaining grape vineyards, green-flowing under the summer sun. Before her the long gray San Gabriel mountain range was silhouetted against the sky, a cutout of Olympian proportion. Its crown was the fiercely solitary Cucamonga Peak. Chantal's car veered in the peak's direction. Like the North Star in a night sky, it had always seemed to belong to her personally.

The Datsun sped through the new residential tracts. There was no need to wonder where the lemon trees and the orange orchards had gone. The land had been despoiled, raped, cemented over, and the proceeds of the country earth sat jingling in the pockets of the developers. The ranchers had been unable to hold out against the swelling hordes of house hunters that moved eastward from Los Angeles, searching like ants for new dwellings to pour into.

As the southern boundary of the Jerrolds' two hundred and eighty-five acres came into sight, Chantal promised herself that this particular Rancho Cucamonga development devastation would stop at EdgeMont.

Most of the Jerrold acreage reached up along a sagebrush-covered mesa, while further acres were swallowed by the canyon that climbed into the mountainside. What a place for View Homes, as Boyd Farrell's shiny-paged brochures would certainly promise.

From Archibald Avenue a palm-tree-lined, unpaved road slanted off toward the big house in the orange grove. It was a Victorian splendor, needing paint but handsome with turrets and cupolas, gingerbread fretwork embellishing bay windows, east and west porches. Built by the first Jerrold, a homesick New Englander, it seemed curiously out of place in this landscape.

The dirt road ended in a parking strip in front of the overgrown garden, but Chantal continued around the house, her car bucking hard over deep indentations made by last winter's rains on the lane leading toward the back.

The first person Chantal saw as she turned the Datsun in under the sycamore tree was Ardis, clad in skinny jeans. She was riding Farrell's shoulders piggyback while he galloped her around the roadway to the barn.

Jason was watching, looking implausibly elegant in his ranch corduroys and laughing at the antics of his daughter and her beau. Millicent stood on the back steps, her silvery-blond hair sheltered from the sun by an enormous straw hat. There was no way for Chantal to read the expression on her mother's face.

As Chantal's car braked in the drift of dust, four faces turned in her direction. Each countenance wore its differing reception for the new arrival.

Ardis slid from Boy's broad back to the ground. With pseudo charm she called out, "So it's Chantal. No one expected you." She looked spiteful.

Chantal moved out from behind the steering wheel. "Bet you're glad to see me." She would not let herself be irritated by her sister.

Ardis pointedly didn't reply. Boy fluttered a hamlike hand in welcome and grinned his ingenuous grin. He gave Ardis a surreptitious push forward. Ardis hung back. Chantal saw the byplay and knew she was in the war zone.

Millicent tripped down the steps. There was a rush of ginger-perfumed air and, seemingly, the tinkle of little bells. Involuntarily, Chantal looked down at her mother's sandaled toes. As usual, Millicent had performed her magic, and whatever it was about her was merely the rustle of imagination. What a woman. Chantal smiled at her mother in broad amusement. "What's up?"

The umbrella-sized hat jounced around them both as, under its cover, Millicent kissed her younger daughter and hissed, "I'm glad you're here. Something important, that's what's up. Ric Milland!"

Chantal froze. "Here, in Rancho Cucamonga?" Millicent nodded; the straw hat bounced.

A long, athetic stride brought Jason to the two

women. He kissed the top of Chantal's head. "They're out of papayas at the supermarket. What did you bring me besides your lovely self, girl?"

"Father, I forgot everything." It was true. Normally she would have stopped at Gelson's and bought out the exotic-fruit department for Jason. She'd even forgotten to pack her yogurt maker. But then, she'd had a lot on her mind.

"Chantal, you surprise me. You're always so organized." Jerrold turned to his wife and said with horrible prescience, "Our girl must be in love, otherwise how could she forget my stuff?"

"Jason! Don't treat me like a child. Don't you understand *anything?*" Chantal's sense of privacy had been invaded. Her sore heart was indignant.

The group stared after her in astonishment as she turned and fled up the steps and inside the house. The screen door banged behind her. Her face was scarlet. She was furious, humiliated. She took a deep breath and rapidly reconsidered. Her father was receiving the brunt of her painful animosity toward Simon.

All right, she told herself, get it over with quickly. She stuck her head back out of the door. "Damn it, Jason, I'm sorry I lost my temper."

"Damn it, girl, I'm sorry I have such an insensitive tongue. Your uncle Edward once said to me, 'Jason Jerrold, you are a sap.' I won't tell you what caused him to say it, but he was probably justified."

"Oh, Dad . . ." Chantal rushed back down the steps, this time in laughter.

Her father patted her shoulder and quoted, " 'These are the times that try men's souls . . .' " Jason amended, " 'Persons' souls.' One must be contemporary, right, Millicent?" He looked guardedly at his wife, as though summoning her to help with this suddenly awkward situation.

"Did you have a good drive out from town?" Millicent asked briskly.

Chantal walked toward the rear of the car. "The smog was fierce until I reached the Archibald turnoff."

Introducing a noncontroversial subject meant there was to be no more truculence. Even Ardis cooperated. She moved forward and picked up a tote bag from the back seat.

Boy assisted with the rest of the luggage. His face full of freckle-faced good humor, he kept saying how glad he was to see Chantal. He turned and prodded Ardis. "Isn't it great your sister's here?"

Ardis was at least honest. The expression in her light brown eyes inimical, she smiled just a little. "We'll see." Ardis knew very well that as far as the sale of EdgeMont was concerned, Chantal and Jay were lined up in opposition to Boy and herself.

As Chantal passed her, Millicent murmured, "We'll talk later, dear. Settle in upstairs. Dinner's at eight."

Carrying the luggage, Chantal and Boy climbed the stairs. She was curious about the sleeping arrangements on the big second floor. Had Millicent finally and grudgingly allowed her older daughter and her fiancé of five years their own double room?

Millicent hadn't—quite, Chantal discovered. Ardis was in her old sleeping quarters, separated by a narrow bathroom from Boy, who had been assigned what had once been a sewing room, small and hot underneath the rafters. Of course at midnight, when the house was quiet, Boy could easily make his way to Ardis's cooler bed.

Chantal unpacked in the sleeping porch that had been turned over to her. She truly regretted the lack of friendliness between Ardis and herself. They had once been close, but seemingly were no longer. Ardis was under Boy's spell, and she would do whatever he wanted her to.

Chantal understood very well what it was that Boy wanted. One night they'd all been together at the Beverly Wilshire, and Boy, a little drunk at the time, had laid it all out, telling Chantal he was aware of her family's financial predicament. He'd gone on to say what a "boon" it would be for everyone if Chantal, along with Ardis, would cooperate in coaxing her parents into considering a sale of the country place. Yes, it was going to be a stressful summer.

Chantal spread out hairbrush, comb and toilet articles, glad that she had her own bathroom. She went into the big walk-in closet, moved aside the garment bags, fragrant with lavender, and hung up her skirts, blouses, pants and some summer dresses she'd packed at the last minute when she realized she probably wouldn't be returning to town for a couple of months. For the time being, she'd put her freelance career plans on hold.

The brass bed looked wonderful, comfortable and comforting. It had been there forever, it seemed, in the same spot, along with the upstairs rattan furniture and the fluffy, white East Indian rugs on the shiny hardwood floor. The windows along three sides of the room were screened casements which could be cranked outward. With the night wind blowing in, the sleeping porch was refreshingly cool.

Looking down the drive, past the high tops of the last remaining stand of eucalyptus trees, Chantal tried to pretend she couldn't see the Spanish tile roofs of the two-story subdivision houses built close together on what had once been the fertile soil of a productive peach orchard. Nor did she want to remember the adjacent small meadow that was no longer there. In the spring it had been carpeted with poppies, purple lupine and Indian paintbrush.

Her mother's tap on the door brought Chantal out of her reverie. Millicent entered, her frosted blond hair swinging in a thick braid down her back. She was wearing turquoise jewelry and a turquoise caftan, her pouter-pigeon breasts thrust forward.

Chantal shook her head. "How did you find the time to change clothes so quickly? I must have inherited the bosom belonging to the Atherton side of the family."

Millicent ignored the first remark. To the second, she responded, "Be glad that you did. Now—I want to talk to you about Ric."

"I'd rather you didn't. How long has it been, three years? Mother, he and I were engaged, but in a very platonic fashion. Why is he back here?"

"You should remember him kindly, Chantal. After all, he's one of the few men left in your generation who ever had honorable intentions."

"That's true. But you're evading. Why is he here?"

"Why shouldn't he be? The Millands have owned property in Rancho Cucamonga as long as the Jerrolds."

"But they sold out. Ric sold out. That was part of the trouble between us. Though I never really loved him, and thank God I gave back his mother's diamond ring."

"I wasn't sure you were coming this afternoon."

"What does that mean? Have you done something you shouldn't? Father can give me an anxiety attack, but you seldom do."

"Well, then, get ready for one."

"Millicent!"

Her mother nodded. "I couldn't help it. There Ric was, at the Bear Gulch Inn. He came in while Jason and I were having iced tea. He looked very handsome, dear. He's wearing a mustache now. You remember, Ric's the brawny type."

"I remember."

"He invited us into the bar and ordered a bottle of champagne. It was a nice gesture. After all, Jason and I almost became Ric's in-laws. We had a good talk. It was like old times. He always liked me."

"Go on."

"And then I invited him to dinner. Tonight."

Chantal banged her hairbrush on the bureau top.

Millicent's eyes widened. "But, Chantal, I didn't know you'd be here."

"I won't be here. I'm going down to El Cholo and eat my dinner there."

"You can't avoid Ric forever. He's back to stay. He's in the land developing business."

"He's *what?*"

"You heard me, dear. Let me tell you—it was Moët and Chandon's Dom Pérignon that he ordered for all of us. That's really being a sport." Millicent glanced into the dressing table mirror and fingered the turquoise caftan. "This color does things for my eyes, doesn't it?"

Chantal stared at her mother for a long minute. Millicent was being her usual charming and manipulative self. Chantal understood that childlike appeal very well. What was the use of fighting it? Besides, even though she'd been vexed, she was still curious about Ric and his development project. She sensed something peculiar in all this.

"Millicent, will you tell me something?"

"I don't think we should talk about Ric anymore."

"It isn't about Ric. I'm resigned to seeing him. I can't very well expect you to withdraw an invitation."

"Then what?"

"Why did you put Boy into that dinky little room down the hall when there's the big guest room on the other side? Is that any way to treat a hopefully prospective son-in-law? Aren't you and Jason planning to show him the way to the altar? You always said to Ardis and me that we could get any man we wanted if we made him comfortable. Not that we believed you, but that's what you said. And look what you're doing to Boy!"

"I'm not doing anything. It's up to Ardis to make him comfortable."

"She has ways."

"What do you mean?"

"Nothing. Forget I said it. But what about that vacant guest room? It has a desk, an extension telephone, everything to make a tycoon happy."

"I was getting to that. It won't be vacant very long. Oliver Larch is coming to spend a week or so. We're working on a project. He has to have a desk and plenty of room."

"What about your friend Athalie? I thought you were planning to help train those models of hers."

"That won't start until the fall. In the meantime . . ."

"In the meantime, Oliver Larch is the twit of the world. I've told you, Millicent. I've warned you. He's an opportunist."

"He likes my short stories—the ones I wrote when

I was in college. He said I had promise. I mean, look at all those millions that woman made who wrote about Rodeo Drive in Beverly Hills."

Suddenly Chantal walked over and kissed her mother. "I know. You're going to save us all. Listen, dinner at eight. I'll be there."

"Bless you, Chantal."

"Ma, I don't think the woman who wrote about Rodeo Drive ever said anything like that. You'll have to smarten up your dialogue."

"Perhaps you can help me. You're very clever, Chantal."

"Untrue. I can't even help myself. If Ric is coming tonight, I think I'll take a nap."

"And wear a pretty dress."

"I will. And I'll make Ric comfortable."

Millicent looked surprised. As she left Chantal's room, she thought, One never knows. Wouldn't it be nice? Ric and Chantal again.

Chapter Nine

It could never be Ric and Chantal again. A week later, sitting side by side on the lip of the fenced-in reservoir, Chantal knew this. Unfortunately, Ric didn't seem to. As her mother had said, he was a handsome fellow. His dark brush of mustache gave him a rugged combative look. With his well-muscled physique encased in work shirt and denims, a straw ranch hat's curled brim pulled down over sleepy-looking dark eyes, and skin tanned to a mahogany shade that made one want to stroke it, he was the picture of what thirty-year-old ranchers had been in the past.

But Ric was contemporary, no doubt about it, and so was his thinking. What he was saying to her made Chantal want to bare her teeth. She didn't, though, and she didn't move, because Ric had cleverly positioned his broad left shoulder and long leg against her right side, so that if she moved at all, she would brush bosom and bottom against his flank in her attempt to stand up, keep her balance and reach the reservoir gate. If she did manage to slide around Ric and avoid physical contact, the slippery ledge above the water was so narrow that with one misstep she'd roll down the sloping cement side.

So she had to sit still and listen. What was he talking about, this irritating, good-looking guy to whom she had once been engaged? They had broken up partly because of Ric's rigid political and socio-economic views, which in no way corresponded to her own. She had realized these differences would be a constant source of friction to them both. She had been angry when Ric had encouraged his parents to sell their home place. And the really big minus was that she'd never truly loved him.

Chantal brought her thoughts back to what Ric was saying. She heard his voice enumerating acreage, and making what sounded suspiciously like a sales pitch.

"You can see for yourself, Chantal, what Jason has under cultivation here—thirteen acres of lemons, thirty-two acres of oranges, thirty-one acres of grapes, four acres of walnuts, seven acres of almonds. On the highest possible use of the land, the taxes on all this reflect potential subdivision value, not the actual value of the ranch land.

Chantal countered, "Father received a tax break when the state legislature passed that act that enabled ranchers to register much of their property as conservation land. That cut their taxes from almost two hundred fifty dollars an acre to fifty dollars an acre. Which is only fair, since most of the land is agricultural."

"But only a portion is designated that way."

"Do you know something, Ric? Not only do you

sound as though you've been studying this situation, you also sound a bit pompous." Here we go, thought Chantal. And I'm the one to start the disagreement this time. She looked swiftly at Ric. "I'm sorry. That was a slip of the tongue. Please go on with your statistics. I'm interested."

"I hope you are." Ric frowned. "This is important, Chantal. What if the pressures on the politicians in Sacramento change? All over this county the developers are buying out the ranchers. First they cut the pieces up into five- or ten-acre parcels, then they chop 'em up into one-acre parcels. You read that article in the local paper the other day?"

"And you're quoting it! Why, Ric? Don't bother to tell me, I think I know. You want to buy out Jason just as much as Boy Farrell does. You'd better look out, the two of you might lock horns—and for nothing, because EdgeMont isn't for sale. If you know so much about our acreage, you should have some compassion and understanding about how important it is to keep these green belts from being invaded."

"The inevitable has to be faced sometime. Don't live in the past, Chantal."

"You know what's going to happen? We're going to end up a nation of people who don't know anything about the outdoors, or even what a lemon looks like growing on a tree. I've had people tell me they thought grapefruit grew like watermelons on vines along the ground. Parents and their children will think walnuts in their natural state come all shelled in little plastic sacks at the grocery store."

"Okay. Tackle it another way. How long do you think Hernandez and Octavio and their families are going to keep on working the groves and vineyards at slave wages?"

Chantal's voice rose. "Everyone around here knows that Jason's done more for his help than any of the other property owners ever did for theirs. The men have those two comfortable bunkhouses to live in, with all their utilities paid for. Everything's modern. They have health insurance, and the school bus comes up here and picks up their kids. They're self-sufficient, and so are we. We have our own water piped in from the tunnels in our canyon. There's plenty of water to irrigate the land, to take care of everyone." Chantal knew she was going off on a tangent, but she wanted to end this conversation, and fast.

Like a great silver dollar, the reservoir in front of them lay gleaming in the sun. Shallow steps were cut into its sloping side. Today only the two top steps were visible above the water. On the opposite side, a wooden support jutted out. It was substantially built so that a workman could stand on it and turn the wheel that operated the outgo valve, which released the water every fourth day to flow along the irrigation furrows in the orchards.

Indicating the reservoir, Chantal looked sharply at Ric. "Have you done your homework here too?"

Ric nodded. "Capacity five hundred seventy thousand gallons." He hesitated. "I'm really talking about something else that I'd rather not bring up."

Chantal's lips tightened. "Then don't." From her sitting position on the cement lip of the reservoir, she still wanted to slide around Ric, and walk out the gate, leaving him to ponder his own concerns about the property. Her situation on the slanting side was too precarious, however.

Ric had always been single-minded, so he went on persistently, even though she'd told him not to. "Your father isn't the greatest manager, you know that. It may not be entirely his fault, with labor costs so high and everything else inflated, but he's had to sell off some of this place already."

"That isn't true," Chantal scoffed. She didn't want Ric to see her inner surprise at this news. But she knew from past experience with Ric Milland that he usually got his information straight.

Chantal felt better when Ric added in explanation, "Your upper twenty was deeded to the state for its flood-control right of way."

Chantal was reassured, yet she wondered why Jason hadn't told the family about it. "Oh, that. . . . It's only sagebrush up there. Not exactly what you'd call a forced sale either. The state already had some kind of easement on that area. Though it was nice of them to think of reimbursing Jason."

"No big deal maybe, Chantal, but it's an opening wedge. Why aren't you on my side? I may not be a big shot like Farrell, but I can get enough money together from sources I have to put a sizable down payment on this property. Think of the future potential it has. Convince your old man for me, will you?"

Chantal felt a choke of anger rise inside her throat at the realization that Ric would ask her to do such a thing. He knew her feelings well enough, or he should by this time. Now she couldn't put the blazing words of reply together fast enough—words that would squelch Ric and make him squirm, words to remind him that this very argument had arisen when the Millands had sold off their own property. Since she didn't answer immediately because she was so infuriated, Ric grinned lazily at her and tossed a pebble across the ninety-foot diameter of water.

"How about a swim to cool you off, Red?" Mockingly, he looked down at her boots and pants.

"Are you as speedy as you used to be?" He was challenging her to do what they'd done in the old days.

Breaking her silence, Chantal roared back at him, "Speedy enough to beat you!" Any action at all was preferable to having to sit and listen to Ric's arguments for selling the land. Disregarding the real danger of a fast slide down the moss-covered side of the reservoir, with two swift motions Chantal ripped off boots and pants and dropped them near the fence. She was furious. With her plaid shirt tail hanging down past her brief underpants, she plunged recklessly into the cold water, came up gasping and then started swimming with a powerful crawl, the quickest way to warm up fast. In the center, at the fourteen-foot depth, she paused to rest and tread water.

Her temper cooled somewhat, she taunted Ric, "I'm as fast as I ever was—and look at you!"

Ric was struggling with tighter pants, losing his balance and slipping. In the next few moments he was out of most of his clothes and into the water beside Chantal. His straw hat flew off and bobbed incongruously along the pool's surface.

Partly forgetting her own annoyance at Ric's obtuseness, Chantal shouted, "This is good!" Continuing to tread water, she stared up at the mountain peaks above them—Old Grayback and Mount Baldy to the west, Cucamonga Peak directly to the north. Suddenly Chantal felt a firm hand slide down her inner thigh. She spun around in the water to face Ric. "Hey, you, don't!"

Ric, his face as innocent as a cherub's, abruptly raised one hand, flattened it on top of Chantal's head and pushed down. She went under, spluttering wildly, flailing her arms.

When Ric removed his hand, Chantal bobbed up fast. "Bully! You never got over being in the sixth grade, did you?"

For an answer, Ric merely floated on his back, looking up at the sky. His brown torso was bare and hard-muscled. He was wearing khaki-colored Jockey briefs that gave him the tanned-allover appearance of a bronze nude. "Chantal, let's begin again, you and me. I've still got your diamond ring in the safety deposit box. All we have to do is renew the license. How about it?"

Chantal hardly heard Ric's words. She certainly didn't catch the import of what he was saying. The sight of him reminded her of another time, another mood, another late afternoon, another male body floating dark beneath the water's surface in a marbled pool. Simon Bryce was never far from her thoughts. Simon was forever. Ric Milland was not even a recalled interlude.

"What d'you say, Chantal?"

"Say to what?" She was still thinking of Simon.

"To you and me. Let's start it up again. We've gotten along fine this past week. It wouldn't take much, would it?" Ric reached for her. His superior strength brought her quickly alongside him. With the length of his body pressed vertically against hers, even beneath the water it was impossible not to realize that he was strongly aroused by her proximity to him. She realized something else. He'd skinnied out of his shorts. Disturbingly, she could feel his taut hardness press against her limbs. She kept her gaze away from the masculine body holding itself close to hers.

"Let me go, Ric," she panted. "It's cold. Let's talk this over on the bank."

But he swung her around, even closer to him, and

worked his mouth hotly, possessively, down over hers. Chantal struggled in vain to avert her face. Ric's grip on her was too strong. As their bodies surged together under the water, his arms clasped her tightly to him, one hand trailing along her lower back to force her hips into contact with his nakedness. Chantal recognized the physical sensation that the nearness of her flesh was having on him, a sensation intensely male.

"Ric! No!" Her head was barely above water. She was swallowing too much of it. Her hair streamed across her face. She realized with a sudden shock that Ric was reaching farther down. She felt the sliding touch of his hand as he removed her underpants, deftly rolling them down the length of her thrashing legs. To add to the indignity, he tucked her struggling body under his elbow and raised his other arm high above his head. Balling the panties in his fist, he sailed them onto the ledge. She could only be thankful that at least her shirt was securely buttoned. In her next effort to free herself from Ric's grasp the plaid shirt pulled down over one shoulder. She made an abrupt sideways move that turned out to be a mistake. She could feel the fabric give way as the front came loose and split wide.

Ric was laughing hard now. In play more than in passion, he pulled at the shirt, which slid easily down over her arms. The day had been hot to start with. She had not worn a bra, so there she was, naked as a miniature Venus.

In her effort to escape, she kicked backward. She must have caught Ric in a vulnerable spot, for all at once he looked surprised and discomfited. He let her go. Chantal swam to the shallower end. Grabbing Ric's hat from the water's surface, she began to swim quickly to the side of the reservoir. Locating the steps near the inflow pipe, she climbed out of the water. After retrieving her soaked underpants, she struggled into them and with Ric's straw hat held in front of her, turned to face her tormentor.

"Bring me my shirt!" Chantal ordered. "No—stay away from me. Throw it here."

Grinning at the sight of Chantal trying to hide her voluptuous body behind his hat, Ric did as he was told and tossed the soggy plaid shirt toward Chantal. She caught it neatly, tugged it around her and reached down to pick up her jeans. She slid them up her wet legs and over her rear, then zipped them taut in front. Boots in hand, she started out the gate.

"Drive your jeep," she hollered back at Ric. "I'm walking."

As Chantal started down the dirt road toward the groves, she heard Ric shout, "Wait for me, Chantal! I want you to marry me! I love you!"

Minutes later, Ric and the jeep caught up with her. The jeep stopped, motor running. The door swung open.

"Get in."

"No."

Ric reached out and with one snakelike motion grasped Chantal's wrist and lifted her from the ground into the seat beside him. He banged the door shut. They looked at each other wordlessly. Ric's brown eyes were still bright with laughter. His humor was contagious. Chantal threw back her head and let her own laughter join his. This way it was easy to pretend she hadn't heard Ric's wild proposal of marriage. Passing the barn and the bunkhouses, they arrived at the back door of the big house, too bedraggled to walk inside together.

Ric let Chantal out and promised, "See you later this evening. We'll talk some more about my propositions. You heard me. Plural!"

Chantal nodded, straight-faced.

Barefoot, her muddied boots in her hand, her hair tangled and wet, her damp shirt clinging almost buttonless to her body, Chantal walked into the kitchen to face Ardis. A very slim Ardis, impeccably clothed in a cream-colored, rib-knit sweater above tailored linen pants.

She stared Chantal up and down, head to foot. "You look rather wanton. What have you been up to—or shouldn't I ask? Was that Ric's jeep that just went down the palm drive?"

"That was Ric's jeep that just went down the palm drive," Chantal repeated good-naturedly. She picked out a bunch of grapes from the basket on the kitchen table, munched a few, then said curiously, "I suppose Millicent has told you that Ric has gone into land development?"

From Ardis's astonished expression, it was obvious she had not been told. "With what? Why didn't he say anything about his plans when he came to dinner?"

"He didn't get a chance to. As I recall, that night it was Boy who did all the talking about those condominiums he's putting up in Hawaii. The rest of us kept quiet. We had to, in homage to Boy's . . . uh . . . sagacity?"

Ardis spun around on one heel like a scrawny witch. "I call it sneaky of Ric not to have mentioned his own business interests, such as they are. Anyway, he doesn't have any money."

"The Millands sold all their property several years ago, you must remember that. Why shouldn't Ric have money, or at least be able to put his hands on some? His credit's excellent."

"I remember the Milland sale very well. That was when you and Ric broke it off. If you mean to tell me that Ric and his family made a walloping profit out of their deal, you're wrong. Totally. They sold too soon, way before land values skyrocketed."

Chantal popped another grape into her mouth, making a sour face. "Mmm . . . not ripe. Too early in the season for muscats." She put the grapes back into the basket. "He wants to buy EdgeMont, Ardis, just as Boy does. Maybe Ric can do it."

"That's ridiculous." Ardis stamped over to the refrigerator and took out a bottle of soda water. "But at least I know your feelings on the matter. *You* won't be helping him."

"You're right about that."

Ardis poured the bubbly stuff into a glass. "You want some?" Chantal shook her head in refusal. Ardis continued. "You should go in the den, open that rolltop desk and take a peek at Jason's book-keeping in the ledger. If you could understand his figures—which I don't think even he does—you'd realize this place has to be sold."

"Never EdgeMont," Chantal said coldly. She started out the kitchen doorway into the central hall. "By the way, Ardis, why are you so dressed up? Are you going out to dinner when Boy gets back from the county seat?"

"The dinner party is here. A friend of Mother's is expected. Oliver Larch."

This stopped Chantal. So soon? she wondered. "Do you know Oliver well?"

Ardis shrugged. "Just the way you do. He was always hanging around Hancock Park. Boy and I ran into them when he and Millicent were having lunch together one day at Perino's. Boy paid for everything—as one usually does with Oliver."

"I heard about that from Millicent. She's not proud."

"Somebody around here ought to be. Jason could go bankrupt."

"Not as long as Jay and I are here."

"I suppose Jay could help out by using Kiki Dalton's fortune." Ardis's tone was acerbic. She finished her soda water.

"You know something? I have a very strong hunch our little brother makes his own scratch. He doesn't have to depend on Kiki Dalton."

"Scratch! You've picked up some real vulgarisms, Chantal. Why can't you say 'money,' like everyone else does?"

"Because I don't *think* money, like everyone else. And as for being vulgar, Ardis, don't scream so loud when Boy does it to you in the lemon grove. You left Millicent's best bedspread out there too. Octavio brought it in."

Ardis's face crimsoned. She swallowed hard, looked momentarily wretched, then suddenly erupted into a flow of tears.

Chantal put out a hand to her sister. "Ardis! I shouldn't have said that."

"It isn't that." Wearily Ardis scrubbed at her face. Chantal ran for the box of tissues on the ledge above the sink. "It's . . . I just get so tired of everything." Ardis went on shakily. "I don't mean to blubber, but I know I could make Boy happy if he'd marry me. Chantal, I'm not very highly sexed, I guess. I keep having to think of new ways to do it. Some of them are pretty freaky." Chantal could only stare. "What

I mean is—original ways to have sex in order to keep Boy interested."

"That's no kind of premise on which to build a marriage."

Ardis was stubborn. "I know I'd be right for him. I know it." She took the tissues from Chantal and rubbed her pink nose. "I have a problem."

"It's Boy who has the problem. Listen, Ardis, please don't cry. You'll wreck your face and your pretty clothes and everything. I'll help you any way I can—except, of course, I won't do anything to help Boy buy this place from Jason and Millicent."

"But that's it! That's what Boy wants."

"I know it, but it doesn't make sense. He's involved in plenty of other profitable ventures."

"He wants more. This would be the big one. He'd even marry me if he got what he wanted with this place."

"If you only knew how terrible that sounds."

"You mean I have no pride?"

"I'm a fine one to be talking about pride." Hastily Chantal pressed on. "If Oliver Larch is coming here, he mustn't know anything about how matters stand with our family. He's the gossip of the world. I've been told he's even paid by some columnists for juicy items he picks up. Did you think it was only parking lot attendants, bartenders, and waiters at some of the best restaurants who do that sort of thing to make a little extra income?"

"If that's true, it's pretty tawdry. Larch shouldn't be here as a house guest. And he has a crush on Millicent. I know the signs."

"No, he doesn't. Not really. He merely has it in his mind that the Jerrolds are rich. He's looking out for Oliver."

"But Millicent says he has a job, that he teaches a writing class in the winter."

"Exactly. He's a fantasy builder. Right now he's building a fantasy around the Jerrolds."

Ardis blew her nose. "We'd better get rid of the jerk."

"Millicent will, eventually. In her own way, she's not partial to phonies. She hasn't found him out yet . . . because she doesn't want to. But she will."

"What are they doing together anyway? She wouldn't put Boy in the best guest room. She saved it for Oliver." Ardis sniffed and looked down at the tear spots on her flat-chested front.

"I'll have to let Millicent tell you her plans. I've got to go now. Hey, those linen pants of yours look great."

"I'm so skinny," Ardis sighed dolefully, "I can wear anything and look terrific. It's without wearing anything that I'm not so terrific."

Chantal hid a smile. "I'll let you in on a secret. There's a book down in the basement, a souvenir of Uncle Edward's visit to the Far East a million years ago. It's pushed in under the shelf where the saddlebags are. It's got a lot of pictures of Oriental art, and I'd say they're pure erotica. That book might give you some ideas even Boy doesn't know about."

"You're making fun of me."

"I'm not, I swear. The book's been there ever since we were in high school. Didn't you know? Jay did. I think he found that book when he was in the fourth grade."

"I never go down there." Suddenly Ardis crossed to the door leading to the basement stairs. "Thanks, Chantal. I'll take a look. But remember, no peace pipe between us where EdgeMont is concerned. I still intend for Boy to buy this property."

Chantal's reply was interrupted by the appearance of Octavio's wife, Beatriz, at the screen door. She'd come from the bunkhouse to help with tonight's dinner. Her smile extended from her calm forehead above liquid-brown eyes to her wide, sweet lips. She was delighted to see the two sisters together. The Jerrolds so rarely came anymore as a family to the country place.

Chantal greeted Beatriz and promised she'd be down to help as soon as she dressed. Ardis nodded perfunctorily and said she had an errand to do but would be back in time to set the table. Beatriz beamed. To her husband, Octavio, she always spoke of the Jerrold sisters as *las inocentes*. Octavio would teasingly reply, "The innocent ones? I think you are the innocent one to say such a thing." But he would never explain what he meant by these words of his delivered with such a knowing smile.

From the casement windows in the sleeping porch, Chantal could look down and see Jason, splendidly tanned, working in his vegetable plot in a far corner of the front garden. He'd had his daily running session and was still wearing running shorts. He certainly knew how to wield a spade and a hoe. He was busily irrigating the tomatoes, tying up the green beans and inspecting the lady bugs that flew healthily around the eggplant and the squash bushes. A happy man. Chantal smiled at the sight of her preoccupied father, then frowned. *Was* Jason happy? It must be difficult to wear a mask of serenity and try to fool your family into thinking all is well when all is not well. Jason knew it. The family knew it. And probably Jason knew that they knew it. He neatly pocketed his son's monthly check. What did Jason think that was for? A return on what he'd spent on Jay in the earlier years? Jason was not astute, but he was not to be gulled that way.

If Jason was not really duping himself, neither was his daughter deceiving herself, for Chantal knew that no matter what problem confronted her at the moment, Simon Bryce was there with her. He was a constant, poised on the perimeter of her consciousness. Simon had stolen her heart; his touch had consumed her being. She couldn't put him out of her mind. Though it was Chantal who had walked away, she had hoped that Simon would find the means to follow her.

Though he had said they could continue to see each other, he had laid down a condition—no commitment at all. Were they supposed to talk and work together, then jump in and out of bed at Simon's whim, saying "Goodbye" and "Thank you" and "Perhaps we'll do it again in a couple of weeks"?

That would be the real rejection.

Finally aware that she was staring blindly out of the window into the garden below, Chantal turned away and began peeling off her clothes. She paused, returned to the window and stared down curiously. Jason, working in the vegetable patch, had been joined by an unknown young woman wearing a tailored suit and carrying a leather briefcase. Chantal glanced at the front parking strip. She hadn't observed the station wagon come up the palm drive and stop at the foot of the garden. She had been oblivious to everything but her thoughts of Simon.

She wanted to continue with those thoughts. As

she kicked aside her jeans and boots, Chantal knew she was being self-indulgent.

Memory raced on, recalling every nuance in their brief relationship, every touch of Simon's hand upon her throat and breast, every shimmering sensation. From their first meeting, their encounters had been charged with a powerful sexuality. They had not only made love fiercely, obsessively and with a sensuality that tuned the blood to ecstasy, they had also shared their thoughts and communicated well. Except, of course, there was to be no future. It wouldn't last. She'd never know when it was to end, when the silence would start. . . .

As she bathed, toweled off and began to dress, Chantal deliberately turned her thoughts away from Simon. She made herself think about Ric Milland and his parting remark that he would see her later this evening to discuss his propositions. Plural.

Chantal brushed her dusky red hair until it shone with the sunset light of late afternoon. She fastened her bra and stepped into a half slip, faintly amused that Ric, who was staying at the Bear Gulch Inn, was still affecting the aspect of a rancher, both in clothes and in deportment. He'd told her he was establishing a business office in the main shopping center at Rancho Cucamonga. What a showoff move of his that had been, to order champagne for Jason and Millicent! It was pretty extraordinary that the bar even stocked Dom Pérignon, but then she supposed the owner might be a bit of a splashmaker himself.

Doubtless Ric had been attempting to establish credibility with the senior Jerrolds. He'd also probably been trying to make points with the inn bartender, who could be counted on to polish Ric's image as an operator with other customers. Ric Milland and

Boy Farrell were both after the same objective. While Ric might be a beginning entrepreneur, Boy Farrell was already set. Though, as Ardis had said, Boy always wanted more.

Chantal walked in and out of the big closet. She held up a taffy-colored silk blouse that warmed the shade of her gray eyes to amber. She could wear the blouse with the really wild trousers—tawny China silk lined in lipstick red—she'd bought on an impulse and packed at the last moment. Chantal wondered at her own financial daring and guessed that it was Simon's extravagant lovemaking that had gone to her head—heart?—and robbed her pocketbook.

The pants and shirt had been advertised as being among those "special pleasures that make life more exciting." Ruefully Chantal put away the silk clothes and brought out a cotton dress, crisp and white and freshly ironed. It was far more appropriate for helping Beatriz to serve dinner tonight.

Dressed, she struck a pose in front of her mirror. Gray eyes steady; no more dreams, she told herself. Red hair smooth, slicked under. But the simplicity of her dress did not disguise the high, rounded bosom or the seductive curve of the slim waist. Nor did it disguise the yearning within her. Chantal closed her eyes, black lashes trembling against the apricot tan of her skin. She needed Simon. Needed his powerful caress seeking the secret places within her body to create excitement, joy, even peace. No one else had ever done this for her. She needed the feel of his taut strength against and within her flesh. Laughter, compassion, intelligence—what else had she discovered as she lay beneath the weight of his splendid body? She recalled how she'd looked up into his face, attempting to decipher the unreadable in his blue-black eyes.

A sudden, quick anger raged through her. She had been ready to give so much. She felt cheated. But had she any right to count on a lasting relationship with Simon Bryce? No one had ever promised Chantal that her love would be rewarded. She opened her eyes, turned her gaze away from that woman in the mirror. Though nothing else might happen, it would have to be enough to have once been Chantal in Simon's arms. A brief span—only an afternoon, one long and lovely night and morning—yet to Chantal it seemed an eternity of loving. And now it was ended.

Why was she moping and glooming this way? The wobbly compass of her emotions spun in mad fashion until it pointed to hope. She'd been at EdgeMont for over a week. Simon had found her once before, he could do it again . . . if he wanted to.

Hope! But, of course, Simon hadn't called.

No one else was upstairs. Chantal walked along the upper hall and through the doorway of the still-unoccupied guest room. The extension phone sat on the bedside table. If she made the call, she would hear Simon's deep voice. Did she dare? Since it seemed she could not be cured of her total obsession with this man, was there any reason to prolong her own silence? Pride didn't matter, not now.

Slowly she moved to the telephone. Sexual liberation hadn't worked for Chantal. She couldn't sleep around casually. She'd found the man for her. She wanted to live with him, love him. But Simon wouldn't allow her to say "I love you." Simon had agreed to passion, not to love.

Her thoughts were full of confused contradictions. She put her finger on the push buttons, then drew it away as though her skin had been scorched. Save yourself, Chantal, she commanded herself. You will be hurt. Your heart will be broken if you make this call. Run away, run fast.

She knew Simon's number. It replayed in her brain. He would be in his studio office. He always stayed late. He was there now. She could speak to him, speak to Simon.

She wouldn't.

She did. She stood by the phone and rapidly tapped out the area code and the number.

From miles away in the bungalow, a woman's unfamiliar, British-accented voice answered, "Simon Bryce Productions." The woman did not recognize Chantal Jerrold's name. Mr. Bryce's regular secretary was on holiday. Mr. Bryce himself was out of the country. Was there anyone else to whom Miss Jerrold would speak? "No message? Thank you. Goodbye." Click.

Mr. Bryce was out of the country.

Chantal stared at the instrument in her hand. Slowly she replaced it in its cradle.

"Chantal?" Millicent called up the stairs. "Ardis has disappeared. Could you come down and help Beatriz? I'm doing the flowers for the table. Your father is entertaining the vice president of Boy's construction company. We'll have to find a room to put her in, since Oliver will be here shortly. Am I the only organized one around here?"

Chantal walked to the head of the stairs. Simon Bryce was out of the country. That lovely British voice might well have said, "And who are you, Miss Jerrold? No one's ever heard of you . . . you . . . you . . ."

Chapter Ten

The late arrival, Oliver Larch, had his vanities. As he turned his Volkswagen up the palm drive leading to the Jerrolds' house, he took off his driving glasses and tucked them in his breast pocket. In doing so, he missed the parking area and ended up beneath the sycamore tree at the rear door. He walked up the back steps into the kitchen, startling Chantal.

Larch was a slightly built man in his mid-forties. He wore a tweedy jacket with the usual suede patch on each elbow, baggy trousers and a decrepit tie. His hair, a pale sand color, curled in a fluff to his coat collar. His eyes matched his hair, except for the ebony pinpoints of their pupils.

Chantal, helping Oliver upstairs with his luggage, found him eccentric and unprepossessing, but she was aware that he was doted on by the women in the Hancock Park literary circles. Before leaving Oliver to settle into his room, Chantal noted the stack of yellow legal pads, the three dozen or so pencils encased in a rubber band and the electric portable typewriter that he carefully placed on the desk.

Larch watched Chantal watching him and produced his slinky smile. "We plan to do a lot of work, your mother and I. She's a very talented lady."

"Multitalented," agreed Chantal. "I'll tell her you're here." She hastily left Oliver's presence. Those strange desert-sand eyes might affect some women with pleasant shivers, but not Chantal.

The unexpected arrival of Erika Talbott, Boy Farrell's executive vice president, had required additional adjustments in the household. She was placed in the downstairs guest room next to the master suite. Since these quarters were usually reserved for Jason's morning and evening exercise program, the dumbbells, weights, slant board and exercycle were hastily moved into Millicent's dressing room.

After these arrangements had been made, it was time to think about baths and showers. There were two forty-gallon heaters in the house, but only one was working. That sufficient hot water was provided for everyone greatly relieved the hostess.

Millicent behaved with aplomb. She changed the seating at the dining table, rearranged flower vases to cover bare spots in the tablecloth's fine linen, found additional sterling silver, told Jason to climb out of his running shorts and into presentable clothes. In the den, she swept the unpaid bills out of sight and locked up the household ledger in the rolltop desk. Then she went in search of Ardis.

Having found the book on Oriental art belonging to Uncle Edward, Ardis came up from the basement with a glazed look on her face. She marched through the kitchen and met her mother in the downstairs hallway.

"Be careful when you use the hot shower tap upstairs," Millicent cautioned. "The water pressure in this antique of a house isn't reliable." In a lowered voice, she asked, "Do you know Erika Talbott well?"

"Why? Is she here?" Ardis assumed an expression of innocence. "I suppose Erika drove out because she and Boy need to confer about something. I've known her slightly during the time Boy and I have been together."

"I wish you wouldn't put it that way."

"All right, Milla. How about, 'during the time Boy and I have been engaged'?"

"That's better, dear. And—oh, Ardis, don't ask for a second helping of anything tonight. We have to make sure there's enough." Millicent studied her daughter's thin frame. "You need second helpings, Ardis. But not this time."

Chantal stayed in the kitchen helping Beatriz as long as she could without making her defection from everyone else too obvious. She peeled potatoes, cut up salad greens, basted the roast, burned her fingers, held ice to them, said it was nothing, put chestnuts and mushrooms through the grinder. Beatriz complained that Chantal moved too fast. Chantal apologized, but inwardly she protested that she couldn't possibly move fast enough to elude the phantom of Simon Bryce's being "out of the country." And not a word to Chantal. But then, why should there be word of either his presence or his absence? There was no commitment, was there?

Chantal went into the drawing room as early

evening spilled its blue light through the big windows. The room had a vast curving bay-window seat at the front end. Here one could look out across a garden overgrown with camellia bushes, wild irises, South African daisies, and the lilacs which grew well at this two-thousand-foot elevation. The walls of the room were papered in gold leaf, once handsome, now fraying and showing its age. So many family pictures covered the walls that the shabbiness really didn't matter. The ceiling was extremely high. The miniature cathedral effect kept voice tones to a pleasant level. Conversations seemed to be hushed. The room was ancient and restful.

Ardis helped Chantal serve the before-dinner drinks, a choice of fruit juice or chilled white wine. Millicent hovered while Larch entertained, describing what he saw as faintly colored auras over each person's head. It was in this manner, he explained, that the personality and the karma could be ascertained. He was intense and dramatic in his monologue. His audience listened, some in polite disbelief, others with absorbed interest.

Chantal drank her pomegranate juice. Oliver Larch's bizarre perceptions were causing her to look forward more kindly to Ric's visit later that evening. At any rate, Ric's arrival would get her out of the house.

Jason and Millicent presided at opposite ends of the dining table. Jason was wearing white cotton-duck trousers, vintage of an era at least twenty years earlier. They fitted his trim body as well as they had in his ardent thirties. His tight-knit polo shirt emphasized the expanse of his chest; his healthy, sun-darkened skin had a youthful look. There was little doubt that the sparkle in his eyes was due to the concentrated attention he was receiving from the woman to his right.

Erika Talbott was thiry-five years old and looked it, beautifully. She had a strong profile, a leonine mass of tawny-colored hair and a perfect figure immaculately displayed in her Evan-Picone suit with its classic black and white blazer and gracefully cut matching skirt. It was a warm midsummer evening, but Erika was cool . . . in every way.

With Jason she discussed organic gardening, and the merits of the marathon runner's diet as opposed to the invigoration of the jogger's diet or the maintenance needs of the short sprinter. Frequently and tactfully, Erika glanced down the table in Millicent's direction. She admired the older woman's ruby-red caftan, embroidered with an intricate pictorial design. Erika recognized the motif as Indian and identified it as deriving from the Chamba region. In remarking on the magnificent copper samovar standing on the sideboard, she asked if it still contained the central tube for live charcoal used to boil tea water in old Russia. To Oliver Larch, seated at Millicent's right, Erika confided she had published a small volume of poetry while taking her M.B.A. at Wharton.

Erika even managed to reassure an easily suspicious Ardis. Having studied all the pertinent courses at the Marine Boating School, Ardis was unusually adept at navigation. Erika's only experience had been with small pocket cruisers in Key West, and she'd piled up two of them. Ardis, with her tendency toward self-deprecation, bloomed under Erika's flattering attention.

Boy Farrell, who had hired Erika from a rival ten years earlier, knew her strengths. He sat back now to enjoy the display she was putting on. Was she contriving good fellowship or too much humble erudition? He wondered, hoping she wasn't hitting the mark too hard. He might have to go over Erika's lines with her later.

Watching her father and the others preen under Erika's artful strokings, Chantal had pondered when it would be her turn. Before this could happen, she had picked up dinner plates and disappeared through the swinging door into the butler's pantry. She stayed in the kitchen with Beatriz until it was time to return with the dessert dishes.

When Chantal once again seated herself at table, Erika's eloquent brown stare immediately found her. She leaned forward and treated Chantal to the box office figures gleaned from the four small cinemas established in a Farrell shopping center in Orange County. Yet Chantal was astounded to hear that one of the films that had done particularly well last year was a Simon Bryce production. Chantal looked across the table at Boy. She had a strong suspicion that he'd handed his vice president a blueprint of the personal lives of the entire Jerrold family.

When the others drifted out to the east porch, where Millicent would serve coffee, Ardis lingered behind with Chantal. "What do you think of Erika? Pretty terrific, isn't she?"

"It's my belief she's hot-dogging," was Chantal's crisp response as she cleared the table.

"If you mean showing off, Erika is too smart for that," Ardis protested.

"Well, I'm not about to be charmed by Erika Talbott. It seems to me as if you and Boy are bringing up the front-line troops."

"I don't know what you mean by that."

"Think about it. You'll figure it out. I have.

Erika's looking for a victim. I think she's found one.
By the way, is she a jogger?"

"She runs the mile in under six minutes. Why?"

Chantal was startled. "If that's true, it's practically world-class. Here, help me with the table-
cloth." There was silence while the two of them
folded the big square of linen.

"You coming out to the porch?" Ardis asked when
they'd finished.

"I'll look in for a minute. I'm meeting Ric later."

When Chantal joined the others, it was comforting to hear their laughter. Larch was doing sleight-
of-hand tricks with a silk scarf. Ardis appeared
relaxed and amused, her chin snuggled over one of
Boy's hands as it rested lightly on her shoulder.
Chantal was glad to see Boy's previously unsus-
pected attentiveness, which seemed to indicate a
genuine affection for her sister. She sat down by
Millicent.

Her mother patted Chantal's knee. "Thank you,
dear, for helping Beatriz. Oh!" she squealed. "Oliver! That's marvelous. Where did the gold piece
come from? Ardie, throw me that scarf, will you?
It's a regular Fort Knox."

Oliver, the magician, grinned.

Chantal looked around for Jason and Erika. They
were seated on the cushioned bamboo couch in one
corner of the porch. Erika was talking earnestly. Her
hands fluttered in eloquence, as if to make a point.
Suddenly one finger dove unerringly toward Jason's
chest. It wavered a bit in midair, then landed with an
intimately suggestive pat that lingered a fraction too
long. Chantal glanced away from them, but not
before she had observed her father move back
slightly. The expression on his face was bemused and
a bit puzzled. Chantal understood why. Jason was

not a worldly man. He didn't quite comprehend what devilment was going on between Erika Talbott and himself.

It was almost ten o'clock when Ric drove up in his jeep. He found Chantal sitting on the rock wall at the end of the drive.

For a long moment there was silence between the man in the vehicle and the woman watching him. Chantal motioned to him. "Come sit here with me. We can look at the lights in the valley. Or rather, we can look if we ignore all those new houses."

Ric remained in his seat, peering at Chantal through the dark night. "You sound bitter."

"I am."

"You can't stop progress. Like they used to say, if it's inevitable, relax and enjoy it."

"That's a dated, sexist remark! You used to be nice."

Ric jumped out of the jeep. "I'm the same, Chantal. You're the one who's different now. We could have made it together back then."

"We can't now? With this different me? I thought you proposed this afternoon. Or was it a joke?"

Ric pressed his hands on the rock wall and pulled his lithe body up beside Chantal. "You've been thinking about what I said? Seriously?"

"I'll probably never marry."

"Big career woman, I get you. Listen to me, Chantal. I think I know what's bothering you. I don't really need your father's place. I have other bullets in my belt. If I promise to stay away from Jason and not press him into making a deal with me, will you consider marrying me?"

Chantal stared at Ric, then burst out laughing.

Ric was shocked at her reaction. "Why the hell are

you laughing?" he demanded. "Are you laughing at *me?*" Abruptly furious, he eased down from the rock wall and faced her menacingly.

Chantal slid from her perch to stand alongside him. She tried not to laugh as she clung to his blue-shirted arm, then his hand. "Ric, it's what you just said."

"I know what I said. Answer me! Is it me you're laughing at?" He towered above her.

"I'm not laughing at you, Ric—never at you! Boy Farrell has promised my sister he'll marry her if she gets Father to deal with him. You say just the opposite. You'll drop the attempt to make hash subdivisions out of EdgeMont if . . . if I'll marry you!"

"Well, then, I'm a hero! I'm the good guy!"

"You certainly are . . ." Chantal's laughter trailed off. "But you and I couldn't spend our lives together. We're different people now than we were."

"If you were the same as me, I wouldn't want to marry you, would I, dummy?" Ric pulled Chantal close to him. He buried his face in her hair, dark and scented in the night. His big hands folded over her bottom, scooping her in close to him. His voice husky, he proclaimed, "The way you smell, the way you feel, the way you talk . . . *you* . . . Chantal! You're sure as hell not like me."

Ric was a big man. Her head tucked against his chest, Chantal felt small and vulnerable. And powerless. She couldn't let this happen. She couldn't deceive Ric. He was too kind, too . . . straight and square with her. She pushed against his muscular chest, but it was difficult to dislodge herself from his arms. It was impossible. She felt the throb of his male strength surge against her body. He was lifting her up . . . lifting her . . .

Hoarsely Ric muttered, "Come with me in the jeep, Chantal. We'll go down to the inn, to my room. I never tried to touch you before. You were too young. Give me credit for some restraint in those days."

"Why is it different now?" To make him hear her words, Chantal managed to press her body away from his and looked up at him. The stars whirled above his broad shoulders as his face came down to hers. Almost brutally, he sought her lips. "Wait, Ric!" She tried to turn her face aside. "Listen to me. I must know . . . why now?"

He almost shouted, "Because I can tell about you—this is *why now!* You walk like you've had it. It's the look in your eyes, everything about you. You smell of sex, you're perfumed with it, Chantal. But I don't mind if someone's been there before me. I don't mind at all."

Ric's breath against Chantal's face and throat was a hot murmur of desire. Before she could stop him, his hand had plunged inside the cleavage of her dress. Fingers covered her breast and squeezed hard. His thumb rubbed slowly over and around her nipple, making it stand upright. He bent closer, licking into her lips, forcefully separating her clenched teeth, strangling her breath with the intensity of his tongue's hot thrust.

Attempting to hold together her ripped bodice, Chantal tried to pull back. Ric clasped her to him, his lips hungrily finding one bared breast. Using all her strength, Chantal was able to push herself free.

"Damn you!" Abruptly Ric let her go. Chantal staggered back against the rock wall. "I don't want to take you by force," he said, breathing hard. "I know I don't have to force you." His hand snaked insinuatingly between her thighs. "You're ready to give it. There's dew on the rose."

"And damn you, Ric Milland! You've got a mean mouth on you. I thought . . . I thought you were—" Sobs stopped her words. *She would not cry.* She bit back the tears and struck with fury at his seeking hand.

Sure of himself, Ric prodded, "You thought I was what? You thought I was different from other men? I'm no different. I've got all the same body parts, all in excellent working order. I've got the same letch any other man has. Except *I* will marry you. Think about it, Chantal. Ric Milland is ready to marry you. Anybody else said that to you lately?"

Chantal kept moving backward, stumbling away from the rock wall. She was out of Ric's reach, but he stood there heavily, making no effort now to stop her retreat.

"That's one of the propositions I promised you. Think about it. I won't talk about the other one now. You going to come down to the inn with me? Tonight?"

"No. Not ever." She was dry-eyed and sick at heart.

"Sleep well. Or stay awake all night. Whichever, Chantal. I hope you stay awake. I hope you know what your body needs, and remember, I'm the one who can give it to you. I don't have to force you. You'll come along. I know the signs."

"Not ever."

She fled up the palm drive. The jeep was still parked next to the wall when she ran around to the kitchen and let herself in through the screen door. The house was dark and silent. She glanced at the clock before turning off the light and slipping along the central hallway. It was nearly midnight.

From the casement windows in the sleeping porch, Chantal looked down into the shadows. She could still see the dark shape of Ric's vehicle waiting. What terrible things happened to people. All the sweetness there had ever been between Ric and her was gone. She felt shamed that she'd had to listen to his ugly words. The good-natured and kind young man who had been Ric Milland had vanished, perhaps Ric had never been the man she'd thought he was. She was changed too. Ric had sensed differences in her.

Chantal undressed in the dark because she guessed that Ric knew which room she was in and was watching. She crept into bed and pulled the sheet high. Tense and stricken, she lay in the brass bed staring at the ceiling. Endless minutes later, the lights of the jeep flashed on. The arc of those lights crossed her ceiling and swept along the casement windows as Ric backed up the jeep and sped down Archibald toward Cucamonga and the inn.

It was impossible to sleep. Chantal rolled over, got out of bed, wrapped her robe around her, went through the hall and started down the stairs. She walked carefully in the dark, remembering where each rise of the step would meet her footfall as she descended. Halfway down she became aware of a dim light in the hall below. Someone else was wakeful.

The last person she expected to see in the kitchen was Jason. Still fully clothed, he was standing over the stove, heating a pan of milk. He gave a start of surprise at her appearance. This show of nerves was unlike her father. The physical fitness he practiced seemed to armor him against the alarms that upset the average individual.

"I didn't mean to startle you, Dad," Chantal apologized. "I couldn't sleep."

"That makes two of us," Jason replied predictably, and turned back to the stove. "If you'll get the Ovaltine out of the cupboard, we'll have ourselves an orgy."

They sat down at the kitchen table with their steaming cups. Chantal eyed Jason as she sipped. "Wow . . . hot." She put down the cup. "I've never known you not to be able to sleep. Is something worrying you?"

"Of course not," Jason answered gamely. "How about you?"

To her own surprise, as much as to her father's, Chantal blurted, "I'm unhappy about the way I'm conducting my life. I could do better."

"Now *that's* interesting. What makes you think you're the one to run your own life? How old are you—twenty three? It seems to me you've lived long enough to have observed that we're all tossed about pretty much willy-nilly, as the phrase goes. Maybe you can captain your own soul by behaving well whatever happens, but that's about it."

"You're saying that I have no control over what happens to me? If it's good, I'm lucky. If it's not good, I have to behave well. Is that it?"

Jason sat back in his chair, his eyes narrowed at his daughter. "We're talking about something specific, I believe, not just life in general."

"That's right, Dad." Chantal hesitated. How much, how little, should she say at midnight? In the morning would she regret a confidence given? She decided to take a chance. "It's a man. . . ."

Her father sighed and nodded. "With a young woman like you, it always is."

"It could be my career that I'm concerned about," Chantal flared.

"Is it?"

"No."

"Go on."

"He's older . . . thirty-seven, in fact. He's intelligent and successful and strong. I care for him . . . very, very much. But he told me—" Chantal paused, then continued. "He was up front with me. He told me he didn't want a serious involvement. No matter what our relationship, he couldn't be committed to me in a serious way. Nor did he want me to . . . to—"

Jason interrupted, a faint smile touching his lips. "He didn't want you to regard him as your prize."

"How do you mean?"

"You're a smart, hard-working, good girl. You're nice-looking. The way you've been brought up, you expect to get your womanly reward. Even today that reward is eventually marriage."

Again Chantal was angered. "I didn't think about marriage. It's simply that I want him to love me."

"And protect you and ease your heart and give you tenderness and sensitive feeling and just be there—always. What else is that but marriage?"

Chantal looked away from Jason. She drew her robe close about her. Her voice ragged, she finally answered, "Why can't he love me? What's wrong with me? I don't want to build my whole life around Simon. I just want a loving relationship with him."

"It isn't you, Chantal, it's the times. You women are living your life free-style, my dear. Think of Ardis, loving Boyd Farrell for five years, yet he feels no obligation to her. Her persistence runs counter to his desire to be free."

"Boy has already had two marriages."

"Gun-shy, as they say. But then we're not talking about Ardis, are we? It's you and this man. Does he have a bad reputation in his relationships with women?"

"Not at all. He seems to have put that part of his life on hold."

Jason stood up and took their empty cups to the sink. His back to Chantal, he advised, "If he says he can't get involved, you'd better believe him."

Chantal's voice rose. "You mean I have to play his game, see him when he wants, be cool and settle for *that?*" She jumped to her feet. "I'm embarrassed to be talking to you this way."

Jason turned. "Why? Fathers are men. They can be compassionate. Though I must admit my feeling as a father makes me want to go out and horsewhip your jerk lover!"

"Dad!"

"Are you asking me to be fair? I love you, child. I want you to have the best in life—a good, stable relationship like your mother and I have. I've racked up as a provider, I'll admit. But your mother can depend on me as a man. I'm a husband who loves her. I want that for you, Chantal. I'm afraid you're going to have to toughen up, be less vulnerable. For you, there's plenty of time. You'll meet the right man."

"I *have* met him."

"He's the right man? You really think so? In that case, are you the wrong woman for him?"

"Absolutely not. I don't believe that. Unless there's something wrong with me I don't know about."

"There's nothing wrong with you, Chantal. But can you give it time? Can you be patient and kind with him? Can you wait? If he's someone you work with, can you continue to do your best in your career and impress him with your quality? I only say this if you're convinced he's the one for you. I respect your judgment."

"Oh, Dad." She went to him and put her hands on his shoulders. "Did I learn anything tonight? Did we get anyplace in our discussion?"

"We didn't, Chantal. There were no wise words spoken. It's not the analyzing that helps, it's the doing. What we say is academic; what we do is what counts. You're impetuous. You want it all now. Isn't that right?"

Chantal nodded. "You're right. I want it all . . . now." She looked at him, linked her arm around his. "Why couldn't you sleep tonight? A problem?"

Jason patted Chantal's shoulder with his free hand. "I'll solve it." He kissed his daughter. "I was there when you were growing up. Always remember that. I was there when you needed me. I'm still here. And I love you."

Back in her own room, Chantal slept fitfully. Finally she awoke fully. By the light outside, she knew it was dawn.

Chantal could just barely hear the telephone ringing, muffled as it was by the closed door of Oliver Larch's bedroom. Would someone downstairs answer? She leaped out of bed and ran to the head of the stairs, only then aware that the sound of the phone had stopped. She listened for the voice of one of her parents in the hall below. There was silence.

Larch's voice behind her made Chantal start. She swung around to see his sleep-ridden face.

"It's for you."

"Do you mind if I take it in your room?"

Oliver stepped back. Wearing nothing except her thin nightgown, Chantal ran past him into the guest room. She picked up the instrument. "Yes? Who? Larette?" She listened, twisting the telephone cord around her fingers. "No, no . . . it's all right." She glanced toward the doorway, where Oliver Larch stood. Her gray eyes asked his forgiveness for the intrusion. Understanding her, he frilled his hands in the air. Then, with surprising thoughtfulness, he threw his robe around her shoulders. Seeing that she wasn't about to sit on the bed he'd occupied, he pushed up a chair for her and tiptoed out of the room.

Chantal continued to listen to Larette Howell. "When did it happen? How is he now? Why would he do such a thing?" All her questions were rapidly answered from the other end. Finally Chantal said, "Of course I'll come. I'll phone you as soon as I reach town. I can come by and pick up everything that's necessary at your office. You have the script— as much as he's done of it?" She waited, then asked impatiently, "The commercial flights are all full? A charter, okay. If there's no other way. I'll leave right now. No, no, it's all right, Larette. I understand. Don't worry."

Oliver Larch was waiting in the hallway. He took Chantal's hand, pressed it close in his. "Whatever's happened, you mustn't worry. It's not bad news. You're going on a journey, my dear, and it will turn out well for you. Last night before dinner I saw the aura above your head. There was no danger, no disaster . . . only joy. It was a misty green halo—a very good omen."

Chantal's smile was tremulous. She gave Oliver back his robe. "Thank you for saying that. I'm terribly sorry you were disturbed. You're right about the journey. I'm going to Mexico. This afternoon."

Behind Oliver's shoulder, Chantal could see Ardis's door open a crack. Ardis was peering out, her face alight with curiosity. Boy's freckled countenance hovered in the background. Chantal pretended not to notice.

She said to Oliver, "You'd better go back to bed. I hope you can sleep. After I'm dressed and packed, I'm going to make coffee on my way out. I'll have some and I'll leave the pot on the kitchen stove for you if you can't sleep. How'll that be?"

Oliver again took Chantal's hand. Gently she released it and patted him on the shoulder. She knew he was trying very hard not to look through her nightgown as she gathered it in front of her, doubling the cotton to make her body less visible.

She turned and ran down the hall to the sleeping porch. Larch was still watching her from his doorway. Chantal didn't care. He'd promised her a good omen.

Chapter Eleven

Larette was waiting for Chantal in the bungalow. Preceding the call made to EdgeMont at five o'clock in the morning, Larette had been up for twenty-four hours straight. Yet she was pearl-perfect as usual, her ash-blond hair smoothed back in a French twist, her beige linen dress looking as though it had just come off the designer's rack. The heightened color in her usually pale cheeks was the only evidence of strain.

Larette indicated the bulging briefcase that sat on top of her otherwise neat desk. "This holds everything you'll need in the way of office supplies. And there's as much of the script in here as Cesar Williams completed before he . . ." Larette paused.

"Exactly what did happen? You sketched in some details this morning on the phone, but not the whole story." Chantal's gray eyes were steady in demanding the truth.

Larette stood up and began moving uneasily about

the room. "Who ever knows the whole story behind anything? We've got to keep this quiet for Cesar's sake. If we hired another writer from the list of possibilities Simon left behind in case of a disastrous script, it would be in the trade papers tomorrow. Naturally Cesar's agent is cooperating with us. It's to his advantage to do so." Larette sat down behind her desk. "Dean and I have to stay here and run the shop. It'll be up to Moira to handle the public relations aspect of this thing."

Why was Larette so slow in getting down to the essentials? Chantal wondered.

Larette stared consideringly at Chantal. "You're familiar with the book. You did an excellent job on the treatment. By the way, tell me something." Larette leaned forward, her gaze boring in, her tone remorseless. "After you were asked to block out scenes the way the production department would handle it, did you know what you were doing when you came up with a full screen treatment instead? Was that intentional?"

"Yes."

"Why?"

"I was angry."

"Can you tell me why? Anger's a strange reason."

"No, I can't tell you."

"A fair enough answer, or nonanswer, under the circumstances. It's none of my business, is it?" Larette's smile was cynical. She had asked because she was curious about Chantal's motives. Was Chantal an ambitious schemer? Or was it something else, something personal concerning Simon? Larette doubted the latter. She'd know about it if there were anything between Simon Bryce and this young woman. Larette shrugged. If there was a puzzle here somewhere, she'd solve it soon enough.

In her turn, Chantal was uncertain of the meaning of Larette's questioning smile. It truly had not occurred to her that Larette might regard her as a threat or a rival. Yet the two women were dueling. And both knew it.

Chantal recognized that Larette was probing, but she was determined that no one in Simon's employ would ever learn what had taken place between herself and Simon.

Though Larette had said otherwise, she was still waiting. When Chantal said nothing more, Larette continued soberly. "Simon will work with you in Puerto Vallarta part of the time. There won't be any question about what the two of you are doing, since you're not known in the industry as a screenwriter. At least, you aren't as of this moment." Larette added, not quite happily, "When this is over, you probably will be a bona fide member of the Writers Guild." She hesitated, then plunged on coolly. "Remember, all we want to do is protect Williams's reputation. If he pulls out of his emotional trouble quickly and can come back to us and finish the script, what you do may not be used at all. The same holds true if Cesar can't continue and we hire another screenwriter. Unless, of course, your work is very good. We'll see."

Larette was tormented. In a personal way, she wanted Chantal to fail. But as the executive in charge of creative development for Simon Bryce Productions, she had to hope for Chantal's success.

Chantal's response was crisp. "I asked you a moment ago exactly what did happen to Cesar Williams. I'm entitled to an answer."

Reminded, Larette frowned. "You're entitled because you're willing to fly down to Mexico and bail us out on this—help us out, I should say." Larette

bit her lip. She should choose her words more
carefully. She didn't want to give Chantal the idea
that they depended on her to any great extent.

Larette picked up a cigarette from the pack on her
desk, immediately putting it down again. It was her
only visible sign of tension. "All right, here goes.
God, I loathe messes like this! Cesar is a true
professional with a fine reputation in the industry as
a writer. His work is strong. He turns his pages in on
time. And he doesn't get drunk so as to cause
anyone to go looking for him. His only deviation is
that he's been married to the same woman for
twenty years and happens to be very much in love
with her. Simply said: two days ago she went off with
a younger man."

"And then?"

"I told you this morning over the phone that Cesar
caught up with her and was fairly violent. What he
actually did was to kick the new lover boy in a
sensitive area and threaten Grace with a gun. He
scared the bejesus out of them both. He did pull the
trigger, but fortunately, and probably intentionally,
it went off in the air. He was pretty much out of his
head by then. That's what I meant when I said on the
phone he went round the bend."

"That part I understand."

Larette sighed. "Cesar Williams is fifty years old,
a tough, macho-type man—the old school. But he
wasn't tough enough to take the shock of Grace
Williams falling for their landscape designer. The
confrontation with his wife and her young stud just
about did in his heart, and it did in his manhood.
Right now he's in Cedars-Sinai undergoing physical
and mental therapy, and he's locked up tight. Grace
had enough sense to hide the gun when he started
banging his head on the floor. That's all I want to

say." While she spoke, Larette had pulled the cigarette apart, shredding the tobacco; she dropped it distastefully in the wastebasket.

"Are they discreet at Cedars? What happened to Williams won't leak out? And if it did, it wouldn't hurt the picture or Simon?"

"Absolutely discreet. That hospital has had much bigger names than Cesar Williams incommunicado in its little psychiatric block. But we don't know how long the media, or the police for that matter, can be kept out of things. I'm sure Grace and the boyfriend won't press charges, so we don't have too much to worry about along those lines. Of course it won't hurt the picture. It has nothing to do with it. We just want Cesar back, whole and happy and operating as a screenwriter at his usual fine level—if it's at all possible. Simon's very honorable like that. I mean, he gives second chances. But in the meantime the work on the script *must* go on. We've signed contracts with the director and others. We've made commitments with several important agents for their clients. We have a schedule to meet."

Chantal nodded wisely. She was beginning to understand more than Larette had told her in words. "So this is where I come in?"

Larette looked at her sharply. "Simon has been in Puerto Vallarta for over a week, conferring with his Mexican associates, and he can't return until his business down there is finished. That's why you have to go there and work."

Again Chantal nodded. "I understand."

"I'm glad somebody does." This time Larette took out a cigarette and lit it, quickly snubbing it out. "I'm giving up these damn things," she said unnecessarily, and went on grimly. "Part of *The Assaulters* will be shot on location in Mexico. Their best cinematographer is being hired for those scenes. His name's Aefollo, who, when he isn't working, lives in some primitive village farther down the coast from Vallarta. It's called Yelapa. Simon has to go there to see him. You'll stay at the Posada Vallarta, where there's more privacy than in any of the big new hotels, and work on the script—under Simon's guidance, of course." Larette paused. As a token she concluded, "Believe me, your help is appreciated."

"What flight do I take?"

"I've already told you, it'll have to be a charter. The commercial flights all leave too early. It's nearly ten o'clock now. You'd never make it to the airport, even if there were a seat for you. LAX is a real hassle this time of year." Larette glanced at her watch. "You couldn't make it by noon, and the only later flight is with an airline that flies by spit. We wouldn't risk you on it. Don't worry, you'll be picked up at your apartment by limo at three this afternoon. The chartered Learjet leaves from Van Nuys Airport at four. It's a six-passenger plane, the smallest they have. I understand that two other people, oilmen from Houston, will also be on it, so they'll share the cost. We don't believe in throwing money around, but this time it's the only way to get you down there fast enough. And fast is of the essence." Larette smiled almost pleasantly. "Wait a minute." She reached into the top drawer of her desk and brought out a stack of new bills. "There's a thousand dollars here. Petty cash. Everything else will be taken care of. Your salary will be deposited in the checking account at your bank. Do you have an agent in mind?"

As Chantal placed the money in her handbag and

prepared to heft the fat briefcase, she shook her head at this last question.

"I suppose you'll be needing one soon."

Chantal's gaze clashed once more with Larette's—silver-gray eyes meeting those of ice-blue—then she stood and walked out of the office and down the hall.

Chantal had two hours to repack before the hired limousine would arrive to take her to the airport. Before leaving EdgeMont she'd explained the situation to Ardis, but since being at the Villa she'd spent a good part of the time trying to reach her brother. As usual, Jay's answering service was maddeningly discreet concerning his whereabouts. Finally she called Kathleen Dalton Enterprises. It was certainly necessary for her to let Jay know where she was going. After several rings, Kiki's office answered. The secretary's information concerning Kiki was delivered in a cheerful, gossipy tone; the implication of what she said dropped Chantal into the nearest chair in astonishment.

"Will you please repeat that?"

"Why, yes, I said Miss Dalton is in Mexico on business. She's in Jalisco, a state on the west coast."

"Do you have a forwarding address?"

"Who is this?" The secretary was suddenly wary.

Chantal sighed. "Jay Jerrold's sister."

"Oh, sure. Okay, it's Puerto Vallarta. Here's the post office box number. No phone. Casa Azul is the name of the house she's rented. You planning to go down there to see Jay?"

"I might. We talked about it. I wasn't sure when he was leaving." Chantal's tone was guarded.

"Last week. I understand it's a great place. Jay's shooting down there."

"He is?" She knew it was stupid of her, but what could Jay be shooting? He wasn't a hunter.

Suspicion crept into the young woman's cheery voice. "You knew that, didn't you?"

"Of course I did," Chantal reassured her. "That's why I was asked to come down."

"Lucky you! Oh, I have another call. 'Bye."

Chantal hung up the phone too, but reluctantly. She was disturbed by the ease with which she'd lied. She wanted to dial Kiki's number again and ask the secretary not to mention the phone call if Kiki should get in touch with her office. But that would sound strange. Better to leave well enough alone.

It was a three-hour flight to Puerto Vallarta. From a height of thirty-five thousand feet, the coastal mountains of Mexico appeared to Chantal as great yellow lions sprawled by the sea. Up front she could observe the profiles of the two pilots. The twin-engine plane had no cabin attendant. The Texas oilmen sat in seats ahead of Chantal, concentrating on the papers in the open attaché cases they held on their knees.

Enmeshed in the landscape of white clouds and blue sea below, Chantal savored the feeling of solitude that surrounded her in the half-filled cabin. She was tired and she dozed, but awakened suddenly on the edge of a dream about Simon. It was hard to believe she would see him in a matter of hours. Perhaps not this evening when they landed, but certainly tomorrow. Simon would not meet her at the airport, of that she was certain. She'd claim her luggage, go through customs and show the tourist card that the studio's location department had quickly arranged for her. She would probably be met by some stranger sent by Simon.

She should be thinking about the script. During the first hour of the flight she had removed and read the pages in the folder left by Cesar Williams before aberration had struck. What he had done so far was very good. She could only hope to continue with the advancement of the story line until Cesar was out of the hospital. She could never match his dialogue. But she had sufficient dramatic knowledge so that she could transcribe much of the original author's intent into the action of the screenplay as it progressed. At any rate, she would have Simon's sure touch and his fine story mind to guide her. All that could be expected of Chantal was a bare-bones attempt to continue with the script until the painful confusion of the Cesar Williams problem could be resolved somehow.

Simon had had enough faith in her to send for her. Considering his reputation, her presence in Mexico could be for no other reason. He would never allow the personal to intrude into the important concerns of his work.

In the late twilight of the plane's arrival at Puerto Vallarta, Chantal stepped out onto the cement apron adjacent to the terminal building. She had been warned, but she could hardly believe the humid blast of coastal heat that assailed her. It was as though a great wave of wet air had engulfed her, smothering her face with a hot compress, forcing its way into her lungs, searing and strangling her breath. Her shirt and pants were sticky against her skin. Her hair felt dank and slick against her clammy neck. The briefcase she carried was heavy, causing her to walk in a drunken sideways lope as she headed for the airport building.

One of the Texans caught up with her. "Here, let

me," he said, and took the swollen briefcase from her. "Walk slowly and draw in shallow breaths until you feel more accustomed to this atmosphere," he ordered. "We're from Houston. We know about this kind of weather."

Soon they were inside the building, going through customs, showing their tourist cards to be stamped. Things weren't much better inside. Water from the overhead air conditioning coils dripped down on them in steady splashes.

"Why don't you ride into town with us? I'll get a taxi. By the way, my name's Mayer—Burt. This is Ralph Hindley." He indicated his traveling companion. Chantal nodded, still speechless. The Texan grinned. "Go ahead, you can breathe now. Try it. It gets easier all the time. Where are you staying?" he asked.

Chantal took a deep breath. "The Posada Vallarta. Do you know where it is? Oh. My name's Chantal Jerrold."

"Greetings, Chantal. The Posada?" The Texan looked surprised. "It's this side of town—easy enough to drop you off there. It's a great place, sort of a pioneer around here. Very popular with people who've been coming down since the early sixties. Also popular with the elite from Mexico City. But I'd expect a young person like yourself to be staying at one of the newer hotels they've built here recently. You know, with swim-up bars and all that sort of thing."

"I came down to do some work," Chantal mumbled, wiping her forehead. She thought she might scissor off those wisps of bangs as soon as she got to her hotel room.

"Work. I guess that's about all that any of us

would come here to do in July. It's not exactly the 'in' season. Right, Ralph?'' The friendly Texan winked at his companion, who was speaking rapid Spanish to a Mexican whom Chantal assumed to be a taxi driver. The local was a small, wiry man who packed all the Texans' bags under both arms and started outside. Chantal wondered if she could again brave the heat out there, although it was almost as sultry inside the terminal. It occurred to her that a car might have been sent for her, or at least that one had stood by in the earlier evening, since Larette must have long-distanced Simon that Chantal could be expected today.

"How is the telephone service here?" she inquired of Burt Mayer.

He laughed uproariously and made a waggling gesture with one hand. "You take your chances. If you're lucky, you get through. Otherwise . . ." He shrugged. "It could be days."

"I'd better come with you, then."

At that moment she heard her name spoken and turned quickly.

"Señorita Jerrold?"

A slight, very handsome young man in a white shirt and black trousers came forward tentatively. "If you are Señorita Jerrold, I have been waiting for you. There is a car outside. Are these your bags?" As he saw Chantal hesitate, he bowed. "I am from the *casa* of Señor Bryce. I am to take you to the Posada. My name is Guillermo."

"I see we're to lose your company, Chantal," the Texan said. "We'll be at the Camino Real for the next couple of days before we go on. When we come back from our trek, may we check with you to see if everything's okay?"

Chantal understood that, being oilmen, they were not saying where their exact destination would be in Jalisco. However, with the mountains and the jungle meeting the sea here, they could not be going far inland. There was no reason to pursue the brief acquaintance with them, but they had been kind, especially Burt Mayer, so she said, "If you have the time, it would be good of you to call. I'd like that." She paused and added gingerly, *"Gracias, amigos."*

Burt waved. *"De nada. Hasta Luego."*

The Texans departed into what was now black night, and Chantal followed Guillermo, who was carrying her luggage, to a sedan parked at the curb. Guillermo smiled shyly at Chantal as he assisted her into the front seat of the sedan. "You speak Spanish?"

"You just heard the extent of it," she admitted ruefully.

The Posada Vallarta lay north of the village on Banderas Bay. When first constructed, it had been a two-storied, U-shaped building. The original inn was still the center of action, but many guest cottages, containing two and sometimes three separate suites, now dotted the palm grove to the south of the main hotel. Separated from the others by thick hibiscus bushes and oleanders, each small villa had its own miniature swimming pool. It was to one of these structures that Chantal was escorted. Guillermo and the hotel porter left her there.

Perhaps she was growing accustomed to the humid atmosphere, because to Chantal the evening seemed milder. But then, she was now within hearing distance of the sea. She looked around her room. It was distinctly soothing to her eyes, or else she was ready for serenity. The walls were painted a peachy terra-cotta hue. The floor was glazed concrete tile covered with small, beautifully woven oval rugs. The wooden furniture was handcrafted, and upholstered with fabrics in quiet earth tones. A handsome, ash-colored bedspread on the large bed was turned down for the night. The white sheets and thick pillows looked inviting, but before retiring, she had to unpack. Her clothing would be hopelessly wrinkled after its stay in the plane's hot baggage compartment. And there was the briefcase with its important contents to attend to. But a shower first!

As Chantal walked toward the dressing room, she passed a square wooden table. She halted in surprise, and then, amused, she removed the cover of an electric typewriter and ran her fingers over the keys.

In the bathroom she was once more surprised. A large white bowl next to the washbasin held a mass of scarlet hibiscus blossoms floating on the surface of the water. No fragrance was discernible, but their beauty was stark and savage. Familiar with the short span of the hibiscus after it has been removed from its stalky branches, she knew that in the morning the frilled petals would be closed forever, yet tonight it was a beautiful Mexican welcome. And another welcome was the bottled drinking water waiting for her.

Everything is here, she thought, but I am starving! She glanced around. There was no telephone. She didn't even know if there was room service at this hour. The plane had left Van Nuys Airport at four that afternoon; it was now nearly nine o'clock, Puerto Vallarta time. She had not had anything to eat since early this morning.

When the knock came at the door, she said aloud, wryly, "The genie!" And in a sense it was. An English-speaking Mexican woman in a white blouse and full white skirt greeted her. The woman handed Chantal a menu, explaining that the dining room was closing but whatever the señorita would like to order would be brought to her on a tray. It was understood that she was Señor Simon Bryce's guest, and all would be done to make her stay at the Posada a comfortable one.

It was nearly midnight. Chantal wandered onto the small patio outside her cottage. Thick oleander and hibiscus bushes provided a natural screen. The tiny pool looked inviting, though the night was not as hot as it had been earlier. Chantal decided to take a dip before going to bed. She knew no one could observe her. While the villas on the other side of the bushes were probably occupied by tourists here to take advantage of the lower summer rates, the two companion suites in her own villa were not.

The dark water glimmered faintly under the light of the last quarter of the moon which filtered through the tall palm trees. Chantal let her robe and nightgown fall onto the glazed brick patio flooring and stepped quickly into the pool.

The water was as warm as the air and tenderly soft to her naked skin. A stray leaf and a small scattering of fragrant blossoms drifted toward the pool's tranquil surface. The low whistle of a night bird broke the peaceful silence. Vines swung in the faint breeze that had come up, their dark shadows dancing across the pale wall of the cottage. Chantal could smell the salt of the sea and hear the distant throb of the breakers as they pounded on the shore and then sucked backward along the sand. Tomorrow she would explore. Tomorrow she would see the beauty around her which was merely hinted at in the darkness. She would see that great blue bay whose rhythms tonight she could only hear.

Chantal moved her arms gently in the black, glittering water. Her bosom gleamed white beneath its surface. She breathed in flower scents, watched the spin of a leaf-shadow, listened to the soothing cricket sounds of the Mexican night. As she had promised herself she would not do, she thought of Simon Bryce and could feel her senses reopen in the ripening night. There was pain in her heart, for thinking of Simon was like hearing the distant music of a sad trumpet. Like a child, she laid her cheek against the pulsing surface of the water. It's not fair of him not to love me, she thought, it's not fair. . . .

She swiftly left the pool, a small, full-breasted, rosy-nippled nymph whom Simon would never see. She grasped her nightgown and robe and ran into her suite, slamming the door behind her, closing out the sensual night. The air had dried her skin. Without looking in the mirror, Chantal put on her nightgown, picked up her hairbrush and slashed violently through her thick, damp locks until they lay as smooth as a shining ribbon across her shoulders.

She settled into bed and was about to turn off the light on the side table when she happened to see a piece of paper slide gently beneath the patio door. She sprang out of bed and carried the paper to the light.

Written in Simon's hand was a note:

Welcome to Vallarta, Chantal. Guillermo will pick you up in the car tomorrow and bring you

to my house for breakfast at nine—and our first
conference on the script. Simon.

Shaken, Chantal stared at the note. Whoever had
delivered it must have witnessed her nude ascent
from the pool. She had heard no footsteps just now.
Had someone lingered in the shadows . . . and
watched? Panicked, her face crimson, she hoped it
had been the Mexican maid, not a hotel porter. Not
Guillermo himself. *Not . . . Simon.*

Chapter Twelve

As Chantal sleepily turned her head on the pillow, she was awakened by diffused light streaming through the vines framing her window. For a moment she wondered where she was. She sat up quickly. The misty green light was a reminder of Oliver Larch's prediction. He'd promised her "a very good omen." This might be the day.

Simon's note still lay on the bedside table. Chantal reread it, feeling none of the uneasiness of the night before. It was possible she had not heard the porter's footsteps when the message had been delivered. It didn't mean that someone had watched her as she swam.

By eight-thirty, Chantal was dressed in a pale pink cotton top and matching skirt. Her bare legs were tanned from the time spent at EdgeMont's reservoir. She was wearing native huaraches, which she'd bought on Olvera Street at home. Her auburn hair was coiled tightly on top of her head, skewered in place by a tortoiseshell circlet comb. With her hair up and wearing no makeup, she looked like a college student. This impression was underscored by the thick notebook she carried and by the pencils and script folder in her tote bag. Chantal was ready to go to work when the Mexican maid arrived, announcing, "Guillermo. For the señorita."

Seeing Guillermo standing beside the sedan, Chantal again wondered if he could have been last night's silent messenger. She dismissed the thought as a needless anxiety and slipped into the front seat. As they drove in the direction of the village, Guillermo explained that Señor Bryce was staying in a house loaned to him by a Mexican friend who summered in California. The man's home was in a secluded spot just north of the village. They turned off the main road into a palm grove and circled to the rear of a small white house. As Chantal got out of the parked car, Guillermo indicated which pathway to take.

Chantal walked briskly beneath an arbor ceilinged with black wooden beams and hanging lanterns. Magenta bougainvillea espaliered upward against the side of the stone house. In front, a narrow beach lay, neatly raked.

Chantal caught her breath. Beyond the sand was the magnificent expanse of Banderas Bay. Its gently rolling movement offered a language of color. Shallow waves of pale green broke on the shore, slid forward in a frolic of white foam, then flowed back to leave small gleaming pools reflecting blue sky. Farther out, the waters turned to an opalescent hue, then to a marine blue that deepened as it reached the darker ink-blue of the horizon. There the distant sky loomed colorless, with the sea a crayon line against the light backdrop.

Suddenly Simon appeared from around the corner of the house. With the sun and the sea filling her eyes, at first Chantal could distinguish only the sharp, dark outline of his body. As he drew closer, his shoulders, chest and limbs became more distinct. Her heart raced wildly as she drank in the sight of his handsome head, high cheekbones, half-smiling lips, and gazed into the unfathomable, blue-black depths of his eyes. He was wearing a faded T-shirt over black cotton pants that closely defined his lean waist and long legs. Pain and joy leaped within Chantal. Remember me, her heart sang . . . as I remember you!

Simon extended his hand in welcome, but his tone was detached. "Chantal, I'm glad to see you. How was your flight down? Are you comfortable at the Posada?"

Confusion overwhelmed her as she stared at that outstretched hand. She wanted to clasp it, to bring it close to her breast. She wanted those arms to surround her. She wanted his warmth, his remembrance of her body. Instead, his formality was frightening.

"Yes. Yes to everything, Simon." Her voice trembled. She steadied it. "And I'm fine. Ready to work." To remind herself of the real reason why she was here, she flourished the notebook and the folder of script pages she'd brought along.

"Good. Come inside. Breakfast first. Then we'll get to our problem." He pulled her along with him, not realizing that the touch of his hand on hers sent fire through her veins. She tried to focus on her surroundings. A stone terrace led to the open-space living quarters that faced the sea. In the main room, the *sala*, the whitewashed walls were high and bare. The open fireplace was filled with giant white daisies in a large brass bowl. Mangoes lay on a tiled counter, their fruity scent fragrant in the air. The single, wide room was combined for living, dining and preparing food. From this area a hallway led to a large bedroom and bath at the rear of the house.

Simon took Chantal's bag and nodded to a chair near the counter. As she sat down, he went into the kitchen section and brought out blue and brown ceramic plates and mugs to place next to the silverware. He served sliced fruit, pungent-tasting coffee and eggs prepared in a manner called *machaca con huevos*. As he cooked at the small stove top behind the counter, he explained the process. "I'm adding shredded beef to the eggs and seasoning them with tomatoes, onions and chili . . . *sabroso!*"

"What does that mean?"

Simon looked up, his white teeth glinting in a rare smile. "It means tasty . . . succulent." He handed over a plate. "See if you don't agree."

Chantal tasted. "Indeed *sabroso!*"

She tried very hard to smile at the right times, to ask the right questions, to exclaim properly at his small jokes. But she was thinking of another breakfast in her own apartment, of another morning with its tender memory of love defiled by the terrible words "You must not love me, Chantal." Perhaps he hadn't said it in quite that way, but the meaning was the same.

Now he was pushing bowls of rice and beans toward her. *"Muy grande!"* Simon proclaimed. Then in a confidential tone he added, "I really do adore my own cooking."

Chantal leaned back, trying to laugh. "I never would have believed you could do this."

"Don't believe too much. There's a wonderful

lady here named Delora who takes care of everything." He gestured around the *sala*. "She prepared
this meal in advance. I'm just achieving the final
touches."

"So you followed instructions." Chantal had to
play the game with him. She must sparkle and be
amused and behave as if theirs were not an emotionally charged meeting.

Simon's dark eyes gleamed. "Be sure to finish
your food. It's hearty enough to last us most of the
day. Because, after this, we go to work!"

"Yes, of course," she said absently, as though
she'd forgotten why she was here. Again she glanced
out toward the terrace and the sea.

If Simon remembered anything at all of what they
had been to each other, he gave no sign. As he
followed her gaze toward the waters lapping on the
beach, he put down his coffee mug. "Don't let
yourself be seduced by the bay. After we outline
twenty pages and you give me the proper number of
scenes, we'll reward ourselves. I'll take you on a tour
of Puerto Vallarta." He paused. "What's the matter?"

Chantal looked at Simon in shock. "I just remembered. Did you know that Kiki Dalton and my
brother arc here? Kiki's rented a place called Casa
Azul. Do you know where it is? Her secretary said
they're down here hunting. They often come to
Mexico, so it isn't that much of a coincidence. But in
this heat . . ." Chantal wiped the perspiration from
her forehead. "I'm getting used to the humidity,"
she added hastily, not wanting Simon to think she
was complaining. "Puerto Vallarta is hardly a place
to vacation in July, is it?"

"A lot of people do it, but I wouldn't choose to.
Personally, I'm here to arrange some financing and

set things up for our location work in February. The climate will be perfect then. Right now you can't count on the weather. We could have a tropical storm tomorrow. Tail ends of hurricanes out at sea, or from Vera Cruz on the other side, touch here frequently."

Simon stood, picked up a mango and cut into it. While he spoke to Chantal, he had actually been thinking about her news concerning Kiki. Glancing at Chantal, he said, "It's surprising Dalton is here during the summer. I know where the Casa Azul is and who owns it. I'll make a few inquiries. Do you want to see Jay and Kiki?"

"Not Kiki particularly, but I suppose Jay . . ." Chantal hesitated.

Simon's eyes narrowed. "You know about Jay?"

Chantal looked puzzled. "Know what about Jay?"

"What he does—his career."

"I don't know what he does. He appears to be busy. He lives very well."

"Haven't you ever been curious as to how he makes his money?"

"Yes. But since he hasn't told me, I haven't asked him outright. I've hinted plenty of times," Chantal confided. "But . . . well, with Jay one doesn't like to push. He's young, only twenty-one, but he's—" Chantal shrugged. "There's only one way to say it. He's tough and he goes his own way. One just doesn't ask questions of my brother. We keep in touch, but it's his doing, not mine. He reaches me only when he has something to say. And that's it. Our communication is mostly about our family."

Simon studied Chantal for a long moment, seemed about to comment and then, as though thinking better of it, nodded toward the tote bag. Seemingly he was finished with the subject of Kiki and Jay. "Now that you've told me they're here, I'll keep an eye out for them. Let's get to work, shall we? Delora!" he shouted.

A stout woman appeared from the direction of the hallway. She smiled warmly at Chantal and told Simon, "I'll clean, señor." Again she glanced at Chantal. Pointing to the remains of the breakfast, she inquired anxiously, *"Bueno?"*

Muy bueno," Chantal said expressively.

Delora beamed.

Simon and Chantal worked for the rest of the morning on the shady terrace. As the sun rose directly overhead, they moved to a wooden table in the palm grove north of the house.

Simon concentrated on Chantal's ideas for future action in the script. Usually, his own directives prevailed, and Chantal hastily kept writing down suggestions for scenes, bits of dialogue, motivations. The only mention of the original screenwriter was an acknowledgment that his excellent dialogue should stand, and that what Chantal wrote now would be smoothed over by Williams when he returned to the studio. There was no concern that Cesar would not be back. At any rate, Chantal had no time to consider the Cesar Williams affair, since Simon's ideas flowed rapidly and she had to keep pace transcribing them.

The late-afternoon sun was spilling across the bay when Simon announced brusquely, "That is enough for today. You have plenty to work on. What did you think of the typewriter in your room? Is it in good working order?"

Chantal admitted she hadn't yet tried it out. She was disappointed as Simon rose and helped her gather up her materials, saying, "Guillermo will drive you back to the Posada. They have a fine dining room there. Hungry?" He wasn't going to ask her to dine with him.

Chantal nodded. "The meal you—or Delora—prepared has lasted just so long. I am hungry again. It must be the sea air. Isn't that what everyone says?"

Simon seemed barely to be listening to her. It was all too obvious that his attention was on other matters. His smile was quick and businesslike. "You have a couple of days' work here. Let's say . . . Friday? We'll meet again. Guillermo will pick you up, same time. Then I'll read over what you've done. Am I giving you enough time?"

Chantal kept her gray gaze cool and distant. "I believe so, Simon. I'll do what I can."

"Knowing you, you'll have it done," he assured her. For a second his eyes flickered from her mouth to her straight brows, to the red hair piled neatly atop her head. "Can you find your way around to the back drive? That's where Guillermo is."

Chantal swallowed hard. Simon wasn't even going to walk her back to the car. "Of course I can find him." She picked up her tote. Her own smile was wide and blank, saying nothing of how she felt. She lifted her head high. "I'll see you Friday."

"Good girl."

God, how patronizing! Chantal walked around the side of the house, her face darkened with inner confusion and anger. Because both of them were so far from home base, she appreciated Simon's professional attitude. In its way, it was a compliment. But that last remark of his—"good girl" indeed!

She recognized her feelings now, if she hadn't before. What a fool she'd been to fly down here with a hopeful fantasy in her head. What had she expected? That Simon would realize how wonderful she was and take her in his arms and hold her forever?

Come down off your cloud, Chantal told herself sternly. She'd do Simon's damned script. She'd do it so well that he'd be on his knees begging her to continue with it even after Cesar Williams returned to the studio, if Cesar ever would return. A new dream featuring an imploring Simon formed in Chantal's imagination as she jerked open the sedan's front door before Guillermo could reach it. He looked at her in shy distress.

Chantal maintained an insulating silence all the way back to the Posada Vallarta. She stared straight ahead, not seeing the life of the road as they passed along it. There was a *caballero*, gorgeously dressed in a black and silver outfit with a matching sombrero, who rode his narrow burro negligently, as though proudly contemplating his own macho splendor. An open bus, filled with staring black eyes, passed their car at a wild rate of speed. Black-haired women with beautiful Indian faces walked alongside the road balancing baskets on their heads. A jeep roared by carrying three blond, young men complete with scuba diving equipment.

By the time she and Guillermo reached the Posada, Chantal had cooled down a bit. She shouldn't have taken out her hurt pride on Guillermo. In fact, she hadn't behaved well at all. There must be no further fantasies about Simon Bryce. To him she was a workhorse, and that was it. Well, she'd been forewarned that men were like this. Most of her women friends had had similar unhappy experiences. Only she had thought that this time it would be different. She and Simon had been so wonderful together, in their verbal communication and in bed.

She guessed it really didn't matter, neither the great talk nor the rapturous union of their bodies. To Simon, their having been together meant nothing.

To look at the situation cynically, as far as Simon Bryce was concerned, Chantal Jerrold was a bright mind to bounce ideas off. She was also very good on a mattress. As long as Chantal understood his terms, they could go on together. If she demanded more of him, then she'd better let go. Which she had.

Chantal got out of the car and tried hard to give Guillermo a warm smile. As she turned away, a sudden notion stopped her. "Guillermo, who delivered the note to my villa late last night?"

"I do not know, señorita. Señor Bryce told me to be here at half past eight this morning. That is all I know. Perhaps Señor Bryce himself came here . . ." Guillermo's shrug was delicately Latin, eloquent. "Shall I inquire of Señor Bryce, señorita?"

"Oh, no! Thank you!" Chantal exclaimed, and hastily moved away. She rushed along the colonnade of the hotel and under the archway with its trailing rainbow of red, yellow and tawny orange bougainvillea clusters.

She didn't want to go back to her room just yet. Though the air was still humid, she paced across the cobblestone courtyard past the big swimming pool, where inert bodies lay enduring their collective broil in the sunset, sustained by margaritas. Off in the distance a lovesick guitar throbbed, accompanied by a male voice crooning a song of unrequited love. Chantal closed her ears to its haunting melancholy. Whatever country one was in, it didn't seem to matter. Romance was always going into a tailspin for someone.

On the broad beach in front of the hotel, hardy guests sat in the sand and the late-afternoon wind.

They were enjoying a last barter with the homeward-bound Mexican vendors. No doubt the trays of silver rings, bright scarves and tiny artifacts had been hastily assembled in some jungle factory. Chantal was beginning to take a jaundiced view of the whole scene.

She glanced up at the sky to observe the people who'd come, not to swim in the sunset sea, but to swim through the air. Chantal watched as someone, harnessed to an opened nylon parachute, soared over the bay. He had been pulled skyward from the beach to para-sail hundreds of feet above the water. The feat looked dangerous. The only safety precaution was a taut line attached to the body harness and towed by a powerboat racing ahead through the waves. When the time came to descend, the boat slowed, then came in close to the shore, and the flyer made a gradual descent over the sand, to be caught in the arms of a waiting assistant on the beach.

"You want to try that?"

Chantal glanced around. A furry-chested, sun-bronzed man wearing swim trunks, a gold chain and a medallion stood there, seemingly as interested in Chantal's hair and legs as he was in her answer to his question.

"Maybe sometime," Chantal replied noncommittally, and started to move away.

The man was not discouraged. He trailed after her, admiring her hair and her pink outfit. "Why don't you join me in a Coco Loco before dinner?"

Chantal half turned. "What's a Coco Loco?"

"You don't know? It's kind of the national drink, for tourists at least. It's green coconut milk with rum, plus gin and tequila."

Chantal looked stunned. "I'd say it serves the tourists right." With dexterity, she ducked beneath his attempt at an encircling arm. "I'm sorry, I really have to work."

"Work?" He stared at her in astonishment.

"I'm a writer," Chantal explained hastily so that he wouldn't get any peculiar ideas about her occupation. She waved cheerily and started down toward the shoreline, her tote bag banging against her knees.

The man caught up with her, gold chain glinting in the sunset. "You're a writer?" he repeated, impressed. "Say, can I carry that bag for you? Looks heavy."

"It isn't, though. It's okay. Another time." She knew the man was still studying her legs as she ran down the beach. Glancing behind her to be sure that no one was following, Chantal cut up through a palm grove. She firmly intended to keep the location of her villa to herself.

Chantal worked on the script in bed. Leaning back against plumped-up pillows, she wrote in longhand on the legal-sized pad she'd brought along. Later she would type the material on white paper for Simon to read. Incorporating his suggestions, she felt as though Simon himself maintained a compelling presence in the room with her.

Restlessly, Chantal put aside the pad and thought about the day. There'd been no signal from Simon that there would be any more between them here in Puerto Vallarta than the anticipated hard work.

Chantal sighed heavily. Again she picked up her pages; again her mind wandered. She and Simon Bryce could continue an alliance of their film careers, fine! And when one or the other felt like it, they could resume another alliance—physically rapturous, emotionally sterile.

No man could reason that a loving woman would be able to handle a situation like that, unless she were a professional whore. Chantal didn't want Simon on a thin and sometime premise. She wanted him forever.

Picking up her pencil, Chantal began to write again with furious resolve. She would create strong scenes, sequences that would play well. She could visualize how the camera would move to project the feeling Simon demanded. Half listening to the sound of the waves, Chantal knew that it was not the seascape that could seduce her from her work. Only her own longings could do that.

On Friday, Guillermo was late in arriving. It was a hot and unusually beautiful day. The lapis-lazuli waters of the bay seemed to merge with the polished azure of the sky, while the jungle and the precipitous mountains created green chaos.

Simon met Chantal on the terrace. He glanced down in amusement at her yellow-and-white-striped beach shift. "You look about fourteen years old," he commented. "I think you'd better pin your hair up again the way it was the other day so I'll know I'm talking to a talented and serious writer."

For an answer, Chantal's hand shot into her pocket and brought out several pencils. She released the rubber band that was around them and shook back her hair. Grasping its thickness, she slid the band on. In an instant she had achieved a smooth ponytail. "What's the effect, Mr. Producer?"

"Now I'd say you're two years older—maybe sixteen?"

Simon was in an expansive mood. Chantal let him take her by the hand and lead her down to the beach. "Come on, I want to show you something."

They walked over the smooth humps of sand until, finally, Simon pointed out a fluttering pennant attached to a small sign. Chantal bent forward to read the faded lettering on the sun-bleached board.

Almost instantly, she glanced up at him, considerably irritated. She didn't quite understand what his purpose was in bringing her down here to read the sign. He would never share himself and his life, but he expected her to clap hands because he was feeling good this morning and wanted to show off this toy. Besides, she certainly couldn't read Spanish.

"What is it?" she asked.

Simon caught the annoyance in her tone. "It's a lesson. I thought you'd be interested."

"Simon, no matter how I look to you, I'm not sixteen. I don't need lessons." She started to move away. "I've had enough lessons," she said over her shoulder.

"Oh, come on, Chantal. Wait a minute. The man who rakes the beach every day puts up that little flag. He has different colors that he can use. You see what the sign says?"

"You read it to me. I'm ignorant."

"You can learn the language. *Calmado,* that would be a green flag for calm. *Precaución,* yellow for caution. *Peligro,* red for danger."

"Today the yellow flag is up."

"The caution flag goes up every day. The sky can be blue and the sea calm, but still the yellow flag says caution."

"Are you trying to tell me something, Simon?"

"I am telling you something, Chantal."

Their eyes met. Simon looked amused. Chantal's gray eyes were stormy. "It may be very obvious to you, but I don't see it. I don't need to be cautioned . . . about anything." She paused. "Maybe you do. Is that it?"

Simon leaned forward and tucked a vagrant strand of Chantal's hair behind her ear. "Yes," he said, "I need reminding. I thought you'd understand."

Chantal stood on one foot, took off her sandal and held it vertically to let the sand slip out. "How about getting to work?" she suggested coldly. She wouldn't let Simon know he'd provoked her. She wouldn't let Simon know her heart was beating hard.

Simon shrugged. "All right, then. Work it is."

Because it was now later in the day and the sun was directly overhead, they went to the wooden table north of the house.

Chantal opened the script folder, fatter by fifteen typed pages, and watched Simon's face while he read. She could tell nothing of what he was thinking. When he finally put down the folder, his dark eyes searched hers, then locked into them. She was certain he was pleased. Her momentary anger with him had passed. Now she knew there was contact between them, light, hardly tactile, like a touch in secret. Her breath quickened. She tightened her hands in her lap and sat up very straight.

"This is very good, Chantal," he said, tapping the pages. "We'll talk more about it tomorrow. There are a few changes I'd like to suggest, a bit more interaction that we might use." He stood up. "Enough for now. I promised you a tour of Vallarta. It's a little late in the day for that, but we'll go to the Oceano Bar near the Malecón and watch the world pass us by."

"What is the Malecón?"

"It's an embankment that runs along the shore, a few steps from the Oceano. We'll walk along the top, and if we're lucky, I'll show you a sunset like no other you've ever seen. The ones here are so splendid that when the sun dips into the ocean, everyone yells, 'Author!' "

"I've heard that story, Simon," Chantal mocked. "They tell it about Sunset Beach in Acapulco."

"Why didn't you tell me you've been around?"

She stooped, picked up a tiny pebble and tossed it at him. "Let's go."

The village of Puerto Vallarta, officially designated a city in 1968, was still compact and picturesque, despite the influx of tourists in the late seventies and early eighties. There was a plaza, a cathedral, and shops displaying leather goods, pottery and the marvelous handicrafts of the local artisans—rugs, papier-mâché animals, hand-painted flora and fauna.

Simon parked the car at the curb of the Oceano. Built in the center of town across from the Malecón, the old hotel resembled a grouped Spanish landscape with its intricately designed, openwork balconies at each floor level and its pink-grilled stairway spiraling upward around an ancient exterior.

Simon led Chantal into the Oceano's terrace bar just off the street. It was partially roofed against tropical showers and green with vines that trailed along the wooden beams. Hanging baskets of foliage were everywhere. Tiny, low-flying birds darted about, trying for taco crumbs.

Simon ordered drinks and explained, "This place was always a favorite with expatriate Americans who lived up in Gringo Gulch. It was a listening post for arrivals, departures, deals and gossip. There are other watering holes now, but this used to be the one." Simon paused, then said sharply, "Don't look! Unless you want to be recognized."

Instinctively Chantal ducked her head. "Who is it?" she whispered without turning around.

"Kiki Dalton and your brother. They're headed this way. There goes our rendezvous."

Dark lashes veiled slightly tilted, startlingly light eyes as Chantal looked quickly at Simon. "Our rendezvous?"

"With the sunset," Simon reminded her.

Chantal's cheeks burned. She hoped Simon didn't suspect that she had attached a romantic significance to his remark. Unexpectedly, he reached across the table to grasp her hand. For an instant only, his strong fingers closed over hers. The pressure of his hand, so uniquely Simon, caused Chantal to shut her eyes under the lightning flash of memory. A Tang horse, a bronze, a Modigliani—all Simon's possessions, as she was Simon's woman. Unnerved by his touch, the blood pounding in her veins, her heart thudding in her chest, she acknowledged his power over her.

Chantal looked away as though her gaze were hypnotized by the emerald flight of the birds among the vines above their heads. She could not let Simon see that her poise was badly shaken. She had completely forgotten the existence of Kiki and Jay.

There was no avoiding the handsome pair who walked onto the terrace from the street. Kiki gave a raucous shout. "Look who's here!"

Jay came forward without surprise. He was wearing faded dungarees and an open-to-the-waist denim shirt. His yellow hair hung shaggily about his sun-darkened face.

All six feet of Kiki Dalton collapsed into a chair at

Simon and Chantal's table. She snapped her fingers at the waiter. "A daiquiri, *por favor* . . . *doble*. What's for you, Jay?"

"Lemonade." Jay was looking at Chantal.

With the grace of a puma, Kiki folded her long arms on the table and stretched long legs beneath it. She was braless, wearing only tiny string bikini underpants beneath a sheer lavender-colored chemise. "It's so damn hot." She pushed back her hair, bleached as white as spun sugar. "Why is everybody staring?" she demanded irritably.

"Because you're supposed to be wearing more clothes when you walk around town. These people are modest. I told you that," Jay admonished.

Kiki shrugged and turned her attention to Simon and Chantal. "So what are you two doing down here?" Her smile was wide, her black eyes knowledgeable. "Make it a good story," she insisted.

Jay took over. "Shut up, Kiki." He nodded affably at Simon and at his sister. "I'm glad to see you, Chantal." He spoke as if nearly two thousand miles from home were a natural setting in which to meet. "How's the family?"

"They're fine, Jay. When I left EdgeMont, a house party was going on. Oliver Larch, Mother's friend, for one. And Boy Farrell was there with his executive vice president. I tried to reach you before I left L.A. I did call Kiki's office, and I heard you were here."

"Yeah? Kiki's office told you? Well, it's fortunate we ran into each other."

"Oh. *Is* it, Jay?" Kiki spoke meaningfully.

Simon leaned forward. "You must have read in the trades I'm setting up location here next winter, Kiki."

"As a matter of fact, I didn't read your publicity. I'm out of town, relaxing." Kiki's black eyes swung in Chantal's direction.

"And Chantal is working on *The Assaulters* script for me," Simon continued. It was in the back of his mind that Kiki might have heard about Williams's difficulty, but apparently not. Larette and Moira were keeping things under lock.

Kiki's triangular brows raised. Abruptly she asked Chantal, "Where are you staying?"

"At the Posada."

"And you, Simon?"

"You're very obvious, Kiki. I'm at Rafael Lijos's house while he's in Santa Barbara for the summer."

"Goody." Kiki lapsed into a slightly sullen silence. Her double daiquiri arrived, and she began to sip it and dab chips into the hot *salsa*.

Simon turned to Jay. "Chantal was under the impression you were hunting down here."

"*Hunting?*" Kiki interrupted. Her look was a stab.

"Shooting. I think that's how your secretary phrased it."

How courteous Simon sounded, Chantal thought, and yet Kiki looked furious and Jay, for once, appeared uncomfortable.

"Remind me to fire that bitch when I get back to town. My business is my own. And so is Jay's."

Jay stood up from the table. "Don't forget, your secretary was speaking to my sister. Naturally she told Chantal where I was."

Kiki finished her drink before snapping, "And *naturally* that dumbhead mentioned what you're doing?" She put down her glass and looked at Jay. "Why are you standing there?"

"Because you and I are leaving." Jay glanced at his sister and Simon. "Will you have dinner with us tomorrow night?"

"We'd like to," Simon replied, "but we're leaving for Yelapa in the morning. Have to track down Aefollo."

Jay nodded. "He lives there when he's not making a picture, doesn't he? I hear he does marvelous things with a camera. I'd like to get hold of him myself." He glanced quickly at Chantal. "It's a primitive spot. I'll see you when you get back."

Kiki rose, saluted with two fingers to her forehead and sauntered away, the swing of her hips and the strut of her long legs a promise of enticement. Jay caught up with her, put an arm around her waist and leaned up to whisper something in her ear. Kiki listened, looked back at Simon and Chantal, then moved off with Jay.

Chantal turned back to Simon in astonishment. "You said Yelapa. Tomorrow. And that I'm going too? That wasn't on the schedule."

"It is now." Simon took pesos out of his wallet to pay the waiter. "I hadn't planned the trip so soon. Nor had I planned to take you with me." Simon glanced up at the sky. "Let's walk across the street to the embankment. I want to show you the sunset. It will be spectacular this evening."

"More than usual?" As she asked the question without really caring about the answer, Chantal was quietly annoyed. How dare Simon Bryce take so much for granted? He should have discussed the Yelapa trip with her. Not that she minded going, it would be an added adventure, but it was high-handed of him not to have asked her first before he announced their departure to her brother.

"We're due for a change in the weather," Simon told her. "I think we'd better get down to Yelapa and back while we still have a calm sea. We can travel by motorboat. But since there's no harbor, the natives have to bring a canoe out to meet us and take us back to the beach."

They left the Oceano, crossed the street and approached the embankment that ran along the sea. Calm? Of course it was. Chantal looked around, reassured by the quiet of the distant hills, the serenity of the green-leafed palms, the solid construction of the tile-roofed houses. Everything was as usual, it seemed. Burros brayed, dogs barked. The smell of exotic cooking wafted through the cobbled streets. The golden mangoes quivered in the tall trees. The plaza, with its paths and its flowers and its wooden benches, looked as it had for a century. The sea itself was still.

The placid beauty surrounding her helped Chantal overcome her annoyance with Simon. She smiled at him enchantingly. "It is *calmado* now."

Simon observed her closely: the ripe, full lips; the short, straight nose; the lovely, wide-cheeked face with its hint of mockery that lingered beneath the surface. Tonight, as the sunset began to flare, Chantal's hair caught fire from the exuberant burst of color. Its luster turned to shades that made her skin and throat appear paler. Simon's gaze dropped to her bosom, its fullness enhanced by her slimness and her slight stature.

As they walked along the embankment, Chantal asked, "Did you hear me, Simon? I said it's very calm this evening. The green flag should fly."

"You remember the little yellow flag that always signals caution?"

Chantal stood very still. Her gaze direct, she challenged, "Do I have to remember—if I prefer not to?"

"I think you should." And so should he remember, for Simon was aware that tonight it would be very difficult to resist holding Chantal in his arms. As the rays of the sinking sun shot sparks of rose and amber and yellow-gold across the gunmetal sea, Simon knew the words in his mind should not be spoken. "Chantal, will you come back to the house and have dinner with me tonight?"

Chapter Thirteen

Dinner was served by Delora on a wrought-iron table set on the terrace. The moonless night, lighted only by the candles in their pottery holders, created a dark encirclement around Simon and Chantal.

Simon nodded toward the doorway. "Guillermo fished early this morning. You're about to see the result."

At that moment Delora appeared and settled a platter in front of Chantal, proudly announcing, *"Huachinango."*

"To put it simply—Pacific red snapper," Simon replied to Chantal's questioning look.

The fish had been simmered in a sauce of green peppers, onions, tomatoes and stuffed green olives. The delicious result was accompanied by side dishes of the inevitable rice and beans.

"The olives lend a distinctive flavor," Simon explained. "I told you, Delora is a dream." He poured the wine, a semidry Bianca di Mare. "Our host, Rafael Lijos, left this behind for us. If he were here, he would say it's the ideal complement to seafood, refreshing as an ocean breeze." Simon glanced toward the bay, hidden from them by the curtain of night. "There's not much of a breeze right now. Tell me, do you find this humid climate difficult to live with, Chantal?"

"I'm getting used to it." Chantal pushed back damp wisps of hair from her perspiring forehead. She had thinned out the heavy bangs as she had promised herself she would. The full red mane was still held by a rubber band, though wayward tendrils escaped to touch her neck and flushed cheeks.

Chantal was unaware that she created an enchanting picture as she sat there framed by the lush background of magenta bougainvillea. By candlelight her graceful shoulders appeared enticingly naked and ivory-toned. The scooped neckline of her simple beach shift clung tantalizingly to the moist skin above her swelling breasts. Simon forced himself to restrain the urge to glide his open palm down her bare, glistening arms.

With concealed annoyance, he told himself that what he was experiencing was a very young man's impatient infatuation. Simon Bryce was no longer a young stud. Romantic yearnings such as these must be charged to candlelight and wine and the feminine presence of that lovely, intelligent face across the table from him. Yet in his heart he knew the truth of his beguilement. The intimate memory of their lying together in each other's arms was fixed in the virile inner core of his being. Tonight that strong imprint from their recent past marked Simon's response to Chantal. His body had not forgotten hers, even though he had commanded his mind and will to do so.

Simon wrenched his gaze away from Chantal. Their moments of shared passion had been intense, but brief. Too brief to permit either of them to be stamped indelibly. To continue to romance a memory was not realistic. Simon tried to convince himself that an individual could have sex freely anytime, and the even more facile freedom to forget and to shed its bonds.

He was pleased to see the steadiness of his hand as he raised his wineglass. He knew it was important to continue the course of sanity they'd set for themselves in Vallarta. Producer and screenwriter collaborating . . . with no personal involvement.

Briskly Simon toasted Chantal. *"Los que toman vino viven cien años!"*

"Translation, please?" Chantal's eyes sparkled in the candlelight.

"Those who drink wine live a hundred years!"

"Do you believe that? And do I want to live a century?" Quizzically Chantal eyed her glass. "Somehow I don't think this will do it for me, Simon. But I'll give your potion a try." She tasted the wine. "I don't see the future," she commented wryly.

He offered the carafe. "Another? You might."

Laughing, Chantal shook her head and leaned back, looking toward the dark beach while Delora cleared away the plates. "If you blow out the candles, will the stars and the surf audition for us? The light prevents me from seeing anything out there."

Simon snuffed the flames with his hand. Sable night immediately closed in. It was as though the velvet blackness had crouched, waiting for this moment to capture them. Their eyes gradually grew accustomed to the darkness. The ancient presence of the vast night came alive with a myriad of stars, twinkling like crushed diamonds. Here and there, huge orbs glowed steadily. In this latitude the constellations were unfamiliar to Chantal's eyes. Where was her friend the North Star?

Along the shoreline below, a white line of surf approached, its movement alive with muttering sound and salt scent. Simon remained silent. To Chantal he was like a silhouette, as mysterious as the night itself. What had he been thinking a few minutes ago, Chantal wondered, when he had stared at her? Who was Simon really? What was he to her? Her mind hesitated to form the words. A co-worker? A lover, for an evening?

Earlier, Chantal had deliberately challenged him. She had understood his meaning well enough about the yellow flag. It was a subtle warning to her. To himself. Still, she had chosen to accept Simon's dinner invitation. What was *her* reason? Curiosity? Desire? Or was it to allow herself to be tormented again by the cruel distance he had put between them? She wasn't sure.

Not far from where they sat, a wave crashed with a great rumbling echo that shook the weather-stained bricks beneath their feet. The water sagged backward. There came another smashing boom. And another. Closer this time. Nervously Chantal turned her head in the direction of the violent surf. Its drumlike sound grew louder as if it were the heartbeat of some sea monster. Chantal sprang to her feet.

Simon rose also. "The tide's coming in," he explained, hesitating. "Shall we go inside? Or would you prefer to stay here and I'll relight the candles? It's perfectly safe, you know. The water can't reach us."

"If we go inside, maybe I can help Delora." Chantal was embarrassed to admit her fear.

"That's thoughtful of you, but Delora has long since left us. She and Guillermo's wife and family live in a small house in the grove behind us. Their day begins at dawn. They're all asleep by now."

"Then Guillermo can't drive me back to the Posada?" Chantal made a little mock grimace of distress. "Is it possible to call a taxi?" She began to move along the terrace. Once again the surf thundered in a threatening explosion that hurried her footsteps.

"I'll drive you when you're ready to leave. If it's the rising tide that's disturbing you, believe me, it won't come up this far."

Simon stretched his tall form, raising his arms upward as though to grasp for the stars. "What a difference this is from Los Angeles. You remember my house in the hills? Even situated as it is in a canyon, I still get all the traffic roar from the freeways below. The executive jets that fly over from the Valley airport almost knock on my roof. But this, this is just night and sea. Sometimes I think I'd like to stay in a place like this forever." He faced Chantal, and she saw the white flash of his teeth in the darkness. "I don't mean that literally, of course."

Chantal nodded. "I saw a T-shirt on a tourist at the hotel. Across the back was printed 'Puerto Vallarta—just another crappy day in Paradise.' I suppose that's what it can come down to. Too much of paradise."

Chantal was chattering to ease her indistinct sense of alarm, to remind herself that they would both soon return to that safe, prosaic life to which they belonged.

Pensively she went on. "It's beautiful here, like an island out of time, a kind of peaceful riddle . . . yet one that I'm not quite able to solve or to identify with." Almost regretfully, Chantal looked back over her shoulder at the swell and dip of the sea as it continued to creep closer. "I suppose I'm too accustomed to our own brand of civilization."

"Can we really call it that?" Simon took Chantal's arm as they walked together into the lighted *sala*. He pushed forward a chair for her and moved matter-of-factly behind the tile counter. "I see Delora has left us coffee." He got out two mugs, poured the coffee and added a dash of Kahlúa liqueur to each cup.

"Mmm . . . delicious. Jay brought me a bottle of Kahlúa last time he came back from Acapulco. It does make black coffee even better."

"Chantal—what about Jay?"

Chantal put down her mug. "What do you mean, what about Jay?"

"Do you see very much of him in Los Angeles?"

"No. I've told you that. He lives his own life, very separate from the rest of our family clan. He seems to adore his friend Kiki. I suppose she's nice enough. What do you know about her?" Deftly Chantal had managed to turn aside Simon's query. For some unexplained reason, his questions had made her uneasy.

"I've known Kiki a long time. She's had three husbands, three divorces, no children and countless affairs. She's very outspoken when it suits her purpose. She told me she was deliberately celibate for two years before she met Jay. She's a Taurus, strong-willed, opinionated, aggressive and very healthy. She doesn't smoke or take drugs of any kind, which is unusual considering the fast crowd she runs with. She doesn't drink. I was surprised to hear her order a double daiquiri today." As an aside he added, "If one can consider a daiquiri a proper drink. I had the feeling that she and Jay had been having a tiff over something." Chantal's eyebrows raised slightly. "She's rich. I do business with her occasionally. How about that for gossip? Satisfied?"

"That's it?"

"That's it. Perhaps we'd better drop the subject of Jay and Kiki."

Chantal stirred uneasily. She was not sure she wanted to return to the subject of Simon and Chantal. She sensed that something between them was unresolved. And that something concerned Jay—and his occupation. She was about to question Simon further when he said, "We'll have to get a fairly early start tomorrow. Guillermo's friend is taking us down the coast in his launch. It's about an hour's trip. There's a fine, large cove at Yelapa. We arrive and depart by sea since there are no roads."

"Who lives there?"

"Besides the natives? Affluent American dropout types. There's a small, thatch-roofed hotel in which one sleeps under plenty of insect netting. Yelapa is a remote jungle-beach village, and that's all."

"Aefollo *lives* there?"

"Lives there and loves it, when he isn't working. I'm not sure he'll appreciate our stalking him in his lair, but I have to get a firm commitment from him to do the camera work when we come down on location. It's not the sort of place you'd ask the William Morris Agency to tackle. More coffee?"

Chantal shook her head. Simon came around from behind the counter and impulsively drew her out of her chair. He pulled her down beside him onto the woven mat in front of the flower-filled fireplace.

"We won't be able to do much on the script in

Yelapa except perhaps have a few conferences with Aefollo. I could leave you behind to work at the Posada until I come back." Simon paused, his brow darkening.

"Yes, I wondered why that wouldn't be the logical arrangement."

Simon's response was clipped. "I have my reasons for wanting you in Yelapa." He placed his coffee mug on the mat. "Let's take another look at the typed pages I read this noon."

Chantal pulled open the tote bag and brought out the script. She tossed a pencil to Simon and took another for herself, then raised her note pad. "Ready?"

"Hmmm, yes . . ." Simon replied absently while he leafed through the folder. "That bag never leaves your side, does it?"

"I can't lose what we've done on the script, Simon."

"Why? Do you live dangerously with no copies of it?"

Chantal nodded, embarrassed. Simon shook his head in dismay and went back to the pages. "A precious first and only copy, then." He continued to read as Chantal glanced about the room, waiting for his comments.

The *sala* was almost bare of furniture. There were two chairs near the counter, a wraparound couch and a mosaic-inlaid coffee table. It seemed only natural that Simon should stretch full length on the mat, his elbows supporting his muscular frame while he held the typed pages propped on his chest.

Sitting on the mat beside him, Chantal began to study his face as she had earlier in the day. Now his eyes were somber beneath black brows. Chantal noted the strong, slightly aquiline nose, the articulated cheekbones, the flat cheeks, the firm mouth. Her heart shivered. It was a warrior's face, not a lover's.

He was wearing another pair of those formidably tight-fitting, black cotton trousers that outlined his narrow hips and the taut length of his powerful legs. In combination with the white shirt stretched across his broad chest, it seemed a uniform he was fond of. Simon's male scent was of salt spray, the lash of palm fronds, fresh air blowing across miles of ocean. Chantal could close her eyes and breathe him in, a mighty landscape of sky and mountain and sea.

She opened her eyes. Simon was regarding her with a strange expression. Hastily Chantal raised her pencil, poising it above her notebook. "What was that you said?" She should have been paying attention.

Simon chuckled. "You're a dreamer. I'll repeat, we've got to keep in mind the production board back at the studio. The department can't start working with their little colored cardboard strips for the sets until we have a script to give them."

Simon turned on his side to face Chantal, the fabric of the shirt pulling tighter across his chest. She looked away, conscious of his nearness. Simon went on. "We've got to create our flashback sequences so we can bunch them all together when we shoot. It's easier on the budget that way. What do you think? Can we keep the action and the costume changes to a minimum in the scene where Auguste and the girl recall their early meeting in Paris?"

"I jumped it around too much in those scenes?"

"In a way, yes. You did the recall scene imaginatively and very well, but pragmatically, the producer has to think of cost. Every minute spells dollar signs. I'm the villain, right? So here, for the sake of budget, we blue-pencil. Right down to this point." He slashed the page to the desired spot while Chantal leaned forward to reread the scene.

"Instead of shooting too many flashback sequences," Simon continued, "we can do a lot with Auguste's and the heroine's dialogue to explain what went before. We can save film that way. Not too much talk, though. Fate and the box office deliver us from a talky film!"

"Simon, what about Cesar Williams? He's marvelous with dialogue."

"We'll do what we can, and if Cesar comes back he'll rewrite. So remember, not too much talk. We've got to involve our audience in movement, action and emotion. If we want them to listen, we send them to a concert."

"I understand. Play it back and forth. Keep the dialogue brief, but do it with enough intensity so the audience's attention will be held and we won't have to show them too much in flashback. Watch the budget!"

Simon grinned at her parroting of his words. "You've got it! You've struck a couple of sets for us right there, Miss Jerrold. You do see what I mean, don't you?"

"Oh, yes, I see. I goofed. You're very patient, Simon."

"I'm not patient, and as for you, you're new at this. You only need experience and time. I've been around the horn. I've learned, and you'll learn too."

Chantal leaned back. "I hear you've had flattering offers from other studios. . . ." She hesitated, not wanting to sound as though she were apple-polishing.

Simon shook his head. "I prefer to produce independently. I do it my way, Chantal. Don't believe every rumor you hear. An eager public relations person we hired might have tossed out that one." He glanced back at the script as though it were his intent not to talk about himself. Actually, he couldn't bear to look at Chantal. He was remembering in too much detail the night in her apartment when he had stripped her, taken her in his arms and carried her into the bedroom. . . .

Chantal looked at Simon alertly, questioningly. He grew aware that she appeared to be waiting for a response to a question she had asked. Simon tried to answer, his tone vague. "I was thinking." He put down the typed pages and finally looked directly at Chantal. "About the last scene you wrote." He paused, frowning. "What *did* you say to me just now?" He had tried to dissemble to himself. But he knew it was no use. Those eyes of hers—those unbelievably clear eyes, their shade the palest gray of dawn's light—spoke to him of her sweetness. He could imagine that a residue of hurt remained in her from their last encounter in the city. Simon was not always selfish. He could sense in Chantal a lingering resentment despite all her brave and snappy pretenses. He sighed. What else was there about her? She was bright. She was good.

"I asked you . . . I wondered . . . they . . ." Chantal stammered. She too had forgotten her question. She felt as though her mind were washed as clean as the beach outside; she knew her heart was thundering like its surf. Her skin felt fevered to her own touch. Her hands were trembling. She must go on talking about the script—but her mouth was so dry. A knot of desire, which had been clenched tight within her, was beginning to dissolve, to untwine, to spin a silken net of languor through her flesh. Helplessly Chantal looked at Simon Bryce, feeling dreamy lassitude spread in seductive quivers along her limbs. She tipped over her coffee cup. "Oh, damn!" she cried as the dregs spilled out, and she had to mop up the mess with a handkerchief retrieved from the tote bag.

Simon continued to stare at Chantal. He didn't seem to notice her awkwardness. His eyes resembled black ice, wintry in their expression. Without speaking, he extended his hand to grasp her wrist. Chantal could feel the steel in his inflexible fingers as they tightened on her wrist, sending an explosive charge of sexual longing through her. Simon rose from his half-recumbent position as effortlessly as an uncoiling current of smoke and pulled Chantal up.

The expression in his eyes was bleak. This was not what he had intended, this torrent of unspoken desire that appeared to be wrenching them both away from the safe shoals of social conduct. The shallows in which they had taken discreet refuge were a mirage, had never existed. They were fast sinking beyond self-control.

"We're in deep trouble," Simon said with simple irony. He waited, as though to give them both one last chance to make a swim for sanity. Chantal couldn't speak. She was beyond coherent thought.

Without releasing her wrist, Simon led Chantal through the wide arch into the bedroom beyond. She had glimpsed it only once before while going down the hall to the bathroom. She stared about her numbly. As in the main *sala,* the walls here were white and bare and soaring. That, at least, registered in her aching and confused consciousness. Once again she seemed to be inside that strange, empty room of her dreams.

She looked up at Simon as he loomed above her in the dusky shadows. He did not understand the shivering murmur on her lips. "Dark . . . wings . . ."

For whatever reason, whatever fears within himself, Simon did not appear to hear her. He lowered his head to hers and covered her dry lips with his own. She swayed against him and he felt her mouth become warm and moist. As her lips parted, he drew her closer, his hands at her lower back, fitting her body into his. His tongue circled again and again within the sensitive inner curve of her lips. His mouth still absorbed by the summoning of her lips, he raised Chantal against him until he sensed a scream within her body that she could no longer withhold. Suddenly, almost unwillingly, in a spasm of passion, she clamped her teeth against Simon's lower lip. He didn't feel the pain. He only knew she was shaking with unrestrained desire, kindled by her response to his embrace.

The heat of her passion was a marvel to him, yet Simon gentled her with soothing palms. He stroked her face and lips and hair with sensitive fingers. He smoothed the material of the beach shift against her breasts and hips, aware that with his touch he ignited even more the urgency of her body. Finally Chantal released her panicked hold on Simon. He saw the white glow of her throat as she tossed her head back in an ecstasy of abandonment.

"I want you, Simon."

He threw back his own head in laughter at the soft growl of her words, then stood away from her, holding his hands out in mock surrender. "I want to be wanted. For a man, it's a beautiful feeling, Chantal." He grinned. "Do with me as you wish."

Strangely, his playacting did not break the love spell. He had given her carte blanche; there was to be no ritual of sexual custom or etiquette between them. They were alone—and she was a woman of summer brought to the fullness of her sensuality.

How the two of them tumbled onto the bed, she was never sure, but she knew that it was she, Chantal, who swiftly unzipped those incredibly lustful black trousers of his. "You wear nothing underneath!" Before Simon could speak, his amused face was hidden as she pulled the shirt above his chest and over his head. Next, she drew off the sandals he was wearing. How swiftly she had undressed him! She gave a husky incoherent cry at the sight of Simon's naked body. Her kisses covered his face, his throat, his chest, his torso, his limbs. His strong body, browned by the sun, flat and muscular from the disciplines of his life, was hers! She perceived the rigid male response to her seductive actions, and it was awesome.

"Quick!" Simon ordered. "Do something about yourself, Chantal."

She looked down in surprise and understood his impatient meaning. She was still fully clothed. She pushed off her shoes, knelt upright on the bed, raised her arms and pulled off the striped beach shift.

His potent maleness was apparent to them both. Still, Simon said politely, "Allow me." He slid the bikini panties down Chantal's active legs. Solemnly he held up the lace-bra insert that had been sewn into her beach dress to confine her ample contours. "Fantastic," he muttered. He then eyed with lustful delight the large and luscious breasts set with harmonious rosebud nipples that were suddenly above his face, that gently jiggled at him above the tiny cinch of waist as Chantal bestrode him.

Their lovemaking grew serious. It was as though the giant combers outside had rolled into the room, laved their bodies, tossed them about and curled into a breathless spiral of sensation created by the exquisite excitement of their arousal.

A Valkyrie riding love's storm, Chantal could hear the surf pounding on the beach. It matched blow for blow the pulse of her wrist, her throat, her heart. Sea sound rushed in her ears as, beneath her, Simon moved strongly to caress her breasts. He thrust his face upward between them with a bruising arrogance that left Chantal trembling. With a panicked sense of both pride and fear, she recognized the moment his body coupled with hers in powerful, rhythmic climax. If she had ever questioned the true intensity of earlier sensations, there was no question now of what was occurring deep within her. She knew she had waited all her life for this night, for this man, for this carnal fire that filled her being and raged in her veins and sinews.

Their bodies revolved in pleasure as though pushed by waves on pliant sand. Now Chantal found herself beneath Simon's weight. From him she learned that her knees were beautiful—kisses there; her toes were beautiful—tiny sea pearls to be stroked against his cheek and nibbled at; her elbows were absolute grace. Didn't she know that? he demanded. His eyes smiled deep into hers with a piratical gleam. Chantal gasped in suppressed laughter at his tensely whispered dialogue.

"I'll see that a shrine is built to worship these perfect breasts, these perfect limbs." More nibbles, strokings, a lingering trail of kisses to help gild his extravagant rhetoric. Simon concluded with mock seriousness, "This shrine will be erected in London's Victoria and Albert Museum. We'll demand nothing less for loveliness such as yours."

Chantal was breathing hard, but her eyes danced

in amusement. "I don't understand your frame of reference."

"Never mind, I'll explain some other time." He murmured that she was his porcelain nymph come alive for him.

Chantal scolded Simon with small, swift, biting nips of kisses. "You are thinking in weird, kinky, filmic terms, my darling. This is real life, *tonight,* in this room. You are with me! Not with a piece of bric-a-brac statuary in far-off London."

She rolled away from him; he rolled her back. "I agree. I am with you." Then he displayed another remarkable reassurance of her presence. Chantal was astounded by the visual evidence of his giant need for her. Again his mouth descended on hers, this time in violent possession. They no longer played or teased, but trespassed dangerously—in self, in body, in spirit. His hands and mouth aroused Chantal to a paroxysm of defenseless intimacy, until her own self seemed foreign to her, more like that of some temptress she did not recognize. She cried out.

Supine on the bed, Simon lifted Chantal ceiling-ward at arm's length and watched her shiver with the hot ardor of her climax. He lowered her body, dripping with perspiration, down to his belly. He swept her up again and again. Their ecstasy in each other was perilous. They were beyond the sound of the sea and the great drafts of waves that slashed along the beach. They did not hear the night wind that came up like a prowling panther to batter the corners of the house. Their own incredible adventure with each other was all they knew.

When they awakened, it was dawn, and quiet after the rage of the night and the sea. They had slept in each other's arms with no cover but the soft, scented

air. Chantal wept, and Simon knew she was happy.
And so was he. The contented warrior, he slitted his
black eyes at her and watched every step of her
progress from the bed to the bathroom to the shower
and into the disguise of the flimsy beach dress and
thong sandals. He brushed her hair for her. They
found a narrow ribbon tied around a flowerpot and
bound back her hair again. This, to give her the
appearance of dignity, he explained. Otherwise she
would look like what she was, a woman who had
been loved throughout the night, so languorously
lovely was she.

Chantal rummaged in her tote bag and came up
with a pair of owl-sized dark glasses. She slid them
across her nose and settled on the side of the bed to
watch Simon tug on those tight pants and draw a
tired shirt over his broad shoulders. When he would
have buttoned it up, she stopped him, undid the
three top buttons and kissed his chest at the place
beneath which his heart beat. He clasped her shining
head close to his heart until she heard its muffled
threat. She leaped back and away from him. "We
mustn't!" she cried. "Not again!"

"Another time, perhaps," he said formally, and
they set off on tiptoe to find the sedan that was
parked at the rear of the house. They drove as
quietly as possible out of the palm grove. A discreet
departure.

As the car bumped onto the main road and turned
left toward the Posada Vallarta, several pairs of eyes
peered over the tops of bushes. Guillermo's children
giggled. Delora pushed them away and muttered in
Spanish that breakfast would be late because she had
not been able to get to her kitchen in the main
house. At the same time, Guillermo announced to
his young wife that he might as well walk to the

village and warn his friend José that the launch due
to leave for Yelapa this morning would probably
have to be held until midday. Nor did Guillermo like
the look of the sky. It was white this morning, and so
was the sea, and the wind was beginning to crackle
the tops of the tall palm trees.

Chapter Fourteen

It was noon. Kiki sat on the balcony of the Casa Azul, her bare feet propped up on the railing. She was watching the wild churning of the bay far beneath her. The sky, white and threatening earlier, had darkened into a purple menace. The air had a hushed quality to it that made Kiki uncomfortable. She was thinking that she was a city girl. All this jungle scenery, ocean, big sky and exotic landscape made her nervous.

Once more she turned her attention to the table beside her, and to the mail pouch she'd received from her office this morning. She was pleased at the report that her shares in the company specializing in genetic engineering had gone up in value. On the other hand, she should have been there to tell her broker to sell gold before it dropped as much as twenty-seven dollars an ounce. Of course it would go up again. No problem. With Kiki, financial matters always seemed to turn out well.

As though struck by a random thought, Kiki made a grab for her binoculars, adjusted the focus and stared into the gully halfway down the cliff. Jay and his crew were shooting there. Through the glasses she could just make out the red bandana around the head of the camera operator. Beside him loomed the bulky figure of Constantin, the assistant, who did everything. He was clapper/loader, grip, propman, and stunt man when needed. There was no sound crew. The dialogue would be dubbed in later. Definitely not your Hollywood studio crew with all its large demands in regard to working conditions, overtime hours and union pay scale. Kiki grinned at Jay's frugality. Then, recalling what was actually going on down there in the gully, she scowled. A few minutes more with the binoculars, and her gaze began to follow a familiar male figure as it ascended the path leading up from the cliffside.

When Jay finally appeared in the archway of the balcony, Kiki's eyes appraised him. "It took you eight minutes to climb up here. No wonder. Look at what you're wearing." She said this in a half-jeering tone. The two of them had not been getting along too well. Mexico's tranquility spooked Kiki, and she was quick to let Jay know her feelings.

Jay was sweating profusely. He glanced down at his Western apparel. The alligator boots were from Lucchese's in San Antonio. The blue jeans and shirt had been custom-made for him at Nudie's Rodeo Tailor in North Hollywood. They always kept Jay's measurements on file.

"Isn't it too hot for you in those duds, cowboy?" Kiki herself was wearing the string bikini she appeared to live in down here. She wiped the perspiration from beneath her shoulder-length hair with a tissue and tossed it over the balcony. Not waiting for Jay's response, she said, "Gad, what a place! I'm not surprised they call their main beach Playa de los Muertos. Beach of the Dead. Gruesome. Ugh!"

Jay seated himself on the iron railing and proceeded to pull off his boots. Kiki followed up with, "Look out I don't push you off there, Big Star Man."

Jay let his boots drop. "You're in a foul mood. You know that beach got its handle from a particularly bloody pirate raid years ago—and for no other reason."

"Ah, so? I couldn't care less."

"Kik, you've been sulking ever since we came to Puerto Vallarta."

"Not ever since. *Before.* I didn't want any part of this venture, you know that. You were doing fine with the damn porno films you shot at your place in Bel Air. The money was rolling in. Why do you have to go straight on us, hmmm?"

"I want to do something serious for a change."

"And lose your shirt!"

"You can have it." Unexpectedly Jay ripped off the blue shirt. He was neither especially tall nor imposing, but he was solid, with a gold-fuzzed chest, broad shoulders and muscular flanks. He was gorgeous. Kiki blinked her eyes, then looked away from temptation. Those tight pants of his showed off his virility.

Her gaze on the shuddering waters of Banderas Bay, she asked querulously, "Why did you leave the crew on its own? You're the star, the director, the location manager, the exec producer *and* the payroll. Have I missed anything?"

"They can manage their pickup shots without me." Jay's vivid blue eyes were concerned. "Where's my fun Kiki?"

"Your fun Kiki is ready to go back to Century City. The mail pouch came. It's very hard playing catch-up with my business activities from this distance. There's a lot of new stuff going on. I should be in L.A. right now."

Jay looked innocent. "Are you missing out on that molecular biology business about our bodies being chemically programmed? I read the prospectus."

Kiki's black eyes raked Jay savagely. "I *have* shares in that company, bub. So don't make jokes about it. It's already earned me half a million while I've been sitting here on my behind doing nothing!"

"Then why are you bitching?"

"I'm not." Contrarily, Kiki again picked up her binoculars and peered toward the gully. "Here comes Sissy, climbing up the rocks after you. She's a scrubby-looking thing. Who is she anyway?"

"You know about Sissy Purdue. I don't have to tell you. Ever since that first night at the disco, she's latched onto us. She says she wants to learn the film business. I don't have to pay her. She's pretty good with that little camera of hers. I have her doing some still photos for the promotion we'll be putting on later. She handles wardrobe and makeup for Gabriella. She'll even do Gabriella's stunt work when our leading lady throws herself off the rocks at the finale."

Kiki groaned. "A downbeat ending yet! You're really going artsy in a big way, aren't you, Jay?" She put down the binoculars. "The local who brought my mail said there was a radio report about a hurricane on its way." She motioned with long fingers. "Look at how that sky looks now."

Jay squinted his eyes at the bruised and lowering clouds. "I heard the same story—but the storm is two hundred miles off the coast. It'll stay on course to Baja."

"The man warned we'll get heavy rain. You'll have to stop shooting. That will cost you—feeding the crew. They'll hang around doing nothing."

"I planned a cover set in case of rain. We'll do an interior in this house."

Kiki jumped up in exasperation. "Jay, I'm leaving. I won't stay around here if you're going to clutter this place with your camera and lights and all that sleazy equipment. Not to mention all those people tramping around! Most of them don't even speak English!"

As she started to brush past him, Jay caught Kiki in his arms. It didn't matter that she was taller than he. They stared at each other for a taut moment. Jay ran his hand down and up Kiki's spine, and then around to rest lightly on one breast. His eyes never once leaving hers, he squeezed gently. Kiki sighed. She put her head on Jay's shoulder. "I just changed my mind. I'm staying."

Jay laughed. "Coax me, Kiki, and I'll finish up early this afternoon." He looked skyward. "We're losing light anyway." He kissed her. "I'll come back and we'll play cards or something." He glanced past Kiki's shoulder toward the bay. "There's a boat going south out of the harbor. Must be headed for Mismaloya."

"In this weather?" Kiki turned around.

"Let me have the binoculars." Jay stared through them. "Yeah, José's launch. Well, he's got a good motor in it. I know. He took me marlin fishing that time. They'll be able to make Yelapa before the sea gets too rough."

"They?"

"Simon Bryce. And my sister. Simon's after Aefollo. They'll probably be down there only a couple of days. Remember yesterday at the Oceano, when I asked them to have dinner with us and Simon said they were leaving today?" Jay again glanced at the sky. "If this weather gets worse, they won't be back that soon."

For one long, steady beat an expressionless Kiki Dalton stared at Jay. Then she smiled, her teeth even and white against the smooth, tanned skin of her face. She waved an arm. "Honey, you go tend to your film making. Give me a big smooch before you go. There! We're not mad anymore, are we? And let that Sissy come up here. She can keep me company."

Jay shot Kiki a curiously reluctant look. "You never need anyone to keep you company."

"I do today."

"You're not up to something, are you?"

"What could I be up to?"

"Well . . ." Jay was thoughtful. "Anyway, I'll be back soon." He picked up his clothes and departed.

Kiki watched him go. Jay had guessed right about her. It was scoundrel time in Kiki's heart. Something Jay had just said had made her think rapidly. She might have reached a truly startling decision. Things came fast to her this way. *If* she could pull it off!

Impatiently, Kiki rose to her full height and shouted, "Marta! As soon as Señorita Sissy comes, send her up here. You hear me?"

The fanciful architect-builder who had constructed the Casa Azul had seen to it that his blue house was grooved in sensational style into the rock cliffs above the water. The upper floor of the *casa* was natural stone, its walls blue rock and quartz.

Two bedrooms and an entry hall were on this first level near the entrance. The open foyer looked out across Kiki's balcony. Safely hemmed in by black iron coils, she could watch the bay and the flowing seascape. More to the point, from this vantage Kiki and her binoculars could observe what was going on in the gully where Jay's film was being shot.

On the second level down, the vaulted kitchen and tiny back bedroom were the refuge of Marta and her sister. Here they giggled and sulked, according to the tenants' moods. Adjacent to the kitchen were the main quarters: a living-dining area, a circular bar and a second-level bathroom. Kiki had locked it only once. After that she forswore privacy. Due to the intricacy of the handsome ornamental door lock, she'd been unable to free herself. No one had heard her shouts for help, since it had been siesta time and the maids had been asleep. Finally, she'd crawled out through the transom above the bathroom door. It was not an experience she cared to repeat. Everything was beautiful here, but nothing worked properly.

The master bedroom suite was on the third and lowest level, close to the giant rocks that speared upward from the water. Kiki's dressing table was a broad wooden board held by massive chains to the whitewashed wall. There were carved chests, and chairs with braided leather seats. The bed was king-sized, its silk sheets sent down from the States. On humid nights Kiki and Jay preferred the floor for intimate moments. It, too, was a kind of paving rock that felt cool and marvelous against one's backside.

While she waited for Sissy to reach Casa Azul,

Kiki thought about Jay and Chantal and Simon Bryce. Her thoughts hovered especially around Simon. She was pleased with herself because she'd decided not to share with him the vital information about the publishing house's interesting sideline. In the first place, she hadn't needed the producer's financial input. Discussion of the transaction with Simon had been more social and expedient than anything else. If one had a lucrative deal going, sometimes it was smart to let somebody like Simon in on it. Quite a few important people around town were obligated to Kiki for stock tips and little pieces of a "good thing." Simon never had been one of those, of course. But now Kiki hugged herself happily. How fortunate that before leaving L.A. she'd consummated the publishing house deal by herself.

How lucky could she get? Kiki gloated. It was very possible she'd just been handed her own Page One story. There was no need to involve Jay's sister. She wasn't newsworthy enough anyway. There might be a society angle, since Chantal's family lived in Hancock Park, but that was reaching. It was better to use the woman in the case as a blind item. More clever, really, to insinuate that a lovely and well-known redhead had gone off to Yelapa with Simon Bryce, the discreet Mr. Simon Pure.

In itself, a licit romance would be of no prurient interest, but if something out of the ordinary occurred between Simon and his woman, readers would drool over the puncturing of his reputation for propriety.

Though Kiki had professed ignorance about Sissy, she remembered her very well. From the first, she'd been watching Sissy through the binoculars as closely as Jay. Now all Kiki needed was a face-to-face encounter to see if her initial instincts about the young woman had been on the mark. Kiki had the habit of picking out stray people to do her bidding. She had not yet failed to find the right one for any task at hand. Of course, the blabbermouth sitting in the office in Century City would have to be fired immediately. But the girl *had* acquired the information about those Arizona leases from the lawyer next door. So she'd get a bonus as well as the pink slip.

Kiki heard a stir in the air behind her. Without turning her head, she said, "After that climb up here, how's your condition?"

"Guarded," a husky female voice answered.

"Did you meet Jay on the way?"

"He said you wanted to see me."

Kiki stood up and turned around. "Let's go have a drink."

The visitor followed Kiki down the curving rock stairs to the main room with its round bar circled by miniature calliope horses. Kiki went behind the bar, while Sissy sat astride one of the brightly painted horses. She reached out to play with its velvety ears and run her fingers down the realistically carved mane.

"What'll it be?" Kiki asked.

"Tequila tonic."

Kiki made the drink expertly, plopped a lime into the tall glass and opened a bottle of mineral water for herself. As she drank, Kiki glanced over her glass at Sissy and noted the woman's face had a bedraggled quality to it, completely nondescript. Nobody would notice her twice. Yet she was probably younger than she looked. Her clothes were awful, scabby-appearing jeans and a perspiration-stained T-shirt. Rundown sandals and banged-up toes with their nail polish peeling off completed the unappetizing aspect of Sissy Purdue. Kiki mused, She'll fade right into the sand or the woodwork. She'll be exactly what I'll need. Kiki smiled entrancingly.

The young woman was about to raise her glass for a fourth and final gulp of her tequila when she caught the expression of satisfaction on Kiki's face. People seldom looked at Sissy in such an appraising manner and with such a pleased expression as this older woman betrayed. Sissy was flattered. She was also shrewd. She didn't waste any time. She attacked first.

"You want something of me?" Sissy purred in a raggedly feline voice.

Kiki Dalton was taken aback, but she didn't allow it to show. She had never met her match and certainly hadn't in this person, but she had expected that getting to the arrangement would take a little longer. All right, Kiki thought, down to business!

"I hear you're very good with that camera." Kiki gestured toward the Nikon slung around Sissy's thin neck by a plastic strap. Each time she moved, the camera banged against her flat chest.

"I consider myself a professional. I learned photography while I was posing for girlie magazines." Kiki's eyebrows tilted. "I can guess what you're thinking, but you don't have to have a great body for that. As long as you don't mind doing a full frontal. I didn't mind."

"I understand Jay isn't paying you for what you do for him."

"He's not."

"I will—if you work for me."

"How much, and what do you want me to do?" Sissy held out her glass. "Hit me again."

Kiki almost burst out laughing. "Are you for real?"

"I'm just trying to impress you with how tough I am. You need something done, and whatever it is, I can do it. Just tell me how much it pays."

As requested, Kiki mentioned the sum. Sissy whistled politely. "I'm yours. What is it?"

"Do you get seasick?"

"No. Why?"

"First you'll have to make some kind of an excuse to Jay for leaving. I'll see that there's a boat to take you where I want you to go. The sea may be rough. Don't take much gear with you. A man and a woman are down the coast in a place called Yelapa. I want you to follow them, and if they get into something compromising—you know what that word means?" Sissy nodded, and Kiki went on. "Anything at all . . . I want a photographic record. You'll have to be smart about it and completely inconspicuous, since I understand not many people are down there. If you shouldn't get what I want, you'll be paid anyway. If what you get is off-color and usable, you'll receive a bonus."

Again Kiki named a sum, and again Sissy whistled, this time enthusiastically. Kiki thought, This gal can pass herself off as a 1960s dropout. She's really a dip. But crafty. Abruptly Kiki's expression turned baleful. Her eyes were as hard as glass as she contemplated Sissy. "No ideas about blackmailing me, have you?"

"None at all." Sissy's response was so prompt that it was easy to suspect she might have been thinking along those lines. Or else her own slyness had told her she might get a question like this from the tall blonde on the other side of the bar. Sissy downed the second drink and looked directly at Kiki. "I can do better for myself by honest cooperation with you, can't I?"

Kiki nodded. "You can. The bar's shut down now. No more of this." Kiki's long fingernail clicked against the glass that had held Sissy's tequila tonic. "No more of the juice until the job's done. We understand each other, I think. You know I'll get you good if you screw up."

"I won't screw up," Sissy said obediently. She put out a dirty hand, which Kiki took reluctantly. Sissy instantly noticed the rebuff. Her face clouded and she sighed. "You'd better tell me some more. And I'll have a cup of coffee if you don't mind. I haven't eaten anything today."

She's playing pitiful waif, Kiki observed to herself, amused. She raised her voice. "Marta! Black coffee and a ham and cheese sandwich. Pronto!" She turned back to Sissy. "I'll talk fast. Jay will be here soon. What'll you tell him by the way?"

Only a second passed before Sissy responded. "That I've missed a couple of my periods and I have to do something about it, so I can't stick around and watch his work anymore, and I can't jump off the cliff for Gabriella on account of my delicate condition."

"Very good." Kiki changed the subject. "I'll give you as much money as you need to get plenty of film in town. You tell me where you're staying. I'll have a local who has a boat get in touch with you." She looked at the sky outside. "It'll have to be fast and soon."

"Why can't I be driven down there?"

"There's no road where you're going. It's all sea and jungle. I understand they take you off a motor launch in a canoe and land you on the beach. Don't get your camera wet." Kiki's voice lowered as Marta came into the room with a tray. "Come sit down over here, and I'll tell you exactly what these people look like and what I want from you." After Marta had left, Kiki continued. "If the pictures aren't so hot, at least try to get me a blow-by-blow on the two of them. Whatever I can use. Bribe someone if you have to. But keep yourself out of sight."

"You're paying extra for items?"

"If it's the truth."

"Or near enough?"

"Or near enough."

"Jay isn't to know anything?"

"Not a word. If this works out, you may have a steady job."

"I know that, Miss Dalton. I know who you are."

"And I'll know who *you* are too, Sissy. As soon as I get to a long-distance telephone."

"I expected that. I don't have a record."

"How old are you?"

"Eighteen. I guess I look thirty."

"Sometimes it goes with the territory. A playwright, Arthur Miller, said it—I didn't."

They eyeballed each other for a moment, then Sissy Purdue bit into her sandwich. My lord, thought Kiki, maybe she hasn't eaten anything today. Sissy glanced up and met Kiki's eye. She seemed to be developing an uncanny habit of reading Kiki's mind, for she said softly to her new employer, "I really haven't eaten today. I wasn't lying."

José's boat moved steadily through the green-black trough of the waves. He didn't mention it to the tall man beside him, but José knew their only safeguard was the lack of wind on the water. Otherwise they would be swamped in rolling swells. They were close to Yelapa, and there was no turning back to find a safer harbor. They had passed Mismaloya nearly an hour ago. If there were storm-driven breakers on the Yelapa beach, it was unlikely that the natives would bring the long canoe to meet them. In that case, José wasn't sure what he would do. The three of them might have to swim for shore.

"Is it pretty bad?" Simon asked.

José shrugged eloquently. "Not too bad, señor." He was lying, of course. He glanced curiously at the imperturbable profile of the man who had insisted they make this trip despite the weather conditions. There was the girl back there too. Not a word or a whimper out of her. Again José shrugged philosophically. People like these were hard to comprehend. But they paid him well, so . . . all he could do was guide his launch as best he could. He had reduced the power of the engine. The boat shivered under his expert fingers as he nursed it along.

Chantal curled in the rear of the cabin, her tote bag containing clothes and the screenplay held between her knees. She'd slung a windbreaker around her shoulders. Its cap peaked in a triangle above her hair, which had tightened into curls from the sea spray. Her gaze was constant, never veering from Simon's broad shoulders as he stood beside José on the fragile bridge.

Simon glanced back at Chantal. "All right?" he asked.

"This isn't exactly the season for boating, is it?" Chantal responded wryly.

A smile flickered across his lips as Simon's dark eyes held hers. The intensity of his stare recalled their soaring pleasure of the night before. Deliberately he looked away.

Chantal's legs felt weak. She wound her arms

around her knees to hug her body closely. In the early dawn, when Simon had returned her to the suite at the Posada, he had taken her in his arms in a farewell that had extended itself into a final, fierce encounter. Their bodies had blended together, enjoying a quickly returning passion that seemed to flame higher because of the brief separation they would face while he went back to his house. Now, in this gray, strange sea, Simon's look had spoken to Chantal. It made her feel safe.

When they foundered into the wide cove at Yelapa, there was reason for José's fears. The engorged black clouds overhead suddenly opened and a pelting rain descended. It was like no storm that Chantal had ever experienced. Gates of water enveloped them. Humidity from the hot rain clothed their bodies, streaking their hair to their skulls.

At the moment the downpour had begun, there was an ominous but fortuitous lull in the heavy breakers lashing along the cove. Chantal peered into the gray distance at dim figures bunched on the sand. It was a relief to see that they were putting a long canoe into the water.

The muscles in José's biceps and forearms knotted and strained while he held his boat at anchor. Through the curtain of rain, the canoe came swiftly alongside. Two men, clad in tattered pants, their bodies wet and glistening, maneuvered close. Like a cat, Simon leaped into the canoe. His motion was so graceful and quick that the craft barely swayed. He turned to catch the knapsack José tossed to him.

Together, José and Simon held the canoe steady while Chantal prepared to make the transfer herself. The two natives contributed their efforts by balancing the level of their paddles across their chests.

They spread their legs within the sides of their delicate craft to keep the rocking to a minimum. Chantal moved unsteadily as José, at her shoulder, gave a prod of encouragement. She shouldn't have closed her eyes, but she did. She tumbled ingloriously into the bottom of the small vessel. At the clumsy delivering of this unexpected weight, the thin, wooden shell tilted precariously. Chantal gasped in alarm and scrambled to her knees. This quick move precipitated another dangerous sideways luch that threw her in the opposite direction. She would have gone into the cold salt water that splashed up into her face had not Simon grabbed her roughly. Chantal moaned and put her head down toward the canoe's bilge. As she lay still, she could feel the turbulence of the sea beneath her.

Simon's hands continued to hold Chantal's shoulders tightly as the forward surge told her they were on their way to shore. She was aware that José had joined them. His familiar canvas shoes rested on either side of her head. Flat on her face, Chantal heard the ocean's menacing gurgle only inches beneath her cheek.

There was a fearful shout, causing Chantal to raise her head for the first time. She had expected the canoe to glide up on the sandy beach. Instead the craft bobbed crazily, and she could see fifteen feet or more of churning water separating them from the little group of people on the shore.

Chantal spluttered a question. The wind swept away Simon's answer. When she glanced up at him, he was looking toward the beach and laughing. Maniac! she thought angrily.

Then she saw the huge, naked man wading out from shore. Great white waves broke against his bare torso. Their force staggered him, but he kept coming. By the time he reached the canoe, only his head could be seen above the heaving waters. Two enormous arms reached out toward Chantal, and before she could utter a sound, they had plucked her up and set her atop broad shoulders. Wildly, instinctively, she clamped her knees tightly under the man's armpits. Her arms nearly strangled his neck as he balanced her tote bag on his head. Terrified, Chantal tucked her chin down over the bag to hold it secure. If her rescuer stumbled in this mad chaos of foaming water, she'd be caught by the undertow and pummeled bruisingly against the sandy bottom. But the churning motion of the man's strong legs didn't falter, and Chantal knew she was about to be ridden through the last scallop of waves and up onto the beach.

She slid down the man's bare back while the smiling natives surrounded her. She'd lost her windbreaker. Her pants and shirt were stuck like wet seaweed to her body. Her sandals were still on her feet, but they squished water as she moved around in front of the big man to thank him. She wasn't quick enough. The naked man disappeared into the little group, which immediately departed, Chantal's rescuer hustling into his clothes as the clan wound its way along a trail leading up a steep cliff.

Simon and José joined Chantal, their clothing as drenched as her own. The two canoeists reached shore, dragging their overturned craft and Simon's knapsack.

Chantal's teeth were chattering. "All of you had to swim in." She knew it was a totally inadequate remark.

"We're here," Simon responded, his face grim. "I

feel responsible for those fellows." He nodded toward the two men running along the cove carrying their canoe.

"I wanted to thank that man," Chantal began.

"He knows you're thankful, señorita," José interrupted. "The villagers see we're safe. They've gone back to their huts. It's very simple."

"Simple? What do you mean?"

"Hurricane does this. These people are ready. Every year they have hurricane weather."

"What about your boat, José?" Simon asked. "Will it ride out the storm?"

"I got enough canvas over the inside." They looked out toward José's launch, which could barely be seen through the rain.

"I'll help you bail it out tomorrow."

José grunted. "Thanks, señor, but it may sink tonight if this keeps up."

Simon put his hand on José's shoulder. "If anything like that happens, I'll see to it that you have a new boat, José."

The three trudged toward the thatch-roofed shelter that perched above the half-moon of sand. They climbed up a shallow hillside overlooking a lagoon to find an anxious hotelkeeper who led them inside.

"Register later, señor. You are my only guests," he said to Simon as he hurried them off to separate rooms.

Chantal smiled wanly at Simon as their host closed the door behind her and left her alone. She looked around. There was a chair, a table, a mirror, a lighted lantern and a bed surrounded with insect netting that hung from the thatched ceiling. She put down her tote bag, knowing its contents must be drenched. Inside it were the only clothes she'd brought with her. Luckily, this time she had made an extra copy of the script pages. It was a relief to know they were safely back in her room at the Posada. After Simon had left her this morning, she had typed the copies instead of sleeping.

The bathroom had a makeshift shower, but the water was pure and warm. Chantal stripped off her wet clothing and was soon soaping her body and shampooing her hair. She came out glistening pink, cleansed from the salt. Nevertheless, each move she made in this humid atmosphere misted her with perspiration.

Someone knocked at the door. Wrapping herself in a bath towel, Chantal went to answer it. A pleasant-faced Mexican woman stood there. "My name is Felicita. Please take this." She handed Chantal a white cotton caftan, the upper part embroidered in vivid shades of peacock blue and turquoise.

Chantal accepted the gift with delight. When the woman departed, she slipped the garment over her head. It was so voluminous that the absence of underwear didn't matter.

Chantal hung her wet underclothes and the contents of her bag around the room to dry. Next, she put on the rubber shower slippers provided by the hotel. In this humid climate it would take her leather sandals at least twenty-four hours to dry.

She carried the lantern to the wall mirror and ran a comb through her thick hair, letting it fall in smooth curves to her shoulders. Her face bare of makeup, her gray eyes shining, she went in search of Simon and José.

By rights, Chantal should have been exhausted, but instead, all the excitement had stimulated her unreasonably. She felt buoyed up as she hurried along a short corridor to the combined office-lobby of this primitive inn. Simon was there, conversing with the hotel owner, who was introduced to her as Roberto.

Simon sat Chantal down at a table and pushed a cup of hot coffee toward her. "No, wait a minute. I think this is better." At Simon's instruction, Roberto brought a brandy. Chantal swallowed it. The liquid burned all the way down, but it steadied her. She leaned back, took a deep breath and tried to relax. Outside, the silver rain consumed their tiny world, locking them in with its rushing sound.

Simon studied Chantal. He shook his handsome head and smiled. "You look very pretty in that Mexican dress."

He himself deserved a good look. Chantal devoured his presence with her gaze. Simon was nearly bare-chested, wearing only a white cotton vest. It was obvious the accommodating hotel owner had been unable to find a shirt to fit the much larger American.

"I shouldn't have brought you into this." Simon stood up and started across the lobby. "I've ordered us some *arroz con pollo.* That's chicken with rice. Does it sound good?"

"Anything, Simon."

As he walked away from her, Chantal observed that he was wearing white trousers that had to belong to their host. They were too short by several inches. She was amused at the way they refused to fit Simon's supple physique. The material flapped loosely about his narrow hips and long legs.

When he returned to her side, Chantal whispered, "I miss those black pants you always wore in Vallarta."

"Those . . . ?" Simon appeared surprised and

resigned. "I don't miss them. I had to wear them. I couldn't hurt Delora's feelings."

"What does Delora have to do with it?"

"When she washed my clothes, she boiled everything in hot water and used a strong soap she had made herself. Everything I owned got shrunk. And whenever I bought a new pair of pants in town, it was the same thing all over again. I couldn't make her understand. What are you laughing at?"

"Oh, Simon!" Chantal gasped. "I think Delora must have shrunk your pants on purpose. You looked so . . . so masculine in them." She was laughing uncontrollably.

"Chantal, what's the matter with you?" There was humor hiding far back in his eyes. Chantal was certain Simon's inner laughter matched her own, but he said, "You sound exhausted and hysterical. I think you'd better go to bed as soon as you've had your dinner. And I mean to bed—alone!"

Impulsively Chantal held out her hands. Simon looked around quickly. Roberto had gone into the kitchen. Simon bent over Chantal, took both of her summoning hands in his and crushed them to his lips.

She said it without thought, an instinctive response from the heart. "I love you, Simon."

He stared down at her for a long and terrible moment, then straightened slowly, the expression in his sea-dark eyes terrifyingly bleak and distant. Almost offhandedly, he said, "You're a captivating woman, Chantal." He turned away from her. "Tomorrow we find Aefollo." That was all.

The blood drained from Chantal's face. Her skin quivered as though she had been struck physically. Her spirit was lacerated. Simon's chill attitude and careless words seemed to have brought the desolation of the storm inside. She felt exposed; she hurt and she was weary. There was no refuge. Earlier she had been able to overcome the buffeting she had taken, both in the launch and in the small canoe. She had ignored exhaustion, gaining strength in the certainty that Simon cared for her.

Why now, in this awful moment, did she remember the long-ago devotion of Mark Duffy? She sat very still, understanding at last a little of Mark's feeling for her their last night together. But she had never turned away love in the cruel manner of Simon Bryce.

Suddenly Chantal sprang to her feet and ran toward the corridor, before Simon could look back at her and sense the tremor in her heart. She hurried down the hallway and slammed the door to her room behind her. She was so tired she could barely stand. The hunger she felt was not one to be appeased by hotel food. She loved, but it seemed her love was inconsequential to Simon. It was merely a distraction to serve a night's passion. Chantal covered her face with her hands and stumbled toward the bed.

Later, Felicita came to Chantal's door with a tray of food. When she knocked, there was no answer. After waiting, she peered inside, then slipped into the room. The señorita appeared to be asleep, the pretty white dress crumpled about her body. Setting down the tray, Felicita pulled the netting around the bed. She shook her head, finding these *norteamericanos* incomprehensible. The handsome man this young woman had arrived with was getting very drunk with Roberto and the boatman, José. No one had eaten the *arroz con pollo* that had been prepared.

Felicita had been asked to guide this pair tomorrow to the clifftop village to find Aefollo. Felicita doubted that either of these two would be in shape to make the climb. Picking up the tray, she quietly left the room.

The rain continued its assault on the thatch-roofed inn. The winds from two hundred miles away came sweeping in, extracting heat energy from the warm ocean and causing the waters along Yelapa's coast to swell under the lash of the distant hurricane. The night seemed to roar. Mercifully, Chantal slept. Misery and exhaustion kept away desire and dreams. Oblivion was sweet.

In his way, too, Simon searched for oblivion. He had another drink, and another. . . .

"Where's my room?" he finally asked wearily.

His drinking companion, Roberto, staggered to his feet. "With an empty hotel, it is easy to find. I have put you next to the young lady." He hiccuped. "Here is the key. You read the number on it, señor. My eyes are not so good tonight." He nudged the exhausted José. "You going to sleep with your head on the table all night?" There was no answer. Roberto sighed. "*Buenas noches,* Señor Bryce. We leave José here."

Simon bowed formally, then looked at his room key. "It works?"

"No, señor, it doesn't. The locks never fit. You just look at the number on the key, go to the third door to your left and walk in. Sleep well. No one will disturb you."

The torrential rains gusted with such a deafening force that it was impossible to hear the remainder of the hotelkeeper's sentence.

Roberto was still uttering soothing phrases as Simon slanted his way down the corridor to find his room. Had the hotel owner said it was next to Chantal's?

Deliberately Simon made his way farther down the unlighted corridor to find another empty room. He knew that, tired as he was, he could never sleep with the perfume of her presence a mere thin wall away. He must put distance between them. . . .

Chapter Fifteen

The next morning Chantal awakened to see a concerned Felicita looking in on her from the doorway. She sat up in bed. Suddenly she realized she was still wearing the dress. She was shocked at its crumpled appearance.

As though understanding Chantal's embarrassment, Felicita came forward. "It's all right. We'll hang it up and the wrinkles will go."

"It's so pretty," Chantal said, fingering the intricate embroidery around the neck. "I must have been very tired last night not to have taken it off." She stood, weakness making her unsteady on her feet. Actually, she was grateful for Felicita's presence. It prevented the painful recall of last night.

Felicita went about the room inspecting the clothes that had been left out to dry. "You can wear these." Felicita indicated underwear and a shirt and blue jeans. She tested the leather of the sandals and shook her head. "Still damp. I'll find you canvas shoes for the climb."

"Climb?"

"Up the cliff. I'm guiding you and the señor to Aefollo's house."

"Is the storm over?"

For an answer, Felicita released the shutters on the window. Chantal stared out. The half-moon stretch of beach where they had landed the day before was covered with giant logs, with driftwood twisted into strange shapes and with long, ungainly strands of seaweed. Relentlessly, the waves banged away in the distance. They were gray and fierce, but no longer sinister. Bound for Baja, the hurricane had passed by far out at sea. Along the Yelapa coast its force had been subdued to only occasional gusts of tropical rain.

"We can still make the climb. The path will be safe," Felicita assured Chantal.

Chantal gathered up her clothes. "I'll get dressed." After a moment, she asked, "How is the señor?"

Felicita rolled her eyes. "He did not eat breakfast. I do not think he and Roberto and José had a good night last night." She pantomimed the raising of a glass to her mouth.

"You mean they drank too much tequila?" Felicita nodded. Chantal was surprised. She had never known Simon to drink heavily. If he had, she hoped he had a classic hangover. Last night he'd been insensitive toward her. Nevertheless, Chantal realized she had no options concerning Simon. She alone would have to take responsibility for her emotions. She couldn't allow Simon Bryce to tear her apart this way. Of course, she had left herself wide open by admitting she loved him. She remembered his casually expressed and cruelly returned reply. So he found her captivating? Quite a nice little item, wasn't she? A delicious morsel, a pert kid. Chantal the woman was not allowed to exist.

She stamped into the bathroom. Felicita called after her, "You must eat, regain your strength. I have told you that Señor Bryce did not eat his breakfast, but he did a very strange thing." Chantal peered curiously around the door as Felicita continued. "He ran along the beach, and he did a lot of . . . what is the word in English? Calisthenics?"

The idea of Simon doing push-ups and vigorous exercise on a remote Mexican beach suddenly filled Chantal with laughter. His body must be getting even with him. She felt almost cheerful about that. "I am hungry," she told Felicita. "I'll be out very soon."

Since she had eaten nothing the day before, the good smell of cooking led her to the table in the dining area. Simon and José were nowhere about. She was glad of that. A subdued-looking Roberto served breakfast. She told him it was delicious. He brightened at her compliment and said she was having Omelet Sonora—two eggs filled with avocado and cheese. "We cover it with red chili sauce and serve it with *chilaquiles,* Mexican beans, garni and assorted fruits," he concluded happily. "We are known here for our food. The Americans who camp out by the lagoon get tired of their own cooking, and they often come to my hotel. The way they dress, some of them look poor, but they have plenty of American dollars."

"Who are they?"

Roberto shrugged. "They come and they stay for months sometimes. A boat arrived with another one this morning."

"Really?" Chantal stopped eating. "How did the boat get through the surf? Was it rescued by the canoe?"

"Oh, yes." Roberto sat down with Chantal and poured himself a cup of coffee. "The boat that brought the young lady was a much better one than José's. It was Fidelio Herra's boat from Vallarta. He has already left."

"Who was the young lady?"

"I don't know. She didn't come here. She went to the lagoon. Maybe she knew some of the campers there. I would not recognize her if I saw her again. Not much to look at. She walked by me, but there was nothing special about her. Like one pelican in a flight of pelicans."

"Maybe she has a beautiful soul, Roberto." Chantal smiled. "It's not right to judge by appearances. Did José's boat make it through the night?"

"He brought it ashore."

Chantal raised her coffee cup. "How?"

"He swam through the waves to get it. He and Señor Bryce."

The coffee cup clattered into its saucer. Chantal's eyes widened. "Both of them swam out? You mean they've done all that this morning? I was under the impression Simon and José weren't feeling too well."

Roberto gave a massive shrug. "You mean because of a little too much tequila last night? These are *men*, señorita."

Chantal didn't blink. She picked up a spear of pineapple. She would like to have pushed it into Roberto's egotistical male face. This was the proper habitat for Simon after all. He was probably having a great time running around on the beach, flexing his muscles and ignoring the devilish hangover she'd wished on him.

"You're a man too, Roberto. Why aren't you out there raising a little hell this morning?"

"I'm a businessman, señorita. I have to prepare for the Americans who are coming for a feast tonight. They didn't eat during the storm."

Chantal stood up, flicking crumbs off her front. "I'm ready to go. Where is everybody? I thought we were going to make the climb to the village."

"The señor is waiting for you outside."

There was no way she could win this macho game. She felt like glaring at Roberto, but that would have been stupid of her. He had no way of knowing why she felt bad.

"I'm off, Roberto."

The hotel owner stood up and bowed politely. "Have a good day," he said, using the American vernacular he'd learned. He wondered why the young woman, who had seemed so gloomy, almost angry, while eating her breakfast, gave him such an amused smile now.

"You too, Roberto."

Felicita, in blouse and skirt and sturdy canvas shoes similar to those she'd found for Chantal, was at the foot of the wooden stairs as Chantal came down to the sandy beach. Already the humid air had caught up with Chantal. She wiped the perspiration from around her neck and the inside of her shirt collar.

"Do you have an extra bandana?" she asked Felicita. The Mexican woman's black hair was neatly bound back under a red kerchief. Felicita took a scarf from around her neck and handed it to Chantal. "Thank you," she said, and tied her hair away from her face and neck as Felicita had done with hers. She looked up toward the cliff. "That's where we're going?"

Felicita nodded. "We'll meet Señor Bryce. He's gone ahead."

"He would—of course—go ahead," Chantal agreed pleasantly. "And we women follow behind. Isn't that right?"

"But why not, señorita?"

"Exactly. Why not? That's the way things are done in this world."

Felicita looked puzzled at this strange remark. The American woman was certainly in a peculiar mood.

Simon was waiting for them at the foot of the cliff. He was wearing the cotton vest and the flapping white trousers, which were now fitted securely about his trim waist with a broad leather belt.

Simon's "Good morning" to Chantal was like a brisk handshake. He asked her if she had slept well and then, as though disinterested in her reply, turned away. The three of them began their climb along the narrow, twisting path that led steeply up the face of the cliff.

By the time they reached the top, the sun had come out from behind the clouds. The sea was no longer a furious gray. When Simon glanced back at Chantal to give her a hand up around a particularly rocky promontory, she saw that his eyes were the slate color of the sea. A feeling of self-disgust rose within her. She told herself she shouldn't be noticing the color of Simon's eyes, or the width of his shoulders, or the long, lean stride of his legs. Quickly she dropped back, so that Felicita was now walking between her and Simon.

Finally Felicita took the lead. When the path widened sufficiently, she and Simon walked side by side through the gorge ahead. Felicita began to explain the area's ancient history. Simon listened intently. Chantal trailed behind. When she turned to look down at the beach far below, she could not help uttering an involuntary gasp of delight. The sand was a pinkish white along the curving crescent of the bay. The sun spread rosy-golden light and dark shadows.

Inland a little way, Chantal could see the waters of the small, lakelike lagoon, and beyond, among the trees, the outline of several tents. This must be where the Americans camped. People were moving about down there, accompanied by frolicking dogs. One figure stood alone, apart from the rest, apparently looking up in the direction of the cliffside. Chantal could not tell whether this individual was a slim boy or a young woman. Hastily she turned away, aware that she'd been admiring the view for too long. She didn't want Simon and Felicita to travel too far in front of her.

When after a few minutes she had not caught up with them, she grew anxious. Thick-leafed, low-growing trees and hanging vines obscured the path ahead. Chantal passed a huge rock that towered above her. The path appeared to end abruptly here. A faint trail led to the right. She followed it until she came to a fast-flowing stream. Flat rocks provided stepping-stones across the water. Certainly there was no other way to go. This had to be the way to the village.

Chantal hesitated. She supposed she should call to the others, but she didn't want to risk making a fool of herself. She must be only a few steps behind Simon and Felicita. It was just that up here the undergrowth was so tangled, so thick and lush, she couldn't see very far. Nor could she hear the roar and mumble of the sea. Only unfamiliar jungle sounds remained: cracklings, high cricket chirps, the skirling cries of hidden birds.

There was nothing to do but go forward. She did so, taking care to be as sure-footed as possible crossing the stream. Even though the water appeared to be not very deep, it was swift. She didn't want to fall. That would be a clumsy embarrassment.

She negotiated the last rock and made a quick, leaping lunge toward the far bank. The ground was more slippery than she had expected. Her rubber-soled canvas shoes gripped wet earth for only one precarious second. She twisted her body sideways to regain her balance. Not quite enough. Her arms flew up to catch the tree vines that swayed overhead. Here she succeeded, but barely. Suspended over the stream, she made another desperate thrust toward dry ground, but with this attempt, the rope vine gave way. Chantal crashed down on the seat of her pants in shallow water. There was an ominous ripping sound. She looked down to investigate. Fortunately, it was not the back seam of her jeans, but only the inseam that showed a bare strip of flesh. Well, to hell with it. Chantal got down on her knees, clawed her way up the bank, then stood erect, only to turn and face a tall figure striding along the opposite side of the stream in the direction from which she had just come.

"For God's sake, Chantal, what happened to you?"

"What do you think happened?"

"You took a bath," Simon said wryly.

They stared at each other—Chantal indignant and muddy on one side of the stream, a surprised Simon on the opposite bank. She had seen alarm in his face before his expression blanked.

"What are you doing over there?" Chantal demanded. "Weren't you and Felicita ahead of me?"

Simon didn't reply. Patiently he stepped across the flat rocks to reach Chantal's side. A quick glance took in her bedraggled appearance, the long tear along the seam of her jeans.

He started to speak, then stopped, his tanned face oddly suffused with a bright flush of color. Chantal's eyes narrowed. "You're laughing at me. You think it's funny!" Her voice choked. "Go ahead, then, laugh! Don't strangle yourself on my account! Let it all out!"

She would have given Simon a stiff push if Felicita hadn't come hurrying down the same side of the bank from which Simon had appeared.

"Señorita, why are you over there? Did you lose us? Oh, I'm sorry. I was talking to Señor Bryce. It is my fault."

"It is not your fault, Felicita. There's nothing to be sorry about." Chantal spoke in a dignified tone. "I must have missed the path. Where was it?"

"Around that big rock back there. Oh, I am so sorry," Felicita repeated.

"Forget it. I said it wasn't your fault." Her leg hurt, but she wouldn't let them know that. At least Simon hadn't laughed, though she assumed he'd been very close to it.

Chantal let him help her back across the rocks. Again they set out, Felicita worrying and fussing and looking back at Chantal, who tried not to limp, knowing that Simon was walking close behind her. She didn't want his sympathy or his scorn.

They came to the huge rock that Felicita had spoken of. The three of them now circled back around it. In front of them lay the tidy trail that led toward the thatched dwellings of the village people.

Chickens scratched the ground and clucked nervously. Tiny pigs grunted and ran squealing inside huts whose floors were simply the bare earth. Felicita was greeted warmly by the natives. Out of doorways along the way, children, goats and small burros peered with curiosity at the two strangers.

They continued along the trail until they had left the village behind. Felicita halted and pointed. "You see? Down that slope, on the cliff. Aefollo's house." She looked searchingly at Simon and Chantal. "I'll go back now. You'll be able to find your way when you're ready to return."

The view was breathtaking. Soaring straight out were miles of blue sky and blue sea, with occasional scudding clouds above. Aefollo and his wife and their many children lived in a huge one-room aerie perched on what appeared to be the edge of the world.

"Why should Aefollo ever leave this?" Simon asked, and Chantal understood his wonderment.

In reply, Chantal sighed and whispered, "I'll stay right here while you go and talk to him." Her leg no longer hurt, but she knew she was unable to remove her gaze from the sight of this expanse of air and space. She could even see the rounding of the earth's curve on the horizon.

Simon looked at Chantal. Something of this solitary vista with its otherworldly magic seemed to have touched him too. "Chantal . . ." he said, then checked himself, his lips tightening. "Please wait here," he finished softly. "I don't want to intrude on Aefollo any longer than I have to. I'll be back." He hesitated. "And, Chantal, you wait for me."

The deeply husky tone in his voice drew her eyes back from their dreamy contemplation of the quiet blue distance spread before her. "I'll wait for you," Chantal promised. "Yes, Simon."

It was going to be all right between them. Fear, anger, suspicion, arrogance—all had vanished in this place of lonely beauty and pale light. Unexpectedly, Simon bent down and gently kissed Chantal's lips. It might have been an apology. "Don't move."

Chantal watched his figure disappear down the slope toward Aefollo's dwelling. They were part of this secluded majesty of nature. Both were possessed by its beauty, captured by its vision. Chantal knew that she and Simon were one again.

It was Felicita's intent to return ahead of Simon and Chantal. She had led them to Aefollo, but they could find their own way back to Yelapa. She guessed they might want to be alone, this tall man and the young woman with the strange, light eyes that could hide nothing of what lay in her vulnerable heart. Felicita suspected these two were lovers.

As she walked down the cliff path and came within sight of the bay, Felicita was surprised to see the woman who had arrived that morning in Fidelio Herra's boat climbing slowly and purposefully up the cliff. When the woman came abreast of Felicita, she halted, shook back her hair and wiped the sweat from her forehead and upper lip. "Howdy. Wish I had a bandana like yours."

Felicita greeted the stranger with a nod but did not reply to this attempt at conversation. She was about to pass when the woman continued. "You had a friend with you this morning. She was wearing a red bandana too. Where is she?"

Felicita looked blank. "I don't know who you mean, señorita."

"You climbed up here with some people this morning. I saw the three of you from the beach."

An expressionless Felicita shook her head. "I do not know." She dipped her head in a farewell gesture and walked on.

Sissy Purdue looked after her. "Stupid Indian!" she muttered to herself, but she said it thoughtfully. She felt inside her denim shirt. The small camera with its handy zoom telephoto lens was safely strapped to her chest. She looked around her. They were still up there, somewhere. . . .

The interview with Aefollo satisfactorily concluded, Simon went back up the slope to find Chantal. She was sitting in the long grass near the brow of the cliff. She regarded him gravely, then a smile widened on her full lips. It was sunny and welcoming. Simon dropped down beside her. He told her about his talk with the Mexican cinematographer and about the deal they'd made. When he finished, they stared at each other, a deep and involuntary possession locking their gaze together.

Serenity, friendship, desire shimmered between them. Chantal's black lashes, gold-flecked in the sun, swept downward to hide the luminous light shining in her eyes. Simon took her chin in his hand, forcing her gaze back to his. Her spine tingled, her breath shuddered with the knowledge that his touch was electrifying to her, that it spoke a long-familiar language of the body. And now, because he had made her look at him, her whole being was drowning in the dark eyes of the enchanter.

Afterward she could barely recall how their lips had met, how his body had folded over hers, how together they had rolled into the seclusion of the nearby hollow of earth in which they found themselves secure from all eyes. Chantal knew only that their place of rendezvous was peaceful and that the heavy scent of exotic wood surrounded them. The blaze of sun was gone; only random sun motes sifted through the shadows of heavily leafed trees and vines that grew thick above them. These same shadows seemed to shift from light to dark, seemed to create billowing green waves of movement in the grass beneath them and in the foliage overhead; movement that had nothing to do with the sea and the earth.

They did not undress. They had neither the time nor the inclination to do so. There was the sound of rough metal unzipping, and her pants were shoved down. His hands moved up to unbutton her shirt and then moved around her back to unfasten her bra. Her breasts swelled free to belong to Simon's seeking hands and his searching lips. The broad leather belt he'd worn lay beside them, and she knew his trousers were released when his flesh joined hers. Her breasts, thighs and inner being began to tremble in rippling compositions of erotic delight.

It was a magical coupling, not to be explored with words, but to be savored with the body. Chantal raised her shirt-sleeved arms so that she could press her hands behind Simon's neck and bring his mouth down to hers. She tasted, licked swiftly with quick little tongue flicks, then fastened her lips on his, gliding back and forth in a sweet, slow rhythm. Her knees, only partially covered by the pushed-down jeans, flexed upward on either side of Simon's body until that last convulsive moment when her limbs scissored across his rump to bring him closer, closer, into herself. The cry she uttered—low, moaning, intense—shocked the earth around them. It was a day of conquest, a day of the conquered. A scintillating, remorseless, passionate, marvelous day.

When it was over, Simon wrapped Chantal in his arms and rose to his feet. He zipped her jeans, fastened her bra, buttoned her shirt and tucked it into her waistband. He straightened his own clothes. Never once taking his gaze from her, he smoothed back the tousled auburn hair from her flushed face and handed her the red bandana. She contemplated it and then slowly, with dry amusement, tied it around his upper arm. She knew he would never understand her romantic notion that he was her knight, her man-at-arms.

Simon, puzzled by her action, took off the bandana and refastened it about her silken hair. "I don't need any ornament," he said, "but you need this scarf to protect your hair. Come on, we'd better find our way back." He paused, looking closely at her with affectionate concern, "Are you all right?" She nodded. "Sure?" he pressed.

"Yes, Simon, I'm fine. I feel great. All I need is a swim in the ocean." With the palm of her hand she wiped away the gathering perspiration from her throat and face.

"Will a shower do?"

"Can you produce one?"

"Try me." He took her hand. They walked rapidly up the slight slope, gazed one more time at Aefollo's world of solitude that had brought them both so much delight, then started back along the trail toward the village.

They were halfway there when the sky darkened spectacularly and once more emptied its burden.

The rain left them both drenched to the skin and turned their walk into a slog along the muddy path. They passed quickly through the village, eliciting no curiosity this time. When they reached the enormous rock that had earlier blocked Chantal's way, the rain ceased abruptly.

This time it was Simon who turned her in the direction of the stream. She followed his lead as they walked upstream, pushing aside damp, mossy branches, heavy tree boughs, giant leaves and snakelike vines.

Chantal was astonished when they came in sight of a high leap of wet rocks with frothing water cascading over them into a stone basin below. "How did you know about this?" she exclaimed.

"Our friend Felicita told me it was here. During the proper tourist season this waterfall has many visitors. It's considered quite an attraction. Come on, strip—if you want to take that shower I promised you."

Simon was already out of his trousers and cotton vest. Without a loss of balance, he untied his boot laces and then slid down into the basin. He was momentarily hidden from Chantal's view beneath the rushing white spume. Removing her own clothing, Chantal poised on the edge. Anxious for Simon's safety, not knowing the depth of the water in the basin, she tried to peer through the watery veil to find him. Relieved, she saw him rise to the surface and push the hair off his forehead with both hands. Opening his eyes wide, he admired Chantal's truly breathtaking nakedness until the moment when, giving only a faint squeal of alarm, she let herself slide down the smooth rock into his arms.

Theirs was a Gauguin waterfall of delight as

Chantal clasped her arms around Simon's waist to steady herself. Her fingers moved along the taut muscles of his back, gently massaging its strong column. He laughed, lowering his face to hers. "I'll give you exactly thirty years to stop doing that." Happily, wonderingly, she thought, Does he really know what he's saying?

Simon reached down to search for the fine sand at the bottom of the stream bed. He brought up a handful and gently scrubbed her body with it, then scrubbed his own. The sun came out from behind the clouds to remain with them while they dried themselves with the huge tropical leaves they had picked from the overhanging boughs.

Standing naked, they gazed at each other. They planted intimate kisses in unpredictable places, and with eagerly seeking fingers they exchanged and explored chaste and unchaste caresses over every tingling surface of their bodies. Before another wildfire of emotion could sweep them into even closer contact, they separated and began to dress.

So involved were Chantal and Simon with each other, they heard nothing unusual. The jungle was busy with what seemed to be its own natural sounds on this late afternoon. Parrots screamed, small animals chattered, clickings and cracklings erupted in the undergrowth. Little spatters of raindrops that had been left behind by the storm appeared to scatter lightly upon the leaf-strewn earth. Still the sun shone, highlighting the nude couple as they slowly clothed themselves following their ardently unconventional embraces.

Ripened tropical fruits plopped to the ground. Tree pods burst open unexpectedly to spray their seeds to the jungle floor. Here there was no wither-

ing of life, only a constant renewal, like kisses on
ripe mouths.

Seemingly there was no foreign sound to distract
or to alert either Simon or Chantal. There was no
human footfall to cause them to be concerned for
their privacy.

Finally, fully clothed, they joined hands and
started down the path to the hotel.

Silence, patience and animal wariness had paid off
for Sissy Purdue.

She congratulated herself for just having made a
bundle of money as well as a good-sized bonus. Kiki
Dalton had so thoroughly described the man and
woman that Sissy had known at once that she had
the right quarry in her camera sight.

Earlier, snakelike, she had followed the pair.
When she had met the stoic Felicita, she'd felt
certain it was Felicita who had been their guide.
Sissy had gone on then, stopping just short of the
village.

Disappointed at having seen no one about, the
young woman had retraced her steps to the barrier
rock. Good luck alone had pointed her toward the
stream and the waterfall that had been described to
her by her newfound friends at the lagoon campsite.
At least she could take some background pictures of
nature at its most primitive. From a vantage point
inside the stream's heavy jungle growth that overlooked the waterfall, she'd considered several options. Actually, she'd been planning for the night to
come. When her camper friends went off to their
dinner at Roberto's, she would stay behind and wait
for a felicitous time when the two lovers might stroll
on the beach or bathe in the surf. Sissy had even

been prepared to peer into windows. If she couldn't take pictures, at least she might be able to observe some action.

She had had no idea she was about to capture both!

Miraculously, Simon and Chantal had appeared on the path, moving in her direction. Sissy had frozen and become part of the jungle. The clicking of her camera had merged with the crackling sounds of growth and decay and rebirth.

As had been planned earlier, that night the Americans from the camp had dinner at Roberto's inn. Roberto served plain fare—vegetable casseroles, bean and rice dishes, fresh fish from the sea. Fruit juice and a little Mexican wine were the only drinks. The guests' tastes were spare, though some of them wore expensive Pucci pants and handmade sandals purchased in Italy.

Sissy stayed behind in the lagoon tents to tend a couple of infants who were part of the affluent commune. She knew that even if she did meet the man and woman whose naked images were imprinted on her film, they would have no inkling she had been within a few yards of them that afternoon. It was the Mexican woman who had been their guide whom Sissy did not want to confront again.

At dawn Sissy Purdue would watch for Fidelio Herra's fast motorboat, which Kiki had promised would return then. Sissy had been given a bare twenty-four hours to accomplish her purpose.

The amazing factor in all of this was that Sissy had succeeded so well in doing what she had set out to do. If she had failed to capture the compromising pictures, she knew she would have been paid anyway. But with two people as passionately involved as this pair seemed to be, Sissy surmised that an episode of the nature she had witnessed hadn't been so unlikely. At any rate, for the first time in her scruffy, unambitious life, Sissy Purdue realized she'd been just plain lucky.

Late the next morning, José, with the help of some locals, pulled his boat off the beach and set it into a calming sea. Again, as at Puerto Vallarta two days earlier, he had to wait for the tardy appearance of his passengers.

In her room, Chantal lay sleeping soundly in Simon's arms. Simon was awake. His arm holding Chantal felt unable to move, but she was such an agreeable burden that he didn't mind. Except, of course, the sunlight slitting through the wooden shutters told him that José would be growing impatient to return to Vallarta. It was a great deal later than the hour they had planned to leave.

Simon awakened Chantal with kisses. She sat up, her sleepy smile remembering the dark of the night before, yet a night that had held such bright hours for them both.

"Devil," she whispered, and bent down and kissed his chest, the place where his heart beat. She would like to have called him "lover." That was forbidden.

"Heave-ho." He tossed her out of bed and just as swiftly sprang up when she landed on her feet. He caught her close to him. They stood in an ardent embrace, limb, thigh, torso, lips straining together. "Quick, now," Simon ordered. He reminded her they mustn't keep José waiting too long. Both began to dress rapidly.

Chantal wondered to herself what would be waiting for them back in Vallarta. Would it be a resumption of cool indifference between them? Would they work a few days on the script, which she'd almost forgotten about, and then return to California? Would it all become a dispassionate, professional alliance once again?

She recalled her father's telling her that no one had control over life's punctuations, that all one could do was to behave well while dodging emotional flak.

As she packed her bag, Chantal mused, Please let the other fellow behave well too. Let Simon learn my worth, let him appreciate me, love me. . . . Was it possible? Could she hope?

Simon's thoughts were his own. They centered on Chantal, but not entirely. His main purpose in bringing her with him to Yelapa had been to put distance between her and her brother and Kiki. It seemed almost incomprehensible to him that Chantal was unaware of Jay's notoriety. But then, the newspaper she read refused to carry advertisements for porno films. They were a subworld of which she obviously knew nothing. She'd find out sooner or later, but Simon didn't want it to be just now, while she was with him in Mexico. He didn't want to have to face this kind of complication.

Upon their arrival in Puerto Vallarta, José's boat and its passengers were met by Guillermo and the sedan.

"You are to call this number, señor." Guillermo handed Simon a slip of paper. "The message came yesterday."

Simon gave the paper to Chantal. She recognized the United States area code and the studio's number.

"The world is knocking on our door," Simon remarked. "At any rate, our business here is finished. Aefollo's word is as good as his signature on a contract. My agreement with the Mexican financiers was concluded before you came down here."

Chantal's smile was a little sad. "So we go?"

Simon's eyes held hers for a fleeting instant. "We go," he replied. And that was all. Reservations were made, plane tickets were secured, the luggage was packed, farewells were said.

On their way to the airport, Chantal thought, Puerto Vallarta is done with—as though it had never been. As though happiness had never touched either her or Simon, as though the pull of the sea's ancient tides had never drawn them passionately into each other's arms. All over. She could not look back over her shoulder at Banderas Bay.

Chapter Sixteen

Dean Davison met them at the Los Angeles airport. While Chantal sat silently between the two men in the front seat of Davison's car, Dean filled Simon in on the business and personal happenings at the studio. The younger man's memory bank unreeled statistics, grosses and gossip. He told them Cesar Williams was out of the hospital, out of trouble and being nursed by a repentant wife. Cesar was ready to function again as screenwriter on *The Assaulters*.

Glancing at Chantal beside him, Simon said, "The time in Mexico wasn't wasted, believe me. We've put together some excellent pages, Dean—mostly action scenes that place the story well ahead of where it was when we left here. Of course, we'll need additional dialogue from Cesar. You think he's really in shape to finish the first draft?"

"No doubt about it. I've seen him and talked to him several times. So has Larette."

Simon looked thoughtful, and little else was said.

They drove north on the freeway in the afternoon sunlight. Chantal pointed out the turnoff to Dean and gave him directions to the Villa Apartments.

After Dean had parked the car, he removed Chantal's suitcase and tote bag from the trunk. The trio stood on the sidewalk. There were handshakes all around. Chantal waited, a small figure in wrinkled pants and shirt and jacket looking up at Simon, who held the script folder in his hand. He was taking part of her away with him, and that part was more than just the excellent professional work she'd done on *The Assaulters*. It was heart and memory and the adventure of life itself.

"I'll take Chantal's stuff upstairs," Dean offered.

His hand already on the handle of Chantal's suitcase, Simon hesitated. Then, he straightened, shoved his hand into his pocket and said, "Fine, Dean, if you will. Chantal, get a good rest, and thank you again for your help." There was a pause before he added, "Thank you for everything. I'll call you."

That last phrase was worth more than anything he could have said to her. *If* Simon really would call. *If* his remark was not just a politic farewell. So many people said, "I'll call you," or "We'll get together for lunch." And that was the end of it. One never heard again.

When Chantal and Dean arrived at the door of her apartment, the phone inside was ringing steadily. After a quick goodbye to Dean, Chantal undid the double locks on the door, pushed her luggage inside and hurried across the living room to pick up the instrument.

"Thank God you're there," Ardis rasped. "I've been calling and calling. When did you get in?"

"Just this minute. What is it? Where are you?"

"At EdgeMont, where else? Chantal, how fast can you get out here?"

"I'm bushed. I just got off the plane. What's the emergency? Are Millicent and Jason okay?"

"Yes, but there's a crisis."

Chantal sat down with a thump. "When isn't there one? Take a deep breath, Ardie. So will I. Tell me what's the matter."

"I'm in the library. I'll have to talk low. I hope nobody picks up one of the extensions."

"Go on."

"It's partly about Boy. You know he's never been physical about anything in his life, particularly in regard to business dealings. But he and Ric Milland have reached a low toleration point where it's push and shove. I mean that literally. It may have been your fault, Chantal."

"My fault?"

"Ric's pretty mad at you. He told me right out that something you did or said to him has made him determined to have Jason sell EdgeMont to him. I wouldn't think Ric had it in him, but he's gotten hold of money and some foreign investors. Look, I don't mind having the citrus groves sold and torn out, but it's got to be Boy who does it, not Ric."

"Ric and I had a little misunderstanding the last time we talked, that's all. Aren't you making this whole thing sound melodramatic, Ardis?"

"Is a black eye melodrama?"

Chantal was silent for a moment. "Who has a black eye?"

"Boy. He and Ric pushed and shoved, like I said. It happened in the bar at the Bear Gulch Inn. Boy got a bruised lip and a black eye. And everybody else who was there got an eyeful. It was awful."

Chantal felt like screaming. Either in laughter or in disbelief, she wasn't sure which. "What about your M.B.A. from Wharton? Can't you get Erika Talbott to come back to EdgeMont and put a civilized edge on things and teach the fellows some sanity?"

Ardis's voice rose in a long squeal across the wire. "But that's it! She's never left. She's still here. I'm furious with her. We don't speak. She's running the mile every day with Jason. It takes them hours to run it, obviously, because they disappear for that long every day."

"Are you telling me that all those vitamins Jason's been taking have finally shot him right into a wild mid-life affair with the vice president of Boy's construction company? I don't believe it of Father. Erika might be trying, yes. Boy must have promised her something special if she succeeds in talking Jason into a sale. Could it be a percentage of his new *and* profitable land corporation? Or another title? You should know, Ardis."

"That's right, Chantal, blame Boy. Blame me. You would."

"What is Mother doing about all this? And where's Oliver Larch?" Chantal asked grimly.

"Oliver realized the state of the economy out here wasn't doing him any good, so he split. Mother sits upstairs in the guest room at that desk, scribbling on those yellow pads Oliver left behind. I can't talk to anybody, least of all to her. Please come, Chantal— as fast as you can."

"I'd better get hold of Jay. If he's back from Mexico."

A snort of scorn came through the wire. "What can Jay do except send a check? Who did you see him with? Kiki?"

"Yes, with Kiki." Chantal took a deep breath. "I'll be there, Ardis. I have to hang up now."

Chantal sat by the phone, her mind circling through a maze of complicated emotions. First there was shocked disbelief that her father could be carrying on with Erika Talbott, though Chantal had certainly been present the night that Erika had made her first tentative feint at Jason on the east porch. Chantal wondered about Millicent's isolation upstairs in the guest room. Because of Erika? Hardly. Millicent had always been accepting of the male's imperfection, especially Jason's. Lastly, Chantal was amazed that Boyd Farrell and Ric Milland had actually involved themselves in a physical altercation—that is, if an overwrought Ardis hadn't been exaggerating.

Chantal groaned softly to herself. She'd wait to call Jay. Or not call him at all. She walked into the kitchen, put a kettle of water on the stove for tea, looked around, relieved to find herself once more in familiar surroundings. Even though it wouldn't be for long.

Someone knocked at the door. "Hi, who is it?" Chantal called out.

"Susan."

Chantal opened the door to the Villa's youthful manager. "Come on in. I just got home and I'm leaving right away again. It's good to see you."

"Good to see you too, Chan." Susan glanced around a little nervously. "If you're on your way out, my news will keep. Where to this time?"

"EdgeMont. My sister called. Anguish time as usual, but I think it can be settled. What's on your mind?"

"Will you be back soon? We'll talk then."

"All right, unless you're in some kind of difficulty I can help with. If you are, I'll hang around."

"No, no. It's nothing to do with me exactly. See you when you get back."

Susan turned away and bolted precipitately down the hall. Chantal closed the door with a frown. She hoped the owners weren't planning to replace Susan as manager. Susan did spend rather a lot of time reading Tarot cards for the tenants. What other stupid move could they be contemplating? Oh, damn, I've got it! Chantal thought. They're going to raise the rent!

Showered, dressed, packed again, Chantal dialed Simon's office.

Marilou answered, her tone confidential. "He's at home, Chantal. By the way, everyone here—I mean Larette and Dean and Moira—is terribly pleased at what you did on the script while you were in Mexico. They've all read the new pages." Her voice dropped lower. "I expect Cesar Williams won't hand you an Oscar. But you know men. Especially male writers where a woman writer is concerned. They're jealous studio politicians."

"You mean they want to keep the 'old boy' network intact?" Chantal was amused. "Marilou, I have to go back to the country. Do you still have the EdgeMont phone number at Rancho Cucamonga?"

"Yes, sure. Right on the Rolodex."

Chantal hung up. She hadn't asked for Simon's number at home because she knew that Marilou wouldn't hand it out. Fortunately, on that long-ago day of wind and fire when Simon had called and left his unlisted number on her phone machine, she'd put it in her address book. She looked it up and dialed Simon's house. There was no answer.

Three weeks later Chantal wondered if she'd dreamed the interlude in Mexico. It was now mid-August, or mid-hell, she wasn't sure which. Simon was constantly on her mind, but there was no bridge of communication between them, and certainly nothing resolved. She'd called him once to tell him she was still in Rancho Cucamonga and that if he needed her to do anything else on the script, she could come back to town.

His voice had been friendly but remote. "Cesar's working his tail off to make up for lost time. He's turning in some good stuff. You'd be pleased, I'm sure, and I'd like to have you read it. Why are you out there, by the way?"

Had he been about to ask her to return? While her heart had thudded, Chantal had tried to sound casual. "A family screw-up that needs straightening."

"When it gets unscrewed and you're back in town, give the office a ring. I've got a London call on the other line. 'Bye, Chantal."

They had both hung up at the same time.

Chantal closed her eyes tight in painful memory. I think I hate him! She cried silently. Mexico, for the most part, had been a beautiful idyll, yet one with strange, dark undercurrents, like the wash of black sand under clear waters.

Her one phone conversation with Simon had been terrible. There was never another one. The knowledge was tough, but Chantal faced it. Simon knew where she was. He'd simply chosen not to call her back. Chantal was wise enough to realize that dredging up every excuse she could think of didn't change things one iota. Busy or not, preoccupied or not, when a man wants to call a woman, he does. When a man wants to find a certain woman, he does. It was a lot of bull to think that sometimes modern men are timid and vulnerable and supersensitive, and that they're just sitting there waiting to hear from a woman. Some men, maybe—freaks. Certainly not Simon, who knew what he wanted and how to get it. He wouldn't fear any kind of turndown. The other type of man Chantal didn't want. If Simon had an urge to speak to her, to find out how she was and when she was returning to the city, he'd pick up the phone and call her. Stated simply, he hadn't done that because he hadn't wanted to. There was no real interest on his part. He'd once told her to call him a bastard if she felt like it. "Bastard!" It felt good to say it out loud.

Chantal went searching for her father and found him sitting at his desk in the den, totaling up figures on his pocket calculator. In the weeks past, there'd been little eye contact between Jason and his family. And especially since the morning a few days ago when Erika, for whatever reason, had packed her briefcase and her gear into the station wagon and driven off.

"Dad, let's talk."

Jason looked up, his gaze not quite focusing on Chantal. His eyes were red; some of the glisten had gone out of his healthy-looking skin. He ran his fingers over the ledger on the desk in front of him. For the first time, Chantal noticed the brown age spots freckling the back of his hand.

Jason's reply was tangential, a digression that wandered and appeared to have nothing to do with Chantal. "The leaking roof at Hancock Park needs replacing. Just got the estimate in the mail. Seventeen thousand dollars to do the work—half in advance, the balance when the crew is one-third through. Seeing that the roofer wants his money before completion of the job, my reputation with the tradespeople must have preceded me."

Jason suddenly faced Chantal directly. "You want to talk about that? My credit's overextended at the bank, with my associates and with my stockbroker, who used to be my friend. The taxes on this place are delinquent. The penalty is interest on top of interest. Is that what you want to talk about?"

Chantal had never known him to be bitter, or to make such scalding admissions. She was heartsick.

Jason had swiveled around in his chair. Still meeting his daughter's eye, he went on. "Or is it that you want to talk to a fifty-two-year-old fool who's been trying to run a romantic footrace with a woman who will only take the old runner seriously if he agrees to her business proposition? Which is to sell EdgeMont. Otherwise the whole affair is—what did she call it?—a giggle and a hoot."

It was a relief to see Jason looking exceedingly angry. Chantal couldn't have stood it if he'd appeared hurt, with his pride ground into dust.

"That what you want to talk about?" he asked aggressively.

That wasn't exactly it, but at the moment she couldn't think of anything better to say than, "Please go upstairs and see Millicent, will you, Dad?" Chantal was finding it hard to get the other words out, the real words she'd come in here to say.

Jason shook his head. "I can't see your mother. You know she moved out of our bedroom a month ago. She doesn't want me near her."

"I don't believe that, and neither do you."

"What is it *you* want, Chantal? 'Let's talk,' you said."

Here it was. She'd have to speak right here and now! She'd been thinking of nothing else for the last forty-eight hours. Even Simon Bryce had receded somewhat from her mind under the enormity of the decision she'd made. At times there had to be big compromises in life. It was possible she and Jay had been wrong about holding onto EdgeMont in the face of what was happening all around them.

Chantal didn't believe in preambles. She gritted her teeth and spoke out. "Dad, sell half this property to Boy and let's go home to Hancock Park. If you do that, we'll have enough loot to pay all the bills, get your life sorted out again and fix things like that damn roof. It'll fix a lot of other things too. Boy will be satisfied, and he and Ardis can start planning their wedding. To hold onto the past never did matter to Mother. What's important is that you and she are happy."

Jason was so silent that Chantal didn't think he'd ever speak again. She tried to swallow the lump of fear in her throat. My God, what had she done? Jumped up and down on the graves of Jason's ancestors?

Chantal plunged on. "If you won't consider what I've just suggested as a practical solution, I'll go upstairs and make Mother listen to me."

"Whoa, there!" Jason rose slowly and advanced toward his daughter. He was limping rather noticeably.

Chantal's voice was full of quick concern. "What happened to your leg, Jason?"

"Nothing big. Deterioration due to age, I suppose. Too much running, too much of trying to make an impression on certain people. Now! What was that extraordinary statement you just made? Did I hear you, of all people, say sell EdgeMont?"

She couldn't bear to repeat the words, though she had meant them intensely. Before Jason could put out a hand to stop her, Chantal whirled away and ran out of the den.

As she hurried toward the stairs, she had time to consider that during these last weeks this house had been a shelter, wise and tolerant enough to contain them all. It was as though EdgeMont's perceptions were alive, understanding of its occupants and the crossfire of their emotions. Chantal paused in her flight up the stairs. There'd been that amorous situation between Jason and Erika. There'd been the machinations of Boyd Farrell, plus the watchful intensity of a suspicious Ardis. Presiding over all, never once letting down her guard, was Millicent, a gracious though preoccupied hostess. She might have removed herself from Jason's bed, but she'd been faultlessly polite to Jason's "friend."

Chantal reached the head of the stairs and banged on the door of the guest room, off-limits to the rest of the family.

"Ma, open up! It's me. Let me come in and talk to you."

The door opened. "You don't have to make noises like that, dear."

Chantal charged by Millicent, then turned to face her mother. Cautiously she studied the older woman's bland expression. "Are you squirreled away up here because you're angry about what's been going on? If you are, there's no need. After all, Erika Talbott lit out several days ago and Father is over his—" Chantal paused. "I don't know what your generation would call it. It wasn't an affair. Let's be generous. I guess you'd say Jason is over his . . . fling?"

"Do you think that woman accomplished her purpose? Did she talk him into selling EdgeMont? Because I suspect that's what it was all about."

"No! *I'm* the one who brought up the sale to Jason."

"You did that, Chantal?" Millicent Jerrold looked startled.

"I wasn't very vigorous in my sales pitch, I'll admit. One sentence and I chickened out. But Jason got my meaning." Chantal walked across the room to the window balcony, where she stared over the eucalyptus windbreak in the distance. "I really do think it would be for the best if you and Jason sold some of the acreage," she said tightly.

"Does your father agree with you?"

"I didn't stay around long enough to find out. I was kind of scared. What I really want is for you to forgive him."

"Because of the Talbott woman? There's nothing to forgive. Jason loves me, dear."

Chantal turned slowly back to her mother. "You mean to say you weren't angry with him, or jealous, or hurt?"

"A little, but I got over it. I've lived long enough to acquire some common sense, I hope. To worry about a female rival in one's married life is a rather corrosive burden to carry about. You can never possess another human being, you know." Millicent's tone grew brisk. "Besides, I've been taking notes on the . . . situation. Notes on my own reaction to it. And how the rest of you, including Jason, have behaved." Millicent pointed to a stack of handwritten yellow sheets on the desk. "It's all there. The experience has been salutary."

"I don't understand."

"It's rather embarrassing to admit, but why shouldn't I attempt a piece of autobiographical fiction? Oh, I know the two terms aren't mutual, but a lot of other people are doing just that. If I'm successful, if I put together something that sells, I can pay off the mortgage Jason has already placed on Hancock Park—which he thinks I don't know about."

Chantal's eyes widened. "Jason mortgaged Hancock Park? I know you once told me he'd talked about it."

"He went right ahead, my dear."

"But the property's in both your names, isn't it?"

"I'd rather not go into that part of it, Chantal."

Chantal protested, "That does it! He signed your name as well as his own. Now I'm sure! You and Jason must sell half of EdgeMont and get a lot of money. Millicent, you don't need to do this sort of thing!" Chantal slammed her hand down hard on the yellow papers. "I'm glad it helped you, and I'm sure your writing everything down was a good remedy to tide you over when Jason and Erika built their little his-and-her bonfire—but that's over with."

Millicent hurried forward. "Be careful, Chantal. Those pages represent hard work. I'm not just 'Mother,' you know. Why shouldn't I be successful if I can swing it? Do something on my own! If Jason does get around to selling EdgeMont, I'll buy the place back with future earnings."

Chantal stared at her mother. Today Millicent was wearing faded blue jeans and a matching shirt. Her pale blond hair was wound in a coronet braid around her well-shaped head. Her smoky amber eyes glittered; mischievous little sun crinkles sprayed out above well-delineated cheekbones.

"Milla, you have a great imagination. Just don't start writing checks before you get your first publishing contract. You try, Milla. You really do try."

"I do more than try," said Chantal's mother. "Now this doesn't follow exactly, but you've always been my favorite. Will you continue to be as understanding of me as you have been in the past?"

"You mean, be your accomplice? Yes, I suppose so."

"Then give me a hug. Go downstairs and send your father up here, will you? He must still be in shock after what you said to him about selling."

Chantal disappeared, racing down the stairs. She hadn't thought about Simon Bryce once in the last forty-five minutes.

Boy Farrell surprised her. While Octavio was putting her luggage in the back of the Datsun, Boy came pounding around the side of the house. He stuck his head in the window on the driver's side and grabbed Chantal's hand. "Kid," he said, "before you leave, I want to get something settled between us. I'm marrying your sister because she needs taking care of and because I love her—not for any other reason. Just wanted you to know. And I've been talking to Jason. He and I will figure out what to do about this place. Matter of fact, maybe we'll just hang onto the property. For the future. You know what I mean?"

Chantal was staggered. She looked into Boy's eyes. Today they had a lot of sunlight in them. "You'll hold the land for the future little Farrells?" she asked, not believing what she was saying.

"Why not?" Boy grinned broadly. "Two marriages and I've never had a child. You want to hear my big news? Ardis is carrying my son right now. Doctor says she'll have an easy time of it—even a skinny toothpick like her." Boy squeezed Chantal's hand. "Wish us luck."

"I wish the three of you luck. Don't kiss me, Boy, I think I'm going to cry. Suppose it's a girl?"

"That'll be next time. I'm lucky."

Luck. Was it all luck?

Driving back to the city, Chantal thought about Doro Kentz's phone call that had sent her over the hill to Universal Studios and her first meeting with Simon Bryce.

It wasn't blind luck that had supported her that night. She'd done well on her own. Hard work and preparation and discipline had brought her to that moment in the dimly lit office when she had faced the dark stranger sitting behind the desk.

And what strange atavism had spoken in Simon's blood when he had seen the woman Chantal standing in front of him, when he had listened to her, watched her?

What recollection, what unconscious evocation, what image from his past had combined to produce the intensity of emotion that had swept them together? And apart?

It was only a little after midday when Chantal reached the Villa Apartments. Talk about Boy's finger of fortune. There was actually a parking space at the curb. Chantal leaned her car into it and sat staring straight ahead, her hands resting lightly on the steering wheel. What next?

A familiar female figure came biking down the

street, wheeled into the Villa driveway and set her bicycle against the bushes. Susan stared in Chantal's direction, the usual welcoming smile absent from her intent face.

Chantal stuck her head out the car window. "What's the misery?"

"Have you been to your mail slot yet?"

"Nope."

"Go. Then I'll come upstairs and you can make me coffee."

Chantal surveyed Susan. "The way you look, you might need something stronger. What'd they do? I know. Raised the rents here, I'll bet."

"Oh, you optimist!" Susan started to wheel her bike down the driveway in the direction of the subterranean garage. "See you in five minutes," she called over her shoulder.

The five minutes were up when Susan arrived at the open door of Chantal's apartment. Chantal had just read for the third time the notice on the expensive paper whose letterhead, "Highrise Happiness Homes," was meant to be soothing.

She looked up and said evenly, "I do not have one hundred and seventy five thousand dollars with which to buy this one-bedroom apartment with its wood-burning fireplace, its view of the Santa Monica mountains and its truly exceptional west side location. Those being all the reasons listed for selling me my apartment, soon to be turned into a condominium. Nor do I have any prospects of raising any such sum with a twenty percent down payment. The interest rate quoted here is obscene. I shall not repeat the amount. When did all this happen?"

"I knew it before you left here a few weeks ago. I was going to tell you then. I just couldn't."

"Of course you couldn't. You have a living, breathing, pulsating, humane heart. Tell me, how many of your tenants have slit their wrists?"

"Well, Three-oh-six OD'd on Valium. Four-oh-seven decided to get a divorce. Four-ten has moved in with his parents. Shall I get the Tarot deck and see what Two-oh-two is going to do?"

"Two-oh-two is going to try to get a job right away. She is also going to call her good friend who teaches school in Santa Monica. Then she is going to try to find another apartment. With a two percent vacancy rate in the city, I think my chances are zero."

"Can you pay six hundred dollars a month? I know where there's a nice single in the industrial district."

"Please. No jokes. Have a sherry." Chantal closed the door and gestured toward the couch. Susan sat down while Chantal brought two glasses and the sherry bottle to the coffee table. "What are you going to do, Susan?" Chantal asked, pouring the drinks.

"I'm going to move in with my boyfriend."

"But you don't have a boyfriend."

"I'm invited to a party in Venice tonight. I'll meet someone."

"You think so? They're very cliquish down there—little private jokes and all that sort of thing. Besides, you're twenty-seven years old, Sue-baby. In this town, isn't that supposed to be 'over the hill'?"

"Bitterness doesn't suit you, Chan. You've never been cruel. Why do I like you when you can make such a revolting social comment?"

"I wonder myself. I suppose I wanted to see

how it sounded when someone actually said the unbelievable out loud. I'm twenty-three, but I feel very old right now." Chantal stood up and patted Susan on the shoulder. "You're bright and you're pretty and you're funny, so you won't have a thing to worry about until your next birthday."

"Chantal! Shut up!" Susan nearly choked on her sherry. "You sure you don't have a hundred seventy-five thou to buy this place? And don't forget the monthly maintenance fee. It should run around three hundred dollars—that is, to start with."

"You're a bundle of joy."

The telephone rang. Chantal put out a slow hand to pick it up. "Hello?" She listened, looked at Susan, looked away from Susan. Then, for Susan's benefit, she repeated aloud, "You say your name's Eddie Bruff and that Doro Kentz asked you to call me? Doro's gone to New York to live there permanently, and the VP in charge of creative affairs at Tri-Symbol Productions left word for me to get in touch with him immediately? That was last week? He wanted to offer me Doro's job as story editor?" There was a pause. Chantal nodded. "I see. The job has now been filled? Thank you. Thank you very much for letting me know, Eddie. Yes, I realize . . . it's a week late. And that I wasn't here to pick up my phone messages. Of course condolences are in order. You're very sweet to call." Chantal hung up the phone gently.

Susan raised her glass. "How about a toast? Up the Establishment."

Chantal meditated, then raised her own glass.

"Someone once said to me, 'Those who drink wine live a hundred years.'"

"We should be so unlucky," Susan remarked. "Who said that to you?"

"A man I used to know."

There had been no message at all from Simon Bryce.

Chapter Seventeen

Everything seemed to be pouring in on Chantal.

She was sitting in her apartment trying to sort it all out. Today's horoscope in the newspaper had said, "Be constructive. If you do not allow your emotions to rule your head, this could be the most valuable day in your life." Hah!

Sixty days notice before she would have to vacate her apartment. "The hearth so close to her heart." That was the way Tilda Gorman, her friend the teacher of English Literature, had put it. Embarrassingly said, but close to the truth.

What could Chantal find to be constructive about? There'd been no further word from Larette. In all probability, Chantal's burgeoning screenwriting career was a thing of the past. Cesar Williams was back at his typewriter. There seemed to be no additional need for a Chantal Jerrold's rather shaky professional touch on *The Assaulters*. Also, she'd missed out on the story editor job at Tri-Symbol by the barest whisker. She'd left her recorder on, but it had run out of tape; thus the beeper had not been activated to alert her to her calls. Extremely efficient, she mused in self-disgust.

To be regretful was not being constructive. But Chantal was sorry she'd made that smart-aleck, "over the hill" remark to her good friend Susan. She'd apologized and tried to make it up to her. Susan had been good-natured about it. Still, Chantal was ashamed of her sharp tongue. It had been her own depression due to Simon's not having called that had been responsible for her caustic attitude that day.

She had been constructive this morning, cleaning and rearranging the apartment she loved and was soon to leave. She couldn't sign her life and her future away for the amount they wanted for this place. Anyway, it was doubtful she could qualify for a loan of the size needed. The monthly payment, plus maintenance, would be huge, even if she were willing to ask her brother for the twenty percent down—which she was not. Jay and she had not been in touch since her return from Mexico. No trouble between them; the line of communication simply wasn't in good working order.

As for the rest of her family, Chantal knew that Millicent and Jason were back in Hancock Park, getting the mansion's roof repaired and purring over their future son-in-law. Almost overnight, Ardis had changed from a sarcastic bitch to a loving person who adored her expanding waistline—a measurement obvious to no one except herself and Boy. Chantal's parents had reached the perfect solution in turning EdgeMont over to Boy, and to all the little Farrells who would come along via Ardis. Boy appeared to have done an impressive turnaround, thanks to his impending fatherhood. Making money seemed to have dropped several notches behind making babies.

Without looking at the clock, Chantal knew from the slant of the sunlight coming through the windows that it was noon. She supposed she might as well do a little further updating on her three-page résumé. The job situation was tight, but she was bound to come up with something before long. All her friends were out hustling leads in her direction. In the meantime, there was always freelance work to be done. Her pals at MGM and Twentieth Century would see to that.

Chantal found it hard to concentrate on the résumé in front of her. Instead, it was Simon's face she saw imprinted like a watermark on each sheet. She put the résumé to one side and picked up the trade papers she'd bought at the drugstore, but she'd already scanned *Variety* and the *Hollywood Reporter* for any items on Simon Bryce Productions.

Her intentions concerning Simon seemed to veer back and forth, resembling a weathercock in an itinerant breeze. She missed him; she wanted him. Next, puzzled because she hadn't heard from him, she wondered why he didn't call her. Was she at fault somehow? She was absolutely sure she would never call him! Yes, she would—why not? No, she wouldn't. It would be too demeaning, a begging request for his attention. He knew where she was. He could reach her if he wanted to. The emotional weathercock within her swung giddily around. Back and forth. A mad whirligig.

Suddenly Chantal shifted the papers off her lap and crawled across the couch to the phone. That damn silent phone. She wouldn't wait any longer. Who cared about pride? Simon had been elusive far too long. She couldn't—wouldn't stand for it.

First she called him at the studio. This time it seemed to a supersensitive Chantal that Simon's secretary was cool and noncommittal. Marilou didn't exactly give Chantal the brushoff, she merely said Simon wasn't available. As a kinder afterthought, she added that he was working at home today.

Closing her eyes, because Chantal knew by heart and touch how the digits were arranged, she dialed Simon's unlisted number. There was a constant busy signal.

After that she dialed every ten minutes, sometimes more frequently. The line remained busy. That could be for a lot of reasons. Chantal hoped it wasn't for the one very basic reason she, being a woman, could conjure up. It was early afternoon—summer was waning into the first week in September. The weather was soft and languorous. There were other women in town—smart, successful, beautiful, good to talk to, good to look at, good to go to bed with.

She didn't know why she was doing this. She must be crazy, perverse. And yet Chantal told herself the reason she was driving up to Simon's house was merely to prowl around and observe. Cruelly then, she understood her real purpose, its fine point. She knew very well what she was doing. So would any other woman know. She was going to spy on him, to see who was there, to see what car might be parked in that circular driveway of his.

Wearing white pants and a shirt, with no makeup on her smooth face, with a heart full of wrath, curiosity and self-reproach, she drove along Sunset Boulevard and up through the freeway pass to the San Fernando Valley.

Her red hair, which had not been cut at all this summer, hung below her shoulders and at this moment was streaming in the breeze.

Chantal drove along Mulholland and down through the canyon that led to Simon's home. She found the house easily, though she'd been there only once before. She could have found it in her sleep. Only one car was parked outside. She knew the steel-gray Bentley convertible belonged to Simon. She got out of her Datsun and went up to the curving arch of the front entrance. At least she hadn't parked stealthily on a side street. She felt, somehow, that that was to her credit.

What had she planned to do next? To skirt around on the hillside and from that vantage peer down into Simon's hidden garden? Tilda would have called it the garden of secret rapture. Chantal wished now she hadn't told her best friend . . . everything. She looked around at the shiny-leaved eucalyptus trees, the untamed shrubbery, the oleanders, the thrusting green vines. What was she doing here? Why had she come? To see some other woman who was with Simon? To put the finishing stroke on her already lacerated feelings?

She couldn't skulk around in the bushes. Chantal was too up-front for that. Instead, deliberately yet tentatively, she placed her fingertips on the massive front door and pushed lightly. To her surprise, the door opened. How extraordinarily careless it was, in these days of thievery and murder, not to keep a front door bolted tight.

Perhaps Simon is expecting a visitor, if she has not already arrived, came an insidious little whisper.

Chantal walked boldly into the foyer. No manservant was about this time. No Larette, no Dean, no Moira. Merely a kind of breathing silence. It was too late in the season for the fragrance of June roses. She remembered that scent well.

Chantal began to walk through the house in the same manner that, in her sleep, she'd walked through the chateau that had dominated her dreams. On the first floor there would be many empty rooms—if this were the dream. Of course, Simon's house was not the dream house. She crossed the big, well-furnished living room and pushed open the patio door that led to the pool area. If two people were there, Chantal would turn and walk away forever. But she had to be here now. She had to know.

Simon was there. Unbelievably, he was there. Sitting on the edge of the pool, his body bare and brown, wearing only swim trunks and dark glasses. Just as she had known it would be, the phone with its long extension cord that plugged into the patio outlet was on the deck beside him. Off the hook. A pile of scripts rested nearby. In Simon's hand was an opened script. It had a bright red cover, indicating it was a "final shooting" script.

Simon was alone.

He put down what he'd been reading, took off his dark glasses, stood up and calmly said, "So there you are."

Not even "Hello, Chantal. What are you doing here?" Not even an expression of slight guilt, such as "I've been busy. I've been thinking about you. I know I haven't called. . . ."

None of it mattered. Neither excuses, said or unsaid.

Chantal, looking at Simon, agreed. "Here I am."

She wondered how that phrase sounded. Angry? Of course not. Sarcastic? Never. Just simply the most natural event in the world. Just simply "I am here, my darling." But she'd have to keep those words inside, never say them aloud to Simon.

She continued a little unsteadily. "I called you."

"I've been ducking calls." Simon smiled as he glanced at the phone off the hook. "Let's leave it at that, shall we?" There were so many different shades of meaning attached to the manner in which he had said those words, it made Chantal wonder.

Simon chucked the scripts out of his way and moved toward Chantal. He took her in his arms. It seemed a reasonable and natural thing for him to do. For a long moment they stared into each other's eyes, seeing there the prisms of golden light, dark seas, desire. Slowly he placed his mouth over hers. She felt her body melt against him, and the well-remembered, almost indescribable ecstasy spilled through her veins once more. This she could expect. The perilous shiver of delight continued within her; its shimmer of the senses cried out for Simon to hold her, caress her, enter into her being and possess her savagely with all the mystery of his male strength.

But Chantal was not prepared for Simon's attitude today. Incredulously, through the pressure of his lips on hers and through his body's embrace, she began to feel an unusual degree of warmth and responsiveness emanating from him. In his rising desire for her there was a tenderness in him she had not known before.

He looked out over the pool as though recalling a memory. "I saw you come out of a tropical pool once, in the darkness," he murmured. "It was a sight I'll never forget."

"Simon! It was you who delivered the note to me

at the Posada? You saw me—" Her cheeks crimsoned. "You didn't let me know. The next day, you
were so cool, so businesslike. . . ."

He turned back to her. "I'm shameless. Didn't
you know that?"

She raised her face to his. Her answer brushed
against his lips. "Yes."

They went inside the house. In the drawing room,
he took off her clothes and they made love on the
soft cushions of the couch.

Afterward, they went upstairs. They stood together in his hand-tiled shower, pretending it was their
Gauguin waterfall in the jungle stream above the
beach at Yelapa.

Perfect as their sexual union had been, Chantal
had the instinctively frightening feeling that this
might be their last time together. Leaning against his
chest, she let all caution go as she murmured, "I
shall call you love." She expected then that he would
withdraw from her. She was prepared for the usual,
almost physical assault of his coldness. But today she
would take her chances.

When he continued to hold her gently, the water
raining down on them both, she grew bolder. Truth
was truth, and she would say it. "You are my love."
She closed her eyes, absorbing the stream of water
on her black lashes, her auburn brows. It felt so
good to say the words, even though she might never
be able to say them again.

He had not asked her why she had come. That in
itself was troubling. If this were to be their final
meeting, there need be no explanations. Because
explanations are not important . . . at the end of an
affair.

Simon, still holding her tenderly, led her out of

the shower. His hands were gentle as he wrapped her in a large white terry body towel. She stared up at him, her lucent eyes questioning. "Why do you let me say it now?" Then, again she said bravely, "I love you, Simon."

He seemed to understand something about her that no one else did. It was as though he could see inside her, the sometimes hovering uncertainties beneath her surface mockery. He stepped away from her and leaned against the wall, watching her closely. He was naked and very beautiful. He always was that to her sight.

"Why can we speak of love now?" Simon murmured solemnly. He bent forward; a faintly impish smile touched his lips. "Because today, for the first time, you came to me of your own accord. A simple woman to a simple man. You showed me yourself, Chantal—without pretensions, without reservations, without those ugly little suspicions, those digs of bitterness; without all that verbal analysis of our relationship that perhaps you yourself are not aware of." Simon paused before going on. "These days women are angry. We men are frightened by their anger. Our manhood is being sabotaged. We are being made to play with dolls and you with whips. But today that's not in you. . . ."

The pause between them was remarkably eloquent.

Chantal pulled the thick white towel closer about her shoulders. "For shame, Simon."

"What's the matter? You didn't like my dialogue?" His black eyes were laughing.

"It was terrible." She eyed him gravely, mockingly. "What are the real reasons you're talking about, Simon Bryce?" All at once she was reassured.

Strong. A kind of mad hosanna was ringing inside her. All barriers between them seemed to have come crashing down.

"Let me share that towel with you," he said.

She opened her arms, made room for him. Body touched body. Chantal thought she would die of happiness.

"The real reasons?" he repeated in response to her question. He appeared thoughtful.

She couldn't nod. She couldn't move. Lightning grazed her and she was struck speechless, remembering what the ridiculous horoscope reading had said: *"This could be the most valuable day in your life."*

They moved to the side of the bed. It seemed almost comical to sit as they were sitting now, wrapped up together in one big towel.

"The real reason," he said, "is this. Basic." He kissed her then, lulled her in his arms, stroked her hair back from her brow as if she were a child. "And this." Again he kissed her, this time very gently. "I do want to protect you, Chantal, and to have you near me always. Yet after we came back from Mexico, it was my intent that we should stay apart."

Chantal could not help thinking, You, Simon . . . you, you, you! What about me and my feelings? So she said it aloud. "Did you think of how I felt, Simon?"

His smile was wry, and full of pain. "No, I didn't, not really. I didn't want the walls of our love, even though they held a wonderful world, to close in on me. Selfish? All right, I admit it. Yet you were always on my mind. Do you know what that means? Can you possibly imagine what it's like to try to work, yet to continually see a phantom Chantal sitting across one's desk? To attempt to concentrate on a script—and there is Chantal's face again? I took a lovely lady to dinner. She's one of the most powerful executives in films. I thought we'd have a great deal to talk about. I was dull that evening. I couldn't even make small talk, because she wasn't you. Her voice wasn't yours. No doubt she had a boring time too, and it was even worse for me. You know why? My pride was jolted because an evening like that could be ruined simply because you mean so much to me." He shrugged, and the towel fell away from them both. "That's all. I've said my piece." He reached down and kissed her breast.

"Simon?" Chantal's voice was very small. "Was it me you were expecting today? The front door was unlocked."

"Suspicious of me? After all that I've confessed to you?"

"Not suspicious exactly, but cautious."

"Cautious for the sake of your own feelings?"

"Well, maybe a little. Let's start over again, and I'll say cautious in a careful sense. And you should be too."

"I'm careless, but not always," Simon agreed. "This time someone was here. Our friend Dean. He left in a hurry to do something for me. I suppose he didn't shut that blasted door. Stay with me, Chantal, and we'll keep all the doors locked. I've let the man who works for me have the long weekend off. We'll be alone. Mmmm." He nuzzled her shoulder.

Chantal sprang to her feet, bouncing and lovely and naked. Her full breasts were entrancingly close to his face. "Do we have to get dressed?" Simon asked.

Chantal nodded. "Yes, because I too have plans for us. You aren't the only one."

Simon pulled out some clothes and did as he was

told. Chantal loved the manner in which his broad shoulders shrugged into the pure linen of the shirt he was putting on. He zipped up the white cord pants. "Ready. Let's go."

They went downstairs. Chantal found her pants and shirt and put them on. She picked up her handbag and ran her fingers through her hair. "First, dinner at my apartment—how's that? I'll have to go back there anyway and get some things to wear for the weekend."

"You won't need anything to wear. But yes, I'll accept your dinner invitation." He pretended amazement. "You mean you can cook too?"

"You'll find out." Chantal produced an extra key from her purse. She gave it to him. "I'll expect you. Around seven?" She wanted to call him "my darling Simon." She couldn't, not yet. Some mysterious constraint held her back.

They walked out to her car. He opened the door and helped her inside. She felt . . . treasured. They kissed, with love.

As Chantal drove out onto the canyon road, she glanced back one last time to wave at Simon standing in the afternoon shadows. Tall, stalwart, her love. Forever. She had known from the beginning.

She began to think of all that he had said to her while they had sat on the side of his bed. She hadn't interrupted him, for how well she had understood everything he had described to her—the constant, imagined presence of the loved one's face, seen around every corner; the sound of the loved one's voice, heard in every strain of music. She was overjoyed that he had felt the same as she. She hoped she wasn't having a delirious dream. She hoped she wouldn't awaken alone in her room, in a lonely bed, sober with despair and reality.

Chantal bought everything at the market that was rare and appetizing to eat. With a bottle of wine tucked under her arm, and pushing her cart along the checkout line, she thought about her depleted bankbook. It didn't matter. She had credit cards with her. Besides, the store manager here knew her.

Since it was almost the beginning of the long Labor Day weekend, she was stalled behind a customer with two market baskets heaped with groceries. Chantal waited impatiently, at first staring blindly at the magazine rack off to one side. A man was delivering the new issues, unwiring bundles and setting up various items on the rack. The purple-prosed, ubiquitous weekly publication that Chantal mentally called the "sick" sheet was the last one to be prominently displayed.

Chantal's gaze began to focus. Big block headlines roared out at her. She stood riveted, her blood turning to ice. The cover story was a blatant teaser. It promised that in two weeks the coming attraction would be a daring exposé. Bold details would be shown, complete with photos of a distinguished local film producer's secret Mexican holiday and the lewd and pagan rites he had engaged in with a red-haired society beauty.

"Christ, lady, be careful!" The deliveryman jumped aside as the bottle of wine fell from under Chantal's arm and crashed at his feet, spotting trousers and shoes in a rivulet of Chenin Blanc.

Chantal remained white-faced, staring in shock at the display rack. People muttered and looked at her with curious interest. The cashier called through the loudspeaker for a maintenance man with a mop, then spoke brusquely to Chantal. "You're holding everybody up. If something's wrong, do you mind stepping out of this line?"

Something was very wrong, horribly wrong. Chantal fumbled in her purse, couldn't find any change, picked up the publication anyway and got out of line, pulling her grocery cart with her.

Her hands shook as she held the rag sheet that assured its salivating readers that the nude orgy in a Mexican jungle would shock the film colony, and presumably everybody else, to the core.

It was Jay she turned to.

Back in the apartment, grocery bags scattered around the living room, she dialed his answering service. Something screaming in the sound of her voice made the curt operator ring right through to Jay's residence. He answered on the first beat.

"I was going to call you," Jay said, and added unnecessarily, "I've been out of town."

"Jay, something terrible has happened. It's got to be stopped right away. You know that time Simon and I saw you in Puerto Vallarta? Somehow someone tracked Simon and me there and made a sensational story out of it. I have a gossip sheet I just picked up at the market. The headline says they're going to spill 'everything' in a couple of weeks. God knows what 'everything' is! Who do we know who's influential enough to get to those people and find out who's behind this? Could Kiki help? Oh, God, Jay, I can't let Simon be hurt! It's so obvious this rag is referring to the two of us!" Jay's silence lasted too long even for thoughtful consideration. "Jay, are you there?" Chantal snapped. "Are you alive and breathing?"

"Come right up here, Chantal, and bring that crummy paper with you. I take it you saw what was on the next page. Are you in any condition to drive?"

"I can drive, but where the hell do you live? You've never told me." He told her. It would be an easy address to find.

While she drove, she wondered what Jay had meant when he said he assumed she'd seen what else was printed. She hadn't had time to look. What could possibly be worse than what she'd already read?

Jay's place in Bel Air was a lavish spread set in deep grounds behind an iron fence. Chantal pushed a button and spoke to someone at the house. An electronic gate opened, allowing her to drive in. Upset and terrified as she was, Chantal understood immediately why no member of their family had ever been invited here before. Jay's residence wasn't exactly the spot for a family get-together.

Jay met her at the front door and led her along a thickly carpeted hall toward the library. He hadn't bothered to close any of the doors along the way. She saw it all, as perhaps he had intended her to. The mirrored ceilings, the angled mirrored walls arranged to cast profiled images sexually askew, the expensive brothel atmosphere. In room after room she observed the complete setup: cameras, lights, lab, darkroom, wardrobe, makeup station; sets consisting principally of beds, beds of all shapes and sizes, enormous beds surrounded by representations of giant phalluses and dildoes, amid delicate paintings of female intimacies.

Shooting? she thought, aghast. Kiki's secretary had told her that Jay was "shooting" in Mexico, and Chantal had assumed he was hunting, fishing—

anything but this. Only where her own brother was concerned could she have been so outrageously stupid!

Once in the library, Jay snatched the paper from her hand. He gestured around him. "I didn't bother to hide anything because I figured you must have read page two of this crap." He flipped the page. Of course she hadn't read any further than page one. Why should she have? Chantal peered over Jay's shoulder. And there was the second story he thought she had seen. The saga and the social background of the famous male porno star known as Jay Jonas. The accompanying close-up photo showed the handsome, smiling face of Jason Jerrold, Jr.

Jay was astonished at Chantal's astonishment. "You mean you didn't see this?"

"What you do is very lucrative—obviously," Chantal replied coldly. "Do you produce as well as star in these little epics of yours?" It hadn't sunk in yet, she realized. But she was a big girl now. She could take this sort of thing.

Jay collapsed gracefully on a huge, silk-covered couch. Chantal remained standing. Her brother looked very tired. He was pale-faced and sunkeneyed.

"We had a violent falling-out, Kiki and I. That's the reason for this." He flourished the sheet of newsprint.

"What has your trouble with Kiki got to do with this—with these problems we both face?"

"She and I fought over the Simon Bryce story."

"Are you crazy, Jay? When did she see it, know about it?"

"See it? Kiki Dalton *is* it! She owns the controlling interest in this sleaze sheet. When I found out she'd sicked the photog Sissy Purdue onto you and Simon, and when Kiki told me this stuff was going into print, we had a hell of a scene. I slugged her and walked out on her. She said she'd expose me as well as Simon. Not that I haven't been pretty well exposed already—to everybody but my own family."

"Did you try to stop her? Is that why you and she fought?" It was an inane repetition of the facts. Chantal couldn't help herself. She found everything too difficult to absorb all at once.

Jay nodded. "I couldn't let her do this to you and Bryce. She said she wouldn't identify you by name. But she does want to nail him. Why him? It's big audience reading. Bryce is known for his quality work, good taste, reticence—you name it. Kiki wants to pull down his class image, nullify it. She can be perverse. She knows people like to read about this sort of thing. Death of heroes. Look what the press did to JFK. Look what they tried to do to Eisenhower."

"I understand," Chantal said harshly. "They don't want the rest of us simple folk to have our heroes. Not that Simon is a hero. He's just a very nice man. He doesn't deserve this."

"Neither do you."

"I don't care about me."

"Oh, Christ, you love him. You're hooked. And so am I." Jay stood up. "I promise you I can take care of this. I can stop it."

"How? Choke Kiki? Why didn't you do it before?"

"I didn't think she'd go through with it." Jay sighed. "No, I know what she needs. I'm going over to Century City now and give it to her."

"Don't whore for me, Jay."

Her brother's smile was stubborn. "I won't, Chantal. You see, I said I was hooked. I love Kiki, dubious dame that she is. Ours is what you might call an exotic relationship. I won't try to explain it. Like most kinks, we're happier together than apart."

"I wish you luck, Jay. I wish us all luck. I disapprove of your line of work, but it's your business, not mine certainly. You're my brother and I love you. Nothing will change that." Chantal turned away. She wanted to get out of there. "You'd better stop sending checks to the family. Sorry, Jay, we don't need the money that much." She had to kiss him goodbye. He looked shaken. After all, he was only twenty-one years old. What did he know? For that matter, what did she know?

Chantal frowned. "Someone is sure to show Simon this headline."

"He already knows about it Chantal, though he didn't tell you. His assistant Dean Davison got the word before the first rag hit the newsstand. Dean's a sharpie and he traced it right down to Kiki's new toy—that cheap publishing house. Goodies to drool over for fifty cents a copy. You don't think Dean would let anything or anyone hurt his boss, do you? He and Simon know about deadlines. So does Kiki. She invented them. She can stop the presses. Dean's already put the heat on. Turned the screws. He has ways. So, like I said, Kiki will stop the press run. As she is fond of saying, she will do it to it with a double ratchet." Jay paused meditatively. "I didn't really believe she meant to go through with the scheme."

"Was this her way of making you come to heel?"

"You guessed it."

For the first time in her life, Chantal could see what her brother might look like when he was old. "Goodbye, Jay. Again, I'm very sorry about everything. The way things are with you, this house, everything." She glanced around her. "But you have my gratitude for squaring this away for Simon and me. I'm counting on you as much as you're counting on Dean. Did he come here?"

"Oh, sure. He's always known about me, where I live, what I do." Jay straightened. "You can count on me too, Chan. I can handle things."

Jay watched Chantal leave the house by herself. He continued to stand there, a too-handsome, rich young man wearing denims a size too small, wearing an open-to-the-navel shirt—the kind no one really wears anymore—a young man wearing years a lot older than he really was. He would like to have called his sister back. He wanted to tell her about the serious film he'd made while they'd all been in Puerto Vallarta. But he knew he wasn't the important part of her life. Simon Bryce was. So he'd do what he could to straighten out matters for her. What he could do was considerable.

He picked up the phone and tapped out the familiar digits—just to be sure Kiki was at the penthouse and waiting for his call. She was. Jay smiled.

On the other side of town, Kiki smiled too. They would make up, forget their fight and the ugly words. She stretched her long body on the bed; already she was planning the story for two weeks from now in her gossip mag. Erase Simon Bryce— the new story would take its place. This one would be a mind-blower!

Chantal drove slowly back to the Villa Apartments. She showered, dressed swiftly and began to put dinner together. The twilight was long. The amber light from the sun setting over the eucalyptus trees filtered through her apartment, touching each familiar object. She'd be giving up her home soon, and she didn't know where she would go. She didn't feel sorry for herself. She'd manage.

She looked at the clock. Six-thirty. Simon would be here at seven. She'd already run downstairs and picked honeysuckle and hibiscus, which grew extravagantly around the building, for the exquisitely set table. She'd put the newly purchased bottle of wine in the frig to chill. The boned trout and new peas were waiting.

Her face was pale, smooth. Her hair was tied back with a gray moiré ribbon. She was wearing a light blouse and a pleated skirt. She sat in a living room chair thinking about Jay and all that had happened and what he'd promised her. She believed him. Families, she thought . . . the small despairs and the large devotions. Millicent, Jason, and now Ardis and Boy and their children to come. How to give, how to lose. What *is* the truth of families? Lost in mist, bright in sunlight, dark in gloom. Yet there, like truth. The truth was sometimes difficult, but bound by love.

Chantal knew she was very tired, a little confused; so much had happened . . . so much . . .

She awakened slowly. He had come in and she didn't know how long he had been sitting there looking at her, his sea-dark eyes brooding. Of course, the key she'd given him. She thought then, I'm not on my knees, like the pictures one sees. But I think I'm praying, if one ever does. I love you, Simon. Love *me*.

Simon came to kneel beside Chantal and put his arms around her. "I love you," he whispered. "I'm going to take care of you. We'll work together, you and I. Someday we'll go back to Vallarta." He put his hand under her chin, raised her face to his.

"There's no place to hide when the hurricane hits. . . ."

Bright and splendid and good, she thought. From that first night I saw Simon, I knew it would be forever. Dreamily, she brought her hands up to touch each side of his face. "I'm awake?"

"You're awake," he assured her. "You promised me dinner."

She stood up, joyous and proud and strong. "I promised you a feast, Simon Bryce, and you shall have it. Now come into the kitchen and help. At least, open the wine."

"That's easy. What I've got for you to do is harder." He took a sheaf of papers out of the inner pocket of his white silk jacket and tossed the pages onto the coffee table. "I need a quick rewrite on a project that's to be submitted to the Hong Kong financiers next week. Do you think . . .?"

"Of course I can do it."

"Then you don't mind having a story conference after dinner?" His eyes twinkled as he reached for her. "This might be a toughie situation."

"Just my kind," Chantal said and kissed him.

Dear Reader:

Would you take a few moments to fill out this questionnaire and mail it to:

Richard Gallen Books/Questionnaire
8-10 West 36th St., New York, N.Y. 10018

1. What rating would you give *The Sudden Summer?*
   ☐ excellent ☐ very good ☐ fair ☐ poor .

2. What prompted you to buy this book? ☐ title
   ☐ front cover ☐ back cover ☐ friend's recommendation ☐ other (please specify) _____

3. Check off the elements you liked best:
   ☐ hero ☐ heroine ☐ other characters ☐ story
   ☐ setting ☐ ending ☐ love scenes

4. Were the love scenes ☐ too explicit
   ☐ not explicit enough ☐ just right

5. Any additional comments about the book?
   _____

6. Would you recommend this book to friends?
   ☐ yes ☐ no

7. Have you read other Richard Gallen romances? ☐ yes ☐ no

8. Do you plan to buy other Richard Gallen romances? ☐ yes ☐ no

9. What kind of romances do you enjoy reading?
   ☐ historical romance ☐ contemporary romance
   ☐ Regency romance ☐ light modern romance
   ☐ Gothic romance

10. Please check your general age group:
    ☐ under 25 ☐ 25-35 ☐ 35-45 ☐ 45-55 ☐ over 55

11. If you would like to receive a romance newsletter please fill in your name and address:
    _____
    _____
    _____